MAYWOOD PUBLIC LIBRARY

3 1312 00091 0507

P9-CSH-816

DATE DUE   9/89

OCT 0 4 1989		
MOV 0 2 1989		
	MAR 2 8 2005	
DEC 0 8 1989	SEP 1 6 2006	
JAN 0 3 1990		
FEB 1 6 1990		
MAR 1 2 1990		

E-K   The Library Store   #47-0103

MAYWOOD PUBLIC LIBRARY
121 SOUTH 5th AVE.
MAYWOOD, ILL. 60153

IMPACT

ALSO BY STEPHEN GREENLEAF

STEPHEN GREENLEAF

WILLIAM MORROW AND COMPANY, INC.   NEW YORK

This is a work of fiction. Names, characters, places, and occurrences are either the product of the author's imagination or are used fictitiously. Except for incidental accounts of aviation history, any resemblance to actual persons, events, or locales is coincidental.

Copyright © 1989 by Stephen Greenleaf

All rights reserved. No part of this book may be reproduced or utilized in any form or by any means, electronic or mechanical, including photocopying, recording or by any information storage and retrieval system, without permission in writing from the Publisher. Inquiries should be addressed to Permissions Department, William Morrow and Company, Inc., 105 Madison Ave., New York, N.Y. 10016.

Library of Congress Cataloging-in-Publication Data

Greenleaf, Stephen.
   Impact / Stephen Greenleaf.
     p. cm.
   ISBN 0-688-07668-8
   I. Title.
   PS3557.R3957I45 1989
   813'.54—dc20   89-32616
                          CIP

Printed in the United States of America

First Edition

1 2 3 4 5 6 7 8 9 10

BOOK DESIGN BY KATHRYN PARISE

For Frances and Warren

IMPACT

SurfAir 617 to SFO Control.

Roger, 617, this is Feeder South. I have you at one two thousand, heading zero one five. Descend to one zero thousand. Maintain zero one five, at one niner zero knots.

Six one seven to one zero zero, maintaining zero one five at one niner zero.

Transmitting ATIS, 617.

This is Automated Terminal Information Service, San Francisco International Airport, time: eighteen-twenty hours. Wind WSW at twenty, visibility one mile, light overcast, ceiling eight hundred feet, temperature five two degrees, low clouds, fog, drizzle, and haze. ATIS over.

Nice to see you again, Mr. Jastrow.

Hi, beautiful. We going to be on time? This is my third trip this week and I haven't touched down on schedule yet.

You know how it is—too many planes, not enough runways. You hear about that pilot in Detroit? He was sixteenth in line waiting takeoff clearance, and finally he just told the tower he'd had all he could stand, climbed out of the cockpit, and left his aircraft on the taxiway. If you ask me, they should build him a monument.

It can't be too bad, Nancy. From the looks of your tan, I'd say you haven't been spending *all* your time pushing a service cart.

I just got back from Hawaii.

Must be nice. Go over by yourself?

With my boyfriend. I guess he's my fiancé now. While we were there we sort of decided to get married.

9

Congratulations. I'm sure you'll be very happy. Me and the missus are going on thirty-eight years.

Hey. Wow. That's impressive, Mr. Jastrow.

All it takes is a little patience and a lot of vitamin E. I'm retiring next month; I tell you that?

Retiring. Wow. I'd retire tomorrow if I could.

You know what?

What?

The only thing I'll miss is watching you stuff coats in the overhead racks.

Now, Mr. Jastrow.

Well it's the truth, dagnabbit. You just perk the hell out of me, young lady. And I'm old enough to tell it to your face.

SurfAir 617, this is SFO Feeder. Descend and maintain eight thousand, heading zero one zero.

Six one seven to eight thousand at zero one zero. ILS?

Tune Instrument Landing System at one zero niner one.

Ladies and gentlemen, the pilot has turned on the no-smoking and fasten-seat-belt signs and we have begun our descent to San Francisco International Airport. Please extinguish all smoking materials and be sure your seat backs and tray tables are in their full upright positions.

SurfAir 617, this is SFO Feeder. Left turn ninety degrees to two eight zero, maintain eight thousand, speed one niner zero.

Six one seven left to two eight zero.

Traffic at six thousand at seven o'clock. Going to have to send you around the block one time, SurfAir. Sorry about that.

Just do the best you can, pal. I got reservations at Ernie's.

The first thing I hear is, no *way* a woman's going to get *that* account. Right? Well, you know how *that* crap jacks me up. So I go in the conference room, which is nothing more than a double-wide trailer with a pool table in it, and there they are. Seven of them. Muscles hanging off them like grapefruits; belt buckles the size of *Vogue*; chewing tobacco, cowboy boots, the whole Marlboro bit. So I go into my Barbie routine: I don't know *why* they sent *me* down here, guys. I'm only a woman, so I *know* I'll never understand the construction business the way *men* do, but I just hope you'll give me a few minutes of your time because we *do* have a wonderful product, and if you'll help me understand your needs and not hold it against me when I say something really dumb, I think I can persuade you that the Ajax Aluminum Framing Stud can save you time and money in any job from a bathroom remodel to a thirty-story high rise. Well, hell. They laughed and spit and coughed and farted, and by the time I was done, four of them had hard-ons, two of them had asked me out, and I had an order for a half-million linear feet of studs. I see a five-figure bonus at Christmas or I'm out of there, let me tell you.

So did you sleep with one of them or not?

Hell, no. I screwed a CPA I met on the plane. Man, did *he* explode some stereotypes.

Six one seven, this is Feeder South. Descend and maintain six thousand, left to one niner zero at one seven zero knots.

Six one seven to six thousand, left to one niner zero.

Contact Bay Approach at one five four point two.

Six one seven adios and thanks.

Why aren't we there yet, Mommy?

Because it's foggy so we're being extra careful, like when we go to the beach sometimes and I drive real slow? But I saw some lights a while ago, so we must be getting close.

Will Daddy be there when we land?

You know he will. He told you last night on the phone, remember?

What are you doing, Mommy?

Putting my knitting in my bag.

Why is your bag up there?

So it won't bounce around if we hit a bump.

There's no bumps in the *air*, Mommy.

I hope you're right. Did you have a good time in the city, Randy?

It was okay. Is Gramma real sick?

Well, she's kind of sick. Not real sick.

Is she going to die?

No. Not for a long time.

Longer than me?

Grandma Kate will die a long time before you do, honey. Almost everyone in the world will die before you do.

Even you and Dad?

Even me and Dad.

Cabin attendants prepare for landing.

I just *hate* this.

Flying?

Well, taking off and landing, at least. Why are we *shaking* like that?

See out there? Those things sticking down from the wings are the slats and flaps. They slow us down and give us extra lift, but they make it a little bumpy, too. Just close your eyes. Give me your hand. Lean back. Now think about what we've been doing all week.

I'm not sure I *like* what we've been doing all week.

You didn't seem to mind it at the time. In fact, last night you said you didn't want it to end.

I don't mean the sex, Jack. I mean the cheating.

I thought we already worked that out.

I did, too. But I keep wondering how I'm going to look Spitter in the eye when we get home.

Spitter doesn't need to know anything about this. Neither does your sister, and neither does anyone else in Altoona. Christ. This is a real downer, Carol.

Sorry.

Come on; lighten up. Don't look so sad.

I'm not sad; I'm just . . . tired. I'm very, very tired. And at this moment all I can think about is how completely *perverted* this is.

Shit. Since when did *you* get so damned high and—

Not us. *Flying*. If human beings were made to fly, why did God invent Adidas? Of course, I suppose to most people flying's not *nearly* as unnatural as adultery.

Come on, Carol; give me a break. I *told* you I'm going to end it. Right after Easter. I can't very well walk out on her at Easter, can I?

Of course not. If you did that, little Laura would have to spend Easter the same way I do—drunk on my ass with a chocolate bunny.

Bay Approach to SurfAir 617. Good evening.

Howdy, honey. How's every little thing?

Everything is A-OK. Six one seven, turn left ninety degrees, to base leg one zero zero. Descend and maintain five thousand, speed one six zero knots.

Six one seven to five thousand, base one zero zero.

Traffic at six thousand, three o'clock, and three thousand, ten o'clock. Expect runway one two left.

One two left. Thanks.

You follow American 262, now at two o'clock. You are five miles from marker.

It was nice of you to take us with you, Lee. The children loved it. Look at them. They're still in Tomorrowland.

I wish we could do this more often, Kiko.

We will.

One day, yes. But when?

Soon. I saw the looks on their faces. They were very impressed with your presentation. And with you.

They see a hundred men like me every year. All begging for money to finance a new business, just the way I did.

They will help you, Lee. I know they will.

I hope so, Kiko. I hope so.

SurfAir 617, this is Bay Approach. Reduce speed to one five zero. Contact tower on twelve twenty.

Confirm altitude, Approach.

Altitude five thousand.

Roger. Thanks for the help, darlin'. Tower, this is SurfAir 617. Request landing instructions.

I *told* you the play was guano, Jerry. It doesn't *matter*, you said. Clarence Van Autsen can make magic out of the *yellow* pages, you said. Well, my fucking Oscar jumped off the shelf at the first act curtain, Jerry, to put itself out of its misery. Clarence is through selling himself for chump change, pal; I'm not going to make a hemorrhoid of myself again no matter *how* good the bread is. It's class from now on— O'Neill, Williams, Miller—and that's it. From now on it's quality or I spend the winter in Palm Springs, baking out the booze.

Clarence?

Yeah, babe?

You know I love you, Clar, but sweetheart, I got a question. What the hell you think you're going to *live* on down in the Springs? Coconuts? I mean Titleists aren't *edible*, sweetheart, you know what I'm saying?

Six one seven, this is SF Tower. Descend and maintain three thousand, heading zero one zero, speed one five zero knots. Wind WSW at three five, ceiling six, rain, visibility one-half mile.

Roger. Six one seven to three thousand at zero one zero.

I've got pop-up traffic one mile at nine o'clock, 617. Altitude unknown.

Roger. Pop-up not in view.

Feel better?

Not as good as I'll feel when we're on the ground. Jack, when we get home to Altoona, we've got to talk.

About what?

Us. Laura. Everything.

Jesus. Why can't you just *enjoy* it, huh, Carol? Why can't you just let it happen?

I'm not built that way. I've made a lot of mistakes in my life, but believe it or not, I try to be a moral person. I need to think this is all going to be . . . *proper*, sooner or later.

I told you we'll make it legal, if that's what you really want.

I do, Jack. Flying makes me feel awfully mortal, you know? I don't want to die a sinner.

God'll save you, baby; sin or no sin. Don't you listen to those guys on TV? That's the nifty thing about God—He has to save us all. It's His *job*, for Christ's sake.

Yeah, well, I hope He hasn't been laid off.

SurfAir 617 to Tower. Request . . . hey! What the hell is *that*?

Jesus. Where'd *he* come from? Pull *up*, Bill. Goddamnit, he's going to fly right into us. Full power! *Get this fucker up!*

Mommy?

Hang on, honey.

Mommy. I'm scared, Mommy.

Hang on to my hand, honey. It'll be okay.

Where is he? Did he hit us?

I don't know, I ... it's not *responsive*. I can't get the damned thing—

What was that bump?

Cargo?

Cargo my ass. He clipped our stabilizer. If I can just—hey! I've got *stick shaker*! We're *stalling*, goddamnit. How the hell ... what's our air speed?

One four oh and falling. Like a fucking rock.

What's wrong?

Nothing, honey. A little turbulence. We just flew over the coastal range, and—

That's not turbulence. We're out of control. My God. It's really happening.

Naw. They'll handle it. Probably a near miss and we're in a tight turn. Happens all the time.

We're crashing, Jack, you *idiot*.

Tower to 617. Are you in trouble? You should still be at three thousand.

Speed one twenty and falling.

We've got to get it *up*. Not the *nose*, damnit! The nose is too high already.

I *know*. I'm trying to force her down, but it's not—

Altitude fifteen hundred and falling. We've got to get up or we'll hit that ridge.

I know. I *know*, for Christ's sake.

Kiko.

Lee.

Hold the boy's hand.

Yes.

I love you, Kiko.

And I you.
We will be together at the Buddha's knee.
I am praying for it, Lee. With all my heart.

Tower to 617. You're *off course*. Return to zero one zero. Increase altitude to three thousand.
Is that what I think it is?
Yeah, shit. Ground proximity warning. No way we make the ridge. Okay, guys, we're going in. I'll try to trim her up, but—
Tower, tell Mary I love her. Tell her I'm sorry I—

Bless me, Father, for I have sinned.

Sit down, Mr. Jastrow. *Please.* You have to *sit down* or you won't be able to—

Randy? Remember when the stewardess told us about the doors that led out to the wing? Now, listen to me. After we land, I want you to run to that door right over there. It may be dark, and people may be yelling and screaming, something may even be on fire, but you just ignore everyone else and run to the door and climb out on the wing and go to the end of it and jump off and then run as far away from the plane as you can. Understand? Just run and run till you can't run anymore.
Why, Mommy?
Don't wait for me, Randy. Do you hear? *Don't wait.* Just run and run and—
Mommy, why is that man crying?

Save me, Carol. I don't want to die. Please? Don't let this *happen* to me. *I really don't want to die.*
I don't think I can help you this time, Jack.
Laura? Honey? Can you hear me? I love you, Laura. I'm sorry for everything. I really, truly am. If I get out of this, I'll make it right again. You'll see. I'll—
You *bastard.* I hope you burn in hell.

Tower to SurfAir. Tower to SurfAir. God*damnit*. What the hell *happened*? I think they're down. Lord Jesus. Hey! Over here, Stan. I've *lost* them. How the hell? . . . How many seats in that new Hastings, anyway? Over a hundred, right? Good God Almighty. Hey. Don't *look* at me like that. It wasn't my *fault*. I don't even know what went *on* up there. Jesus. I knew something like this was going to happen. I fucking *knew* it.

PART I

ONE

At yet another banquet, Alec Hawthorne lolls beneath a glittering chandelier watching his food turn tepid and his wine go sour while he patiently awaits his cue. At least he is in Paris, the hotel the finest in the city, which means it is the finest in the world, so the room is therefore perfect: frescoed ceilings, gilded paneling, flatware cast from bullion, porcelain as luminous as pearls, livery worthy of an Antoinette or even a de Gaulle. But if the occasion and the trappings are familiar, the audience is not.

Normally, the faces that arrange themselves so they can see and hear and envy him belong to lawyers. Hawthorne is asked to speak to an assemblage of his colleagues at least fifty times a year, accepting only those invitations from his alma mater, the ABA, and the half-dozen trial-advocacy seminars that offer the most luxurious venues or the most exorbitant emoluments. On such occasions he hears himself described as a "superstar," a "million-dollar lawyer," and similar sobriquets designed to establish that he is someone who can teach the plodding practitioner how to make big bucks. And he can, oddly enough—although it is not what they want to hear, not the "secret" they assume he knows or the formula they assume he follows. He can teach them that the only certain way to riches in the legal profession is to work your ass off—nights, days, weekends; birthdays, anniversaries, holidays—until your eyes ache and your head pounds and your underlings exchange estimations of your madness. What he leaves them to discover for themselves is that the only thing you have time to do once the bucks roll in is watch some idiot investment adviser flush them down a speculative sewer. As for the pittance that manages

21

to escape such clutches, well, even if the IRS doesn't invalidate your avoidance scheme and your former wives don't convert it all to alimony, you still won't find time to do anything with the money that's elevating, or even fun.

Work. It is the sponge of his time, the fulcrum of his life, what has gotten him where he is and also where he isn't, which is in the bosom of a happy family instead of sitting at a formal dais in the ballroom of a palace he has somehow come to consider his due. Still, although he is never unaware that getting where he is has involved some rather weighty trade-offs, at this point in his life Alec Hawthorne does not often regret the bargain.

Comforted by the well-worn rationale, Hawthorne sighs, then sips a nice Bordeaux. In the next moment, because his mind operates as often by Newtonian as by Freudian principles, his serenity is routed by a pang of fear. He is suddenly convinced he is an imposter, present at the dais under false pretenses, a con man who will momentarily be found to know nothing about the law or the world or even about himself.

A molten flow of insecurity descends from his throat to his abdomen. He closes his eyes and holds his breath. After a minute the specter of ineptitude disappears, leaving behind a burning belly and a skim of sweat. Wiping his brow with a magnificently woven napkin, Hawthorne turns his attention to the center of the dais, where proceedings are ready to begin.

A rotund man stands, clears his throat, passes a hand across his gleaming pate, and manages a sentence on the second try. "Ladies and gentlemen, may I have your attention, please. Thank you. As program chairman of the Association of Commercial Airline Pilots' thirty-fifth annual convention, I have the privilege of introducing the keynote speaker of the evening. I say privilege, because our guest tonight is truly a bird of a different feather, as it were. He is not a pilot or aeronautical engineer or airline executive. Alec Hawthorne is a lawyer, and in the opinion of most, he is the heir apparent to the throne of the legendary Ed Haroldson, the foremost aviation attorney of our time.

"Alec is no stranger to the association. Most of you have heard of him; several of you have worked with him on a consulting basis in one of his many lawsuits; a few of you have been grilled by him on the witness stand or at a deposition, and it is no secret that more than one of our members has taken an early retirement after enduring that ordeal. Alec's accomplishments are many, but perhaps foremost is this: In the past twenty-five years, Alec Hawthorne has recovered more than half a billion dollars—that's right, *billion*—on behalf of the victims of air disasters, their families, and heirs. And in the process of collecting those sums, Alec has been a primary factor in pointing the finger of blame in such proceedings where it justifiably belongs.

"It was Alec Hawthorne who first made public that the cockpit instrumentation of the DC-8 was arranged so that a pilot could, entirely by accident, put the engines into reverse thrust while airborne; that the instruments in different models of the Caravelle were in different locations, leading to pilot confusion and passenger jeopardy; that the T-tail design of the early 727s caused a dangerously excessive sink rate, resulting in premature touchdown. Such revelations led not only to large verdicts for Mr. Hawthorne's clients but to the actions necessary to remedy the defects. In other words, our guest has been the leader in showing that pilot error—the so-called 'Oh Christ' activity —that is all too often cited as the cause of an air disaster, is almost always design-induced, the result of engineering that fails to account for the human factors inevitably present in modern aviation."

The chairman wipes his brow again, gulps some water, glances nervously to his side to see how it is going so far, then shuffles his notes and clears his throat. "Pilots, as the saying goes, are the first ones at the scene of an accident. Because Alec Hawthorne may be the world's foremost authority on why planes crash, we have asked him to speak to us tonight on the general subject of safety in the skies and on the international airline pilots' role in improving airline performance. Ladies and gentlemen, I am proud to present Alec Hawthorne, Esquire, the best friend a commercial pilot ever had."

The applause is hesitant, then swells, as if a collective decision has been reached that, on this evening at least, he is one of them. Smiling vaguely into the adulation, Hawthorne unfolds his six feet three inches and makes his way to the podium, which, draped in velvet and satin, reminds him of the lining of a coffin. He extracts his notes from his jacket. In the light from the chandelier, the jottings seem animate and surreal. To subdue a moment of vertigo he samples the tumbler to his left, then takes a deep breath and rids himself of all but the requisite sense that he is as supreme as the monarch who once held court in this very building. Still, as he looks into the mirror of a thousand eyes, he feels less a monarch than a badly frightened child.

"The aviation industry has come a long way since 1783," he begins, "when a Frenchman in a smoke balloon made the first recorded flight. It took Magellan two years to circumnavigate the globe, but by 1980 you could fly around the world in forty-four hours and six minutes, not with Chuck Yeager in an experimental jet, but on regularly scheduled airlines. When Cal Rodgers became the first person to cross the United States by plane, it took him sixty-nine hops and forty-nine days and he crashed fifteen times along the way. Today, routes such as the red-eye from LA to New York are both routine and essential to many industries, not the least the movies.

"From the beginning, safety was a major concern, of course, and even in the early days steps were taken to make the airways safer. In the 1920s, cross-country flights began to follow the rail lines for guidance. After a few head-on collisions in the fog, the pilots figured out that if they each agreed to fly on the right side of the tracks, they wouldn't run into each other anymore. Such primitive navigational aids seem ludicrous in this day of radar and transponders, yet airplanes still fly into each other, most recently the midair collision over Cerritos, California, involving an Aeromexico DC-9 and a Piper Archer. It's not as bad as it once was, when thirty-one of the first forty mail pilots lost their lives in crashes, but you and I both know it's still not as good as it should and could be. They used to say there were only three things important to a pilot—sex, seniority, and salary. I'm here tonight to tell you that you—*each* of you—had better add a fourth s to that list, and that s must stand for safety.

"You know all too well the pressures that engulf the industry today. Although the figures I'm going to mention apply to aviation in the United States, their message must be heard around the globe. Indeed, in a world where Singapore Air goes from the fifty-fourth largest air carrier in 1972 to the seventh largest ten years later, the American experience may be only the tip of the iceberg.

"In two important senses, the pressure on the industry is the result of actions of the federal government. In 1978, Congress deregulated commercial aviation. Airlines multiplied like rabbits, only to be gobbled up in merger mania, which often led to firings or wage cutbacks for ground personnel and two-tier wage structures for flight crews that saw one pilot earn three times what another pilot was paid to do the same job. Such developments fostered employee unrest and walkouts by pilots to protest wage and safety conditions—even to charges of sabotage by disgruntled workers.

"On the consumer side, fares on well-traveled routes plummeted, resulting in a fifty percent increase in air traffic since 1979, a crush that has led one commentator to call modern air travel the most constrained form of mass transport since the slave ships. Competition has become so intense that established carriers such as Braniff, Frontier, and Continental—even TWA and Eastern—fly high for a time, then fall into the bog of bankruptcy, reorganization, or hostile takeover. Meanwhile, the surviving carriers look for savings wherever they can find them, and too many find them in their maintenance and training programs. Airframe manufacturers feel the competitive crunch as well. Since 1952, twenty-two new aircraft have been designed, built, and made operational, yet only two of those planes have made money for the companies that built them.

"So much for deregulation. A second policy threatens the industry just as much, the policy that results from the notion that government is simply a burden upon us all, that it has no role to play in providing for the health and welfare of its citizens. At least as far as aviation is concerned, that proposition is both nonsensical and dangerous.

"As a result of the president's attitude toward their union, and of the budget cuts he imposed on all levels of government, the ranks of air traffic controllers have thinned to the danger point at a time when the drop in fares has caused traffic to expand beyond the capacities of virtually all airports and air routes. It is not by chance that critical near midairs—when aircraft pass within a hundred feet of each other—have doubled in the past two years, to the extent that one such incident occurs every other day.

"The simple fact is, commercial aviation is skating on the edge of disaster. Consider the following:

"1. Because of administration budget cuts, there were only 1,332 Federal Aviation Administration safety inspectors last year, compared with 2,012 in 1979.

"2. In 1978 the FAA employed eleven thousand computer, radar, and systems-maintenance technicians. Today only fifty-five hundred people perform those functions.

"3. There are three thousand fewer airline mechanics servicing seventeen hundred more aircraft than were in the air five years ago.

"4. Although the average age of aircraft flying today is more than a year older than in 1980—meaning metal fatigue in the frame and skin occurs more frequently—the airlines spend only $69.18 per flight hour on structural maintenance, compared with $76.66 per flight hour in 1980.

"I don't have to tell you the bottom line. In 1985 these forces came together with predictable consequences—more than *two thousand people* lost their lives in air disasters, making it the worst year in aviation history. Fortunately, last year this tragic trend reversed and not one passenger was killed while flying on a major American airline.

However, the Aeromexico midair that killed more than eighty persons, including fifteen on the ground, makes the domestic fatality statistic for 1986 less reassuring than it appears.

"As the chairman noted, my specialty is crashes—their causes and their aftermath. Most air disasters can be traced to a specific event, but seldom are the precipitating events the same. In the JAL 747 crash in Japan, the aft bulkhead collapsed because of improper repair work by the manufacturer. In Dallas, a severe wind-shear condition went both undetected and unreported and drove a Delta L1011 TriStar into the ground as it approached the field. Every day, it seems, the papers carry yet another article about a near miss in the skies that threatened a collision like the one that brought down Aeromexico, to the extent that a recent poll of the members of this organization listed a midair collision as their greatest fear.

"But behind the specific causes of these disasters are general problems that can and must be addressed—neglect, cutbacks, layoffs, shortcuts, delayed implementation of technology. I'm here to remind you that commercial pilots play an important role in reversing the trends I've just referred to. The reason is simple. Without you, the planes don't fly.

"Let me make some suggestions. First, you must expand and energize your air safety committee. Second, you must bring pressure to bear, to the point of work stoppage if necessary, to implement the following improvements:

"One thousand additional traffic controllers must be hired and trained immediately, before the system collapses.

"The FAA's withdrawal of the proposal to require wind-shear-detection devices in commercial aircraft and at major airports should be vigorously protested. Wind shear has caused eighteen major accidents since 1972; it is absurd that the IBM corporate fleet carries wind-shear-detection technology but commercial airliners do not.

"General aviation aircraft—*all* planes in the air, no matter how small—must be required to install Mode C transponders that reveal to the traffic controllers not only their position but also their altitude.

"You must demand that the FAA address the many deficiencies in the traffic control system beyond the lack of adequate personnel. Steps must be taken to ..."

By the time the soliloquy has ended, no one believes its message more fervently than the man who has delivered it.

Because he lived in Altoona when the land next to the water tower had been occupied by a De Soto dealer instead of a stone-and-steel structure that could have served as a monument to the steam radiator, Keith Tollison thought of the courthouse as new. In terms of years it was, he supposed, but like many of those summoned to its dusky chambers, the building had not taken very good care of itself, had withered prematurely and emitted the subtle stench of age. At the moment, however, the municipal musk was masked by the heady fume of panic emanating from the man who sat beside Tollison hoping his leisure suit was an ice-blue igloo that would shield him from a vengeful world.

Tollison inclined his head and whispered. "It's like I told you this morning, Larry. If I don't win this motion, we'll have to put on a defense. Since we don't have one, that's not a good development. I'll make one last stab at a plea bargain, but since I won't have any leverage if my motion's denied, we'll have to go to the jury. I've tried a hundred of these, Larry, and unless you've bribed one of those people in the box, there's no way they'll find you anything but guilty. Which means you're on your way to jail, given your priors. In other words, Larry, old buddy, I suggest you wish me luck."

At his side, his client bowed his head and closed his eyes, a caricature of contrition that was by now so familiar it was infuriating. Tollison shook his head with a disgust he hoped was disguised as pity and got to his feet.

"Yes, Mr. Tollison?" His body as weary as his inflection, the trial judge was virtually horizontal, his robe more a shroud than a cloak, his chair more a catafalque than a high-backed throne.

"The defense moves for a directed verdict of acquittal on all charges in the indictment," Tollison said crisply.

"Grounds?"

Tollison strolled to the front of the counsel table, then leaned against it and stuffed his left hand in his jacket pocket, where it came across a half-eaten roll of Life Savers. As he began to speak, he pried forth a wheel of cherry candy, which, like its manipulator, felt old and slightly soiled.

"I've listened closely to Mr. Dawkins's witnesses, Your Honor, and what I heard them say is this. On November fifteenth last, Officer Abernathy was driving north on Oak Street in his black-and-white at approximately two-fifteen A.M., when he saw a blue Plymouth sedan in his rearview mirror. The Plymouth was crossing Oak on Jefferson, moving west to east, and was being driven, as Officer Abernathy so emphatically termed it, erratically. Officer Abernathy made a U-turn, hit his lights and siren, and set off in pursuit. The sedan slowed momentarily, then increased its speed and disappeared.

"The unexpected acceleration caused Officer Abernathy to fall some distance behind the sedan. By the time he rounded the corner, what he saw was the blue sedan at rest against a Norwegian maple in Andy Palko's yard, hood up, smoke pouring from the radiator, doors open, windshield shattered, and a man later determined to be Larry Mitchell sitting on the ground beside the car, moaning and holding his head. Officer Abernathy approached, ascertained that Mr. Mitchell was neither armed nor seriously injured, advised him of his rights, and put him under arrest. When he asked Mr. Mitchell what happened, Mr. Mitchell mumbled, and I quote, 'Too drunk; too fucking drunk.' A subsequent test revealed the alcohol content of Mr. Mitchell's blood to be point one eight, well in excess of the presumptive level of intoxication in this state. I—"

"I'm aware of the testimony, Mr. Tollison," the judge grumbled, still substantially supine. "What is your point?"

Taking advantage of the hiatus, Tollison gobbled the Life Saver. "My point is simply this. Larry Mitchell is charged with operating a vehicle while under the influence of intoxicants. Now, certainly he was under the influence of demon rum that evening, Your Honor. But as far as I can tell, there's no evidence that Mr. Mitchell was *driving that car.*"

Struggling toward a more august position, the judge looked to his left. "Mr. Dawkins? Have you some thoughts on the matter?"

The young prosecutor's words tumbled across the room like dice across a crap table. "There is *ample* circumstantial evidence that Mr. Mitchell was operating that vehicle, Your Honor. The Plymouth was registered to him. No one else was at the scene. His head was bleeding, doubtless from impact with the windshield, which was shattered. Mr. Mitchell told the officer he was 'too drunk,' clearly meaning he was too intoxicated to be *driving.* Furthermore, there was no one else who *could* have been—"

The judge coughed and snorted. "I don't think it's enough."

"Neither do I, Your Honor," Tollison offered affably. "Particularly in light of the fact that no car keys were found either on Mr. Mitchell's person or in the vehicle itself."

The judge hauled himself erect; the gavel banged an ultimatum. "Case dismissed."

"Your Honor, *please.* Mr. Mitchell is a multiple offender, a menace to every man, woman, and child in this city."

"Move for a mistrial, Your Honor," Tollison boomed as amazement and uncertainty puckered the faces in the jury box.

"*Please*, judge. Allow me to reopen. I—"

"Sorry, Mr. Dawkins. Better luck next time."

The gavel banged again, and the judge rolled out of his chair and left the bench. Tollison put his arm around his client. Larry Mitchell's face, momentarily pink with pleasure, dimmed with puzzlement then folded in pain as Tollison tightened his grip on the man's right shoulder.

"You were lucky, Larry," Tollison said. "Dawkins is so new his briefcase still shines. Next time he won't make that mistake. I just want to make it clear that this is where I get off. This is the second one I've walked you away from, and you've got two priors before that. If you're busted again, I'm not going to be the one who puts you back behind the wheel."

"But I won't, Mr. Tollison. I swear."

"Get some help with the booze, Larry. Somehow you got yourself a nice wife and a great kid. Give up the sauce, or buy some term insurance and next time hit the tree hard enough to do them both a favor."

Tollison released his client and looked away from Larry Mitchell's smarmy bluster toward the flags that flanked the judge's vacant chair. His outburst was another in a long list of words he shouldn't have uttered, thoughts he shouldn't have voiced, a list that was lengthening rapidly of late.

"I'll quit," Mitchell was promising. "I'll kick it this time, you can count on it, Keith. I mean, Mr. Tollison."

"Don't *tell* me about it, Larry. Just do it."

"I will. I really will. Thanks, Mr. Tollison. You're great. Really. The greatest."

Tollison ignored the praise. "Where'd you learn about the keys?"

Mitchell's glance ricocheted around the room as cunning occupied his eyes. "My brother-in-law works for this lawyer in LA. Runs errands and serves process and stuff? Anyway, his boss told Lyle that if he ever had a wreck while he was driving drunk, he should take the keys and throw them as far into the boonies as he could, then get out of the car and sit down on the ground and wait for the cops to come." Mitchell's face blossomed with pleasure. "I didn't know what he was talking about then, but I sure as hell do now."

"It won't work next time, Larry."

"Why not?"

Tollison was about to tell him when a band of Mitchell's cohorts shoved their way through the bar of the court and escorted their comrade off the field of battle, triumph clearly as potent as Mitchell's normal brew, which was a daily gallon of T. J. Swann.

The courtroom slowly cleared. When they were the last two remaining beneath its inadequately soundproofed ceiling, Rex Dawkins walked to Tollison's table and sat on it gingerly. "I just wanted to say you'll never catch me short on the elements of an offense again. I've learned my lesson."

Tollison smiled. "I learned the same one in roughly the same way. You ran into an honest cop."

"Well, I wouldn't put it quite that—"

Tollison laughed. "Five cops in this town will testify exactly the way you want them to even if you forget to tell them what that is. Three won't remember what you want them to say no matter how often you remind them, and two won't say anything but the truth no matter how hard you push them otherwise."

"And Abernathy's one of the two." Dawkins's grin was sheepish. "I guess I should be glad he's such a paragon, but right now I just wish he'd said he'd seen Mitchell behind the wheel of that Plymouth before he set out in pursuit."

"Don't let it get you down. In this business you learn more by losing than winning. And you'll get another shot at Mitchell before long."

"I hope so. There's a lot of heat to get guys like him off the roads." Dawkins paused. "The boys in the office told me to expect something like this. They say you're the best trial lawyer north of San Francisco."

"That's not quite the way they put it, as I remember."

Dawkins reddened. "What they say is you could be if you wanted to be," he amended carefully.

"They still don't have it quite right."

"Then what is it, if you don't mind my asking?" Dawkins's stare was empty of all but innocence. "What I don't understand is, if you're as good as they say you are, why are you still doing . . . this?" His gesture encompassed the court and the cause and the client.

Suppressing annoyance at the young man's gall, Tollison considered his response. There was no reason at all to be candid, no reason to pick at his past, except that no one else had ever asked him the question, which happened to be one he had asked himself a thousand times.

Dawkins was a comer, the D.A. had said the last time they'd shared a meal. Reminded the D.A. a little of the young Keith Tollison. But comer or not, young Dawkins had screwed up, because he was a little cocky and a little lazy, but mostly because in the beginning they're never thorough enough, because they don't believe it can possibly be as tough as it is to convict someone of a crime. From sentiments that were part professional and part paternal, Tollison found himself about to voice an assessment he had uttered only once before—to a woman who had been and still was the wife of another man.

"Under the theory that those who are ignorant of history are condemned to repeat it," he began, looking not at Dawkins but at the emptied jury box, "I offer my résumé. I grew up here in Altoona, went away to school and, for reasons that aren't important anymore, came back a dozen years later. I'd spent seven years in Berkeley—the civil rights movement was in full swing, lawyers were going south in droves to integrate everything from beaches to buses, the antiwar movement was under way as well. Since I believed in those things, too, I came home determined to change Altoona the way some of my classmates were changing Jackson and Montgomery."

Dawkins was transfixed. "So what happened?"

"I did what any ambitious lawyer does—I sued everyone in sight. I sued the welfare office over its hearing procedures. I sued the police department because its entrance requirements discriminated against blacks. I sued the jail because it was so crowded it was cruel and unusual punishment to keep someone in there overnight, and I sued the grade school for opening each session with the Lord's Prayer. I even sued the city to let a girl play Little League baseball."

"What's wrong with that?"

"Nothing, in theory—I won most of those cases—but in reality it made me a stranger. I wasn't that nice Tollison kid who'd gone off to college, the local boy making good. I was a troublemaker. I was naïve, of course—I thought people would eventually appreciate or at least respect what I was trying to do—but it turned out the only people who admired my efforts were drunk drivers and dope dealers and mental cases, since they were the only ones coming through the office door. People believed that because I defended my clients I was advocating their causes, when all I was advocating was their right to some civil liberties and a fair trial."

The courthouse clock chimed four funereal peals. Tollison paused, suddenly embarrassed. "So that's why Mr. Mitchell and I showed up here this morning," he concluded quickly, "and why I'll be in here tomorrow with another one just like him."

In the sudden silence, Dawkins glanced at his watch and slid off the table. "Thanks for the history lesson. There are some things about the world I'd like to change, too. But maybe Altoona's not the place to do it."

Tollison shrugged. "I never tried it anywhere else."

"Why not? Why didn't you move away?"

"Because I fell in love," was the answer he stopped himself from uttering. Instead, he shook his head.

Dawkins stuck out a hand. "I better run. Glad I got to know you better, even though I didn't make much of an impression."

"Tell the boys upstairs hello."

Dawkins moved off down the aisle, doubtlessly wondering how he was going to explain the dismissal to his boss, the press, and the local chapter of M.A.D.D.

Tollison grabbed his briefcase and wandered out into the afternoon. Ordinarily, a successful trial produced an electric surge that boosted him through the rest of the week and kept him from taking his savings out of the local S&L and buying a cabin in the Sierras and fishing out his life. But not today. Today he could not escape the longing revived by his indulgence with young Dawkins or the regret sparked by what he had just accomplished in court.

In what passed for social circles in the town, Tollison was considered an ogre. Altoonans weren't disposed to forgive him for putting Larry Mitchell back on the streets, just as they weren't disposed to forgive Larry Mitchell for being a drunk. Consistent with the precepts of the pseudo-Christian renaissance, Altoonans were only disposed to forgiving themselves.

The state had screwed up, so Larry Mitchell was free. It was that simple for Tollison, though not for his neighbors, to whom the state merited endless license and excuse unless it zeroed in on them. As long as judgment would descend on others, they were willing to let guilt be determined by hunch and hearsay, prejudice and surmise. But when *they* got into trouble, they hurried to the lawyer most adept at exploiting the safeguards so deplored when less worthy persons sought refuge in them. The irony was that Altoona was so damn small and its legal fraternity so damn conservative, the lawyer they rushed to most often was him.

Tollison squinted in the sunlight and glanced down the block. When he saw the woman who was walking toward him, head down, brow knit, contemplating a conundrum that apparently trotted before her like a dachshund on a leash, he smiled. As he had been doing figuratively for a decade, he put himself squarely in her path.

"I'm sorry, I . . ." She zigged to avoid him.

"Damn. One more step and it would have been the most intimate encounter I've had all week."

Startled, Laura Donahue brushed a lock of caramel-candy hair away from her robin's-egg eyes, then held up her hands to block out enough spring sunlight to enable her to recognize him. "Keith. I'm sorry, I was thinking about something else. Did I hurt you?"

"Only because you tried so hard to get out of my way."

Matching his smile, she lowered her hands and stuffed them into the pockets of her satin jacket, a burnt-orange balloon around a thick white sweater. "Were you in trial?" she asked carefully. Then, because their circumstances made Altoona ominous, her eyes flicked up the block as his looked down.

He nodded.

"Did you win?"

He nodded again.

"You always do, don't you?"

"Not always. And even when I win, I lose." When she frowned, he shook his head to forestall explanation. "So how are you?"

"Fine."

"Long time no see, I believe."

She looked toward the neon announcement of a bar called Blackstone's. "I know. I was going to call you last night, but I haven't been sleeping too well, so I went to bed early."

"Why no sleep?"

She shrugged an ironic tilt. "Life seems to have gotten awfully *crowded* lately. There are all these arrangements to be made." Her lips flicked a stunted grin. "Do you suppose they have efficiency experts in adultery? Give workshops on it, maybe?" When she saw his look, she hurried on. "Plus, I keep hearing things out in the yard that only seem to make noise when Jack's away."

He struggled to remain unfazed. "I didn't know Jack was out of town."

Nodding, she evaded his gaze.

"Where is he?"

"LA."

"When did he leave?"

"Sunday."

"Why didn't you—"

She hurried from the question. "He's convinced he finally got the financing for his resort lined up. He was very excited when he called the other night."

As Tollison struggled to make sense of what she said, the sun, like her revelations, became too much for him. He put a hand on her shoulder. "Let's go over there."

He pointed to a bench in the park beyond the courthouse, but she pulled away and shook her head. "Not here, Keith."

He dropped his hand. "We need to talk, Laura."

"I can't; I don't have time." She finally faced him. "I know I should have told you Jack was going away. I know we should have ... taken advantage. I wanted to, but—"

A car passed and honked. They both looked and, recognizing the driver as the local baker, both waved. In face of another reminder of the need for caution, Tollison retreated. "It's just that I thought this was what we've been waiting for."

Again she brushed hair from her eyes, which had become as insubstantial as her explanation for avoiding him. "It was. But you were in Sacramento Monday night, and you know how it gets when you're by yourself—I got drugged on solitude. These *fantasies* kept rolling through my head, images of everything I can imagine happening to me over the next twenty years. Some were thrilling and some were terrifying and I finally decided to stop thinking altogether. I gobbled Cheetos and took bubble baths and listened to Johnny Mathis records and watched Cary Grant movies." Her grin became elfin. "It was wonderful. Now I know why you go fishing so often."

He sought solace in the narrow beauty of her face. "I guess what I need to know is if there's a message in all that for me."

The response seemed bittersweet. "Just that I love you very much."

The yearning in her voice made him want to press her to his chest, Altoona be damned. "Can I come over tonight?"

She shook her head. "Tonight's the museum benefit."

"Christ. Tomorrow, then?"

"Jack gets home this evening. We're supposed to go to Bodega Bay with the Ewings tomorrow."

She reached for his hand and stroked it in an unaccustomed burst of daring. "Are you taking Brenda to the dance?"

He nodded absently, still plotting a rendezvous.

"Do you think I could catch a ride? Jack said he might not be in till late, and I hate driving up our road after I've been drinking."

"Why don't you just skip it?"

"I'm on the committee, so I have to be there. But I thought if we all went together it might help our cause. Or would that be pressing our luck? Assuming we still have some."

Tollison considered it. "It might be a good idea, if I can get Brenda to buy it. I'll check with her and give you a buzz. What time?"

"Eight?"

"Fine." In a surge of desperation, he looked at his watch. "Uh, what are you doing for the next hour or so?"

His intent was so obvious she grinned. That she frequently laughed with delight when they made love had been an unexpected blessing, but his pleasure in memory quickly waned—they were not yet to where it was impossible to believe that it would all end woefully.

"I have to get my hair done," she was saying.

"But I need to see you."

"I know; I need to see you, too. I'll find time next week. I promise."

"*Early* next week. Monday."

"If I can."

She looked at the courthouse clock. "I have to go. André doesn't allow us to be late."

"Fuck André."

Her eyes closed. "Don't, Keith. Please. I'm relying on you to keep us from doing something dumb in all this."

Tollison started to turn away, then stopped in the certainty that crucial information lay just below the surface of their encounter. He began to speak without thinking, juggling words frantically to make her linger. "So Jack's finally going to get rich. He's been talking about that resort thing forever—I can't believe someone finally took him up on it."

Laura shrugged. "He's convinced he's got enough money, so construction can begin by the end of summer and a year after that he'll open the doors. I find it incredible, to tell you the truth. Jack is, well, he's no wizard or anything. I mean, you ought to know, right?"

Tollison knew, all right. He had grown up with Jack Donahue, right here in Altoona, back before the boom. He had been the football star; Jack, the champion sprinter. He, the reticent lummox; Jack, the gregarious jokester. He, the diligent student; Jack, the beneficiary of the athletic director's sway over the teaching staff. He was the offspring of a small-town lawyer and his dutiful wife who helped with the office typing; Jack had sprung from a pair of wastrels who lived in a rusty house trailer and pursued a succession of rickety enterprises that finally collapsed into a heap of fraud and insolvency. Once Jack had left for college, his parents and their trailer had been run out of town by the sheriff, acting at the behest of a dozen creditors.

Too envious of each other to become either enemies or friends, he and Jack Donahue left Altoona at the same time, after high school graduation, in the summer of 1958. A dozen years later, as though in response to a cosmic prompt, they had both returned. Over the long years since, they had not exchanged a word that wasn't required by the mores of the town they lived in.

In the interim, Tollison had gone to Cal, then law school, then the public defender's office in San Francisco, where he learned how to work a jury as he learned how little he liked slaving away in a metropolis where you could only see the sun by looking up. After progressing from defending panhandlers to defending psychopaths, Tollison had left the inefficiencies of the city for the law-and-order verities of the D.A's office in Altoona, the timing prompted less by his distaste for San Francisco than by his father's tearful plea.

With shock and anger but surprisingly little sympathy, Tollison learned that in his absence, his father had invested the family assets in a silver-futures scheme and had diverted a client's trust fund when the investment became worthless. Swallowing the remainder of his pride, Cliff Tollison had called on his son to come home to ward off the bar association, the district attorney, and the beneficiaries of the trust. The wrangle lasted for five years. A month after the final claim was settled, his father died from a stroke. His mother had, in every waking moment since, looked to her son to redeem her fallen name.

Meanwhile, Jack Donahue had gone to San Francisco State, where he drifted in and out of a series of sixties life-styles, from antiwar activism to an urban commune grounded in polygamy to, some would later say, a profitable dealership in synthetic hallucinogens. A few even suggested that Jack had eventually become a narc, squealing on his pals to escape prosecution for his own misdeeds, returning to Altoona mostly to escape retribution. Tollison didn't know and didn't particularly care. What he knew was that he had brought a law degree back with him and Jack had brought back Laura. At any moment since, Tollison would have gladly exchanged their trophies.

Laura was regarding his silence with alarm. "Right," he agreed again. "Jack's no wizard, but he's an overachiever, I'll give him that. And he's lucky. I just wish the bastard would stop treating you like—"

Her dark look silenced him. "What is it?" he demanded. "What's happened?"

"He knows. Or thinks he does."

"Jack? About us?"

She nodded. "You know how we've tried to figure out whether he did or not? Well just before he left, he said that since I'd be alone for a week I wouldn't have to slither out of town the way I usually did. I could invite you over and play house to my heart's content."

"He mentioned me specifically?"

She nodded.

Tollison's gaze fell on the courthouse, symbolic of turpitude and time. "What's he going to do?"

"He didn't say."

He grasped her arm. "We have to discuss this, Laura; we need to decide what we're going to—"

She pulled away. "I have to go now, Keith. Really. We'll get together next week, I promise." She looked up and down the street once more. "Call me if there's a problem with the ride. I'll catch an early lift home, so you and Bren can dance till the wee hours."

"I'll be ready to leave by the time we get there."

She shook her head. "Isn't middle age boring? I find myself asleep by nine o'clock some nights. By the time Jack wanders in, it seems like it must be time for breakfast." With the sun at her back, her hair was aflame. "And once in a while it is. See you at eight."

Suddenly saucy, she pursed her lips in a sly long-distance kiss, then hurried down the street and disappeared into a doorway beneath a sign that featured an electrically oscillating hand and bright white lettering that read: THE PERMANENT WAVE.

"Good evening, this is Carl Noland, Channel 9 News.

Less than one hour ago, a SurfAir Coastal Airways Hastings H-11 fan-jet, bound for San Francisco from Los Angeles, crashed in a remote area near Woodside as it was descending to land at San Francisco International Airport. Details are sketchy at this time, but one onlooker has told authorities that the plane seemed to stop in midair, then sink slowly toward the ground. The pilot apparently was able to get the craft under control just before it crashed, and for that reason some observers are optimistic that there may be survivors. There are also reports that the H-11 collided in midair with a smaller aircraft, but they have yet to be confirmed.

"There is no word yet on the number of casualties. SurfAir was originally known as Valley Airlines, a commuter line serving Reno, Nevada, and the San Joaquin valley cities of Stockton, Modesto, and Merced. Four years ago, the airline changed its name and, thanks to an infusion of funds from financier Baxter Chase, expanded its operations dramatically. SurfAir now serves all major cities in California and Nevada, and recently announced plans to extend service to Boise, Idaho, and Portland, Oregon.

"For the past six months, the airline has been engaged in an aggressive fare war with its competitors for the air-commuter dollar, and sources at San Francisco International tell us that the SurfAir flights from Los Angeles, particularly those departing in the early evening, are frequently booked to capacity. There have also been periodic rumors in the financial community that SurfAir's aggressive marketing strategy has forced the company dangerously close to insolvency, but company officials have consistently denied those rumors.

"The Hastings H-11 is a new airplane, first certified in 1985. It has a capacity of one hundred twenty passengers plus a crew of eight, and was designed and built especially for heavily traveled routes such as LA–San Francisco. This is believed to be the first accident involving that model. At the time of its introduction, the H-11 created controversy in aviation circles because Hastings subcontracted with a Japanese manufacturer to design and build the tail and wing components of the plane, leading American companies to express concern that this foothold would lead to the eventual dominance by the Japanese of the commercial airframe industry, to the detriment of American manufacturers such as Boeing and McDonnell Douglas.

"Access to the crash site is apparently limited to a narrow fire road, however we are told that police and fire authorities, as well as investigators from the National Transportation Safety Board, are already on the scene. Also on the scene is our own Helen Macy, and we go live to her now."

"Thank you, Carl. As you said, I am here at the site of the crash, which is approximately two miles off Highway 84, also known as La Honda Road, some six miles west of the San Francisco peninsula community of Woodside.

"It's like a war zone, Carl. As you can see, fires are blazing all around me, doubtlessly from the fuel expelled as the aircraft broke apart. The smoke makes it difficult to see, but hunks of metal and fabric appear to be scattered over the entire area. Everywhere you turn you can see bodies or portions of bodies; rescue workers are trying to determine if any of them are still alive. The personal possessions of the passengers are scattered over the site as well. Over there is a broken briefcase containing stacks of computer printouts that are blowing across the ground. Just beyond the briefcase is a doll in a pretty pink dress that miraculously seems untouched. It is impossible not to imagine what must have happened to the little girl who—"

"Helen?"

"Yes, Carl?"

"What about survivors?"

"I have nothing definite on that as yet. The front portion of the plane is so badly smashed that survival would be a miracle for passengers seated in that area, but the rear portion has broken away and seems intact. Rescue efforts seem to be concentrated in that area.

"There are several ambulances already on the scene, and more are arriving even now. The only person I have seen being treated by the medical personnel is a fireman who burned his hands as he made his way into the wreckage. A priest is giving last rites to victims who were thrown clear. As you can see, the rescue people are fashioning masks from their handkerchiefs or other scraps of clothing. This is because of the stench, which is overwhelming.

"Oh. The smoke just lifted for a moment and I could see a pair of seats, seats from the plane that have come to rest at least twenty yards from the wreckage, thrown out during the crash. There are people still strapped in them, Carl, and they are on fire. Smoke is pouring off them and ... well, since they're not moving, I assume they're dead. I hope they are, at least. It . . . unless you've seen something like this, you can't begin to—"

"Helen, thank you. That was Helen Macy from—"

"Behind the yellow police line a crowd has started to form, perhaps fifty onlookers. Incredibly, many of them are laughing; a few are even drinking beer. They seem to be—*oh my God*. Someone just dashed out from behind the police line and picked up something off the ground and stuck it beneath his jacket and ran back. This is unbelievable. I think it was human flesh, Carl. I think it was a *foot*. I . . . you think you've seen everything there is to see in this business, and then—"

"Helen, thank you for your report. We—"

"I talked to a man who saw the plane pass over his farm just seconds before impact, and he said he saw nothing unusual at the time he noticed the plane—"

"Helen, we—"

"—which may mean that the passengers were aware of what was happening right up to the time they hit the ground. I can only guess what—"

"Thank you, Helen Macy, for that live report. Obviously a tragic scene."

"*Wait*. I want to tell you—"

"I'm afraid that's all we have time for, Helen. When further information is available, we will certainly get back to you.

"In other news, police today seized a record quantity of cocaine that was hidden in a . . ."

TWO

He thinks the speech went well, but for confirmation Alec Hawthorne turns to the only person in his life whose judgment he trusts implicitly. He first met Martha a decade ago, after he had battled his way to a senior partnership in a law firm as big as a village and she had been hired fresh out of the good law school that was her antidote to a bad marriage. He was between wives three and four at the time, perplexed by yet another woman's metamorphosis from flirting fan to grasping harpy. Numb to the world beyond the office door, determined never again to be humiliated by female or divorce lawyer, he confronted the women who crossed his path with hostility verging on misogyny. Around the firm, Hawthorne became known as Pope Alec the First.

Wife number three had cost him half a million in cash and equivalents. Regularly and relentlessly, he would be assaulted by memories of selling the house on Russian Hill, the trimaran in Sausalito, the condo at Tahoe and, most vividly of all, of the Sunday morning he watched her lawyer drive off in his favorite performance car, one of only forty like it in the world. Still, shortly after Martha joined the firm, he picked her to assist him in wrapping up the final settlements in the Paris crash, as if to prove to himself that, thrice burned, he had finally become immune to romance. For her part, Martha became so immersed in the Civil Code and the Federal Reporter, she seemed blind to the dazzle of both his reputation and his wealth. Over the succeeding months they worked their way into an efficient professional partnership marked by exchanges of silly gifts and wry observations of the several absurdities of their profession. The decade of difference in their ages gradually became not a barrier but an increasingly comfortable tether.

Somehow, despite his wariness of romance and his growing affection for his chief assistant, wife number four came and went. To this day he cannot remember her face without a photographic nudge. After the divorce, he once again drowned recrimination in work and drink. Nevertheless, in the dim light of an alcoholic fog, he and Martha advanced from friendship through an unpremeditated coupling on his office couch sometime between 3 and 5 A.M. on a New Year's Eve to a passion so ubiquitous his partners demanded that he give her up or leave the firm.

Since he was generating more business than any six of his colleagues combined, jealousy was the more precise motive for his ouster— indeed, had he not been asked to leave, he would have departed of his own volition. A month after the ultimatum, he and Martha founded their own firm, associating one other attorney with them and, within a year, half a dozen more.

Goaded by the rejection of his former wives and partners, Hawthorne had been determined to exceed even his own immoderate ambitions. After spending a borrowed fortune on office space and equipment, he began working harder than ever to build his practice. At his side, Martha dispensed narcotics of praise or emetics of criticism, playing his ego like a harp by telling him the unvarnished truth or a perfectly tailored lie, whichever she thought would get him through the next item on their increasingly dense agenda. A series of fortuitous circumstances allowed him to pay off the new building six months after the all-night party that announced the opening of his law firm's brass-hinged doors, and Hawthorne quickly found himself as counsel of record in the majority of significant crash cases on the West Coast.

Martha coughs and breaks his reverie. Hawthorne rubs his eyes and glances at his watch. It is 2 A.M. Somewhere. Loosening his tie and unbuttoning his shirt, he leaves the Louis XIV desk, trudges to the bed, and reclines atop the heavy coverlet. At his look, Martha abandons the current *Journal of Air Law & Commerce*, pours him a drink from a bar secreted within a false armoire, then sits next to him after handing him his cognac. He takes a sip, enjoys the downward singe, and makes room for her to lie beside him. She slips a hand to her spine and unzips her gown, steps out of it with care, and drapes it over the back of a chair. When she joins him, she is dressed only in bra and panties.

Her hair is as short as a man's. Her body is long and narrow, far less lush than those of the four women he has wed. Her brassiere is more a belt than a pair of silken sacks; the thatch at her crotch strays beyond the V of silk that tries to bale it.

"So how was it?" he asks.

"Fine."

"I thought they were a little bored."

"They weren't bored; they were embarrassed. They haven't done half enough to improve the safety situation and you reminded them of it."

"Ad nauseam."

"Pilots are like kids—they only hear what they want to hear, and they only hear that after you repeat it ten times."

The solitaire on her middle finger—the sole souvenir of her marriage more visible than cynicism—scrapes his inner thigh. When he doesn't encourage her, she takes her hand away.

"Speaking of kids, I should fit Jason into the schedule somewhere," he says.

"There's no room till after the Grand Canyon trial."

"When's that?"

"Late May. After that you've got the helicopter case—if it doesn't settle, which it doesn't look like it's going to—then Greece, then the Hawaii thing."

"Jesus. Is Christmas still clear?"

"Ten days, as ordered."

"Good. Keep it that way."

Her punch is either affectionate or cautionary, he can't be sure. Martha takes an incredible variety of orders from him, encompassing everything from his lunch menu to his tax returns, but there is a right way and a wrong way to issue them, and sometimes he transgresses. When he does, she retaliates.

"Okay," he says. "What's next?"

"We take the eight-ten to Washington. Dinner with Senator Langston, more talk about his bill to forbid overbooking and limit carry-on luggage. He'll hit you up for a contribution to his next campaign, but you're already okay with both the senator and his party, so don't worry about it. In any event, you've given him all you can."

"Don't tell me I'm broke again."

Her attention shifts to her favorite subject. "Not yet. I'm trying like hell to keep it that way, but as usual I'm getting no cooperation from you or anyone else in the firm."

He sighs. "Back to the senator. What do I think of his bill?"

"You think it would be a mistake for you to support it publicly, because you're so closely identified with the consumer side of aviation issues no one would buy your objectivity, which you don't have anyway. You think you've done all you can do, which is recommend it to certain sources you prefer to keep anonymous."

"Will he buy it?"

"He buys anything that comes wrapped in a check. And you don't care if he does or doesn't."

"Why?"

"Because he won't be around in two years."

"Who's going to beat him?"

"Maxwell."

"You sure?"

"Yes."

"Then we should toss some money his way, too."

"We have."

He kisses her forehead. "Next."

"Night shuttle to Boston; a ten A.M. hearing on objections to your petition for attorneys' fees in the Logan crash."

"What am I asking?"

"Two million two."

"How's the judge?"

"Sympathetic. We did a lot of groundwork for him in that case and he knows it. If the engine guys hadn't agreed to contribute thirty percent of the settlement, the whole mess would have gone to trial and it would have taken ten years to get a civil case onto the calendar in Boston for the rest of this century."

"Do I have a fallback position?"

"You hang tough. We accepted half of what we were entitled to under our fee agreements in the Chicago DC-10. That's our charitable contribution for this year."

"Okay. What else?"

"Afternoon flight to LA. Booked at the Bonaventure. Hearing the next morning to choose the chairman of the plaintiffs' committee in the Barstow crash."

"How do we look?"

"We have eleven cases. A couple are sure seven figures, a couple are kids, three are nondependents, the rest are marginal. Haroldson has the most: thirty. Scallini has a dozen at least, and he'll be loaded for bear: He's tired of getting competition from another Californian in the races for lead counsel. Vic is still inclined to remind you that he was trying aviation cases when you were trying to tie your shoes."

"The man is so greedy he drools, for God's sake."

"You know that and I know that, but Judge Hallett doesn't know that."

"He will the first time Vic opens his mouth," Hawthorne predicts. "Who got that—what's her name?—the widow of the president of Keefer Instruments?"

"Scallini."

"Damn. I thought she liked me."

"She did; her lawyer didn't. He and Scallini had some preexisting relationship. Political stuff, I think, from back when Vic decided he wanted to be governor. That one was over before you laid eyes on her. Plus, I heard Vic agreed to kick back half his fee for the referral."

"The guy better get *that* little incentive engraved on the steps of city hall." Hawthorne laughs. "Poor Vic. He just won't quit, will he? Not till he knocks Ed Haroldson off the top."

"Neither will you. Or have I been wasting my time for ten years?"

Though Martha is gazing at him intently, Hawthorne is far too tired to debate the trajectory of his career. "So who's not committed?" he asks.

"Mostly, the Japanese. Tour group of seventeen. You have a meeting with their representative at the Bonaventure when we get in. I've sent fruit and flowers to his room, and I have sketches of the memorial we propose to build at the crash site with a portion of our fees if we're their counsel. Grass and rocks and flowers; a plaque, no monument. Don't worry; he'll go for it."

"I'm not worried, I'm just tired."

"No you're not. When you're tired, I can't do this."

Unzipping his fly, she makes a fist around his sex and transforms it into a dowel. He kisses her lightly, tasting greased lips and inhaling perfume.

"Shall we?" she asks, gazing idly at the fleur-de-lis that bespeckle the far wall. Hawthorne wonders if they remind her of when she was a Scout.

He considers her offer, knowing she would refuse him nothing, knowing also that the act will be quick and meaningless. "Let's wait for Boston. Take in a show, get all hot and bothered, then go back to the Ritz and do things that run afoul of half the ordinances in the city."

"Fine."

The word is without affect. Hawthorne takes it at face value. It would be equally fine with Martha if they took concurrent vows of chastity. With Martha, allure and perversity are congruent.

"Should I stop or keep on?" she asks.

As he considers the question, the phone rings. When it peals a second time, Martha glances at her watch. When he nods, she goes off to answer it. She listens, says, "You know the drill. I'll call with any special instructions," then hangs up.

After arranging her underclothes, Martha goes to the closet and selects a simple dress and steps into it. Taking a legal pad and silver fountain pen from her briefcase, she sits at the elaborately ornamented desk, crosses her legs, and says, "A Hastings just went down."

Hawthorne scoots back against the headboard. "The new one?"

She nods.

"Where?"

"Woodside."

"What airline?"

"SurfAir."

"The shuttle?"

She nods.

He leaves the bed and begins to pace. "Tell Dan to get to the airport, talk to the people meeting the plane, get names if he can. Tell them not to sign anything or talk to anyone, especially Hawley Chambers. Tell him—"

"Dan knows what to do."

"Right. Is Ray going to the site?"

"If he can get there."

"Send someone to the SurfAir offices in LA, bird-dog their people, get a passenger list, whatever else they put out."

"That won't be easy. It's the new age, remember. Just board with your credit card and ring up the fare. The records probably all went up in smoke."

"Jesus. It'll take a year to figure out who was on the damn thing."

Martha waits for more. Hawthorne circles the room, issuing additional orders as familiar faces begin to crowd his mind—crash victims he has represented in the past, once more begging him to *do* something. But he is never able to do what they want most, which is to rewind time.

His eyes begin to sting. Doing the best he can, he dictates more instructions. Martha records them silently. Despite the hour Hawthorne is fully awake, electrically charged, oblivious to all but the disaster he has just been dealt. He is launching a war, and he loves it as helplessly as Patton.

" Hi, Mr. Tollison. How'd it go?"

"Hi, Sandy. Another controversial triumph. How come you're here so late?"

"I like to end the week with a clean desk, is all." She looked away. "Plus, I like to be down here after dark sometimes. It makes me feel professional and everything."

He smiled. "Well, don't make a habit of it or your mom will be all over me again."

He watched the freckles on her face make room for a smile. "Anything I should know about?" he asked as she unwrapped a chocolate ingot dug from within her desk.

"Lots."

He sighed and detoured to the waiting-room couch.

Sandy swallowed a bite of nougat the size of a walnut and looked at her shorthand book. "Mrs. Rushton's son—she said *her* mother used to do some kind of piecework for *your* mother?—was arrested last night. He stole a car. He's still in jail, because he can't afford bail and she won't post it."

Tollison resisted a lecture on the presumption of innocence. "Public defender."

Sandy shook her head. "She wants you. I told her our fees and she says she can pay. But you don't have to do anything right away. She thinks it will do him some good to spend a night behind bars."

"The last mother who thought that ended up at a funeral. While her son was learning his lesson, his cellmate slit his throat."

Sandy's countenance darkened to the shade of her Snickers bar. "Well, she wants you to talk to him."

"Okay. Next?"

"Hugh Vickery wants to change his will."

"What's it this time?"

Sandy read from her pad: " 'A Styrofoam container, sealed with duct tape, painted red, white, and blue, and tossed off the Golden Gate Bridge on the first equinox following his death. Toward the ocean side."

"Jesus. What was it last time?"

"Scattered over the ninth green at the country club. The time before that he wanted them mailed to the secretary of state."

Tollison shook his head. "I don't know why Hugh can't let himself get boxed and planted like the rest of us. Well, you know what to do."

Sandy nodded.

"Next?"

The demand was more abrupt than he intended, since a review of his active cases inevitably made him churlish, but after his quick apology, Sandy's grin returned. "Mr. Wilson wants to know if the contract's ready; Mrs. Hanley wants to know if she can take her baby to Florida without the judge's permission; Charley Hoover wants another chance to persuade you to run for city attorney."

"The answer is no. To each of them. That it?"

"No. Mr. Golding called." Sandy consulted her notes. "He says Mr. Cosgrove won't agree to paragraph nineteen of the property-settlement agreement."

"Which one is that?"

"The golf clubs."

Tollison swore. "I *told* him if he turned down my offer we were going for half of everything. Well, you draft a letter to Stephen Golding, Esquire, and tell him half means half—my client insists that she be awarded the even-numbered golf clubs in the set her husband acquired during the marriage, and that includes the sand wedge. Without the clubs we go to court."

Sandy nodded and made a note.

"Anything else?"

She shook her head.

"Okay. Get Brenda for me if you can, then call the jail and see if they'll have the Rushton boy ready in an hour. I'd better get him out of there, so get his mother on the line so I can tell her the facts of life in the county lockup. The boy got a job?"

"I don't know."

"Probably not—no one under thirty has a job in this town. Except you. Call my mother and tell her I'll stop by and see her in the morning. If I don't have anything to eat in the refrigerator, order something for me before you leave. I'll get that Wilson thing done tonight."

"You have the dance, remember?"

He nodded. "I brought my suit in this morning, so I can go straight to the dance from here. By way of the jail, I guess." He glanced at his watch. "After I've talked to Mrs. Rushton, you can take off."

"Thanks."

Tollison watched as she reached for the phone book. She was young enough to be his daughter, and he often experienced the pleasant sensation that Sandy was precisely that. "You still dating Travis?" he asked quietly.

She scattered her freckles once again. "Sort of."

"I like Travis."

"I know."

"I think I like him better than you do."

"I do, too."

"Just because I like him doesn't mean you have to date him."

She reddened. "You're a nice man, Mr. Tollison. But no one's *that* nice."

They exchanged winks, and Tollison trudged into his private office, tossed his coat onto the battered Chesterfield, and collapsed into the chair behind his desk. Like its occupant, the room bore a rumpled aspect that with a little work could have been distinctive.

Most of the furnishings were abused and unprepossessing, but a few were treasures—the library table had been built by Quaker craftsmen in the previous century and bequeathed to him by his father, who had acquired it from his. The pictures on the wall were a set of Goya etchings purchased during his only trip to Europe, a ten-day fling taken after an employment-discrimination case had yielded him a five-figure fee. A more active art collection hung from pegs behind the desk—a set of Giants caps, one of every style the team had worn from the past of John McGraw to the present of Chili Davis, some so moth-eaten they were disappearing right before his eyes.

Except for the hats, style had been sacrificed for the convenience of disarray. The office was littered with paper—briefs, notes, phone messages, rough-draft pleadings, research data. Atop the paper a dozen law books lay facedown, splayed open to appellate opinions that at some point in time had been relevant to Altoona. The rest of the place, as Tollison's mother often pointed out, was just a bunch of junk.

Gazing thoughtfully at the tousle on his desk, he reached halfway down a stack of file folders and pulled out one marked "Wilson." He was about to open the file when the telephone rang. When he heard who it was, he said, "Hi."

"Hi."

"How's your day been?" he asked.

"Lousy. Herm wants me to handle the yearbook next year."

"What did you tell him?"

"I told him no way."

"And?"

"He told me if I didn't, there wouldn't *be* a yearbook next year."

"I thought that was Balderstone's project."

"He went three hundred over budget last time. Plus the kids snuck some dirty language by him."

"How dirty?"

"Does the word *cooz* mean anything to you?"

"A portion of the anatomy popular with gynecologists?"

"Yes, well it didn't mean anything to Mr. B., but it meant a lot to Terri Winthrop's mother, Terri being the possessor of the hottest cooz in the senior class, according to the Altoona High School *Tidings*."

"Jesus."

"The principal's word, exactly."

He paused. "You're going to do it, aren't you?"

"I imagine so. I seem to have lots of time on my hands these days. Or haven't you noticed?"

Brenda Farnsworth's voice had taken on an edge designed to etch the word *neglect* on his conscience. "I ran into Laura Donahue today," he evaded, then immediately wished he hadn't.

"I thought you were in court."

"I was. I saw her after. While I was walking back. She wants a ride tonight."

"To where?"

"The benefit. We're going, aren't we?"

"*We* are. I didn't plan for three. What's the matter with Jack?"

"Out of town."

"Jack's been out of town for years. And he's been out to lunch even longer."

"According to Laura, he's about to make a ton of money on that resort thing he's talked about for so long."

"Good. She can afford to take a cab."

He waited for the phrase to dissolve in its hydrocholeric bath. "Why are you being like this?"

"Because I'm not looking forward to spending my evening watching you making *cow* eyes at Laura Donahue. You'd think she was *royalty*, for crying out loud."

"She's attractive, Brenda, and I like attractive women. I know that's a federal offense these days, but I can't help it. I *like* them. Present company included."

"The present company hasn't kept company with *you* for a long time, has she? This is the first night we've gone anywhere this month."

"I've been busy. So have you."

Brenda paused long enough to make him dread what was coming —he often dreaded what came after Brenda stopped to think.

"We used to *make* time, Keith," she intoned. "Busy or no. Why do you suppose we don't do that anymore?"

"We're making time right now."

"I wouldn't call—"

"I told her we'd be by a little before eight," he interrupted before she could shove him further toward the admission of inconstancy she so clearly wanted him to make.

"*No*," she ordered angrily. "We can't. I'm sorry to spoil your plans, but I want to go by Carol's before the dance."

"Why?"

"Because I'm worried. She's been depressed lately. I thought we could cheer her up."

"I could pick up Laura, then go by for you at Carol's."

"No, you have to come too."

"Why?"

"Because Carol thinks you're funny. For reasons not readily apparent," Brenda added with a demeaning fillip.

He sighed. "What's her problem?"

"I *think* she's found another man. Probably a married one—it wouldn't be the first time. Remember Paddy Runnels? God. If I told her once I told her a thousand times, 'If Sadie doesn't want him, why on earth would you?' But Carol never listens to me about men, not since I caught her playing doctor with Billy Pinnock."

Tollison cupped the phone and paged idly through the Wilson file. "Okay," he yielded. "I'll call Laura and tell her we can't make it. But I think you're being silly."

"And I think you're being blind. She's nothing but a gold digger, Keith. Why else would she stay married to Jack?"

"Jack puts up a big front, but unless that resort thing gets rolling, he's barely keeping his head above water. At least that's what I hear at the barbershop."

"Maybe," Brenda muttered. "And maybe he just doesn't like spending it in places the boys at the barbershop can see." She paused, and her voice spread into a more appealing timbre. "I'll see you at seven-thirty. Okay? I don't want to be mean, Keith. But at my age I don't think I have to put up with a man playing footsies with another woman under my nose."

Tollison listened to the sizzle of the phone line, then replaced the receiver. Although he never knew which of his shortcomings Brenda knew of and which she merely guessed at, he was fairly certain she didn't know of his affair, since she had voiced similar suspicions long before he and Laura had given her grounds. But certainty was only a matter of time. Tollison leaned back and closed his eyes and began to recall their crooked history.

They had begun dating in high school, the result of a dare that was prompted by Brenda's risqué lineage—her father owned a bar and her mother had just run off with the Hamm's distributor, leaving her husband, two kids, and the six-to-midnight shift. But Brenda had been more exotic than Tollison had suspected—she used swear words casually, knew as much about sports as he did, got A's in trig and Spanish both, and always said exactly what was on her mind, which was often something titillating. The bogus date had spawned a second, and eventually they had done the prom, the all-sports banquet, and the other hallmarks of his senior year. In the process they had fought a losing battle with their cravings until they were stalled by a pregnancy scare just before graduation. Terrified by the experience, Tollison had sworn himself to abstinence. When he left Brenda behind as he went off to college, he planned, Tollison told her in a dozen panting promises, to return after his freshman year and make her his bride.

That grand design had endured six months. After returning to school from Christmas break, he began to hear rumors of Brenda's dalliance with an assortment of Altoona's toughs. Eventually, his parents mailed him a clipping announcing her betrothal to one of her more slovenly swains, a gas jockey who raced stock cars on the weekends. Although he had hacked at it with beer and a willing woman, the rejection festered, and when Tollison returned to Altoona for the summer, Brenda was still uppermost in his mind. But when he ran into her at a party, his lingering affection was quickly doused. Having given up on herself for reasons he had never learned, Brenda seemed determined to make him duplicate her slide, belittling his ambitions so inclusively that his interest in her vanished.

By the time he entered law school, Brenda had married the mechanic and had a child, a strangely warped appendage who had come to be called Spitter. In response to an atavistic urge, the mechanic had volunteered for duty in Vietnam and been killed for the impulse. When Tollison returned to Altoona he found the reach of Brenda's social life was reduced to her peculiar child, her sister, Carol, and a coven of embittered teachers at Altoona High, where she taught four periods of freshman comp and two of junior lit.

For a second time they began to date, partly because there remained a trace of their high school hunger and partly because they were two of the few unmarried adults in Altoona and a string of helpful hostesses thought they remembered there had once been something serious between them. And, on Tollison's part, because Brenda was preferable to the string of spinster ladies his mother sent his way and to the periodic one-night stands he negotiated in San Francisco.

The reborn romance had ebbed and flowed for a decade, now passionate or at least resolute, now limp and mechanistic. The wounds they had inflicted upon each other over the years made each occasionally compelled to treat the other cruelly, as though to prove that between the two of them there could be no bygones. The relationship was thus a bumpy road that Tollison followed in large part because it relieved him of the burden of courting strangers. Still, he liked and even admired Brenda—her loyalties were fierce, her sense of injustice as acute as his, her intellectual aspirations far outdistanced his own, and her periodic expressions of soft sentiment were as moving as they were unexpected.

But those charms had not been enough; given the chance, he had quickly strayed. Smitten to his toes from the moment he laid eyes on Laura Donahue, Tollison had kept his hopes in check for years, until she came to see him about filing for divorce. Her reasons had been vague, though if the rumors about Jack were true, she could name half the women in Altoona as co-respondents. But after consultation over a period of several months, Laura had decided not to leave her husband after all, for reasons as unformed as those she gave for consulting Tollison in the first place. Then, only a week after telling him she had decided to stay with Jack, Laura had called to tell him she had decided to have an affair. Over the pounding of his hopeful heart, he asked her who she planned to play with. She answered simply: "You. If you'll have me."

"I'll have you any way you come," was what he thought he'd said.

They had met that very night, some eighteen months before, in a bar in Sebastopol where they correctly assumed no one would know anyone, and proceeded from there to a seedy motel in Santa Rosa that had, because of what it had permitted them, grown in his imagination to resemble the Taj Mahal. Over the succeeding months they sculpted their liaison. Covert schemes, unwitting allies, elaborate evasions— all were servants of their charade. Like adolescents, they believed they invented each emotion that stirred them, coined each phrase that passed their lips, originated each erotic expression of their love. Like Victorians, they reveled in their secret, then berated themselves for contravening the laws of God, or at least Altoona.

Since the beginnings of his affair with Laura, Tollison told himself that he wanted nothing less for Brenda than what he had found himself, which was a passion equal to the one they shared before he had gone away and left her to Altoona. But that was not quite right. Although his pursuit of Laura caused him to increasingly regard Brenda as an irritant, his failure to break with her completely stemmed from the sense that if Laura eventually cast him off, in a loathsome corner of his hardened heart he wanted Brenda to be ready to take him back.

As usual, Sandy peeked in before he could subdue the past or divine the future. The jail appointment was set, and Mrs. Rushton was on line one. Tollison put the women in his life aside and persuaded the mother to allow him to spring her son. Then, filling his cup with well-aged coffee, he got to work, relieved to be confronted with a task that would yield to brute persistence.

A half hour got him to the final clauses of the Wilson contract, a string of turgid phrases covering anticipatory breaches and willful defaults, forfeitures and restitution, all so his client could unload five acres of apple orchard on the local car-wash king—the circumlocutions and equivocations a pathetic bulwark against mankind's innate tendency to break its word. The originator of such boilerplate thought the labored language would keep disputes between the parties away from lawyers and out of court. Instead, the added ambiguity increased the possible grounds for quarrel. Lawyers feeding lawyers; sharks feeding on their own.

As he fumbled with the wording, Tollison realized his research into land contracts needed updating before he sent the instrument to Wilson for approval. He would have to check the texts, look into recent developments to make sure he didn't screw up ... when? He flipped through the calendar. A cocaine trial, two OMVUIIs, a bar meeting. Status conferences, suppression hearings, appellate arguments. No time, except for the hours he regularly promised Brenda while he schemed to award them to Mrs. Donahue.

Tollison picked up the phone to tell Laura he wouldn't be able to provide a taxi. When there was no answer, he left a message on her machine. Minutes later, in the musty basement of his law office, he donned his best blue suit and tried to foresee the evening—if he dared ask Laura to dance, what she would say when he held her close, whether in the grip of mischief he would make a miscue so brash that he would, like so many of his hapless clients, incriminate himself with foolishness.

Aviation Investigations, Inc.
F. Raymond Livingood, Ph.D.,
Founder and Chief Investigator

Site Inspection Report, March 27, 1987—
SurfAir Flight 617 (Hastings H-11 Fan-jet):
Suspected Midair Collision

THIS REPORT CONSTITUTES THE WORK PRODUCT OF ALEC
HAWTHORNE, ATTORNEY-AT-LAW, AND IS PROTECTED BY THE
ATTORNEY-CLIENT AND WORK-PRODUCT PRIVILEGES.

On March 23, 1987, pursuant to the telephone request of Daniel
Griffin, Esq., of the Law Offices of Alec Hawthorne, I proceeded to
the site of the crash of SurfAir flight 617, near Woodside, California.

I arrived at the scene at approximately 8:15 P.M., some two hours
after the accident. I was able to obtain a ride with Ralph Hutchins,
the IIC (Investigator in Charge) out of the National Transportation
Safety Board's San Francisco office, a friend from my days with that
agency. Needless to say, my presence in the Go Team vehicle should
remain confidential.

The immediate environment was typical of a major air disaster.
(Videotape to be provided.) The aircraft impacted on a heading of
approximately 050 degrees magnetic, and left a gouge in the ground
about 400 feet long. The main wreckage came to rest on a heading
of 240 degrees magnetic.

The cockpit and approximately the forward one third of the main
cabin were crushed. A portion of the rear fuselage and tail assembly
had broken away from the main wreckage and appeared relatively
intact. The two fan-jet engines had separated from the wings and
lay on either side of the fuselage, some 50 to 100 feet forward of the
main cabin. The right wing had struck a eucalyptus tree and was
folded back against the fuselage; the left wing separated from the
fuselage upon impact with a rock outcropping. Landing gear were
fully retracted. The aircraft struck the ground at a near level attitude,
indicating the pilot was in sufficient control of the flight systems
to attempt an emergency landing.

Although the aft portion of the fuselage remained intact, virtually
all seats appeared to have torn free, causing the occupants to be
hurtled into or through the bulkhead. Most passengers appeared to

be still in their seat restraints, but some had been thrown free. It was impossible to estimate the number of casualties from observation of the remains; however, estimates by airline personnel at the scene were that a full complement of 120 passengers and eight crew members was aboard.

By the time I reached the site, remains were already being gathered into disaster pouches by the coroner's personnel. Body parts were being segregated by type—legs in one bag, arms in another, etc. All remains were charred from postimpact burning.

There were apparently several survivors—estimates run as high as twenty. Passengers with vital signs were taken to hospitals in Palo Alto and San Jose. The names and addresses of the survivors are beyond the scope of this report.

Initial observation revealed no evidence of metal splatter or hot spots indicative of pre-impact fire or explosion in either the engines or the cabin. The cabin floor did not appear to have collapsed, at least not in the rear portion of the fuselage, so interruption of hydraulic systems is not indicated. I saw no major component pieces outside the impact swath, so in-flight structural failure is not indicated. Temperatures on the ground were sufficiently substantial to preclude in-flight engine shutdown. It should be noted that because of the fire, I could not get near enough to the wreckage to make a definitive assessment of these points. Follow-up will be provided.

Personnel on the scene suggested that the crash may have been the result of a midair collision between the Hastings H-11 and a general aviation aircraft, possibly a Cessna 160. Markings on the upper portion of the H-11 vertical stabilizer may prove to be rubber residues from the nose wheel of the smaller aircraft. This has yet to be confirmed.

(Two additional possibilities were suggested to me, *off the record*, by Ralph Hutchins. On two previous occasions, aircraft approaching SFO on this flight path have been shot at and hit by unknown gunmen. One round penetrated the fuselage of a 737 and lodged in the baggage compartment; the other punctured the aileron of a DC-9. Both aircraft landed without further incident. Also, approximately one month ago, a 727 on approach to SFO received instructions from an ersatz traffic controller, instructions that would have placed the aircraft at risk had the pilot not recognized them as bogus. The cockpit voice recorder will presumably reveal whether this transpired on flight 617.)

In subsequent reports I will inform as to the disposition of the wreckage (current price of scrap—$650 per ton; initial cost of the H-11—$25,000,000), the personal effects of the passengers, and the preliminary findings of the NTSB Red Team. Because of inadequate lighting and constant interference from police personnel, videotapes made by me are of limited utility. Editing and picture augmentation may improve quality, and such steps will be undertaken at your request.

F. Raymond Livingood
Chief Investigator
Aviation Investigations, Inc.

THREE

It is one of the ironies of his life that in order to make his living proving that airlines are often negligent and aircraft frequently defective, Alec Hawthorne must spend fifty days a year using the instrument of travel whose inadequacies he knows best. Although the dilemma is old hat by now, he can't suppress his expertise. The glistening widebody that carries him across the Atlantic is a miracle of engineering, but it is heir to a legacy of jumbo failures that pecks persistently at his mind—tires blowing, lavatories burning, doors exploding, engines failing, landing gear collapsing, bulkheads buckling, flaps retracting— to say nothing of the more mundane foul-ups that plague aircraft of any size.

Hawthorne stuffs a deposition transcript back in his bulging briefcase, reclines in his seat, and closes his eyes. Washington is less than an hour away. Dulles, the long ride into the city, suite at the Mayflower, dinner with Lame-duck Langston at the Cosmos Club. A busy schedule, but time in between for—what? Surely somewhere within the federal bureaucracy there is someone . . . yes. The woman from the San Diego case. The staff attorney with the FAA.

Willing, she'd made no secret of that. And able, he would wager. They were always able these days. What was her name? . . . Something incongruous. Christian. That was it. Molly Christian. GS-18 and rising. He'd call her the minute he got in. From the limo. They were always impressed when he called them from the limo. His sex life thrived on the cellular phone.

It would be nice to be with someone more enthusiastic than Martha for a change. Bedding Martha was like tying your tie—nice, but no big deal. Not that Martha would mind if he dallied with someone else: He had done it often, with her knowledge; occasionally, at her urging. Martha would no doubt relish the night off.

He flies through a cloud of eroticism until his anticipation fades. Molly Christian would almost certainly have left the FAA—San Diego was ten years ago. By now she'd be with a legal factory that peddled influence instead of law and legislation, and took full advantage of Molly's experience while advising its clients how to reduce to nil their contributions to the government that had trained her. To track her down would consume his evening, and for what?

At his side, Martha stirs, turns a page of *Aviation Week*, squirms to a more comfortable position, and reads on, oblivious to both her companion and her distance from the ground. Martha has no fear of abstractions. He doubts that she ever anticipates disaster, doubts that she sees a crucial distinction between mortality and its converse, doubts that she would react visibly if the airplane began to pitch and yaw and plunge toward the sea that very second. He shakes his head. Robots have their advantages, but it would be nice if this one would hint a bit of frailty. Like modesty and a file full of recipes, frailty was an endearing trait in a woman. Too bad they all had fallen out of favor.

As Hawthorne observes her covertly, Martha closes the magazine and plucks a larger document out of her briefcase. It is a helicopter flight manual, and it will be the chief exhibit in one of their most difficult lawsuits.

Because their clients in the case are neither dead nor obviously injured, they lack reliable damage claims. Whiplash and headache, back trouble and blurred vision—although their lives have been permanently diminished by the crash, their complaints are of the type considered risky in the business, of uncertain value compared to overt maladies. He will be lucky if he gets them a hundred thousand each. Had they lost an arm or leg, he could get them a million.

The helicopter matter is interesting from another angle. Had the chopper gone down in California he would not have taken the case, but because the crash was in Alaska and Alaska law applied, he could afford the price of admission. Alone among the fifty states, Alaska allows successful personal-injury plaintiffs to recover attorneys' fees, a potential gold mine given precise record-keeping and a judge who was formerly a trial lawyer. Alaska also allows recovery of damages for pre-impact terror, and Hawthorne has already hired a psychologist who, with the help of sound effects, Equity actors, a Hollywood set designer, and a cassette of 8mm videotape, has re-created the moments before impact in such chilling detail that before Hawthorne is through with them, the jury will think *they* went down in the damn thing.

But as always, there are problems. The shuttle service that owned the helicopter is broke, and its insurance carrier is claiming a defect in coverage because of a late premium. The pilot, whose blood tested .08 alcohol immediately after the incident, has no money either, so there is only one source of funds to pay the victims—the company that built the chopper.

Hawthorne is trying to blame the amphibious skids—the balloon landing gear that were attached to the helicopter when it crashed, causing it to bounce and somersault after it hit the ground, aggravating the situation tenfold. Hawthorne's experts will say the bounce, and not the initial impact, was the proximate cause of the injuries; the manufacturer's experts will say the opposite. He has to establish that the manufacturer should have made it mandatory that the inflatable skids be used only over water.

Proof of an inadequate warning will be in the manuals and service bulletins circulated to purchasers of the particular model—in the hundreds of thousands of pieces of paper the manufacturer has turned over to Hawthorne during the discovery phase of the case, documents Hawthorne's legal assistants are at this moment pawing through in the bowels of his office—indexing, summarizing, computerizing, microfilming—preparing to present the relevant ones at trial. Ironically, if they nail the proof in the documents, there will *be* no trial. The company will settle so it will not risk alerting other customers to the problem with the skids and spawning additional lawsuits. Hawthorne has decided to take $150,000 per plaintiff if it is offered, but no less than twice that once the trial begins.

He wonders if it is a function of his age or his cash flow that he is hoping so hard for a settlement. In the old days he relished a trial—anytime, anywhere; on more than one occasion he had rejected reasonable settlements just to strut his stuff in court. But the thought of trying the copter case is painful: two months in Juneau, living like a monk on two hours' sleep a night while a judge who spends most of his time with timber sales and fishing rights tries to wend his way through the law of aviation accidents.

Even if he wins, there will be an appeal—two years' wait in the Ninth Circuit just to get a date for oral argument, another year till the appellate opinion is handed down—then a petition to the Supreme Court, certiorari denied, back to the trial court, judgment finally entered and, eventually, after all avenues of delay have been exhausted, paid by the manufacturer. Some ten years after it is earned, Hawthorne's fee will be received—and immediately begrudged, because it will seem disproportionate when compared to the award to the victims. Ignorant of the facts and blind to the ramifications of the neobarbarism advocated by the insurance companies, the newspapers will create another public relations disaster for the legal profession. For those and a thousand other reasons, settlement is preferable, but either way, Hawthorne calculates, the chopper case won't yield enough to get his business in the black.

As though she has read his mind, Martha looks up from her manual. "We need to talk."

"About what?"

"Money."

"You want a raise." Feeling expansive after his conquest of the convening pilots, Hawthorne is prepared to bargain in good faith.

Martha shakes her head. "I want to work for a solvent enterprise."

"So do I."

"Then you'd better listen to what I have to say."

He knows from the ditch just dug above her eyes that she is serious and angry, so he nods. When Martha is seriously angry, he obeys orders.

She swivels to face him squarely. Her suit is black and austere, offering the gloomy aspect she believes she must cultivate in order to be taken seriously. Behind her antique reading glasses, her eyes fix on him like landing lights.

"After you went to sleep last night, I got up and ran some numbers," she begins. "What with the start-up costs in SurfAir and the likelihood that the ultralight case will be reversed and have to be retried, I calculate that at the close of fiscal 'eighty-seven, the Law Offices of Alec Hawthorne will show a net operating loss of half a million dollars."

He feels his eyes widen and his veins swell. "You're kidding."

"I don't kid," she observes, "about money."

"What's the balance on our note?"

"A hundred and a half. The people at Security Pacific are not going to want to see you coming back for more, especially in light of the promises you made last time."

"Do I have any choice?"

"Several." She doesn't wait for him to request enumeration. "First, the house. The place in Belvedere has six bedrooms and eight baths."

"At last count."

"You live alone. You don't need the space, and you could net a quarter-million if you sold it. So why don't you?"

"I entertain sometimes."

"You throw an office bash at Christmas. Big deal. Given the tendency of the courts to extend dram shop liability to private parties, it isn't a good idea to be even *that* gracious anymore." She blinks to scroll another item into her thoughts. "Then there are the condos. You haven't seen Jackson Hole in years."

"I was thinking about doing some skiing just the other day."

"A condo is not essential equipment. You want to slide down the Tetons, rent a place at the village for a week. Let some surgeon carry the mortgage."

"It's a good investment."

"You need cash, not unrealized capital gains. Also, you should sell one of the cars. Frankly, I think a Rolls looks a bit ridiculous anywhere but London, but then I've never understood about men and cars. The bottom line is, one of them should go."

When he hesitates, she hurries on. "I'm not going to say anything about the office, even though it's excessive in every respect. I realize it's a security blanket or a phallic symbol or something, but we can put on a show and still slash the expenses."

He closes his eyes and leans back in his seat, enduring his punishment the way he endures the dentist. "Like what?"

"Like travel. The last time you went to Paris, you paid eight hundred a night at the Georges Cinq and averaged two hundred dollars per lunch tab."

"It's deductible, for Christ's sake."

"When a business is running at a loss, deductibility is no longer a viable rationale. And it's not the amount that's important, it's your ignorance of the details. How much do you think we've spent on the helicopter case?"

He shrugs. "Fifty thousand?"

Her lips curled like blood-red worms. "Three times that. We've spent forty just tracking down the mechanic who installed the skids."

"I thought he was CIA."

"He is, but they don't give you a map to the homes of their agents. We had to send someone to Honduras to hang around and try to spot the guy. Plus there are the trips to Juneau and back, depositions of the corporate guys in New York, the mock-up of the chopper, the video, the—"

"Okay, already. I'll keep better track."

"There are thirty other cases like that one in the office, Alec, and they're all sopping up money like a tampon."

He opens his eyes. "You're crude, you know that?"

She drills him with a glance. "If I weren't crude, I wouldn't last a day in this business." Martha returns to her manual.

He closes his eyes and sighs disspiritedly. Martha is right, of course; something must be done about the money. For all his fame and fortune, Hawthorne runs his business like a Ponzi scheme. What makes it difficult—and what Martha doesn't understand, because she believes success has something to do with merit—is that extravagance is essential to the game. Cases come to him not from the heirs of crash victims but from the lawyers handling the probate or the hand-holding. If Alec Hawthorne didn't look like the best aviation attorney on the West Coast, act like the best aviation attorney on the West Coat, *glow* like the best aviation attorney on the West Coast, the referrals would go to someone suitably audacious, and he is not willing to let that happen. He has been poor before; he doubts he can lift the load again.

A stewardess interrupts and asks if he needs anything. He motions for another drink. Because it is first class, she knows his name and his libation. The highball is before him in a jiffy, service with a smile.

A year ago he would have made a pass at her—she is ringless, buxom, and has a cast in her eye that suggests an adventuresome bent. But a recent fact of his life is that he has stopped trying to seduce strange women. Hence his abandonment of Molly Christian before the chase was even on. Hence his increasingly monogamous relationship with Martha. To the extent he understands it, Hawthorne believes it has something to do with his anxiety about the course and distance of his life. He has always viewed longevity as an overrated goal, but as his fiftieth year approaches, he is not so sure it isn't the only goal he has.

The plane trembles through an updraft. As his stomach flattens, Hawthorne is reminded of the SurfAir crash. He wonders if his investigator is at the scene yet, whether poor Livingood is wading through debris and decedents. For several seconds he wonders how a man could abide a life like that, until he realizes that most people see him and Livingood as part of the same vile process, jackals gobbling at the entrails of disaster victims, buzzards picking at the dead.

They had been standing on the stoop for a quarter of an hour, braving the chill in the evening air, apparently attempting the impossible, which was to get someone inside the little bungalow to answer the door.

Buried in a full-length winter wrap that enveloped all but her bobbed brown hair, her darkly troubled eyes, and the jut of her stubborn jaw, Brenda Farnsworth pressed the buzzer for the fifth time, as though her sister would materialize just to keep down the racket. At her back, Keith Tollison leaned against the wrought-iron railing and marveled at her determination. Brenda became intent upon the oddest things, most of them beyond achievement.

When she seemed about to ring again, he grabbed her arm. "She's obviously not home. Why is that making you crazy?"

She turned to face him, her breath white in the night, her gloved fists clenched against her chest. "I told Carol last week we might drop by before the dance. She said fine. She said she'd make hors d'oeuvres. She asked if you liked pâté."

He smiled. "What did you tell her?"

"I told her you didn't, but were too polite to say so if she served it up." Brenda met his look with eyes half-buried by the tumble of a frown. "Something's going on, Keith."

"What?"

"I don't know, but something definitely is—I've been having trouble connecting with Carol for months. She doesn't answer her phone, isn't home when I stop by, and when we *do* get together, she's mysterious about what she's been up to."

"Maybe she's found a man."

"She's not looking for a man."

"Sometimes they show up anyway. And sometimes older sisters don't know as much about their siblings as they think they do."

She refused to yield. "Carol hasn't been happy lately, and when you're unhappy, you do things that don't make sense. Things that come back to haunt you." Brenda's eyes glazed with the sting of memory. Although she was speaking of her sister, her template was herself.

She shrugged her coat higher on her neck, and looked beyond him at the lawn and the trees and the street, as though even geography were conspiring against her. "Can we come here after the dance? To make sure she's okay? Something's wrong; I can feel it."

Her brow knit, her features blunted by concern, Brenda leaned against the door and rewrapped her coat around her, struggling for warmth and peace of mind and failing to find either.

"I can't let anything happen to her, Keith," she said as he reached for her hand. "Every other person in my life got screwed up because of me: you; Spitter; my mother; my husband. If anything happened to Carol, it would kill me."

She looked at him from within the pain that had become a permanent part of her. According to Brenda, her husband had gone to war because the marriage had been a disaster and she had repeatedly told him so; her son was retarded because she had taken drugs while she was pregnant; her mother had run off because Brenda had been a terror as a child. Tollison didn't know how much of that was true; he only knew that Brenda believed it all was.

"I think you're imagining things," he said. "Carol probably just snuck off for the weekend. She can take care of herself, Bren."

Brenda released her coat and grasped his forearm, squeezing at sympathy. "But I'm worried. You know how I am."

He freed his arm. "You're working yourself up over nothing. *Forget* Carol for the next two hours. We'll have fun at the dance, then come see if she's home. In the meantime, let's just try to have a good time."

She shoved her hands in her pockets and shivered. Tollison put his arm over her shoulders and pulled her to his side. "Don't make me dance *every* dance, okay?" she murmured.

"Every other."

"And if your mother's there, promise you won't go off and leave me alone with her."

"She's not in the historical society anymore."

"But if she is."

"Okay, I promise. I won't leave you alone with her."

"With anybody."

He nodded. Her head against his chest, she spoke through scattered strands of hair. "Remember the prom?"

"Yep."

"I still have my dress. Daddy bought it in San Francisco. It cost a fortune. I couldn't remember thanking him for it, so I stopped by the bar and thanked him tonight. I was so proud that night, Keith," she added quietly.

"Of what?"

"Of myself."

"Why?"

"Because I was there with you."

His guilt cowered with him in the darkness.

"I still am, you know," Brenda went on, watching him with fractured eyes. "I'm proud to go places with you, even after all these years. You're the only prize I ever won."

He hugged her tight. After a last stab at the door button, they went off arm in arm. As they drove away, Tollison tried to escape the fact that of late his idea of a good time had become holding another woman in his arms.

The high school gym was as spruced and shined as a dozen volunteers and a hundred dollars could make it. Bunting dripped from the rafters like the remnants of a rally for the gold standard. The reflections off a revolving mirrored ball cascaded them with shooting stars. Beneath it all, Altoonans wore what they perceived to be their finest, which in most cases was what they wore to church.

The ladies of the historical society clustered at the door, beaming at the new arrivals, as proud as parents at what they'd wrought. Tollison presented a smile and the tickets to his fifth grade teacher, then edged toward the center of the floor, where most of the guests had gathered at the jump circle to gossip rather than to dance. Brenda stayed silent on his arm.

The band was a major attraction, a nine-piece ensemble that retained the name of its deceased leader, fronted by a sideman from the original group. It wasn't as thrilling as it had been in the old days, Tollison supposed, since swing was as alien as chamber music in a world numbed by heavy metal, but it was good enough to cause him to slip his arm around his partner's waist and urge her toward a space where there was room to do whatever you could call what it was he did when presented with an opportunity to dance.

"But we're the only ones," Brenda protested as he guided her around a knot of laughing merchants.

"Just close your eyes," he said as he twirled her toward the stage, "and pretend we're home alone."

"You *know* I'm not good at this," she said as he began to move her through the crowd in an ungainly combination of a toddle and a schottische.

"You're as good as you need to be in Altoona," he said, and apologized for stepping on her toe.

Holding her tight, reminded as he never was when they were arguing that Brenda was almost tiny, they bounced through "One O'clock Jump" and glided through "Loch Lomond" before she begged for a rest. Refreshments were heaped atop a table to the side of the dance floor, and they helped themselves to egg-salad sandwiches, slaw, a walnut brownie, and some of the adult punch. As they munched away beneath the north basket, the band segued into "Stardust," and Carl Woodley and his wife, Jasmine, joined them.

Carl was the clerk of the municipal court; his wife, the librarian at the high school. The women were friends and the men were reluctant acquaintances. While Brenda and Jasmine launched a new chapter of schoolroom gossip, Carl asked Tollison whether he was going to run for city attorney.

Tollison shook his head, knowing Woodley owed his job to the spoils reaped by the opposite party during the second Reagan landslide, sensing that Carl's pleasure in his answer indicated that Carl saw him as electable. Tollison wondered if he ought to reconsider.

"Can't blame you," Woodley intoned. "Municipal bonding and street repair probably aren't very challenging. But we do need new leadership. Altoona is going to hell, what with the fight over the new mall and the environmental people trying to get a no-growth initiative on the ballot next fall. And we've *got* to crack down on the hooligans, Keith. Senior citizens are afraid to go downtown anymore, the way those kids carry on in front of that video place and Pauli's Pizza. I've never heard such profanity in my life. And you know as well as I do they're doing drugs down there. What we need is a curfew. I tell you, these punkers make you wonder about the future of the country. I saw one yesterday, his head was shaved bald and painted black and numbered like an eight ball."

Tollison smiled. The kid Woodley referred to was the son of one of his clients, who thought the pool motif was the only creative thing his son had ever done.

"I don't think it's quite that bad, Carl. You and Ricky Peters got into a few scrapes in your day."

"Ah, that was only hijinks. Kids today are committing major crimes. The things Jasmine tells me about what goes on at that high school have no place in a civilized society."

Barely listening, Tollison was looking for Laura Donahue. "I don't think we've ever been quite as civilized as we believe, Carl."

"No? Well, I'd like you to name a place that's better."

"There were thirty-five murders in Japan last year. In the U.S. there were nine thousand."

"So what? You know those Orientals aren't like—"

"In Canada there were six. Australia only had ten."

"But that's hardly a sign of—"

"Every industrialized nation but the U.S. and South Africa provides government-funded medical insurance to its citizens. And requires TV stations to give free time to candidates for office. And—"

"Come on, Keith. That's just liberal pap. Money won't solve our problems. Values, that's what it's all about. Basic human values."

Tollison was about to respond in predictable kind when a hand on his shoulder turned him away from his antagonist. It was Sandy, his secretary, a vision in a strapless blue billow and a tiara of silver foil. "Hi, Mr. Tollison."

"Hi, Sandy. You're looking great this evening. Scrumptious, in fact."

"Thanks." Sandy blushed, and the young man who lurked at her back reddened to match.

"I'm sorry to bother you," Sandy hurried on, "but I was wondering if Mrs. Donahue ever got in touch with you."

A muscle tightened in his neck. "No. Why?"

"It's just, she called *me*, see, and said she'd been trying to reach you at the office and at home and everything, and she asked if I knew where you were and I said you were probably at the jail, so she said if I saw you to have you call her as soon as possible. She sounded sort of upset."

"Did she say what was wrong?"

"No, she just said it was urgent. Oh. She said if I didn't reach you right away to tell you she'd be at the airport, not at home. At the, ah, what's that new one? SurfAir? That's it. The SurfAir counter. She said she didn't know if you could get through to her or not, but she wanted you to try."

"Is that all?"

"I *think* so. I was getting ready for the dance and Travis was early, the geek, so maybe I forgot something. She seemed real worried, that's all I know."

Tollison turned to Brenda. "I've got to make some calls." Though Brenda was about to ask a question, he turned his back and trotted toward the door.

The telephones were down the hall toward the restrooms. When the operator came on the line, he asked for the SurfAir counter at San Francisco International. The operator asked for money. Digging for his wallet, Tollison extracted his credit card and read off the number. The operator put him through but the line was busy. He hung up and went through the procedure once again, this time asking for the airport number. That line was busy also. When he got the operator once again, she was irritated.

"Give me station KXYV, the news department, please," he asked in his kindest tone, the one reserved for Laura and veniremen. When the operator asked for his card number again, it was through clenched teeth.

"Station KXYV, Channel Nine, San Francisco; how may we help you?" a voice sang a moment later, indistinguishable from a pitch for tithes.

"News department, please."

"One moment. . . . Those lines are busy at this time. May I take a message?"

"Maybe you can help me. Has something happened at the airport tonight? An emergency of some kind?"

"I'm not sure if I should give out that information, sir. Perhaps when the news lines are free you could ask—"

"Come on. Just tell me. Not the details. Just tell me what happened."

The voice dipped into a sensible range. "I *think* there was a plane crash somewhere, but I'm not sure. People have been running in and out all night, but they never *tell* me anything. I don't have any details—I'm in sales, not news—so if you could call back later, maybe some lines will be free? Or watch our nightwatch edition or our early-bird news at six A.M. I'm *sure* we'll have complete information by then."

Tollison hung up. When he got back to Brenda, she looked at him warily. "What's wrong?"

"There's been a plane crash."

"Where?"

"San Francisco. Near the airport. Jack Donahue was supposed to be coming back from LA tonight. I have to go find Laura."

"But surely someone else can—"

"She was trying to reach *me*," he said, his ferocity as surprising to him as to the Woodleys and his date. "If there were someone else, she would have called them," he added as reasonably as he could. "I've got to go. Jasmine, can you and Carl take Brenda when you leave?"

"But—"

"I'll call you."

He bent to bestow a kiss that Brenda twisted to avoid, then sprinted toward the door.

His mind a whirl, the miles passed unnoticed. By the time he neared the airport exit, he was unable to keep from seeing the evening as a watershed. If Jack Donahue had been killed, after a period of mourning Tollison could marry Laura and begin a new life, the life he wanted rather than one that had been thrust on him, a life elsewhere than Altoona.

As he approached the SurfAir section of the terminal, the traffic thickened to a fudge. Beneath the canopy four TV news vehicles, two police units, an ambulance, and a crunch of other vehicles strayed under the bewildered supervision of a private guard. Horns honked, arms flailed, people dashed in and out, many of them crying.

If he observed legalities, parking his car was out of the question. Given the expense of the ticket, normally he would not have considered double-parking, but when it was clear that it would be many minutes before he could get through the jam, he left his Cutlass next to a dilapidated Chevy he hoped had been there as long as it looked, which was a decade.

The counter was a mob scene. Newspeople swarmed over the area like ants fighting their way toward fresher food. A woman in a SurfAir uniform looked both infuriated and on the brink of tears. As quickly as he could, Tollison edged to where he could hear the woman's response to the questions that flew at her like bats.

"I have no way of knowing if they will be made available. . . . Of *course* they are not being held against their will, but until the situation is clarified, we feel . . . I'm not at liberty to disclose their location at this time. . . . I have no word on survivors; an announcement will be made when definite information is available. I'm sure you understand our desire not to issue misleading comments on that subject. . . . At this time we believe the flight was full. . . . A complete manifest is not available—617 was a shuttle flight, with credit-card ticketing on board the aircraft. There were a few advance reservations, but not many. . . . Yes, the system might make identification of the passengers difficult. . . . Well, no one thought something like this would happen, obviously. Now, if you will excuse me, I need to consult my superiors. I have no reason to believe that the relatives and friends of the passengers will be returning to this area. As I said before, in the interests of privacy, their location will not be disclosed. They are, of course, free to contact you at any time they choose. As far as I know, none of them has chosen to do so. Now, if you will excuse me. *Please.* Let me by. Get that camera out of my face. You people are *savages*, aren't you? *Total savages.*"

Tollison watched as the poor woman squeezed through the throng of reporters and made her way to an unmarked door to the left of the ticket counter. Gradually and grudgingly, the crowd of onlookers began to disperse, allowing Tollison a clear view of the counter area. When he saw no one resembling Laura Donahue, he concluded that those who had been awaiting passengers off the SurfAir flight had been taken by authorities to another part of the airport to await an account of the victims.

He looked up and down the ticket area but saw nothing to indicate where the families and friends of the passengers might be. The SurfAir counter was empty; the notation on the arrival schedule board beside flight 617 read merely DELAYED. He decided to drive to the short-term lot, leave the car, and come back to the terminal and wait. The media would have to be told something, and that something would surely indicate where they had taken Laura.

In his car and clear of the mob, he followed signs to the garage. As he was about to turn in, a knot of people emerged from a door at the far end of the terminal. Huddled together, they milled on the sidewalk until, ushered by a half-dozen SurfAir personnel, they moved toward a shuttle bus parked just outside the door and, in dreadful silence, filed into the gray-green vehicle.

Tollison slowed as much as he dared and looked at the men and women as they appeared at the windows. They had drawn faces, stark and anxious; more than a few bore tears or the empty eyes of dire perspective. One kept looking at the sky, as though she expected the plane to appear below the clouds, proof that the report of a disaster was a hoax.

In the next instant he saw Laura, her face a momentary moon beyond the dark plastic of the windows. As he was about to call her name, she turned to respond to something said by the man beside her. When she did not turn back, Tollison veered away from the parking lot and waited. When the bus pulled away from the curb he fell in behind it, close enough to keep tabs, far enough not to give alarm.

The ride was short. Five minutes after leaving the airport boulevard the bus turned abruptly, then pulled into a driveway that led through a high hedge to what appeared to be a small motel. Lights off, Tollison parked behind a service van that bore the SurfAir logo and waited as the bus riders trudged off the vehicle as desolately as they'd embarked. When they had filed through the revolving door into the gaily decorated lobby, he got out of his car and crouched behind the van, in position to see what was going on inside.

Enervated, the friends and families clustered around the registration desk as though its aura would revive them. They seemed fewer in number than the total that had gotten off the bus, and after a moment Tollison realized the group was in line, receiving room keys one by one. When he didn't see Laura, he guessed she had already been assigned a space. As he contemplated his next move, he found himself wondering whether she was as despairing as the others or whether, in some new nick of consciousness, she was relieved that Jack Donahue was out of her life so that Keith Tollison could enter it properly, through an open door.

Ten minutes later the last person had been dispatched toward the elevators. When they were alone, the SurfAir employees talked among themselves for several minutes, then one of them took a sheet of paper from the desk clerk, glanced at it and nodded, and led the others in the direction opposite the elevators. When they were gone, Tollison went inside.

The desk clerk was a young man with slick black hair, a slick black suit, and a transparent moustache that highlighted his chipped front tooth. He looked up with an expression that suggested he had prayed for a messiah.

"You're from the airline, right? So can I go now? My shift was up an hour ago, man, and these people are hassling me like mad and I don't know what—"

"I'm not with the airline," Tollison interrupted. "I'm an attorney. My name is Tollison."

After a jolt of panic, the desk clerk shook his head. "I got instructions. No reporters; no lawyers. Period."

"I don't care *what* your instructions are, I have a client in this hotel. Her name is Laura Donahue. Her husband was on that plane. She came in along with the rest of the people. She's been trying to reach me all evening and—"

"I'm *sorry*, sir; I got my orders. You aren't supposed to *be* here."

Tollison leaned across the counter. "Listen to me, son. I told you my client has been trying to reach me. She left word for me to contact her as soon as possible. I am attempting to do that now, and I want—"

"I can't help you, buddy."

"As I said, I'm trying to reach her, and she *wants* me to reach her, and for you to forbid that to occur is a false imprisonment of Mrs. Donahue. I will sue *both* you *and* the airline for that, for the intentional infliction of mental distress on Mrs. Donahue in this time of tragedy, and for your gross and willful disregard of her basic human rights. It will cost you a bundle, son, and to prevent it, all you have to do is tell me what room she's in. The SurfAir people don't even have to know I'm around."

The desk clerk thought it over, then looked at his list. "Donahue, Donahue," he murmured as he ran his finger down the paper. "Got it. If you hurry, you'll be up there before they get back from their meeting."

"Do you know anything at all about the crash?"

The desk clerk shook his head. "It crashed, that's all I know."

"While it was landing?"

"It was in a forest somewhere. By Palo Alto, I think. It was real bad, I know that. I think they're all dead," he added softly. "I mean, it would take a miracle to survive something like that, right? God. You should have *seen* those people. Crying. Praying. *Swearing*, can you believe it? At *me*. Was *I* the pilot of the fucking thing? I only been in a plane once in my life and I got sick as shit over Denver. I didn't know anything like *this* would happen when I took this job. All I want is out of here, let me tell you. She's in three oh seven."

Tollison took the stairs to the third floor. When he reached the door he tapped, and tapped again. When a voice asked him who it was, he told her.

After several seconds a desolate stranger appeared in the doorway, searched for succor in his face, then rushed into his arms. "His plane crashed, Keith."

"Is he dead?"

As the echo of the question threatened to betray him, Laura Donahue shook her head. "They won't *tell* me anything. They just stuck me here to wait."

"I'll go find out what—"

She held him fast. "Hold me, Keith. Please hold me. Hold me and tell me what to do if Jack's been killed."

He held her as tightly as he thought she could bear, until he heard the telephone ring inside the room. When Laura made no move to answer it, he guided her to the bed, eased her onto it, and went to pick up the receiver.

"Listen good, 'cause I can only tell you once," an oily voice demanded. "This could be the most important minute of your life. I'm the senior associate of Victor A. Scallini, the foremost aviation attorney in the world. Mr. Scallini would like to represent you in filing an action against SurfAir for the wrongful death of your loved one in the crash. His clients have received *major* damage awards in crash litigation— I'm talking *millions* here, believe me. There's no time for details now, but whatever you do, don't sign anything and don't talk to another lawyer. If you call Mr. Scallini's Los Angeles office tomorrow, you will be told what to do. The number is 213-555-1232. Write it down. This could be the most important thing you've ever done. I guarantee you won't be—"

Tollison dropped the phone into its cradle and returned to the bed. Eyes closed, shoes off, her green gown bunched and twisted at her waist, Laura blindly pulled him toward her. He crawled onto the bed and took her in his arms. As he pressed his lips against her hair, he could not help hoping that the catastrophe meant that he could lie with her forever—a dream as corrupt as the lawyer on the phone.

REPORT ON WOODSIDE AIR
DISASTER

Postmortem Examination No. 87-A-379
Name of Deceased: Jane Doe No. 16-W
Pathologist: Jacob Greenman
Date: April 2, 1987
Location: South Bay Mortuary, San Jose, California

External Description: The severely traumatized dismembered body of a Caucasian female, age approximately forty years, dressed in the charred and shredded remains of white silk undergarments, a cotton print blouse, and a blue wool blend skirt, the rest of the clothing being missing or decomposed or present in microscopic quantities.

There is a flattening of the torso as a result of multiple fractures of all of the long bones of the body, with displacement of the sternum downward. There is a decapitation injury close to the neck with avulsion of the neck and viscera. The heart and lungs and uterus protrude through a large defect in the chest. The lower left leg is missing below the knee.

Possible identifying features include abdominal scarring indicating appendectomy.

Cause of death: Traumatic evisceration of heart and brain due to airline accident. Remains will be held at the above location, pending identification and disposition.

WARNING: Unless essential for legal or religious reasons, remains should not be viewed by next of kin.

FOUR

"But why?"

Alec Hawthorne crumples the top sheet of the legal pad on the desk in front of him, a sheet of scribbles that begins in lazy curves and ends in angry angles and irritated whorls. "I made the guy a senior partner last year, for God's sake. *I doubled his draw.* I thought that was what he wanted."

"He did," Martha agrees mildly. "Last year."

"He just packed and left? No explanation, no nothing?"

"That's the way I hear it."

"Did he steal anything?"

"Only Gwen."

"Who the hell is Gwen?"

"His secretary. The blonde with the legs you like."

Perplexed and pained, Hawthorne shakes his head. "Did anyone see him go?"

"The receptionist. She thought the boxes meant they were remodeling his office. Again."

"Who knew him best around here?" Hawthorne asks, casting his mind back across the years, seeking a foretelling incident.

Martha constructs a smile, filament-thin, maddeningly tranquil. "You did."

Hawthorne shakes his head against the implication that he is somehow at fault. "Was he pissed about something? Lately people seem to be getting mad at me without me even knowing about it," he adds, as if it is a phenomenon violative of natural law.

Martha only shrugs. "I heard he didn't like the size of his office."

76

"Which office did he want?"

"Mine," Martha notes without inflection, then stands, smooths her skirt, adjusts her jacket. For just a moment, her back arcs triumphantly.

She and Dan Griffin have been rivals for a decade, the contenders for his empire jostling for the seat at his right hand. De jure, Griffin has been senior, his name before Martha's on the letterhead and door. De facto, Martha has been primary since spending seventy-two hours in the office without sleep or supper to meet a deadline that had fallen through the cracks in Hawthorne's scattered schedule. From that time hence, Martha has been in charge of the office calendar, and deadlines are no longer missed.

He watches as she perfects her look. She is svelte and, in a form-fitting suit of blood-red suede and a high-necked blouse of off-white silk, particularly majestic this morning. He wonders if she knew Dan's surrender was imminent and had dressed to suit the occasion.

"You do twice the work that he did," Hawthorne says tentatively, trying a justification on for size. Because he knows no reason for Dan Griffin's defection, he sits guilty of all conceivable ones.

"Closer to triple, I'd say. Not that Dan saw it that way."

"How *did* he see it?"

Her smile is cryptic. "That he'd been with the firm longer than anyone but me, and that I didn't count because I'd slept my way into the partnership." She laughs to herself. "He also thought his credentials were more impressive than mine because he'd been a law review editor, and that because he was a man and a father and a sole provider and whatever else it is that men think makes them more valuable than women, he should be top cock."

As with most of Martha's utterances, there is a provocative slant to her version of events, but the possibility that Dan's desertion implies a personal failure on his part prompts Hawthorne to probe further. "We were *carrying* him. He never stayed in the office after five, never worked weekends, and always got sick when his cases came up on the trial calendar. He was a nervous wreck whenever he had to be anywhere but the law library."

"True."

"So why leave now?"

Martha stops fiddling with her dress and looks at him. "He got a client. Some movie star. A law school buddy down in Beverly Hills referred the case to Dan."

"What case?"

"SurfAir."

"Already?"

"Well, you know those show biz types. If it involves anything more demanding than eggs Benedict and bullshit, they start looking for someone else to do the work."

Hawthorne slams a fist onto the desk. "He can't take files out of here like that. If he weren't in this firm, he'd never have gotten that referral in a million years."

"You and I know that, and Dan *used* to know that; I doubt that he does anymore."

"We'll stop him."

"How?"

The problem is suddenly in a familiar mode—a quarrel amenable to maneuver. "What firm did he go with?"

Martha shrugs. "I heard he shopped himself to Scallini a month ago, but Vic was fending off another malpractice crisis, so he wasn't interested."

"If you hear anything definite, call whatever outfit he signs on with and tell them we regard SurfAir as an office matter, not Dan's personal property. Tell them we'll file a lien on any monies due him out of the case, tell them—"

"It may not be worth the trouble," Martha interrupts, retaking her seat and crossing her endless legs. Though she wears no stockings, her shins bear a perpetual burnish from an unseasonable source that Hawthorne cannot fathom.

"Why not?"

"This so-called actor. Name's Clarence Autrey or some such. Got a supporting actor Oscar for playing a dipso in some western a hundred years ago, which apparently was typecasting. No wife, a couple of adult kids. Hasn't worked in anything but dinner theater in years. We'll be lucky to net fifty thousand."

Hawthorne refuses to be dissuaded. "It's the principle, damnit. We can't let lawyers walk out with whatever happens to catch their eye. We've got bills to pay, for Christ's sake. We've got—"

She sniffs. "So what do you want me to do?"

"Draft a letter to Dan, for my signature, saying we regard that matter as ours and all other cases he was working on as well. Tell him to list any other pending matters he regards as his, tell him to list any and all items of personal property he removed from the office when he left. Make it nasty. I—"

Martha smothers his outburst before he combusts. "Right. What else?"

Hawthorne seethes to silence. Martha eyes him as curiously as an anthropologist at a mating rite. "Nothing now," he surrenders. "Not on Dan, at least." In need of another focus, he eyes the notebook atop her naked knee. "What else do you have?"

She flips a page. "Status conference. You're going to Rome on Friday, and the troops need to know where we stand on the active files. Plus, we've got two new bodies to break in."

"Can't you do it?"

She shakes her head. "These young geniuses didn't join this firm to work for *me*. Let them see you know they're alive. Hell, one of them turned down Pillsbury *and* Cravath to come with us."

"He won't last a year."

"I know, I know; you think trial work is too messy for the intellectuals. Maybe you're right, but if you don't start doing a little PR around here, you're going to have more Dan Griffins on your hands."

He sighs. "Give me five minutes, then round them up. How many do we have now?"

"Eighteen lawyers, thirty staff. Only ten of the lawyers are in town."

"Jesus. I keep thinking this is a small operation."

"The only thing small about it is our bank balance."

Martha is out of the room before he knows it. In the rarefied air of her absence, Hawthorne leans back in his chair and closes his eyes. Dan Griffin. Not a genius or a wizard in court or a business-getter or a deft closer, either. Just a guy who worked hard hours if not particularly long ones, a nice guy in a profession where nice guys are as rare as a well-turned phrase. And he hadn't even said goodbye. It is an apparent legacy of the decade that nice guys are as greedy as the rest of them—$120,000 had purchased a year of labor but not an ounce of loyalty. Christ. Running a law firm has become as treacherous as owning a ball team.

He looks out across the bay, toward the island where traitors like Dan Griffin had in times past been imprisoned. Tears come to his eyes—without Dan there is no one in the office who remembers the old days, no one except Martha, and she regards the past as putrid, a cadaverous repository of hypocrisy and misplaced sentiment.

On many a Friday evening he and Dan had shared a little Scotch and a lot of exhaustion and reminisced about the early years, when Dan had been in the library researching the case law and Hawthorne was traveling Indian country trying his first crash cases. Planes with names indigenous to the land—Apache, Comanche, Navajo—went down in a veritable blizzard, for reasons ranging from disintegrating propellers to collapsing nose wheels to defective altimeters to the wrath of weather to drunken pilots to—who knew? Sometimes planes just crashed and the reason died with the pilot, who probably never knew it either.

Plane by plane and trial by trial, Hawthorne had forged his knowledge of the industry—aeronautics, avionics, meteorology, traffic control, operations and maintenance procedures, safety regulations, pilot training. It had become a quest, in the end—the more he learned, the more he wanted to know. Living out of ratty motels, his private life confined to the telephone and every other weekend, he tracked down witnesses, interviewed survivors, inspected wreckage, debriefed passengers and pilots and controllers, doing it all himself. As he'd mastered the technical data necessary to ferret out the cause of the disasters, he'd mastered the workings of the human body to the extent that by the time he moved up to the big cases—commercial disasters like SurfAir—he knew more medicine than most of the doctors in the city, knew so much that he hadn't consulted a physician about his personal health for years.

Doctors. He still laughed at the memory of the pompous "experts" the manufacturers trotted out to oppose him, so secure in their theories of why the plaintiffs weren't injured that badly, hadn't suffered that much pain, wouldn't be disabled for all that long. Then wham— a day of cross-examination would leave them looking angrily at their lawyers and longingly at the door and imploringly at the judge, who wasn't doing nearly enough to stop the slaughter.

In the old days he could ambush them—they had never heard of Alec Hawthorne, had no idea what was coming till he'd deftly removed their scalps. Now, they knew details about his career he'd long forgotten, were thoroughly prepared and prepped, so careful and cautious he was lucky if they spelled their name for the record without allowing for the eminently reasonable possibility they might have gotten it wrong.

But it didn't matter. Despite their wary reticence, the hirelings of the defense teams almost always lost, not because they were incompetent or unintelligent, but because after the years in Indian country, Alec Hawthorne was the best in the West at persuading jury after jury that his opponent's cause was foul. Victories piled up and his reputation grew, not because he was smarter or better prepared or even luckier than the defense, but because in the bedrock of his soul Alec Hawthorne believed his cause was just and the incandescence of that conviction made twelve men and women believe it was as well.

He still hears from them once in a while, those early clients, telling him how their broken bodies or broken homes were mending, describing rendings in their lives that all the money in the world could never heal. And on the days he does, he does not regret what his life has cost him.

The door opens and Martha reenters, followed by a string of young men and women—handsome, alert, aware—the lawyers in the firm. Hawthorne gestures toward the grouping of couches and easy chairs at the far end of his massive office and waits while they take their seats.

They eye him bravely, eager for his counsel. They are more than a little brash, which was why he'd hired them, the absence of neutrality and niceness being the essence of a trial lawyer. Building a law office is a bit like cloning, Hawthorne supposes, or even playing God, for what he has tried to gather around him is a group of men and women who could double for the Alec Hawthorne who had begun to ply his trade in Indian country some twenty years before.

He looks at Martha and nods. "First," she begins, "the offer is up to nine hundred thousand in the helicopter case."

"Have we nailed the skid thing down yet?"

"Not quite. We still haven't located the mechanic—the last we heard he was TDY in Chad. But we'll get him."

Hawthorne frowns. "I hate to settle till all the teeth are pulled—this can go to a mil and a half if we lock up liability a little tighter. One thing that occurred to me—we're claiming it wasn't the crash but the bounce that did the damage, right? Why don't we send the tower tapes to a voice-print analyst, show the pilot wasn't under that much stress when he hit the ground the first time, which would imply he thought he could handle the situation until the skids turned the damn thing into a basketball."

"Okay," Martha says, then looks at one of the young men. "Mike?"

Mike nods and takes a note.

"As for the settlement itself," Hawthorne continues, "someone from Union Casualty called me yesterday, said they had a new annuity package we'd be interested in, that could be tailored to any type of structure we use. I want someone to talk to him and see if it's as good as it sounds. A point either way on the annuity tables can amount to hundreds of thousands of dollars over the course of the payout."

Several heads nod. Martha look at one of them. "Pam?"

"Right."

"Just be sure we're straight with the IRS. Revenue Ruling 79-220 says if we release the defendants from liability, the payments will count as income to the recipient."

"Right."

"That it for the chopper?"

Martha nods.

"Next?"

"The defendants in the Grand Canyon crash have agreed how to share the damages," Martha continues. "They're going to stipulate liability next week."

"Are we ready for that to happen?"

"Not if it limits our discovery, which is what they're trying to do, to keep us from getting hold of their maintenance schedules. They want us to waive our punitive-damage claim in return for the stipulation, of course."

"What do you think?"

Martha snarls. "I think they should fuck themselves. We've got a real chance at punitives for willful disregard of the Airworthiness Directive. A court in Oregon just upheld punitives against United in the Portland crash, which is the first time a jury award of exemplary damages against a major airline in a crash case has been affirmed on appeal. We don't have a smoking gun yet, but it's worth it to keep looking."

"You always think there's a smoking gun," Alec says with a grin that Martha clearly sees as condescending.

"That's because there always is," she retorts hotly. "If we can't find it, it's because Hawley Chambers has *buried* the son of a bitch."

Hawthorne looks toward his button-down acolytes. "Hawley Chambers is chief counsel for Federal Airline Underwriters, which insures most of the major airlines in this country. Martha sees insurance companies as only slightly less craven than the Mafia."

He expects her to smile at his jest. "Tell them about Pago Pago," she directs instead.

Hawthorne laughs. "Back in 1974, a Pan Am 707 went down while trying to land in Pago Pago. Ninety-seven killed, not from the crash but from the fire afterward. Seems the exit doors didn't open, and everyone was trapped inside. Well, before any independent investigators could get to the scene, someone—the insurers, the airline, someone—ordered the wreckage buried where it lay. They just dug a hole with bulldozers and shoved the 707 down in it, then covered it up. So no one ever knew why only four people got out of that plane alive."

"That's foul," someone mutters.

"So let's make sure discovery goes ahead," Hawthorne instructs into the awed silence. "And we hang on to the punitive claim until they've produced the documents."

After a brief hesitation, Martha nods. "That was Dan's baby," she says carefully.

He doesn't know how much the troops know about Dan's defection, suspects as is usual in bureaucracies the troops know more than the commander about internal unrest. "Well, now it's someone else's. You decide."

She whispers to the young man at her side. Mike is his name, Hawthorne seems to remember. As they exchange smiles, he waits for Martha to continue through her list.

"SurfAir," Martha says.

Hawthorne nods. "A death case came in yesterday—a mother and a preschool child, the client the surviving husband. We need to get a fee agreement to him."

"Not much money for a mother and child in a nondependent context," the young man Mike observes laconically.

Martha rebuts him quickly. "That's not true anymore; the women's movement is forcing courts to place a reasonable monetary value on homemakers and children. We got three hundred thousand for a housewife in the Cessna case, and in New Orleans they just awarded two fifty to a parent for loss of a minor child."

"Doesn't matter, anyway," Hawthorne adds. "We should have several more plaintiffs coming in, so we can afford to take some marginals."

Martha shakes her head. "I don't know about that. Somehow Scallini's people got through to the hotel where SurfAir whisked the friends and families. Our guy in the clerk's office told me Vic just dropped a billion-dollar case in the hopper. The papers will be full of it tomorrow, and that'll get Vic a dozen more cases, easy. He's serious about this one, evidently; a lawyer in San Mateo called this morning to tell me he represented the wife of a SurfAir victim. He asked what we paid in referral fees. When I told him thirty percent, he said Scallini had offered fifty. When I wouldn't let him jack me up, he decided Vic was his boy."

"The buzzards are gathering," Hawthorne mumbles. "And Dan's gone off to join them."

His mind dwells on Vic Scallini, scourge of legitimate tort practitioners. Lecher, alcoholic, ambulance chaser—over the years, Scallini had generated more bad publicity for the personal-injury bar than the rest of the field combined, yet the ignorant and uninformed still flocked to him, as often as not only to see their claims vanish in the muck of Vic's slovenly and haphazard practice, where overworked and underpaid nonentities labored mightily just to keep the statutes of limitation in mind.

"We should get out a choice-of-law memo in SurfAir," Martha says in the middle of the depression fostered by his colleague's vast venality.

The question jerks Hawthorne back to business. "Right."

Martha looks left. "Mike?"

"Okay," the young man says.

Hawthorne decides to coach. "Normally, California law would apply in SurfAir, since the *lex loci delicti* is here and most of the victims are California residents, which makes California chiefly concerned over how the injured and the heirs are compensated. But another jurisdiction may be better as far as damages, particularly punitive damages, which California doesn't allow in death cases. Check pre-impact terror, too —a Texas jury just awarded twenty thousand for two seconds' worth. I don't think there are any contacts with Texas in this case, but Florida allows recovery for pain and suffering for the heirs even if the victim dies, which California does not, and a recent case awarded one point eight million in the death of a teenager. Florida is where the engines were manufactured, so that's a hook, but be careful. Before you suggest an alternative to California, see how close the state's legislature is to passing a tort-limitation law that will throw it all in an uproar. Give Martha a memo on all the considerations." He looks at Martha. "Anything else?"

"You want to file a complaint yet?"

"No, but we should file a federal tort claim on the theory the control tower screwed up, which is almost certainly the case if it was a midair or a near miss. They reuse those tower tapes every fifteen days, so we need to get an order preserving them."

Martha nods.

"Let's leave it there for now. Thanks for your attention, group." He pauses, senses they are expecting more from him, and continues when he realizes what it is. "As you know, Mr. Griffin is no longer with this office. If you were doing work for him, see Martha for your new assignment. If any of you knows anything about his plans, I hope you'll let Martha know. These things happen. Usually because of money. If any of you gets to feeling underpaid, take a look around at what it takes to keep us going. Then look at the time sheets and compare your contribution with Martha's. If you still feel abused, come see me. No promises to give you a raise; only a promise to listen to your tale of woe." He pauses for some response. When he hears none, he says, "Okay. That's it."

In the back of the room, a hand goes up. "Where do you see this firm ten years from now, Mr. Hawthorne?"

He is startled first by the young man's candor and then by the sadistic gleam in Martha's eye when he silently asks her to put a stop to it. "Well," he stammers when Martha fails to lift a finger, "I hope we'll be known as the preeminent personal-injury firm on the West Coast."

"You're not planning to retire anytime soon, are you?"

"I can't afford to." He hears laughs from those who think he is joking.

"If you got hit by a truck, who would be in charge?"

The questioner is Mike. Hawthorne dares a glance at Martha. "I really haven't thought about it much—I try to keep out of the way of both trucks and ex-wives." When no one laughs, he blurts the only answer the circumstance allows. "Martha would be, I imagine. Most people think she's in charge already."

Another hand goes up and its owner doesn't wait for an invitation to speak. "Some people say the tort system won't even exist ten years from now. What's your response?"

The question is impudent and smooth—Hawthorne frowns at the affront. "I know that's what some people say, but if you look into it, you'll find those people are politically naïve or deeply biased. Inefficiency, greed, waste, everything that can be blamed on tort lawyers has been. And there are abuses, I don't deny it. But what's the alternative? No money for pain and suffering? No punitive damages for willful and wanton misconduct? Restricting contingent fees until only incompetents can make a living representing injured people? Why should the companies that cause these horrible injuries not be required to pay for them?"

When no one responds to his rhetoric, he plunges ahead.

"The law professors want tort litigation replaced by a social service agency, like the workman's compensation boards. Sounds great? Well, tell me a single social service agency that is adequately funded. Food stamps—slashed. Disabled kicked off the Social Security rolls right and left. If you *really* analyze the reform proposals, you find that what they do is force someone who's been injured to reduce his standard of living to the poverty level merely because he was unlucky enough to get his brain scrambled by a reckless driver."

Pausing for breath, Hawthorne looks at his audience. In a pool of rapt attention, he warms to the subject.

"What's true is, the assault on the tort system is the product of a multimillion-dollar publicity campaign by the insurance companies to sell the idea that there is something wrong with the civil justice system in this country. The first thing to say is that the supposed litigation explosion is a lie—tort filings between 1978 and 1984 increased at half the rate of the population.

"The second thing to say is that the size of verdicts has been grossly overstated—even the service that provides the numbers says they're being misused in the insurance propaganda.

"The third thing is that the crisis, if any, is over. Insurance profits in the first quarter of 1986 were up a thousand percent; for the entire year the profits of property/casualty carriers more than doubled. Was the crisis real in the first place? Well, in the so-called crisis years of 1982 to 1985, when premiums were going through the roof, twelve of the largest casualty insurers increased the cash compensation to their CEOs by fifty percent.

"It's the insurance industry, not the lawyers, that should be reformed—they're not regulated by the states and are exempt from federal antitrust laws and the scrutiny of the Federal Trade Commission. The exemptions should be cancelled. State approval should be required for premium increases of ten percent or more. The industry should have to reveal how much premium and investment income it earns each year and how much it pays in claims, so its rates can be evaluated. The giant reinsurance companies—primarily, Lloyd's of London—that earn half their income from American companies and call all the shots in major disaster litigation should be regulated as well. And the states should hire enough people to do the job—right now, Aetna alone employs more actuaries than all the states combined."

He stands up and begins to pace. "Tort reform will be a cruel joke on every consumer in America. How do I know the proposed reforms won't help? Simple. Canada enacted virtually every proposal the insurance companies are pushing and the situation up there hasn't changed at all—premiums are outrageous and risky operations can't get coverage."

He stops for breath, then smiles. "That's the bad news. The good news is that compromise may be coming. A group is getting together in Sacramento next month—representatives of doctors, lawyers, consumer groups, Common Cause, insurance people, manufacturers, chambers of commerce—to try to come up with a treaty that will solve some of the problems or at least keep the various interests from cutting each other's throats. If everyone gives a little, maybe we'll come up with a compromise. I'm going as a representative of the California Trial Lawyers, and I'll know more about how things look after the meeting. But for now, the short answer to your question is that the personal-injury business isn't dead yet, and if the people of this state have any sense, it never will be. Okay?"

Stunned by the exegesis, Hawthorne's assistants file silently from the room and leave him to his labors and his lingering thoughts of treason.

At some point Keith Tollison fell asleep. It was some time after Laura had stopped crying; after he had gone out in search of a liquor store and returned with a pint of bourbon they had shared until it vanished; after they had tacitly forsworn the question each had yearned to ask, which was whether the plane crash was the answer to a prayer the other one had offered.

He sensed even before he opened his eyes that Laura was no longer beside him. Disoriented, for a moment he thought the previous evening had been a nightmare, but the shiny surfaces of the room and the rush of water from behind the mirrored door indicated otherwise. He propped the pillows against the headboard and hiked himself against them.

The room was dark, shaded by a thick drape across the single window, smelling of sleep and booze and cleaning agents. Images of the evening slipped in and out of focus, as did the shape of his desires. As he considered whether to leave Laura long enough to find a drugstore, the mirrored door opened and she appeared before him, wrapped in a sheet.

"Good morning," she said.

"How are you feeling?"

"Fine. Well, a little hung over, actually. I usually don't drink so much so fast."

He glanced at the rim of sunlight around the window curtain. "What time is it?"

"Ten-fifteen." She smiled warmly. "You slept like a baby. You must have been exhausted."

"I should go somewhere and clean up." He rolled off the bed and sagged into the chair beneath the swag lamp.

"There's everything you need right here." She gestured to the bathroom at her back. "Those little gift packs these places give you nowadays. While you take a shower and get dressed, I'll go to the lobby and see what's going on."

"You haven't heard anything at all?"

She shook her head. "They came by at eight and told me to stay in my room unless I wanted to go to the coffee shop for breakfast. I didn't feel like looking an egg in the eye, so here I am." For the first time of the morning, a flutter in her voice hinted of tumult.

He stood up. "Wait for me. I'll just be a minute."

"It's all right. I'll just—"

"*Wait* for me."

Ten minutes later he emerged, showered and shaved. Laura waited for him to tie his tie. Only when she joined him in the mirror's reflection did he appreciate their flair—he in his best blue suit, she in a scoop-necked gown that would have worn well on a princess and wore so well on Laura Donahue it was, in the circumstances, arguably indecent.

She joined his thought. "Well, they can't say we didn't deal with it in style." With the final word her tears returned, and it was only after a ten-minute repair of face and fortitude that they made it to the lobby.

The desk clerk was new, dressed nattily in SurfAir blue and white, composed yet compassionate. Tollison waited while she consoled an elderly Oriental couple who seemed too small to have problems so far beyond their scale. After a final plea for solace, the couple drifted off, their faces frozen by withheld grief.

When they were gone, the desk clerk turned his way. "I wish there was something adequate I could do," she said, her eyes flattened with frustration. "In a way it's easier when there are no survivors. It's the not knowing that tortures them." She took a sip from a glass that held what looked like orange juice. "How can I help you?"

"I'm trying to learn the procedure," Tollison explained. "What are we supposed to do at this point?"

"Are you a family member of a passenger on flight 617?"

He shook his head. "A friend. The passenger's wife is over there."

He gestured toward Laura. The desk clerk took in her gown and the amount of flesh it failed to cover. When she turned back to Tollison, her lips were white with anger. "I certainly hope this isn't your idea of a joke."

His face roasted under the accusation. "Of course not," he managed. "Mrs. Donahue was on her way to a dance when they called about the crash. I . . . it was a benefit. She was on the committee. Naturally, she went right to the airport, so . . . her husband's name is John Charles Donahue. He was on the plane. At least we think he was."

As he stammered into silence, the clerk glanced at Laura a second time, then shook her head and rubbed her red-rimmed eyes. "I'm sorry. You wouldn't *believe* the things that happen at times like this. Lawyers, undertakers, real estate agents, every sleazeball in town comes flocking around to make a buck off these poor people." She breathed deeply. "Then there's the ones like I thought *she* was, family members who figure they might as well party on our money since what's happened has happened and they can't do anything about it. I'd like to say I think that attitude is healthy, but I'm afraid I think it's sick." She gulped another swig of juice. "I'm sorry. It's just so . . . unfair." She consulted a list. "Very well. I have her name. But who are you?"

"A friend."

Something in the air made her hesitate. When she spoke again, her words were arch with judgment. "Breakfast is being served in the coffee shop. At our expense. I suggest—"

"We don't want breakfast, we want information."

"I'm afraid I don't have anything beyond what's on the board."

"What board?"

She gestured across the lobby. "As soon as we are informed as to the identity of a survivor or decedent, we post the name over there, and notify the family if they are staying here or contact them at home if they are not. Right now there are fifty-five names of the deceased and sixteen survivor names." The clerk consulted a paper behind her. "Mrs. Donahue's husband is not on either list."

"How long do you think it will take before all the names are in?"

"Sometimes it takes days. And sometimes weird things happen. Once, a pickpocket died in a crash carrying only the identification in the wallet of his last victim, so it was assumed . . . well, I'm sure you can appreciate the difficulties."

"But surely there's *something* you can do."

She looked at him with pained intensity. "In the Paris crash they found over fifty body pieces *per passenger*. Perhaps that will help you appreciate what we're up against." Her eyes strayed to the glass doorway, as though carnage could be transformed by the air of morning.

"So we wait here," Tollison concluded.

"I believe that offers the quickest resolution of the uncertainties. There will be some religious leaders here shortly," the clerk continued, brightened by the prospect of providing tangible assistance, "should you or Mrs. Donahue feel spiritual counseling would be helpful. And we have arranged for a psychologist to be available this afternoon, a specialist in dealing with mass tragedies. If we can be helpful in any other way, please let us know. All expenses of your stay are of course the responsibility of SurfAir. I only wish there was more we could do."

"I'm sure you're doing all you can."

She seemed thankful for the sentiment.

They ate breakfast in a silence broken only by outbursts of emotion at adjoining tables. After finishing his waffle, Tollison went to the lobby and bought a morning paper, but its pages were so full of pictures and accounts of the tragedy that he tossed it in the trash.

They were finishing their coffee when the desk clerk announced that three more names had been posted to the lists. Several people rushed from the room; moments later, one returned in tears. When the crowd had cleared, Tollison stood up. Toying with her toast, Laura avoided his eyes. He went to the lobby and searched the lists.

Jack's name was still not posted. He read the rolls through twice, then once again as he indulged in a vision of a world from which Jack Donahue was absent.

Flushed with self-reproach, he returned to their table.

"I ... is there something else I should do?" Laura asked after he told her Jack was still not listed. "I feel so useless just sitting here."

"Does he have family?"

"A cousin somewhere. An uncle, maybe. I haven't heard him speak of them in years."

"How about you? Is there anyone you want me to call?"

She shook her head. "I'm not that close to anyone in Altoona. No one who would be a help." She lowered her eyes. "No one but you."

As he basked in the phrase, Tollison reached for her hand and held it for as long as he could without becoming lurid. "How sure are they that Jack was on the plane?" he asked when he felt he could.

Laura blinked back from wherever the moment had sent her. "He was listed on the ..."

"The manifest."

She nodded. "They called to ask if I knew whether he'd actually taken the flight. I didn't know what had happened—I hadn't been listening to the news or anything—so I just told them I wasn't sure, but that he'd gone to LA as scheduled and I hadn't heard of any change in plan. Then they told me about the crash and said I should come to the airport if I wanted to be certain I got the details as soon as possible." She sighed ruefully. "I didn't realize I still had this dress on until I was crossing the Golden Gate and the toll guy whistled at me."

"He might not have been on board," Tollison said, the statement less a likelihood than a slap at the part of him that wished otherwise. "Maybe he decided to stay over. Maybe he's trying to call you right now."

He expected she would take encouragement, but instead she shook her head. "Last night was poker night. He *never* misses poker night."

He refused to be dissuaded. "Can you activate your answering machine from a remote location?"

She nodded. "There's a code number."

After she told him what it was, he went to a pay phone and dialed a number he knew by heart. When the machine was engaged, he pressed in the code and waited while four callers identified themselves. Two were clearly business people wanting Jack, one was him wanting Laura, one was Brenda wanting him. Brenda's voice was strained and formal. There was nothing from Jack himself.

He hung up, dialed Brenda's number, and listened through ten rings before giving up. It was Saturday, so she was not at school, was likely somewhere with her son, which meant there was no telling where she was. Wherever it was, she wasn't happy.

When Tollison reentered the coffee shop, another man was sitting in his chair. For an instant he thought it was Jack, bloodied but unbowed, emerged from the ruins to reclaim his wife. His heart lurched, but the man pivoted in the chair and proved himself a stranger.

When Tollison reached the table, Laura looked up. "Keith. This is Mr. . . . ?"

The man's smile was quick and practiced. "Chambers. Hawley Chambers. I'm a representative of SurfAir in this unfortunate matter."

Chambers floated off his seat and stuck out a hand, his rimless glasses a set of gleaming wheels beneath his looming forehead, his grip the beginnings of a contest. "I was just telling Mrs. Donahue that we realize how difficult the waiting is and that we stand willing to do anything we can to ease the situation."

"Do you have any idea how long before identification will be complete?" Tollison asked.

"'I wish I could tell you. In the Cairo crash, only four of fifty-two victims were *ever* identified." His smile was languid. "But of course that was Cairo."

Tollison looked at Laura. "Maybe you should wait at home. Maybe it would be easier."

Uncertain, she glanced at the man from SurfAir.

"May I make a suggestion?" Chambers offered easily. "Wait here till this evening. Talk with our counselors or church personnel if you wish, or simply get some rest. If no word has come in by then, by all means return home. The desk clerk has your number, and we would of course call the minute anything comes in on Mr. Donahue."

Laura glanced at Tollison. He shrugged. "Whatever seems best to you."

She nodded. "I'll stay. But only till suppertime."

"Good," Chambers proclaimed, then glanced at his watch. "One more thing. We try our best to keep intruders out, but we have information that at least one aviation attorney has been seen in the building. There may well be more—they tend to appear like hyenas at times like this. They will attempt to persuade you to sign fee agreements retaining them to represent you in this matter, but I can't emphasize too strongly that our advice is to do *nothing* at this point—there is no need to be precipitous." Chambers looked at Laura. "Do you have a personal attorney?"

Laura pointed. "Him."

Chambers's eyes narrowed to the width of a subpoena. "I see. Well, of course I wasn't speaking of family counselors. Not at all. In fact, in our judgment general practitioners like Mr. Tollison can give you perfectly adequate advice in this matter. Our policy is to make generous settlements at times like this. Very generous."

Chambers paused for a response, but Tollison provided only a polite silence.

"Well, I must be going," Chambers said after an awkward moment. "I hope for the best, Mrs. Donahue. I truly do."

"Thank you."

"If the outcome is not salubrious, however, we will no doubt be contacting you, Mr. Tollison."

"Fine."

Chambers bowed, then swept out of the room. "A nice man," Laura murmured in his wake.

"Maybe," Tollison said. "And maybe you'll be lucky and never have to know if he is or not."

Laura treated his false optimism as a canard. "Jack was on that plane."

"Is he dead?"

His question came unbidden, presumed powers Tollison didn't believe existed, but Laura considered it seriously. "I don't know." She looked toward the window. "What if he is? What do I do? With his business and all?"

"Do you really want to go into it? Maybe Jack'll walk in here in a minute and—"

She sighed disconnectedly. "I just wondered what happens at a time like that. What all has to be done."

"Who wrote his will? Do you know?"

"Fred Fitch, probably. He handles Jack's business things."

"Well, if Jack made you his executrix, you'd authorize whichever lawyer you choose to represent you to file the will for probate and go through Jack's records and open his safe deposit boxes to see what insurance and stocks and other assets he had, so the inventory can be made. Basically, the probate process assembles the property, puts it in the name of the legatee, pays the taxes and expenses such as the funeral and any other debts Jack had, and—"

"I imagine he's cut me off without a cent, don't you?" Laura interrupted.

That she had considered such an insult oddly cheered him. "Why?"

She shrugged. "I told you he knew about us, so I'm sure he changed his will. Jack's always been big on revenge. You, for example, were in line for retribution even before we became . . . whatever we became. I never knew why—I assumed you'd taken something from him at some time or other." Her smile was cruel. "Lately I've been wondering whether you only pursued me as part of the silly *game* you two have been playing all these years."

He clutched her hand. "You know that's nonsense, Laura. It's a difficult time, I know, but—"

"Difficult?" Laura looked at him with an almost drunken languor. "Are you telling me you never *hoped* for something like this, Keith Tollison? Are you telling me you never wished that Jack was dead?"

In the silence that was his only answer, he wondered what she wanted him to say and whether she would answer the question differently herself.

Back in the room, Laura attempted to shoo him to Altoona. He resisted, for his welfare as much as hers. She turned on the television, to a rerun of something that had been terrible the first time.

When the phone rang, Tollison picked up the receiver, but Laura snatched it from him. "Yes . . . yes . . . that's right. . . . Can you tell me anything more? . . . Should I go down there now? . . . I will. Thank you. Thank you very much."

Her eyes ballooned and bright, she dropped the receiver to the floor. "He's alive," she said simply.

"Great." The word lodged in his throat like a bone.

"He's hurt very badly, but he's alive."

"Where?"

"A hospital in San Jose."

"Let's go."

"You don't have to."

"Yes I do."

When she started to protest, he reached out and tugged her to his side, less her lover than a teammate in a game being played by brand new rules.

It took twenty minutes to reach San Jose and ten more to find the hospital. When they entered, a SurfAir woman was waiting in the lobby. After Laura gave her name, the woman instructed the orderly slumped in the chair beside her to escort Mrs. Donahue to the fourth floor, east wing.

They wound through stairs and hallways, obeying signs, inhaling scents of medicines and death. Their destination read NEUROLOGY.

Their guide went to the nurses' station and rang a bell. A moment later a nurse came toward them, imperious, speaking while she was still several feet away. "Your husband is badly injured, Mrs. Donahue. There is nothing you can do for him at the moment, so I suggest you—"

Laura dismissed her dictates with a wave. "I want to see him."

The nurse shook her head. "He is unconscious. Doctor will have to authorize any—"

"Where *is* the doctor?"

"I'm afraid he cannot be disturbed."

"If you don't get him in the next two minutes, I'll go looking for him myself. And I'll find him. Believe me."

It was a demand of a sort Tollison had never heard her utter. Even the nurse recognized its value and surrendered. "I'll have him paged. It may take some time. Meanwhile, please wait in the visitors' area." She gestured toward a couch next to the exit and started to turn away.

"No."

The nurse raised a brow. "I beg your pardon?"

Laura Donahue had become colossal. "I want to see my husband. I don't need to talk to him or touch him or even go into the room, but I want to *see* him. If you won't show me where he is, I'll search every room on this floor until I find him. And I'll scream bloody murder if anyone interferes."

What she saw in Laura's eyes caused the nurse to look up and down the hall, then melt. "Come with me. I'll open the door, but you will remain in the hallway. You will not speak or make a sound. Is that understood? No matter what you see or hear, you will keep silent. Do I have your word?"

When Laura nodded, the nurse led them around a corner and down a narrow hall. A moment later they stopped before the door to 414. "I mean it," she cautioned. "No sound at all." She opened the door, peered into the room, then stepped away.

Laura replaced the nurse in the doorway, blocking the view. When she didn't give him space to join her, Tollison put his hand on her shoulder and moved to where he could see for himself.

It was merely a mound of white, a drift of bandages and plaster that was plugged into machines, pricked with needles, pierced with tubes, suspended in traction, bolstered with sand bags, strangled with a cervical collar, strapped to a bed. Unidentifiable as anything but suffering, if it was alive it was only at the behest of elixirs and electrons. Above the stolid mound, machines were perversely jolly.

Tollison looked from Jack to his wife, back and forth, as though he had become a monitor himself. Finally fixing on Laura, he waited until she blinked and backed away.

The nurse led them back to the waiting area. Laura sank to the couch and awaited instructions, her expression unreadable. People came and went, rendering them routine. Tollison sat by her side and took her hand. "He'll be fine. They perform all kinds of miracles these days."

The words insulted her. "Machines are doing everything for him, Keith."

As Tollison struggled to respond, the doctor appeared, tall, thin, and bald, dressed in surgeon's greens.

Tollison stood up. After they shook hands, the man looked down at Laura. "I'm Dr. Ryan. Your husband has been through a terrible event, as you know. I've seen some of the other casualties, and if you're so inclined you can regard it as a miracle that Mr. Donahue is still alive."

Laura's mouth rumpled. "Is that what he is?"

The doctor blinked uncomfortably, as though her response had raised a moral issue. "Nurse told me you've seen him."

Laura nodded.

"Then you know his condition is grave. But he is not *in extremis*. His vital signs are stronger than might be expected, given his ordeal."

"What's wrong with him, exactly?"

The doctor searched her face for guidance, then looked at Tollison. Events far past his logic, Tollison could only shrug.

"Your husband has lots of problems," Dr. Ryan said, finally at ease in detail. "Broken bones. Burns and lacerations. Lung damage." He hesitated.

"What else?"

The doctor glanced once more at Tollison, who did nothing to encourage or deter him. "Mr. Donahue has experienced significant intracranial injury, perhaps at more than one location. We have relieved the subdural hematoma and extracted the invasive object, but the degree of insult has not yet been assessed."

"Is he conscious?"

"No."

"So he may be in a coma for a long time?"

The doctor looked at her as though she had become a block of X-ray film that offered a diagnostic puzzle. "He may be in a coma for quite some time, yes. Or he may regain consciousness momentarily. We are dealing with a major injury to your husband's brain, which means prognosis is entirely speculative."

Laura's eyes squinted against the bright light overhead. "What are you trying to tell me, Doctor?"

The tall man sighed, reached for her hand, then knelt beside her on a single knee. "To put it simply, a definite likelihood is that as a result of trauma to his cerebral cortex and elsewhere, Mr. Donahue will be unable to move all or a portion of his body, quite possibly for the rest of his life." He looked at the floor. "And given the extent of the injury, that may be the least of his problems."

Law Offices of Alec Hawthorne
Pier 32, The Embarcadero
San Francisco, CA 94105
Attorneys for Petitioner

UNITED STATES DISTRICT COURT
NORTHERN DISTRICT OF
CALIFORNIA
PETITION PURSUANT TO
FEDERAL RULE OF
CIVIL PROCEDURE 27(a)

Petitioner, WALTER J. WARREN, intends to bring a civil action against the United States of America, pursuant to Title 28 United States Code, Secs. 1346(b) and 2671 et seq., to recover damages sustained in the crash of a commercial aircraft near San Francisco International Airport on March 23, 1987. The action cannot be commenced at this time because of the provisions of 28 USC Sec. 2675, which prohibit such actions until after a claim submitted to the governmental agency involved has been finally denied or until six months after the claim is presented.

Petitioner, WALTER J. WARREN, is the surviving spouse and father of two victims of the aforementioned crash of SurfAir flight 617, which crash was a result in whole or in part of the actions and omissions of employees of the United States (including but not limited to air traffic controllers and National Weather Service forecasters).

Petitioner seeks to have the following tapes, records, and documents produced and preserved in undamaged and unaltered condition until six months after petitioner's administrative claim is acted upon, since such items are relevant and material evidence as to the crash which occurred on March 23, 1987:

1. Voice recorder tapes for all air traffic control positions in San Francisco International Airport Control Tower and TRACOM from 6:15 P.M. through 6:45 P.M. on March 23, 1987.
2. All tapes and corresponding printouts from Automated Radar Terminal Systems computer which contain processed data on all aircraft during said period.
3. Manual of Operation and Standard Operating Procedures Manual for SF International Tower and TRACOM.

4. Position Binder and Position Log for all traffic control positions in SF International Airport Tower.
5. Reading Binder for SF International Airport Tower.
6. Watch Supervisor's Log for SF International Tower.
7. Current Orders and Directives issued by Tower Chief at SF International in effect on March 23, 1987.
8. Such other material as may lead to the discovery of evidence relevant to the crash of SurfAir flight 617.

DATED: April 6, 1987

Respectfully submitted,

Law Offices of Alec Hawthorne
Attorney for Petitioner

FIVE

Martha appears in the doorway. When Alec Hawthorne nods, she steps into his office and leans against the doorjamb, coffee cup in hand, indicating her message is brief. Her hair is slick with mousse, her earrings are silver daggers, her heels lift her toward the beams that once held up the pier the office rests on and now support its ceiling. In muslin jerkin and leather knee britches, Martha seems capable of sadism, knows it, and is pleased.

"Your son," she says, without inflection. "Line two. Do you want to talk to him?"

"Of course I want to talk to him."

"You don't always," she reminds.

He reddens. "How does he sound?"

"Straight. And scared."

"God. After everything we've been through, I hate to think what might have *scared* him."

Martha shrugs, then looks at her watch. "You said you wanted to go to the airport an hour earlier than usual. If that still holds, you should leave in fifteen minutes. Do you want me to drive you or shall I call a limo?"

"A limo will be fine."

Martha nods. "Fifteen minutes," she repeats, "and that's cutting it close." She makes certain he has heard her, then disappears.

Hawthorne looks thoughtfully at the picture within the antique silver frame that sits on the corner of his desk. It has taken him twenty years to learn that when it comes to his son, caution does not pay and prayers are seldom answered. He can only jump in willy-nilly and hope that for once reality does not outstrip his fears.

He picks up the phone. "What's the trouble?"

"It's no catastrophe or anything, I . . ."

Over Jason's hesitation, Hawthorne hears the hum of long distance. "Where are you?" he asks.

"Rio Nido. Up at the Russian River."

Hawthorne can recall no previous reference to the place, from Jason or from anyone else. It is difficult, in fact, to recall the last time he spoke to Jason about anything.

"What happened?" Unintended, his timbre presumes the worst.

Jason hesitates, as always trying to be as careful in what he says to his father as his father is careful of what he says to a jury. "It's the car."

Hawthorne imagines a Camaro crushed to the size of a beer keg. "What happened to it?"

"It got trashed. Maxed out, basically."

"How?"

"It went down an embankment."

"You mean it went off a cliff."

"Kind of. Yeah."

Hawthorne finds that he has made a fist. "Are you all right?"

"Sure."

"Was anyone else injured?"

"Naw. No problem."

The brisk assurance leaves Hawthorne more dubious than ever. He imagines gigantic judgments, colossal medical bills, extensive therapies, rapacious attorneys like himself materializing on behalf of victims of his son's endless irresponsibility. "Were you driving, Jason?"

Pause. "Not exactly."

He should have known. Jason utilizes virtually nothing as he floats through life, compulsively bestows his possessions on persons who are no more than acquaintances. His only apparent reason for existence is to redistribute his father's wealth. "Who was driving, Jason?"

"Storm."

"I don't care about the weather, I asked you who was driving."

"Storm. He's this dude I know up here."

"Were you in the car with him?"

"Naw. Just Storm."

Hawthorne's fist relaxes. Surely nothing of consequence could happen to persons who refer to themselves meteorologically. "Was he hurt?"

"Naw, but the cops up here have just been *looking* for a reason to bust him, so they're holding him on a dope thing."

"Dope? There were drugs in the car?"

"That's what the fuzz claims. If there *was* anything there, they planted it."

"Let me guess," Hawthorne says. "The car is impounded on the drug charge?"

"Yeah. Sort of."

"And Storm is in jail?"

"Yeah."

"If you want me to bail him out, I have to tell you—"

"Naw, Storm's got tons of . . . I mean, he's got the bail, no problem, but he's staying stout till the arraignment, then he'll nail them for false arrest."

Hawthorne slumps at the suggestion of Storm's net worth, imagines hoards of contraband and piles of cash, the spoils of drug deals and international arms transactions.

"It'll really be fresh," Jason is saying. "See, Storm went to law school till he realized there was no reason to wait three years before churning out the bucks. He figures he'll mash them for a hundred grand, easy. Storm's hard, Dad—you should talk to him sometime."

"I look forward to the pleasure. In the meantime, what exactly do you want from me?"

"Coin. Just enough to get me out of here. I got some people coming to see me in Berkeley tomorrow, so if you could just send me bus fare, wire it Western Union maybe, there's this place down the street that does that, and—"

"How much?"

"A hundred? The hound to the city is forty-five, then BART to Berkeley, and I got to eat and stuff."

"Are you charged with anything, Jason? Did they arrest you?"

"Naw. They may file later on, though, this one cop told me. Since they found stuff in my trunk."

"Stuff?"

"Just some powder they think is blow but is really unbleached flour. These dweebs are so out of it—the bust is completely bogus, Dad. The fucking road was washed out, was the problem, so the county's the one at fault, not us. You ought to sue the bastards; I mean, the infrastructure up here is totally lame. Punitive damages and everything, I bet."

"Right."

The phone suddenly seems too heavy to hold. His son's mind has regressed to that of infancy, where truth and fantasy were equally plausible. He wonders if it is the leavings of a decade of illegal drugs, remembers that the first time he discovered his son was stoned, Jason was twelve years old.

"Where are you, exactly?" Hawthorne asks wearily. "I'll have Martha make the arrangements."

Jason gives his location and tells his father to hurry, the bus leaves in an hour.

"Is your mother still living in Kenwood?" he asks, a last gasp of paternalism.

"I guess. I haven't seen her for a while. Me and number four don't get along. He's a Nazi, basically."

Which meant he didn't allow Jason and his friends to invade the premises, raid the pantry, trash the living quarters, and depart without a word. Hawthorne laughs inwardly. Perhaps wife number two has done all right for herself. Not that Hawthorne would know. He hasn't spoken to her in years.

"Are you still living in the flat in Berkeley?"

"Naw."

"What happened?"

"They threw me out. Landlord games, you know? Trying to stiff the rent control. I may take them to court."

Hawthorne wonders if he should be flattered that Jason's threats are so frequently litigious. "Are you in school this term?"

"Naw. They canceled the film class I wanted, and the rest of it's an anachronism, basically, so . . ."

Hawthorne shakes his head. In tune with recent policy, he speaks to his son without a euphemistic filter. "Are you selling drugs, Jason?"

"What? Hey. What the fuck are you *talking* about?" When Jason remembers he is talking to his father and not a cop, he mutters a quick apology.

"I'm talking about how you make your living. You haven't got a job. You haven't been hounding *me* for money lately, and I'm sure your mother hasn't been giving you any. So how are you surviving? Are you up there buying dope? Is Storm some kind of trafficker, Jason?"

Jason's voice lowers to an urgent rasp. "Jesus, Dad; chill out. I'm at the *police* station, for Christ's sake. What are you trying to do?"

Since what he is doing has more to do with himself than with Jason, Hawthorne gives up. He pats the pocket of his suit coat and feels the calming bulge of airline tickets. As it has been so many times in the past, the answer seems to be to get out of town as soon as possible.

He tells his son the money will be coming right away, then asks if he needs anything else. Jason seems about to say something significant, but says only goodbye. "Go see your mother," Hawthorne prompts. "And me," he adds, but far too late.

After a moment of bleak reflection, Hawthorne calls for Martha. When she appears in the doorway, he tells her to wire the money. She nods and leaves the room. A moment later she is back, looking at her watch. "Limo's here. You better get going."

He nods, puts the file he has been reviewing back in his briefcase, gets his garment bag from the closet, and heads for the door. Various people bid him goodbye on the way out, but the turnover in the office is so acute he doesn't know quite who is wishing him bon voyage. When the street door closes behind him, he exhales with relief. He is always glad to get away, until he gets to where he is bound for.

"Where to, sir?" The limo driver places the garment bag and briefcase in the back seat of the long black Lincoln, and Hawthorne clambers in after them. "The airport," he instructs. "United."

He settles back in the glove-soft leather, places his briefcase beside him, and removes a memorandum of points and authorities. Laden with law and argument, it is an attempt to persuade a judge in Baton Rouge that an airport is not relieved of liability for inadequate runway lights because the pilot who crashed was soloing without a license to do so. It's a matter that will be appealed by whoever loses, so the argument is not crucial. Ordinarily, Hawthorne would have left it to one of the younger lawyers, except the next day he starts a series of depositions in Dallas, where he will grill flight crews and traffic controllers to determine whether a wind-shear crash that killed 137 people could have been prevented if proper warnings had been given. If he handles the deposition right, he will force the government to settle.

Then to São Paulo for more depositions; he hopes Martha has remembered to line up the interpreter. Then to Mexico City to meet with a group of potential plaintiffs who were shopping for a lawyer and had asked some American attorneys to come pay homage to them and their cultural traditions, which according to Martha included bribes. Then home for three days, a trial lawyers' symposium in Las Vegas over the weekend, a quick run to LA for a meeting with the personal-injury panel of the bar association. Then to Alaska for a pretrial conference in the helicopter case, tort-reform negotiations in Sacramento, then . . . he looks at his calendar, which is as scribbled on and scratched over as a pocket Jackson Pollock. He won't be home for ten more days.

A twinge in his side makes him squirm to a more comfortable position. The conversation with his son has left him empty and forlorn. That was another thing he and Dan Griffin had talked about—kids. Dan was always frank, consoling, nonjudgmental, occasionally even helpful in a California sort of way, perhaps because Dan was still a kid himself. Now there was no one who could provide him that same balm. Martha regards children as hazardous waste afoot.

As they near the airport, he remembers his plan and tells the driver to take an earlier exit. The driver shrugs, then does as he is told, and ten minutes later Hawthorne issues another instruction, and still others, and in twenty minutes he is there. It is his first visit to the site of a crash of a commercial airliner except vicariously, through the distant drama of admissible evidence.

The wreckage is gone, taken to a hangar at Moffett Air Base for reconstruction in aid of determining the cause of the crash. The bodies are gone as well, both those that are whole and those that are only scraps that have been meticulously tagged and bagged, in the hope that fingers and feet and ears and arms can eventually be matched with enough of their genetic complements that they can be given a name and returned to the folks who loved them. As a shudder rises and falls within him, Hawthorne tells the driver he will be a minute, then gets out of the car.

The grass is smashed flat, the earth is soft and glutinous. Soaked by oils and foams and blood, it seems to want to explain itself, to disclaim responsibility. As he walks toward the grove where the wreckage came to rest, Hawthorne's imagination soars. He hears the voices in the cockpit as they labor to save their charges, sees the attendants grope for words of comfort and assurance, senses the passengers grasping at whatever straw they believe will save them, until they abandon hope and await the crash in terror. He wonders who they blame, in those final seconds, for what is about to happen to them; wonders upon what authority some have died and some are spared.

He kicks at a rock half buried in the ooze. Beneath it, something gleams. He picks it up. It is a brass button off a natty blazer, emblazoned with a crest of indeterminate significance. Hawthorne flips it in the air, catches it, imagines a man who might have worn it, a man much like himself. He walks back toward the car.

The driver leans out the window and asks if they're going to the airport or not, he's got another fare at noon. Hawthorne ignores him, tries once again to meld with the event; but though its leavings are all around, he can't come to grips with its enormity. He has spent his professional life reading accounts of air disasters, of what had happened in the sky and in the plane and on the ground, of what had fractured and dislodged, of who had died and how. Yet this ravaged knoll, empty of corpse or wreckage, is far worse than he imagined; implies horror beyond true telling. Suddenly mourning less for the passengers than for himself, Hawthorne climbs back into the limousine and orders the driver to return to the airport.

As they retrace their route, Hawthorne realizes he has lingered at the crash site so long he may miss his flight. He looks at his watch once, then again, then a third time before the airport exit finally looms out of the mists ahead. It is going to be close. If he misses the plane, he will have to arrange for someone to cover for him, doing what past experience has taught him to avoid, which is to trust someone other than Martha not to make a mistake.

Acid spills across his stomach. He dilutes it with a breath of air, then checks his ticket to see how much time he has to change planes in Denver. He gathers up the papers he has been scanning, pats his pocket to confirm the presence of the ticket he examined only seconds before, leans back, and closes his eyes.

"What airline do you want again?" the driver asks.

As he repeats the earlier instruction, Hawthorne feels a swelling sensation in his chest, as though his lungs are being stuffed like sausage. He tries to burp but can't; his lower lip quivers, then tingles, reminding him of the comedown off of Novocain.

As he rubs his lip with the back of his hand, he feels his vision narrow, as though the driver is plunging them into a tunnel. A part of him remembers there are no tunnels at the airport while another part senses a spider crawling down his arm, a tickle of tracks from his armpit to the fingers that now curl around the bright brass button, fingers that are sweating, pale, squeezed tight—holding on to what has somehow become his life.

Hawthorne inhales as much oxygen as his chest will bear. "I think you'd better take me to a hospital."

The driver turns an ear. "Say what?"

"Don't stop at the terminal—take me back to San Francisco General."

The driver's eyes appear in the rearview mirror, red, wide, as encompassing as a marsupial's. "You got a problem or something, pal?"

"I think I'm having a heart attack."

The eyes disappear, to be replaced by a voice, throaty and afraid. "Wait a minute. This ain't no ambulance, buddy. Christ. . . . Here. United you wanted; United you got. I'll put your stuff on the walk for you, no sweat. There ain't no charge, even. Just get out. . . . Come on, Mac, get out of the limo. I bet they got all kinds of doctors here, for Christ's sake. Hell yes. They'll take care of you just fine. I got other fares, pal. . . . *Jesus*, don't lie *down* like that. Hey! Over here! I need some *help* here. This guy's trying to fucking *croak* on me, the son of a bitch."

Keith Tollison stumbled through his normal routine for three days before judging himself incompetent to pursue his practice. Then, with Sandy's assistance, he postponed, continued, canceled, and evaded as many of his responsibilities as he could, until he had cleared his slate of anything that would divert him from the circumstances foisted on him by the crash.

In one sense his preoccupation was shared with thousands—the entire Bay Area was obsessed with the disaster. Photographs of the wreckage wrested the news pages away from the pratfalls of the increasingly beleaguered president. The broadcast by Helen Macy, the first television reporter to reach the scene, was rerun dozens of times, until her tears became both legendary and her ticket to the LA market. Rumors were rife—pilferage from the baggage strewn across the crash site, thefts from the now-vacant homes of victims, wars between funeral directors and medical facilities over the organs of the dead. Lawyers were portrayed as vampires, airplanes as dangerously defective, airlines and the FAA remiss in matters of safety, hospitals inadequate to confront a disaster of this dimension to say nothing of the quake that was only a geologic tic away. And there was a bit of truth in all of it.

A part of Tollison was a public mourner, saddened by the loss of others. But his misery also had a more specific source, for what he had lost was Laura—she had vanished from his life as surely as if she had perished in the plane herself.

His phone calls went unanswered. She was never where she used to be at the times she used to be there. His only knowledge came from a brief conversation when they had run into each other at Safeway—Laura's responses to his queries both perfunctory and distant—and from his pestering of her neighbor to the point of inquisition.

What he knew was this. Galvanized by her circumstances, Laura was making daily trips to the hospital in San Jose, refusing Tollison's offer to accompany her and avoiding all but rote descriptions of what she encountered when she got there. Her reticence finally led Tollison to call the hospital himself, in the role of Laura's lawyer, to request a fresh prognosis. What he was told by Dr. Ryan was sufficiently supple to depress him.

Against the counsel of the specialists who attended him, Laura had begun to plan for her husband's return to Altoona, consulting with anyone who would discuss the subject—doctors and nurses, therapists and psychologists, even a priest—learning how to cope with whatever it was Jack Donahue had become. Her conduct allowed but one conclusion—Tollison had become subordinate to a man who was alive at the pleasure of devices that dented the definitions of life and death.

Lacking anyone to fight with to regain the status quo, he retreated to Brenda and, to his surprise, she welcomed his attentions. The reason was simple—her sister, Carol, had not been heard from in more than a week. As time went by and there was still no word, Brenda began calling him day and night, increasingly desperate, until he had agreed to aid in her search simply to regain some peace of mind.

Tollison had spent the week as a private eye, talking to police, hospitals, girlfriends, and the lengthy string of Carol Farnsworth's lovers that had accumulated over the years, most of them ne'er-do-wells who languished like driftwood on the fringes of Altoona. He had learned a lot—that Carol often smoked pot and occasionally sniffed cocaine, that she liked to shoot pool and was good at it, that her girlfriends called her Cee Cee, that she spent several nights a week at a bar called Cheerios—but his inquiry was essentially unproductive. No one knew where Carol was, no one had heard from her of late, and no one had been told of any plans that would keep her out of circulation for so long, which by now was a dozen days. Periodically, he suggested to Brenda that she declare Carol a missing person and bring in the authorities, but Brenda always refused, with a vehemence that caused Tollison to wonder if she feared her sister was a fugitive.

Since Carol ran with a crowd that assumed all questions had their origins with the police, his most promising lines of inquiry had been met with a sullen silence. Now Tollison was completing what amounted to his last gasp: searching her house from top to bottom.

He began in the kitchen, at the back, and worked his way toward the living room, in the front. As in the earlier stages of his investigation, he learned things. Carol read historical biographies, worshiped Robert Redford, applied something to her body called Mating Musk, subscribed to *Playgirl*, owned a vibrator, and loved the sounds of Sting and Springsteen. She was more than slightly slovenly and drank impressive quantities of Canadian Club, indicating her nickname derived from her libation rather than her first initial. She binged on Archway lemon cookies, collected matchbooks and stuffed rabbits, spent more than she should have on clothes, and bought them in styles ranging from sedate straight skirts to multi-zippered vinyl outfits that, given their size and his recollection of Carol's figure, must have been provocative.

The hint that Carol had a swinging sex life received further confirmation in the bedroom. Secreted within the pages of an atlas was a set of surprisingly artful photographs of Carol in the nude, posed in a wooded glade, the sun highlighting her best features, which were her breasts and sculpted shoulders, shadow camouflaging her worst, which were her heavy legs. The subject was obviously relishing the display; the photographer was obviously familiar with the rudiments of erotic art. Nevertheless, Carol was more alluring in her clothes than out of them.

All of which was interesting, but none of it told him where she was, which left him without a clue but not without a guess.

After closing the atlas, he rejoined Brenda in the living room. "I've done everything I can think of to do," Tollison began as he tried to come up with a gentle way to broach the idea that had just come to him. "Except filing a report with the police or hiring someone to track her down."

Brenda nodded, her mind elsewhere, as it increasingly was. "How's Jack?" she asked idly, as if she had read his mind and hoped a digression would divert him.

He saw no reason not to discuss the situation, since the whole town was doing so anyway. "Still in a coma, last I heard."

"Is he going to be a vegetable?"

Brenda's eyes contained a glint he chose not to fathom. "They won't know till he regains consciousness and they can test his motor functions. I get the impression that anything at all is possible, from complete recovery to a horror story."

"How's Laura holding up?"

He shrugged. "Okay, I think. Money's going to be a problem. Jack doesn't seem to have had any disability insurance. His whole financial setup was a mess—I can't find more than eight hundred dollars cash on hand, and there's ten times that in unpaid bills. Social Security is all they'll have till the crash litigation is settled, and that won't kick in for six months. If Jack's income was as sketchy as people think, even the disability won't amount to much."

"Laura will be a little trooper, I'm sure."

"That's not very charitable, Brenda. Jack's situation is terrible for her."

Brenda's smile twisted bitterly. "To say nothing of Jack."

"Come on, Brenda. For God's sake."

Her eyes would not acquit him. He knew she didn't know it all, but he was afraid she knew enough.

"Let's get back to Carol," Tollison said quickly. "The only things we know for sure are that she apparently left here voluntarily, and took some clothing and toiletries with her but not her car. I've talked to all the travel companies I can think of and all the friends on the list you gave me, and I haven't come up with anything. I didn't come up with anything in here, either," he added.

"So we give up? Is that what you're suggesting?"

He hesitated before voicing the idea that had materialized a moment earlier. In the middle of his caution, Brenda broke her silence. "I think Spitter may know."

The shift confused him. "What?"

"I think Spitter knows where she is. You know how he is—Carol's the only person he likes who's halfway normal. I think she told him where she was going so he wouldn't get worried when she didn't come see him for a while. Usually, he gets agitated if he doesn't see her for even a day or two, but this time he hasn't been upset at all and it's been two weeks."

"Did you ask him to tell you where she was?"

Brenda closed her eyes. "Of course."

"And?"

She shook her head. "He just gritted his teeth and got that look in his eyes."

Tollison knew that look. He had seen it on men he had defended in San Francisco, the suggestion that the world was owed a debt payable only in belligerence.

"Where's Spitter now?" he asked.

"Home."

"Let's go see him."

She shook her head. "It won't do any good. He doesn't like you any more than he does me."

He stood up. "At this point we should try anything." Though her look was skeptical, Brenda didn't protest when he pulled her to her feet and drove her to her own small home, the one she shared with Spitter.

Brenda unlocked the door, then led him to the living room. As they regarded each other silently, Tollison wondered what he would unearth if he searched this house as thoroughly as he had her sister's.

Spitter was nowhere in sight. Brenda called his name and received no answer. "He's probably in his room," she said, and started for the rear of the house.

Spitter's room was a former utility porch that had been converted both to meet his needs and best his predilections. The door was a plank without a lock, the floors slick linoleum rather than absorbent carpet, the walls unpainted plywood that could withstand whatever missiles Spitter sent their way. The window was screened from the inside, as was the light in the center of the ceiling. If the effect was institutional, the result was an odd emancipation—Spitter rarely was attracted to any other portion of the house.

Tollison knocked and waited. After a second he heard a creak of bedsprings. He knocked again. "Spitter," he called. "It's Keith Tollison. I need to talk to you. About your Aunt Carol."

Tollison treated the resulting mumble as an invitation. When he looked at Brenda, she shrugged and went away. At his push, the door opened inward, to the resistance of a spring.

The lights were off. His back to the door, Spitter was curled in a semicircle on the bed, head wrapped in arms and hands, ears plugged by the tendrils of a Walkman. Tollison closed the door and said hello.

Spitter curled into a tighter ball, his camouflage pants tightening across his bony buttocks, the collar of his field jacket bunching at his neck. His jump boots rubbed against each other, making the only sound in the room more audible than the leaking whispers from the Walkman. "Spitter," Tollison repeated. "I've come about Carol."

"What about her?" Spitter mumbled from behind a forearm.

"I was wondering if you knew where she was."

Spitter didn't answer.

"I just wanted to make sure you knew, because if you didn't, I was going to tell you."

"I know, so don't worry."

"Good."

In the ensuing silence, the boy wriggled within his baggy clothing. "She told me it was a secret."

"It is. We're the only ones who know. You and me."

Spitter straightened his legs and rolled toward his visitor, then sat on the edge of the bed and tugged the headset off his ears.

As always, Tollison was surprised at Spitter's age. His lagging mental development led Tollison to regard him as an adolescent, but as he gazed through the cowl of oily hair at the sallow skin, the reluctant eyes, the spotty stubble of his beard, Tollison remembered Spitter was almost twenty-five. Doctor after doctor had said Spitter was not violent, not a threat to others or to himself, not subnormally intelligent, but in every minute of his day he looked capable of terrible assaults upon a world that seemed to incense him.

A high school dropout, Spitter was enough his father's child that he was a valued mechanic at the local Chevron station, his love of engines so enormous he would haunt the garage into the wee hours, until the owner sent him home. Much of the time he was joined by two men of indeterminate age who worked as grave diggers at the local cemetery, or by a covey of prepubescent admirers whose parents doubtlessly saw Spitter as Fagin reincarnate.

As Tollison schemed to lure the boy into a meaningful admission, Spitter looked around the room. "You don't know where she is; you're trying to trick me," he charged suddenly.

"Yes I do," Tollison said.

"No you don't." Spitter seemed on the verge of tears. "If you know so much, why don't you *prove* it?"

"Okay, I will. I'll write the place Carol went on a piece of paper. If I'm right, you have to give me your comic book."

He pointed to a particularly outrageous example of the genre, one of many scattered throughout the room, this one opened to a page on which a helmeted man mounted on a soaring Pegasus was attacking a futuristic tank with a lance tipped by a diamond the size of a fist. "Okay?"

Spitter glanced at the book as covetously as if it were his flesh and blood. "If I win, I get the comic book," Tollison repeated, "and if I lose, I give you five dollars."

His world made simple by the final phrase, Spitter nodded.

Tollison reached into his coat and took out his pen and a business card. On the back of the card he wrote *Los Angeles*, and after a moment, just *LA*.

His nerves playing a variation on the theme he felt while awaiting a jury verdict, Tollison folded the card and handed it to Spitter.

Spitter read the words. His quick glance at the imperiled magazine told Tollison all he needed to know. He picked up the comic, ruffed through it quickly, sighed, then tossed it casually to Spitter. "I've read that one already."

The young man clasped the comic to his breast, a tear trickling from his eye. Tollison clapped him on the shoulder. Spitter didn't say a word as Tollison left the room, his earlier guess confirmed.

Brenda was on the couch, leafing through a month-old *Newsweek*, waiting. He sat beside her and took her hand. "Carol went to LA," he said without preamble.

"LA? Are you sure?" The question was tranquil, the connection not yet made. "Why would she go down there?"

"It doesn't matter."

"What do you mean it doesn't matter? We have to talk to people. We have to—"

Grasping for a euphemism but finding nothing but a line as straight as a spear, he said, "If Carol went to LA, there's one possibility we have to consider."

"What's that?"

"That Carol was on that plane."

"What plane?"

"The one that crashed."

"No." The rebuttal was quick and savage. "That's not possible. She wasn't even *in* LA, so she wasn't on that *plane*."

"She told Spitter that's where she was going."

"I don't care. I'd know if something like that happened to her. I'd *know* it."

He almost believed her. The link between Brenda and her sister had always seemed to have roots in ESP. Each often knew what the other was thinking, where the other was, what the other was in need of. Tollison had observed enough instances of casual telepathy to believe that Brenda's welling sorrow over the past week meant that, contrary to her protest, in some crevice of her mind she sensed her sister was dead.

"We should call the airline," he told her. "The last I heard, they'd only identified two thirds of the bodies."

"Don't be absurd. If Carol was on that plane, they'd have *some* record of her."

"Maybe, but maybe not. What if she used a false name?"

"Why would she do anything that ridiculous?"

"What if she got involved in something criminal? You know the guys she hangs out with. She could be running dope for them or something."

Brenda wrenched away. "You son of a bitch. How *dare* you—"

He hurried on. "Okay, what if she was traveling with a man? A married one? What if they snuck off for a week of fun and games and the plane crashed on the way back? If they were trying to cover their tracks, the airline might not have any record."

"Are you trying to say she was with Jack Donahue?"

The thought hadn't occurred to him. Its reach momentarily diverted his attention. "I'm just saying someone," he continued absently. "Anyone."

"Carol wouldn't give Jack Donahue the time of day." Brenda crossed her arms against the possibility. "Fingerprints. They would have checked the fingerprints by now. I read they've got a dozen pathologists working on the identifications."

"There was a fire, Brenda. Fingerprints can burn off; dental work can melt; baggage can burn to ashes."

She lowered her head to her hands. "So what do you think we should do?"

"Go over there."

"Where?"

"The warehouse where they took the personal effects of the passengers. It might not come to anything—they obviously don't have a lead that points to Carol, or you would have been notified. But we have to make sure there's nothing in that stuff that indicates she was on that plane. We look, and hope to hell we don't find anything."

The exposition of the idea made it inconceivable to her. "I won't do it."

"I wish I could do it for you, but you know I can't."

"It must be *horrible* in there. *Grotesque.*"

"We have to do it, all the same." He reached out his hand.

"Now?" she asked, eyes wide, hand darting out of reach.

Tollison nodded slowly, then grasped her wrist and pulled her to her feet. She rose hesitantly, as though he were a stranger tugging her toward the dance floor, a stranger about whom she'd heard bad things.

He put an arm around her shoulder. "It's time we did something. You're falling apart with the uncertainty. I am, too."

"What if it's true, Keith?" she asked softly, gripping his arm. "What if she's so broken and smashed no one knows who she is anymore?"

Her words pummeled her features, leaving them wrenched and bloated. He pulled her close and whispered. "If that's what's happened, we'll have to deal with it. I'll help you any way I can. We may not be everything to each other, but we're still something. I'll be there whenever you need me."

"I don't know if that's enough anymore, Keith."

"I know. But who else is there?"

Her response was leaden. "No one. Not for me." She found his eyes. "There is for you, though. Isn't there?"

"There was," he admitted, his usual evasion suddenly unthinkable. "I'm not sure there is anymore." He paused. "Let's go do what we have to do."

They stood together grasping for diversions but finding only a strange accord.

A minute later they were in his car. Brenda lapsed into a trance, a den of raw psychology. Because he knew no words of comfort, Tollison remained silent as they drove toward the place where the airline and the county had collaborated to collect the leavings of the crash.

Traffic was thick and demanding, for which he was grateful for once. After two wrong turns and as many denunciations of the SurfAir person who instructed him when he'd called to ask directions, Tollison pulled up to a large concrete structure near the railroad district. A sign on the side of the building read MCMANIS BROTHERS WHOLESALERS, but it was faded to oblivion, a historic guidepost only.

Tollison parked and turned to Brenda. "Let me go first. I'll make sure it's the right place."

She nodded mechanically, rigid at the prospect of following him, her imagination clearly rampant.

He got out of the car and went through the heavy metal door. Inside, a makeshift foyer had been fashioned out of a row of room dividers. In front of the wall, a woman in a Red Cross uniform sat behind a table, knitting. A coffee cup and several stacks of forms were precisely placed in front of her. A sign at her back read QUIET, PLEASE.

When Tollison approached, she looked up and smiled. He was about to speak when he became conscious of the smell—sweet, penetrating, laced with the familiar scent of a deodorizer—that permeated the room.

The woman watched him wrinkle his nose. "It's jet fuel," she said, her warm voice and ample bosom so reassuring it made him want to genuflect. "There's not much more we can do. Much of the fabric is far too fragile to clean effectively. Are you a relative of a passenger on the flight?"

He shook his head. "I'm a friend of a relative. A sister. She's out in the car. I thought I'd come in first and . . ." Tollison shrugged, uncertain of nomenclature.

The Red Cross woman picked up a pen and took the top sheet off a stack of printed forms. "If I may have the name of the sister and the name and address of the purported passenger, the person you are attempting to verify."

He gave her what she asked. She looked at the papers in front of her and flipped through three of them. "I don't have that name listed. Did she go by any other, possibly?"

He shook his head. "We're not certain she was *on* that flight. We only know she disappeared a week before the crash, and we have some indication she might have gone to Los Angeles. So we have to see—"

Even the woman's squint was comforting. "Naturally. If there is anything I can do to assist you, please just ask. We have a medical unit here, and a chaplain, if you—"

"Thank you. That's very kind. I think I'll go in first, so I can ... is that ... do I just go look around?"

She nodded. "The material has been divided into sections. They are clearly labeled. Clothing—men's, women's, and children's. Footwear, the same. Jewelry—men's and women's, though of course some of the items are not easily classifiable by gender, so you should check both tables. Books. Luggage. Miscellaneous. And, of course, those items which are no longer classifiable. You should examine all the categories if you find nothing in the most logical places. Just to make sure."

He nodded. "How long will this material be kept here?"

"As long as there is any question as to the identity of any of the remains, I imagine."

"How many are still anonymous?"

"Twelve."

He nodded. Before he was quite ready for it, he had backed beyond the barriers.

Ranks of tables ran the length of the warehouse, the kind found in church basements and school cafeterias. On them were mounds of matter, dark and indistinct from where he stood, not easily distinguishable even upon closer inspection due to the dimness of the room. He wondered if they kept it dark on purpose, to stifle extrapolation from the scorched and tattered garments to the fate of those who had worn them through the crash.

The few people in the room were as separated from each other as the layout would allow. Some strolled idly through the aisles as though they shopped for day-old pastry. Some stood transfixed, in the grip of inner visions. Others staved off knowledge by looking anywhere but at what they had come there to inspect. Some seemed uncertain of their mission; others pawed through the rummage as though they had a license to appropriate the bargains.

Tollison went to the table marked WOMEN'S CLOTHING. It was a jumble, a sale table on the morning after, a heap of torn and tangled apparel even markdowns couldn't move. Deep dark blots beyond the power of detergents had given the articles a common hue, except for a few pristine pieces so incongruous they seemed to have been added to the table by mistake.

Wiping his eyes, Tollison took one more look around, then retreated to the car. Brenda was staring at the blank wall of the warehouse. He slid inside and put his arm around her.

"It's not pleasant," he began, "but you get used to it. There's all kinds of stuff in there, most of it pretty messed up. But it's not . . . gruesome."

"Maybe that's because it's not your sister."

When she didn't say anything further, he opened the door. "We'd better get started."

Suddenly valiant, Brenda shrugged his arm off her shoulders, pushed open the door, and slid into the sunlight. He did the same, and took her hand as they went into the building, less the leader than an obsequious retainer.

The Red Cross worker gave them a maternal smile. Tollison smiled back. Brenda seemed not to notice. Careful not to overcome resistance, he guided her beyond the slim dividers.

The room seemed larger and the occupants more numerous than before. He paused to let Brenda sense the scene, to weigh its power against her own resources. When he felt a tremble he anticipated a retreat, but she made no move to leave. Encouraged, he led her to the table he had already inspected. "This is as good a place to start as any."

She regarded it tentatively, as though the display were of questionable taste. Finally, she fingered a cotton blouse. Tollison doubted anything was registering, doubted the day could possibly prove anything except her courage.

He was wondering if there was a less arduous method of eliminating Carol from both the room and the event when Brenda spoke. "It's like the catacombs in here."

"I know."

"Ghosts and stuff. Do you believe in them?"

"No."

"I didn't, either. But maybe I'll start."

"Why?"

116

"Because Carol's here. And now I have to find her."

Her eyes were clear, her strength immense. In its wake, Tollison grew timid. "Maybe we should go. Leave it for another time."

Brenda shook her head. "It's not going to get any easier, Keith. Haven't you learned that yet? *Nothing* gets any easier."

She stepped toward the table until her thighs were pressed against its edge. With one hand she reached out and touched another garment, a raglan sweater she fondled reverently, as though it had warmed a prophet. After a moment, she dropped its sleeve and touched a tattered piece of denim that was spotted by what was clearly blood. And another and another, poking, probing, searching for the clothing that, according to her revelation, her sister must have died in.

Finished with the first table, she moved to the second. Tollison walked with her, though carefully at her back, his eyes on Brenda rather than debris. She gave off an intensity he had only sensed when she had been searching for a cure for whatever ailed her son. He held his tongue and watched her work.

An hour later, she had finished the clothing and luggage but had found no sign of Carol. When he asked if she wanted to rest, she merely shook her head. They moved through footwear with the same result. At one point, somewhere behind them, a woman screamed and started crying.

People came and left; words were not exchanged. Earnest men and women moved through the room, examined the searchers from a distance, looked for signs of derangement and, finding none, departed. It was as mysterious as a mass, as transforming as communion. They moved along to jewelry.

The table glowed, the watches, rings, and necklaces bright testimony to the variety of taste and aspiration. A guard gave them a stiff acknowledgment; a sign disclosed that more valuable items were kept in a vault in the back.

Another groan rippled the heavy air, and Tollison turned to see if help was needed. When he turned back, Brenda was holding a wristwatch, turning it in her fingers, canting it to the light.

A slight smile lifted her lips. "I bought it at Shreve's. For her thirtieth birthday. It was half off. I always get Carol nice things for her birthday—I buy them the day after Christmas. It's pretty, isn't it, Keith? See? It's quite pretty still, after all these years. I wonder what we do now?" she concluded softly.

Taking her hand, he led her toward the door. As they passed the Red Cross table, the woman asked if they had found anything.

When he nodded, the woman sobered. "In that case you should complete this form. Please. It will speed things immensely if you do it now."

He guided Brenda to the table, where the woman took Brenda's hand in both of hers. "I'm afraid I have to tell you that all the survivors have been identified, so if your sister was on board the plane she is, necessarily, deceased." The woman held up a paper. "This is an FBI identification form. If you will fill it out, it will be compared with postmortem examinations and matched with the appropriate remains. Then you will be notified as to the whereabouts of the body and instructed how to claim it."

Brenda took the form and the pencil that came with it, bent over the table and began to fill the blanks, registering Carol's statistics. When she completed the form, she returned it.

"Be advised that the airline requires a twenty-five-gauge monoseal casket for removal of the remains," the Red Cross woman said, "and an acceptable vehicle of the type normally used to transmit the deceased for burial. I am authorized to tell you that the airline will provide funeral services itself if you have made no arrangements of your own. This form describes their interment specifications. You must provide a casket, however. There are no more caskets in the South Bay area, due to the demands of the incident."

Brenda shook her head, refusing the document. The woman returned it to its stack. "I will pray for your sister and for you. She is with the Lord. You can take solace in that."

"Who did this?" Brenda asked, so softly Tollison almost missed it.

The Red Cross woman looked up from her papers. "What was that, my dear?"

"What made the airplane crash?"

"I don't know."

"Who does?"

"I'm afraid I don't know."

Who knows why this happened?

For the first time, the woman could transmit no solace. "The Lord works in mysterious ways. We can't always know His—"

"Well, there's *one* mystery He damn well better solve by the time I get back home," Brenda declared in fury.

"Please. There is no need to blaspheme, though I understand your need to—"

Brenda could not have heard. "He'd better tell me how I'm going to *explain this to my son.*"

PART II

MEMORANDUM

To: **MIKE**

From: **MARTHA**

Subject: **SURFAIR**

We need to move forward with SurfAir. Alec will try the case if it comes to that, but his schedule is such, to say nothing of his health, that we can't assume he will do any of the pretrial. I have no time for SurfAir myself, so it's all yours.

The NTSB report on the crash is still not out, but our information is that they are inclined to think flight 617 had a near miss, and that in maneuvering to avoid the collision, it reached a stall condition and crashed. The other plane has not been identified, so it was most probably a rogue, an unregistered general aviation aircraft unlawfully occupying the San Francisco Terminal Control Area.

In some circumstances we would wait for the NTSB report before initiating our lawsuit, but in order to compete with Vic Scallini and others for plaintiffs, we need the publicity of a complaint with our name on it. Also, the Judicial Panel on Multidistrict Litigation is meeting next month, and consolidation of the SurfAir cases is on the agenda, as is selection of the plaintiffs' committee. For Alec to be considered for chairman, we have to be of record. So we file, by the end of next week at the latest.

At this point we have four plaintiffs, not counting the actor Dan Griffin stole: Walter Warren, the surviving spouse of a wife and minor child who died in the crash; Alice Jastrow, wife of Stanley Jastrow—a sixty-four-year-old businessman who was going to retire in a month; and the parents of Lee Chen, a high-tech entrepreneur, age thirty-seven, who perished along with his wife and two children.

From an economic standpoint none is ideal. Mrs. Warren didn't work outside the home, Jastrow wouldn't have earned much more over the course of his life expectancy, and the parents of a married man are not usually considered to suffer significant economic loss from the death of their child. We want to maximize the damages that _were_ suffered, however, so be sure to update our evidence on the money value of domestic services performed by women in the home. Also, the wife of the pilot in the Chicago crash got a million four in nonpecuniary damages—for loss of society and pain and suffering—so don't set our sights too low.

In the Chen case, Alec suggests an additional avenue. Talk to people at Berkeley and Stanford—sociologists, anthropologists, theologians, whatever—and find an expert to testify that whatever the case with American families, the Chinese (in particular, those observing the tenets of Buddhism) have a strong tradition of reverence for ancestors, which includes financial support far beyond what is normal in this country.

The action is for statutory damages under Code of Civil Procedure 377 for wrongful death, and for loss of society under the case law. Krouse v. Graham, 137 Cal. Rptr. 863 (1977).

Defendants are as follows:

SurfAir Coastal Airways—the claim is for negligence, based on a breach of the duty of a common carrier. Acosta v. Southern California Rapid Transit Dist., 465 P.2nd 72, 77 (Cal. 1970).

Hastings Aircraft Corporation—we sue Hastings on the basis of both negligence and strict liability in tort for the manufacture of a defective product. Until evidence of a defect is available, proceed under the doctrine of res ipsa loquitur—the thing speaks for itself, i.e., the plane wouldn't have crashed unless something was wrong with it. Eventually we will amend res ipsa out, and plead specific defects.

Cross and Dolby—they made the engines, and Alec always joins the engine people. Same liability as Hastings.

Federal Aviation Administration—the plane was within the control of the San Francisco tower, hence failure to warn of approaching traffic or erroneous approach instructions are possible causes, particularly if it turns out to have been a near miss. Secretary of Transportation Dole has just admitted that 955 additional controllers are needed in the system, and Newsweek is coming out with a cover story in two weeks calling 1987 "The Year of the Near Miss" (they're up 35 percent), so if we play our cards right, we can make hay with this one.

National Weather Service—there was a storm that night, as far as we know at this point not a particularly severe one, but we want to allege on information and belief that the weather service negligently forecast conditions, causing the pilot to fail to take adequate safety precautions. If the crash ultimately turns on pilot error, we can plead the so-called Caged Brain Syndrome—that pilots in rainstorms are subject to extranormal magnetic forces that impair their judgment in emergencies.

That's all the defendants we name specifically. Use John Does to cover the subcontractors, etc., as well as the pilot, owner, operator, and manufacturer of the small aircraft. Put in standard claims for failure to properly equip and maintain, for breach of express and implied warranties of safety, for lack of crashworthiness, and for punitive damages, though at this point they're window dressing.

Ask for $20 million, for publicity purposes—the newspapers still like to print the damage claims, even though they're meaningless. File in federal court in San Francisco, jurisdiction based on diversity of citizenship between the plaintiffs and defendants, venue on the place of the accident.

Keep our clients informed of developments, which includes sending them copies of pleadings. People in their situation often feel hopeless and helpless, and the litigation gives them a focus, even though it may amount to nothing more productive than a desire for revenge. Don't feel it inappropriate to discuss the case with them. Some of our most rewarding strategic points, particularly on the issue of damages, have originated in casual conversations with our clients. Also remember that if you don't do these things, the client may grow to hold you as responsible as the defendants for their ordeal. There is no worse publicity for an attorney than to be reviled by his client, so beware. Also keep in mind that if it takes a decade to get the plaintiffs the money they deserve, our clients will hate us no matter <u>what</u> we do. That's why we go full tilt in crash cases from day one. Keep the pressure on, or the pressure will be on you.

Incidentally, the rumors that Alec intends to retire are being spread by our competitors to divert potential SurfAir plaintiffs from this office. Assure anyone who asks that Alec will be back in action, full time, in a few weeks.

If you have any other questions, see me.

<u>Martha</u>

SIX

The view mesmerizes as it always does—the bay, the green lump of Angel Island, San Francisco's skyscrapers rising in the distance like the sails of an approaching armada. Once he could stare across this slice of the world for hours and in the process stare deep within himself, but of late the dazzle is only momentary. He has asked the view to heal his heart when all it ever promised was to empty excess from his brain.

With a final glance across the sequined water, Alec Hawthorne reaches for a button. At its command, his head and shoulders, inclined at forty-five degrees, sink toward the horizontal. When he is level, he looks at the appointment calendar now accessible on the table beside him, finds the day, and crosses off the one just past. The big black X is number sixty-four.

He has spent nine weeks in his living room, for much of that time leaving it only to use the bathroom or to endure his designated therapy with the drill sergeant assigned to hound enough strength into his heart to carry it into the twenty-first century. But enough has finally been enough. Although he has been urged to continue his therapies for another month, on Monday last he dismissed his entire retinue—cardiologist, internist, physiotherapist, and nurses of all shapes, sizes, and demeanors—but for the minimal follow-up required by their malpractice-avoidance procedures.

He is determined to complete his recovery by his own devices. Minimally, during the weeks of his recuperation he should have for-mulated a plan, a "wellness program" in the current argot, that had

125

at its core a dazzling array of dietary sacrifices and rehabilitative schemes designed to rid both his soul and his arteries of any residue of pleasure. Instead, he has gone back to work, bowing to the blandishments of his white-garbed advisers only by reducing the hours of his former routine by half. He knows he should change his habits, but can think of no other regimen that is capable of beating back the fear that the law firm with his name on it can function just fine without him.

Still, he is being a good boy. Every other afternoon is spent at home, walking for a vigorous hour, then resting and reading the classics. Deeply into *War and Peace*, he wonders why so many of the great books were written by the subjects of czars or monarchs and whether the empty drone of modern fiction is the fault of its authors or of a form of government that permits them to be irrelevant. Such musings are digressive, however. The Franklin Library edition of Tolstoy's masterwork lies closed on the table beside him, because Hawthorne is awaiting the arrival of his very first wife.

Hygiene is her name, the legacy of a fastidious father and his submissive spouse. Too late, Hawthorne realized that Hygiene had been raised to be resentful by parents who were convinced that—despite their damnation of everything in the universe less perfect than their God—they deserved much more than they got from life, on fronts from the financial to the philosophical. Hygiene's parents not only wanted to be rich, they wanted to be revered.

Hygiene continued the tradition with an accusatory vehemence more common to political columnists and youth gangs. In spite of this, Hawthorne had married her. The reason was sex—from the moment he met her, Hygiene made it clear she was willing to erase his deficit in exchange for an option on his surname.

The marriage lasted until Hawthorne had partaken of every wanton exercise he had ever dreamed or read of, and Hygiene discovered that her husband's savoir faire came from books and movies rather than a family fortune. Oddly, Hygiene remains convinced that despite a combative divorce and their itchy encounters over the ensuing twenty years, they are friends. She is as wrong as their marriage was, but he has never had the nerve to tell her so.

The doorbell rings. The maid hurries to answer it. After a moment, footsteps echo on the foyer tiles. Hawthorne presses the button to raise himself to a conversational tilt, then rolls to his side and waits for his visitor to move into his range of vision. Dressed in pajamas and dressing gown, he is determined to remain bedridden over the course of the visit, to appeal to whatever cinder of sympathy might smolder within Hygiene's morally blackened body.

Suddenly she is beside him—stylish, vibrant, dressed in slacks and shirt beneath a jacket cut in the style of a vice cop, an instant reminder of why he made her the first of four. Given her age, he wonders how she does it.

She doesn't speak, not yet, not until she has assessed the scene. Looking down her narrow nose, moving with the slide of the cocktail waitress she was when they first met, the former Hygiene Dillon circles the bed like an agricultural inspector regarding the first fruit of the season.

When she has confirmed that the rumors that have brought her here are true, she strikes a pose. Arms akimbo, chemically blonded head cocked at a quizzical tilt, she stands on one foot while the other swivels like a machine gun on the point of its high heel, until it zeroes on his chest. Then it stops and waits, presumably for him to surrender.

"Hygiene," he begins, determined to be minimalist in everything from etiquette to chitchat.

"Alec. You look *much* better than I expected."

"You, too."

She shakes her head and purses her perfect lips. "Now, now. Don't I at least deserve a smile?"

"You deserve a great deal more than that, Hygiene."

She shakes her head with resignation. "Are we going to be like this, or are we going to be grown-up?"

"By 'we' you mean the sick guy, right?"

She raises a brow that is as defined as a scimitar. The lazy string of her lip is supposed to indicate that she knows far better than he why he is doing what he has just done, saying what he has just said in just the way he said it. She had used the smile a dozen times a day when they were married.

"If you do that once more I'll have you thrown out," Hawthorne declares, wishing he were as assured as she, knowing he is for some reason only able to manage it when he is in a courtroom speaking on behalf of someone other than himself.

Hygiene remains impervious. After a moment, she nods briskly. "Let's pretend I just rang the bell. Door opens, I come in, smile, blow you a kiss. Now we start over. Hello, Alec. You're looking well. How are you feeling?"

He grins sheepishly, despite his determination to remain aloof. It

127

seems she is not here to gloat, so he decides to be as nice as she will let him be. "I'm fine, Hygiene. Yourself?"

"Wonderful," she says, then abandons the charade for candor. "Did you have a bypass? I heard you did and then I heard you didn't."

He shakes his head. "They're trying to handle it medically. I take some stuff that's supposed to dissolve deposits in my arteries. In the meantime, they stuck a little drill in there to open them enough to keep things moving."

"A Rotoblator," Hygiene murmurs.

"Very good. It's supposed to be a new procedure."

She shrugs. "I try to keep up with the latest techniques, in case I meet a cardiologist I want to impress. They average three hundred thousand a year, you know." She licks her lips to show she's joking, and in the process shows her most endearing smile. "But are you . . . that is, did it work?"

He shrugs. "There's an eighty percent opening in the affected artery now, as opposed to twenty when I keeled over. Unless I have an urge to perform in stag films, they tell me I can live with that. And if I conk out again, they can always cut. Pig valves and plastic pipe and such. If that doesn't work, I'll get a job where a heart isn't required. With an insurance company, for instance."

Hygiene's smile is a tepid acknowledgment of his well-worn wit. "I hope for the best, Alec. I really do." She grabs his eyes and squeezes them with hers. "And what I *really* hope is that you know that."

"I do. I guess." What he knows is that she is up to something. What he doesn't know is what.

"We're still friends, at least," she comments as her eyes complete an inventory of the room. In the event he decides to liquidate, as Martha has suggested, Hygiene will be the first he asks to tell him what his house is worth. "It's really quite amazing, isn't it, given what we said to each other during that last month?"

"To say nothing of what we did to each other."

She brushes at his words, daintily, as though they are crumbs from a croissant. "That was nothing, Alec. You know that. It was just my way of fighting back against your precious job. Surely you don't still hold *that* against me."

"I suppose not. But if I held anything at all against you, that's what it would be."

She wrinkles her forehead as she considers if he has a hidden agenda, one that encompasses a reexamination of her several infidelities. "If I thought you meant that, I'd be mad."

He returns her careful smile and waits. With women he has always been a counterpuncher. But he is far from undefeated.

Hygiene uncrosses her arms, unshoulders her leather bag, sits on the edge of his bed. Her weight on the mattress causes him to roll uncomfortably close to her. Her perfume makes him cough, giving him an excuse to reestablish distance. For some reason, Hygiene has always fancied a fragrance that makes her smell like laundry soap.

"So, Alec," she says, patting his knee. "Are you going to do what four wives and who knows how many mistresses have been begging you to do for years?"

"What's that—consult a sex therapist?"

She punches his thigh. "I mean slow *down*, you idiot. Hop off the treadmill."

He gestures toward the bed they sit on. "I've pretty much slowed to a stop."

She looks dubious. "You haven't been to the office yet? Not even once?"

He avoids her eyes. "In and out, is all."

She shakes her head disgustedly. "In at seven and out twelve hours later." She looks at him with an intensity he interprets as concern. "Do you really miss it that much?"

"Some of it."

"Like what?"

"Earning a fortune off the misery of others is its main attraction, I think."

"I'm serious, Alec."

He shrugs, still wary of her motive. "I like what I do, Hygiene. I seem to be good at it, and despite what you read in the papers, I do some good for others."

"There's more to it than that."

"I suppose. The bullshit. The camaraderie. Litigation's kind of like football without helmets."

She raises a brow. "Camaraderie with who? I heard Dan Griffin left you."

As he scrambles for an answer, he curls into a defensive posture. "There are other people to talk to besides Dan."

"Not in your firm, there aren't."

"What the hell do *you* know?" he flashes. "You could never bring yourself to darken my office door." He waits for her rebuttal. When it doesn't appear, he simmers. "There are plenty of other reasons to continue working. Not that I have any obligation to explain them to you."

"The glory, for instance," Hygiene observes quietly.

"I've never denied that I like the psychic income as much as the legal tender."

"I know you haven't. I just thought maybe you didn't need it quite so much anymore. I always wished I knew more about your childhood," she continues with what appears to be regret. "You crave attention more than anyone I've ever met. I think your mother must never have even *touched* you."

It's a topic he avoids, his childhood. Not because he's certain it was deprived or traumatic, but because its particulars are so vague he's not certain it existed. If it did, the proof was circumstantial, its relics stuffed in backs of drawers and pasted to dusty albums, the only obvious outgrowth a rather broadly based repression. In his thirties he worried about the blank page of his formative years, but now he seldom dwells on it. His wives were far more interested in his youth than he was, presumably so they could blame the kind of husband he'd become on someone other than themselves.

Hygiene admires the view, then leaves the bed and sits in the chair that faces him. "This is a beautiful place, Alec. I've driven by a few times, hoping to see signs that your life had fallen apart, but they were never there. That was years ago, of course. Now so many lives are falling apart, one more or less doesn't matter."

"Thanks."

"I didn't mean just you, you idiot. I meant all of us." She paused. "I hear you're about to tie the knot again. Martha? Is that her name? The horsy thing you gave up your partnership in Perkins and Maxwell for? She'd be number five, if my abacus is accurate."

"Martha and I are *not* engaged, Hygiene. You may pass that along to the social arbiters, and tell them to kiss my ass."

Martha. She is due in an hour. On three evenings a week she drops by to update his calendar, sift through the active cases and keep him current with the effluent of legal gossip, and provide any other services he may be in need of. But her official duties are not the reason Hawthorne has shuddered at the mention of her name.

A month ago his doctor cleared the way for sex. Though it has been four months since his last orgasm, and though Martha is willing to perform the most gentle of manipulations, to goad him toward that eruptive end while he remains stresslessly recumbent, he seems to have lost the urge. He doesn't know whether the incapacity originates in mind or body, in middle-age ennui or posttraumatic terror, but whatever the reason, he suppresses the slightest hint of concupiscence. Which means his relations with Martha have been uncommonly wholesome since his coronary. Which both of them seem to find refreshing. Which sounds uncomfortably like chronic illness or old age. Which vastly depresses him.

In what amounts to a welcome diversion, Hygiene bats her eyes. "You've been seen entering hotels with her," she says.

"If I married every woman I've taken to a hotel, I'd be eating my meals at a mission."

Abandoning his role as invalid, he goes to the bar and fixes her a drink. When he delivers it, she seizes his hand and kisses his palm. "I really did come just to tell you I wish you well, Alec," she says. "And to tell you I think you should retire."

He reacts with stony ire. "That's ridiculous. I'm not even fifty, for God's sake."

"You *know* your law practice put you in that bed. And you know if you don't give it up, you'll be back there again."

"Like hell I—"

"What do you *want* at this point, anyway?" she interrupts. "You make more money than Croesus. You're preeminent in your field— every time a plane goes down you pop up on TV, telling some idiot interviewer why it happened and how it could have been prevented. You've got fame and you've got fortune. So why don't you find a good woman and take her around the world a few times." Hygiene fiddles with her necklace. "You always were good with women. I'm sure you could make a nice retirement program out of one."

He reels from her tirade. "Jesus, Hygiene. What brought all that on?"

She hesitates, then shrugs, as if truth were a fallback position. "You're not my only ex-husband who's had a heart attack this year."

"Who's the other?"

"Ben."

He sighs. "I'm sorry. I didn't know. I like Ben."

"I know."

He is remembering the rumpled man who had succeeded him, a good guy who had been married to Hygiene for a dozen years and then abruptly divorced her. "Whatever happened between you and Ben? I thought that one was for real."

131

She glances toward the floor, then looks at him until he fidgets. "I had a mastectomy. I learned to live with it; Ben didn't."

He closes his eyes and envisions her on a table ringed with eager surgeons. "I didn't know, Hygiene. You should have told me."

Her gaze falls to the protuberances at her chest. "Why? So you could keep it as a souvenir?"

"What kind of a ..." He stops when he sees that no matter how badly he feels she has hurt him, she feels she has been hurt in equal measure.

"I'm sorry," she says softly. "You don't deserve that. Not now, you don't."

"I wish you'd told me, Genie," he says, using the diminutive he has not uttered since six months prior to their divorce. "I would have liked to try to help. Be someone to talk to, if nothing else. Or help with Ben."

She shakes her head. "It's okay, Alec. I wanted people around about as much as you do right now. The only reason I'm here is to tell you that Ben had his first attack a year before this last, and they told him to slow down and he didn't, and it happened again just like they warned him it would." Her eyes are aglow with urgency. "I'm hoping you'll learn from it, Alec. I'm hoping my coming here will help save your life. There. I've been as melodramatic about it as I can."

He has no idea what to say, so he says, "I guess I should thank you."

"What you should do is decide whether you want to live or die. If you decide you want to live, just kiss your job goodbye. If you decide you want to die, just keep on the way you have been. I know you don't believe it, but sometimes life really *is* just as simple as that."

He makes a face, trying to make light of her mission, but she keeps digging. "You haven't been dumb with your money, have you?"

He shrugs. "Just spent more of it than I have."

"But you could walk away anytime you wanted to, right?"

Actually, he has thought about it more than once since his confinement, though not enough to reach a decision. But it is increasingly difficult to see his future as anything but a replay of his past, complete with the inevitable slow motion. "I'm not as flush as you think, Genie," he dissembles finally. "In order to retire I'd have to sell this place, disown my kid, and move to Mississippi."

She shakes her head. He watches her hair dance across her shoulders and remembers when she would crouch above him and conceal her breasts with her wavy mane, make him dig through a silken shade

132

to suckle them. He is enjoying the moment until he remembers that now she has only one of them to hide.

"Balls," she says. "You and I could have a lot of fun together, Alec. Travel. Go to plays and concerts. Read to each other. Sex would be a separate thing you could work out however you wanted. You and me, we'd just tug each other toward the cocktail hour."

"You make it sound like I've only got five minutes left on earth."

She rises off the chair and looms above him. "That's the way I *want* to make it sound." She bangs her empty glass on the table and strides angrily toward the door.

"Say hi to Ben for me," he calls after her.

"Ben is *dead*, you idiot" is what he realizes she has said, but only after she has left him.

Keith Tollison leaned back in his chair and tried to summon the energy to do what he had to do next, which was to see both Laura Donahue and Brenda Farnsworth within the space of the next two hours. Only months before, both prospects would have gladdened him. Now they were demoralizing reminders that the SurfAir crash had cast both women beyond his reach—the more he tried to help, the less of him they seemed to need.

Brenda had retreated to her school and son; Laura, to the task of coaxing her husband from his coma. Purposeful to them, to Tollison the weeks since the crash had been pointless and depressing. Certain that he should be doing everything that needed to be done, he spent long hours doing little but wonder why life continued to deprive him of its most coveted rewards. The only virtue of such thoughts being his increasingly virulent contempt for them, Tollison cursed himself and sighed, then grabbed his coat and left the office.

The Donahue house was high in the hills past the western edge of town, overlooking the lights of Altoona and the vineyards and apple orchards bordering the city to the north and south. Jack had built it as a showplace, stagy testimony to his talent for promotion and development. Borrowing to the hilt to finance it, he watched its worth appreciate dramatically as a series of San Francisco profiteers cast about for environments that would shield their families from the victims of the system that had yielded up their fortunes. The string of restaurants, boutiques, bodegas, and fitness centers that had accumulated along Main Street—bearing names that would have won prizes in a punsters' contest—was testimony that Altoona's transformation from sleepy village to suburban chic was practically complete. The result for the majority of Altoonans was that year by booming year, their homes earned more than they did.

Visible on the crest above, the Donahue house was long and low, shingle and stone, cantilevered from a brushy hillside, complete with swimming pool and putting green and view to the end of the valley. In the early years of his return to Altoona, Tollison had been there several times, at one or another of Jack's promotional extravaganzas. But since he never succumbed to one of the investment schemes, his presence had recently been infrequent. It was the way both he and Jack had wanted it and, since the first fumblings of their affair, the way Laura wanted it as well.

The road narrowed. At its end was only Laura's place and forty contiguous acres Jack had acquired in the hope of subdividing them. A faded sign still advertised the dream—OAKWOOD ACRES, VIEW LOTS, A PROJECT OF DONAHUE DEVELOPMENT CORPORATION. For reasons unknown to Tollison, the project had never gotten off the ground, and the road now led only to Laura and her forty-acre yard.

Another car rounded a turn, coming from the opposite direction. Driven far too fast for the width and contour of the road, it forced Tollison off the pavement. Bouncing along the rocky shoulder, he cursed the reckless driver, a bearded block of a man, no one he knew. When the man didn't acknowledge his protest, Tollison honked. With studied insolence, the driver turned the other way. Tollison resisted an impulse to turn around and chase him down.

From a distance the house seemed to have maintained its original flair, but after Tollison turned into the drive the signs of neglect were evident. The pool was dry; the putting green had grown to the length of rough. Weeds sprouted through the flagstone walkway; gutters brimmed with sodden leaves and sagged beneath wet weight. Moss patches soiled the roof like the droppings of large birds. One of the cars in the garage, a big Mercedes, had a FOR SALE sign in the window and its left rear tire was flat.

Tollison parked in the shade of a live oak, grabbed his briefcase, and hurried to the entrance and rang the bell. The ornamental plums that flanked the doorway seemed diseased and dying, of a virus that seemed to have spread to the house. He rang the bell again. Heat rose at him as though all of Altoona were on fire.

Moments later Laura Donahue, a smile on her face and a drink in her hand, tugged open the heavy door. When she saw who it was, she smiled crookedly and readied herself for a kiss. Her hair was twirled into a golden twist, her lips were heavily red, her silken blouse and slacks were black and white and billowy. The greeting was the first sign in weeks that he was other than a nuisance.

"Come in, Keith," she said. "Let me fix you a drink. Still bourbon?"

"Still."

The mention of the whiskey recalled the pint they'd shared in the airport motel. As he followed Laura through the narrow foyer, he forgot the waning of her attentions and his resultant pique, and felt the familiar swell of ardor. When they rounded a corner and descended to the living room, which was sunk three steps below the entrance level and was vast, he almost tripped and fell.

As always, the room demanded awe. One wall was entirely glass, revealing the forty empty acres and the city far below. The other three wore wainscoting of rough-hewn planks that formed the backs of three long benches, deeply padded, capable of seating a platoon. The floor was oak parquet, the ceiling roughened plaster, the furnishings beige linen and brown leather.

In the year it was built, the design and decor had been the talk of the town, but that was before refugees from San Francisco began building newer and finer mansions on the adjacent hillsides. Even had that competitive migration not occurred, the impact would have dwindled. The place had simply gotten old, had somehow become a relic, even though Tollison still thought of it as the Donahues' new house.

As Laura disappeared toward the kitchen, Tollison sank to the love seat by the fireplace, enjoying the sun's farewell and the soft tinkle of a familiar sonata. A moment later Laura brought him his drink and sat down in the chair across from him, curled her legs beneath her, and offered a silent toast.

"I should have come to your office," she began. "I don't like to take advantage of . . . us." She swirled the liquid in her glass.

"No problem," he said, as careful as he had been in the years before he knew his desire for her was reciprocated.

"But it's hard for me to go out these days," she went on. "People always want to talk about Jack. When I tell them there's no news, they look at me as though it's my fault, as if they think the doctors have been trying to call to tell me he's recovered and I haven't bothered to answer the phone." Her voice broke, then mended itself in the succeeding pause. "It's odd what people blame you for, isn't it? It's almost always for the wrong thing."

He refused to indulge her urge to judge them. "Jack's condition hasn't changed?"

She shook her head. "They say he's stable, his vital signs are good, but he's still unconscious." Her expression took on a stricken cast. "Sometimes I think he doesn't want to come back. Sometimes I think he's happier the way he is." She paused and hugged herself, as though her husband's wounded ghost had forced its way into the room.

Tollison looked at her with what he hoped was detachment. "We haven't been alone for a long time."

Her eyes shifted toward the world outside the window, as though it harbored enemies. "I know."

"I've missed you."

"I've missed you, too."

"I keep hoping you'll need me for something, and you keep doing just fine on your own."

"I don't know if fine is quite the word for it."

There was a place he wanted them to go, but he no longer knew how to get them there. As he struggled for an endearing phrase, Laura looked everywhere but at him.

"Your friend Marlene is worried about you," he managed finally. "She thinks you blame yourself for Jack's accident."

Laura opened her eyes and closed her fingers. "What on earth would give her that idea?"

"Something you said about retribution."

When there was no response, frustration made him blunt. "You didn't cause the plane crash, Laura. And neither did I."

She looked at him through a wary squint. "Are you sure?"

"For crying out loud—why are you getting mystical about this? You didn't feel guilty about us six months ago, so why feel guilty now?"

She shrugged and raised her glass. "Guilt seems to be a lot like cockroaches—it thrives no matter what you use against it."

He went to her side and sat beside her chair, taking her hand. "If you knew how much I've thought about you over the past months," she declared from her perch above him. "How many nights I've almost jumped in the car and raced to your house and crawled in your bed and begged to stay with you forever."

"I wish you had."

"I know. But it's not that simple anymore."

"Why not?"

"You know why not."

His response was instantaneous and cruel. "Just because he's in a coma doesn't make him a saint."

She stiffened. "Please, Keith."

Chagrined, he kissed her hand. "I'm sorry, but I'm fighting for my *life* here, Laura. I *love* you; I've loved you ever since Jack first came by the office to show you off. I can't sit by and let you put an end to everything." He sighed and searched for words. "Nothing's *changed*, don't you see? We're not *kids* anymore, Laura. This could be the last chance we have to make our lives what we want them to be. I'm sorry Jack's hurt, and I hope he gets better, I really do. But there's nothing you can *do* for him. And even if there was, you're not obliged to do it."

In the wake of his desperation, her words were wretched. "I *can* help, Keith. So I have to."

"How? You're not a doctor, for crying out loud."

She pulled her hand away. Though he sensed her gaze, he wouldn't turn to meet it.

"I'm an LPN," she said quietly. "That's how we met. I was working at the Free Clinic in the Haight, and Jack came in to help a friend down off a bad trip. He hung around all night. By morning he had swept me off my feet, maybe because he was the first guy I'd seen in a week who wasn't stoned out of his mind."

His mouth was as dry as gypsum. "You never told me you were a nurse."

For the first time since he entered the house, her tone was affectionate. "That's because we did it backward, you idiot; we were lovers before we were friends."

He looked up at her, his mind spinning with misery and newness. "Is that what we're doing? Going back to friendship?"

"It might not be a bad idea, do you think?"

"What I think is that you're telling me it's over between us."

She shook her head, though slowly enough to admit of ambiguity. "I'm just saying we have to wait."

Panic clouded his vision. "So I pray for a miracle, is that it? For Jack to be revived as the son of a bitch he always was, and then I get to screw his wife again. Somehow I don't think those particular prayers will be answered, Laura. So maybe I'll just wish he was dead."

Her silence was the judgment he deserved. "I didn't know I'd hurt you that much," she murmured finally.

"You're hurting me worse than I thought I could possibly be hurt."

"But I've been hurt, too, don't you see? That's my *husband* in that hospital. The man I swore to love in sickness and in health is as sick as you can get. I can't just let him rot away while I frolic with his boyhood buddy."

"You can, but you won't."

"That's not fair."

"It depends on your perspective. And Jack and I were never buddies."

She was quiet long enough to let him recover a shred of dignity. "How's Brenda?" she asked finally.

The question seemed to seal his fate. "Brenda's up and down," he said as he got to his feet and returned to the love seat. "When she found proof that Carol had been on the plane, she was ready to hunt down the president of SurfAir and shoot him between the eyes. Now she seems to be blocking the whole thing, as though Carol slipped away after a lengthy illness and is living on a silver cloud."

"That's not healthy, I don't think."

"I don't, either."

They unlocked their eyes and fidgeted. Absent guidance from the woman across the room, Tollison pulled his briefcase onto his lap and opened it. "We might as well go over these papers, since I don't seem to be of any use around here except professionally." He paused. "If you want to look them over, you'll have to sit here by me."

He fumbled with obstreperous documents and felt her snuggle against his side. When she was comfortably canted against the padded arm of the love seat, she crossed a leg and looked at him expectantly. As he flipped through the stack of parchment bond her hand rested on his thigh, lightly at first, then grew weighty with his preoccupation. He let the moment build, to see if it contained a possibility, but she took her hand away.

"This is an application to make you Jack's conservator. That means you'll have the right to make decisions about most details of his life, from his property to his person. Dr. Ryan has signed an affidavit stating that Jack is unable to act for himself, so there won't be any problem getting the appointment approved. It's pretty routine. Just sign there."

She turned the pages, pausing only at Dr. Ryan's statement. "He doesn't sound too hopeful, does he?"

"He's just trying to help."

For the first time, she sounded as desolate as he was. "Who does it help to say Jack may never regain consciousness?"

"The judge," he answered simply. "And speaking of help, I think it's time you made a decision about a lawsuit against the airline. The insurance company isn't going to talk settlement seriously until you have a complaint on file."

"Then file me a complaint."

"I've told you a dozen times; I'm not competent to handle a case like this. How much are the medical bills up to, by the way?"

"Over two hundred thousand, the last I asked. They're getting embarrassed to talk about it, I think."

"So there's that, and Jack's lost earnings and pain and suffering, plus the loss of consortium you've suffered. You could recover millions."

"Consortium? What's consortium?"

He felt himself redden. "Affection. Companionship. Stuff like that."

"You mean sex." Her grin was mocking. "They put a price on such matters, do they?"

"They try."

"And people say lawyers aren't clever little devils."

"I've heard them called devils a lot more than I've heard them called clever."

Her smile faded. "I really would like you to handle it, Keith."

He shook his head. "You should retain an aviation expert—someone who does this full time."

She scowled. "I've talked to one of those experts—a man named Scallini calls here twice a week."

"How'd you run afoul of him?"

"There was another patient in Jack's room for a while—a crash victim who was barely hanging on. People were streaming in and out—specialists, priests, medical students stopping by to gawk—it was like *St. Elsewhere* in there sometimes. Then this Scallini person showed up, claiming he was this poor guy's lawyer." She swore. "What a repulsive man; his toupee has a streak of gray in it that makes him look like a skunk. Anyway, since his client was too out of it to listen, he started in on me. Told me he could get Jack ten million dollars. Started handing me papers—a fee agreement, power of attorney, some sort of arbitration thing in case I claimed malpractice. I think he even made a pass, right there in front of Jack, though maybe massaging a woman's knee is what passes for charm in lawyer circles. Anyway, when he started referring to Jack and his client as *droolers*, I had the nurses throw him out."

She crossed her arms and shook her head. "But he won't take no for an answer. Someone keeps calling and claiming I've indicated I'm interested in Mr. Scallini's services and telling me what I have to do to retain him. I can't *bear* to deal with people who see Jack in terms of dollars and headlines, Keith. Why can't someone I *like* look after my interests? If we get millions out of this, some lawyer is going to get a juicy hunk as a fee. Why should it go to a stranger instead of you?"

He sighed. "You'll get your millions because the stranger will know how to pressure an insurance company into paying you that much. I wouldn't have the faintest idea how to go about it. Hell, I don't even know how airplanes stay in the air."

"You don't have to know that, though, do you? You just have to know why they crash."

Her summation was as jarring as a cudgel. Speechless, Tollison found refuge in the papers in his lap.

Once again her hand lit on his thigh. "Are you telling me you won't help me, Keith?"

Her voice was thick and throaty, impossible to refuse. Still, his terms were tentative. "Have you heard anything from the insurance people?"

She nodded. "They called last week. They asked if I would accept two hundred thousand plus the medical bills. When I said I'd have to ask my lawyer, they asked who my lawyer was. When I gave them your name, they asked if you were representing me in the crash case. I said I wasn't sure. Then they said I'd better settle quickly, because if I didn't I was going to learn things about my husband that I wouldn't want to know." She laughed. "That's a pretty good definition of my marriage, come to think of it—learning things about my husband that I didn't want to know."

He turned to face her. "I want you to see this guy I was in law school with. He's a pro at this stuff, one of the best in the country. If you still want me to handle things after you talk to him, I guess I will. But I want us to see him first, so he can tell you exactly what you're up against. Okay? Can I make the appointment?"

She hesitated, then nodded. "Whatever you say."

"I'll call him tomorrow and let you know. By the way, who was that guy who left here just before I drove up?"

"What guy?"

"Drove a gray Taurus. Looked about fifty. Beard."

She shook her head. "There was no one here this afternoon. Maybe he came up to look at the lots. They still do that once in a while."

"I hope that's all it was. You could use the money."

"You're telling me."

The sentence implied a struggle Tollison was only dimly aware of. "All the more reason to get your lawsuit under way," he said.

"I suppose." Her interest in both him and her legal rights was flagging.

He put his papers back in his case and placed it between them. "The main thing I need to know is that you're psychologically sound, Laura, that you're dealing with your troubles in a healthy way."

She stood up and regarded him with a stalwart gaze. "What I have to deal with isn't trouble; what I have to deal with is responsibility." She walked toward the kitchen and left him in a muddle.

A moment later she returned, refreshed and cheerful. "I've got some soup on the stove and some ham in the fridge. Would you like to stay for dinner?"

He grabbed his briefcase. "I can't. I'm sorry."

"Oh." Her disappointment was plain and unexpected.

"I made another appointment. I didn't think you'd want me to stick around."

She smiled slyly. "Brenda?"

He nodded.

"I'm the one who should be sorry. Go on. Don't look so miserable. Say hi to her for me."

He stood up. After two steps his hands were on her. He pulled her to his chest and embraced her tightly, burying his face in her soft shoulder. He thought he felt her shudder, heard her say his name. When he released her, he made her look at him. "If all you want me to be is your lawyer, then that's all I'll try to be."

She looked at him through fresh tears. "I can handle it if he dies, you know," she murmured, as though to remind herself of a tolerable alternative. "That night in the motel when I was certain he was dead already, I lay awake all night imagining how life would be without him. And I decided life would be just fine. You know better than anyone that I've been prepared to do without Jack for a long time." She sniffed, and he kissed her cheek.

"And I can handle it if he gets well. If he wakes up one day and is the same old Jack, then I could be the same old me and you the same old you, which would be the best for all of us. But what I'm afraid I *can't* handle is if he's something in between. I'm afraid the miracle people keep talking about will be that Jack opens his eyes and grunts some subhuman noise and slobbers down his chin and stays that way forever."

She had made the forecast dreadful and inescapable. Tollison had no idea how to alter it.

"I'm sorry," Laura said after a minute. "It's just ... I want to be able to do what I have to do, you know? I want to be a hero if I have to be."

He pulled her toward him a second time. "That's the job I've been trying to get for twenty years," he said. "But you'll be better at it than I've been." Awash in hope and anguish, he kissed her a quick goodbye.

Ten minutes later he entered Altoona's Chinese restaurant. Brenda looked up from a booth in the back and waved. Tollison slid onto the bench across from her, asked if she wanted a drink, and motioned for the waiter when she nodded.

The waiter's name was Sam. Tollison had represented him in the negotiations to buy the building from the video entrepreneur who had owned it previously. Because he had taken advantage of the collapse of the video fad and gotten a deal well below the market, Sam would have given Tollison three free meals a day for life.

After he and Sam exchanged spry greetings, Tollison ordered a whiskey sour for Brenda and a bourbon and water for himself. Irrepressible as always, Sam went away smiling, and Tollison turned to Brenda.

In the months since learning of her sister's death, Brenda had become strangely subdued. There were duties to perform, of course— the funeral, the inventory of Carol's small estate, collecting Carol's possessions and auctioning the items Brenda didn't want, putting the house on the market, filing the will for probate. Through it all, Brenda maintained a beatific calm. Which made Tollison anticipate a storm.

He reached for her hand and gave it a pat. "Long time no see."

Her response was desultory. "I suppose. I haven't kept track."

"How's school?"

"The kids went on strike for movies at the noon hour."

"I thought they already had movies at the noon hour."

"That was last year. The principal closed them down after *The Breakfast Club*."

"What was wrong with *The Breakfast Club*?"

"I think it had the temerity to show kids talking about things kids really talk about."

Sam returned with the drinks. Tollison and Brenda shared long swallows. "I see that's not your first," she said as he lowered his glass. "You've got that little red spot you always get, right below your nose."

Involuntarily, he reached to rub it off.

Brenda met his eye. "You've been with Laura."

The question implied a visit as intimate as the one Tollison had hoped would transpire. Thanks to his newfound innocence, he stayed steady, wondering if this was the moment of truth he had dreaded for so many months, wondering if she really knew or was merely guessing, wondering if it mattered.

Brenda's voice was stout. "I don't care anymore, you know."

He blinked. "About Laura. Or about anything?"

Brenda's look made either answer likely. "You had an affair with her, didn't you?"

"What makes you think that?"

"I ran into her at Safeway the other day. She was so *careful* when your name came up. She acted like she'd never laid eyes on you before." Her lips whitened. "The affair I don't mind. What I mind is that you didn't have the guts to tell me."

"It's not like that, Brenda. We aren't—"

"Don't *lie* to me, Keith. I've had to put up with a lot lately, but I don't have to put up with that."

As they exchanged stark looks, Sam returned for their order. Tollison, who had spent a year wondering how to confess his faithlessness to Brenda, spent the interval wondering whether he any longer had anything to confess to her at all.

He waited till Sam left, then said, "About Laura. I just want to—"

Brenda held up a hand. "Do you know what's funny? In a way, I hope it's true."

"Why?"

"So I don't have to keep feeling sorry for what I did to you thirty years ago. The way I see it, maybe when the score gets evened up we can give it another try. What do you think?"

He knew only that what would have been inconceivable six months earlier was now no longer that. "Maybe so."

They finished their drinks in silence. "On the phone you mentioned Spitter," Tollison said finally. "What's happened?"

"He quit his job."

"I thought he loved it at the garage."

"He did." She waved for Sam to bring her another drink. "You know those guys he hangs around with?"

"The little kids?"

She shook her head. "The grave diggers. As best I can interpret it, those idiots told Spitter they buried Carol without her head."

"What?"

"You heard me. According to Spitter, Carol's head wasn't in the casket." Brenda's eyes were boiling. "Do you think it can possibly be true? Or were they playing tricks on him? Those guys are pretty macabre sometimes—they used to make fake body parts out of clay and hide behind gravestones and toss them at kids who went to the cemetery to neck. Maybe this is more of that."

"Maybe."

"Can you find out for sure?"

He shrugged. "I can call Ethan Calthorp at the funeral home. I know enough about Ethan's cremation practices to give me a little leverage, but the question is why you want to know."

"For Spitter's sake, for one thing."

"Do you think he'll believe you even if you tell him Carol's all there?"

"Probably not."

"Then what's the point?"

"The *point* might be not to let the bastards get away with giving me back only half my sister."

"It was a terrible crash. Plus, weird things were going on at the crash site. None of it will make you—"

"Are you telling me someone *stole* it?"

"I'm telling you to leave it alone."

She shook her head in wonder. "I don't believe my life is so fucked up that I have to dig up my sister's coffin to make sure she's all *there*."

He reached for her hand and tugged her away from the state of her sister's cadaver. "What else is Spitter doing? You sound like you haven't seen him in a while."

"He moved out."

"When?"

"Two weeks ago. I haven't seen him since. Neither has anyone else. Until today."

"What happened today?"

She put a hand over her eyes, as though to become blind to the picture she was about to paint. "I got a call from Marge Hilton—she runs the photo shop? She told me she'd been out to the cemetery this morning—her mother died a year ago, and she was planting some bulbs by her grave. Well, there she was, pulling weeds and planting tulips, and she looked over to the next section and there was Spitter."

"Doing what?"

"Camping out."

"Where?"

"On Carol's grave. He had a tent and sleeping bag; he'd even built a fire. Marge said he looked like a soldier who didn't know the war was over." Brenda's eyes extruded tears. "He hasn't been the same since she died, Keith."

"I know."

"I've talked to the doctors and all they recommend is tranquilizers. But that's not going to help. He needs something to do, a job with someone who cares about him. Something to take his mind off Carol." Her look made her meaning clear.

"I don't have a place for him, Brenda; I'll keep my ears open, but—" He shrugged. "Don't count on anything."

Her lips flattened. "I haven't counted on anything since you went away to college." She lowered her head to her hands. He reached out and touched her hair. After a moment she looked up. "I don't know what to do," she said. "If he stays out there in the cemetery they'll arrest him, and if he goes to jail I'm afraid he won't survive. They'll pick on him, and—"

"There must be *some* place in this state that treats people like Spitter."

Her eyes narrowed. "And what people might those be?"

He squirmed. "I don't know. Retarded, I guess. Mixed up. You know better than I do what's wrong with him."

"There's nothing *wrong* with him that a little understanding wouldn't cure."

"He could use therapy, Brenda. Job training. Something."

"And how am I supposed to pay for therapy?"

"Sue the people who killed your sister."

"Sue them for what?"

"Wrongful death and the loss of Carol's society. For both you and Spitter."

"But I want to let her rest in peace."

"Why do you want the airline to get away with killing Carol without it costing them one red cent?"

"Vengeance is mine, sayeth the Lord."

"Come on. The Lord didn't lose His sister in a plane crash."

"I want to be like the Japanese. *They* don't sue everyone in sight at the drop of a hat."

"Did the president of SurfAir come to your house to apologize for killing your sister? Or resign because of the shame? Or take a cut in pay to cover the damage done to the airline? Or offer a reasonable amount to settle your claim? *That's* the way the Japanese do it."

She reddened. "SurfAir hasn't apologized, but the insurance man has."

"Goddamnit, I *told* you not to talk to—"

"Not in person; his letter."

"His letter was trying to get you to make admissions they can use against you, and to convince you not to hire the kind of lawyer who can get you what you're entitled to under the laws of the land."

"So you say."

"Listen. Whether you sue them or not means nothing to me. I told you, I'm not competent to handle your claim. What I want to do is get you in touch with someone who specializes in crash cases, so he can tell you what your rights are. A guy I used to know is an aviation attorney in San Francisco. I can probably get a meeting set up with him sometime next week. Just *talk* to him, Brenda. Let him tell you about how these cases work, then you can decide what you want to do. What are you afraid of, anyway?"

"I'm afraid I can't live with myself if I try to make a profit off my sister's death. I don't want to dance on her grave, Keith; I just want to plant flowers."

"How the hell do you think they'll grow, with Spitter using them for a mattress?"

LAW OFFICES OF ALEC HAWTHORNE
PIER 32, THE EMBARCADERO
SAN FRANCISCO, CA 94105
ATTORNEYS FOR PLAINTIFF

UNITED STATES DISTRICT COURT
NORTHERN DISTRICT OF
CALIFORNIA

WALTER J. WARREN, individually)   No. 87-5653
and as Administrator of the)   COMPLAINT FOR DAMAGES
Estates of Rhonda J. Warren and)
Randolph F. Warren, on behalf of)   (Wrongful Death and
the estate and heirs of said)   Punitive Damages)
decedents,   Plaintiff,)
            vs.   )
SurfAir Coastal Airways Inc., et al.,)
            Defendants.)

COMES NOW PLAINTIFF AND ALLEGES THAT:
First Cause of Action

I.

At all times mentioned herein, plaintiff WALTER J. WARREN was the husband of decedent Rhonda J. Warren and the father of decedent Randolph F. Warren, a minor child.

II.

Defendant SURFAIR COASTAL AIRWAYS is, and at all times herein mentioned was, a corporation organized and existing under the laws of the State of Nevada and authorized to do business and doing business in California.

. . .

VII.

Defendants HASTINGS AIRCRAFT CORPORATION and CROSS AND DOLBY, INC. at all times herein mentioned were engaged in the business of designing, manufacturing, assembling, inspecting, placing on the market, and selling aircraft and their component parts and instruments to the general public, and plaintiff is informed and believes and thereon alleges that as part of said businesses and at

147

some time prior to March 23, 1987, said defendants designed, manufactured, assembled, inspected, placed on the market, and sold for use by members of the general public, a certain fan-jet Hastings aircraft, Model H-11, registration number C1446-989, and each of its component parts and instruments, hereinafter referred to as "the airplane."

VIII.

At all times herein mentioned, defendant SURFAIR COASTAL AIRWAYS INC. was operating as a common carrier for hire in the transportation of persons and goods on various aircraft owned or leased and operated by said defendant, said aircraft including, at all times pertinent hereto, the airplane hereinabove described.

IX.

Prior to March 23, 1987, the defendants, and each of them, negligently designed, manufactured, assembled, inspected, placed in the market, and sold the airplane, and operated it as a common carrier, including but not limited to aircraft engines, communications, navigation and warning systems, their component parts and instruments, and other component parts and instruments related to occupant safety and survivability, so as to be defective, unsafe, dangerous, and unreasonably dangerous for their intended use and purpose, as said defendants and each of them knew or should have known.

X.

As a direct and proximate result of the negligence hereinabove described, the airplane crashed and burned near San Francisco International Airport on March 23, 1987, and Rhonda J. Warren and Randolph F. Warren were killed.

...

Twelfth Cause of Action

I.

Plaintiff reaffirms, realleges, and incorporates herein by reference each and every allegation contained in Paragraphs I through X of the First Cause of Action herein.

II.

In designing, manufacturing, marketing, and in failing to warn or instruct about the dangerous and defective condition of said aircraft and its components, so as to cause and allow said aircraft into the stream of commerce and to be operated by a common carrier without reasonable occupant protection from crash and fire, said defendants and each of them acted recklessly and indifferently and in disregard of the probable consequences, and were acting with fraud, malice, and oppression, so as to subject them and each of them to punitive and exemplary damages, which should be assessed in a sum no less than twenty million dollars ($20,000,000).

. . .

WHEREFORE, plaintiff prays judgment against defendants, and each of them, jointly and severally, as follows:

1. For general damages for the wrongful death of his wife, Rhonda J. Warren, and his son, Randolph F. Warren, a minor child,
2. For damages for the loss of society of his wife and minor child, and for the loss of consortium of his wife,
3. For special damages according to proof relating to the wrongful deaths of Rhonda J. Warren and Randolph F. Warren,
4. For costs of suit,
5. For punitive damages in the sum of twenty million dollars ($20,000,000),
6. For such other and further relief as may be just and proper.

DATED: August 28, 1987

> Law Offices of Alec Hawthorne
> By _____
> Alec Hawthorne, Esq.

SEVEN

Martha looks in on him with a harried scowl, her stock expression since Hawthorne's heart attack. During his convalescence she has taken command of the office, and it has begun to grind her down. Her critical thrusts, previously trained on him, are now directed inward —she blames herself for every imperfection of the firm, from the cost of paper clips to the misplaced commas in briefs on their way to court.

Mismanagement is not her only worry. In their private moments, Hawthorne is still unable to prove that he is none the worse for his heart's revolt. Though she claims to believe his incapacity is both trivial and temporary, Martha clearly fears it is an omen, that her inability to coax Hawthorne to erection means he is on the verge of severing all but professional relations with her, and perhaps even those as well. Hawthorne hopes his condition stems from the opposite impulse— that he has come to care so much for Martha he can no longer treat her like a toy—but he has not told her so, because he doesn't know what to do if it turns out to be true.

What he fears is that impotence is a permanent consequence of his attack, that he has become so attuned to the potential byproducts of ejaculation—ruptures and aneurysms, infarcts and fibrillations—that even in the most erotic circumstance he will no longer anticipate rapture but only a second collapse. He doesn't know what to do if this suspicion is correct, but he has thumbed through the Yellow Pages listing of psychiatrists, just in case.

"You've got a call," Martha announces flatly. "Line three. Some guy who claims he was in law school with you." A corner of her mouth curls upward. "How many were *in* that class, anyway? Ten thousand?"

150

As his renown has grown, Hawthorne has been approached with increasing frequency by dimly recalled classmates seeking contributions to this or that good cause. Since Martha sees charities as shameless beggars, a threat to the budgets she has laboriously constructed for both Hawthorne and the firm, even philanthropic interruptions are a menace.

"What's his name?" Hawthorne asks, his mind scanning the dwindled panoply of faces he recalls from the class of '65. Of the half-dozen people who were important to him then, he knows nothing about any but the one who had, in the name of Ho Chi Minh and the liberation of the Asiatic masses, tossed a Molotov cocktail at a police cordon on the Berkeley campus and is still serving time for it. For all Hawthorne knows, his other friends could be dead or, worse, be on the bench. For one of the few times since his attack, he finds himself eager to take a call.

Martha scratches her temple. "Tollman, I think. No. Tollison."

"Keith Tollison?"

She nods. "He sounded embarrassed. I suggest you watch your wallet."

"Keith Tollison. I'll be damned. Where's he calling from? Here in town?"

She shakes her head. "Altoona."

"Where the hell is that?"

"Somewhere between Santa Rosa and Bodega Bay. It's one of the stoplights you hit between the wine country and the coast."

"Did he say what he wanted?"

"My guess is he's the class treasurer and you're the key to his quota."

For many reasons, not the least of which his old friend's bashful bent, Hawthorne knows she is wrong. "We were in the same section freshman year, and on law review together. He was probably my best friend in those days. Hell, he was probably the last best friend I had. Our last year we were partners in the trial practice competition."

"Did you win?"

He laughs and shakes his head. "We screwed up the dying declaration exception to the hearsay rule."

"How?"

"We forgot to prove the dying declarant died."

Wondrous at Hawthorne's nostalgic burp, Martha looks as though he has just volunteered the Apostles' Creed. "I take it you want to take the call."

He nods. "No interruptions. No matter what." As he is punching the third button on his console, Martha disappears.

"Hello?"

"Alec?"

"Keith? "

"Hey. Alec. How are you?"

"Great, Keith. It's been a long time."

"Twenty years."

"Jesus. We must be getting old."

"I wouldn't know—I broke all the mirrors in the house."

Hawthorne laughs. "It's nice to hear your voice."

"You too, Alec."

"Good."

"Yeah."

The silence comes from nowhere. It is surprising and unsettling, suggests this has not been a good idea after all. Hawthorne grasps for a sustaining sentence, but the ball is in his old friend's court. Ever the litigant, Hawthorne decides to wait him out.

"I hope I'm not disturbing you, Alec," Tollison manages finally. "I've followed your career over the years, so I know how busy you are. But I just—"

"I'm only trying to keep out of Chapter Seven, just like half the country. What are *you* up to these days? I have to confess I've lost track."

The ensuing laugh is stunted. "I'm a sole practitioner, is all—criminal stuff, fender benders, unlawful detainers. I'm not practicing any of the law we studied in law school, that's for sure. And I certainly don't do anything anyone has reason to keep track of."

Hawthorne remembers the young Keith Tollison as quietly confident, enviably mature, certain of where he was bound. Since those labels don't match the meekness he has just heard, Hawthorne wonders if his memory is faulty or if he never really knew his friend. "Where's your office?" he asks as a second hush threatens to defeat them.

"Here in Altoona."

"Right. Right. You came from up there, didn't you?"

"Yep."

"Did you go back right after school? I thought you were here in the city for a while. Didn't we bump into each other at Vanessi's once?"

"Right. Back in 'sixty-six. I was with the P. D. After a couple of years of representing sociopaths, I decided to go back home. So now I represent drunks and Christmas tree farmers. It's about as exciting as it sounds."

"What made you go back?"

Hawthorne asks the question without thinking, in an effort to re-establish the candor that had once been their strongest bond. Belatedly, he realizes the question could be construed as condescending, or even cruel.

Tollison seems to consider the subject for the first time, though that can't possibly be the case. "It seemed like a good idea back then. The city was getting pretty wild—drugs, the antiwar movement had turned ugly, blacks and whites were scaring each other to death. Plus, city life was so inefficient—I seemed to spend all my time waiting in line. Then my dad had some trouble and needed my help, so I headed home to see if things would be better in the country."

"Were they?"

"I don't ask that question anymore." The answer reeks of surrender.

Hawthorne tries to make his friend feel better than he sounds. "Compared to what's going on in the city *these* days, the sixties seems like the Age of Pericles."

Tollison laughs. "It's not so hot up here, either. They took down a meth lab on the edge of town last week, and we've had a couple of teen suicides this year already." Tollison hesitates, as though there is something he needs to express exactly. "I guess I thought Altoona would be a good place to raise a family, but I never had a family to raise. And I wanted to work on cases that had importance beyond the particular client, but those cases stopped coming through the door. And suddenly it was too late to do anything but what I'd been doing for the last ten years, which was nothing much."

Tollison's tawdry résumé makes Hawthorne angry at the weight of years and the twists of fate. "Are you married?" he asks, hoping to lighten his old friend's load, then remembers he has already heard the answer.

"No. You?"

"Four times," Hawthorne admits, his marital miseries suddenly a symbol of fallibility which he happily bestows on his friend.

He senses Tollison has to suppress dismay. "Kids?"

"One," Hawthorne answers. "A boy. Twenty. We don't get along too well."

"He still at home?"

"I've been paying rent on an apartment for him in Berkeley." He pauses, then decides he has not yet matched his friend's confessional.

"I just found out he abandoned the place three months ago, so I've shelled out twelve hundred bucks for an empty room."

"Too bad."

"Yeah, well, I keep thinking there's something I can do about it, but everything I try seems to make things worse, so I've decided to disengage for a while. I guess that's one thing someone like you doesn't have to worry about, right? Kids and alimony."

Tollison chuckles dryly. "Someone like me, huh? Is this where I'm supposed to tell you I'm not gay?"

Hawthorne closes his eyes. "It never even occurred to me, Keith. And it wouldn't matter anyway. Christ, we're too old to be passing judgments. At our age, morality is whatever gets you through the night."

"I haven't gotten through a night in years."

"Me either."

They laugh in unison. For the first time the silence between them seems a prelude, not a finale. Like all silences it lasts too long, however, and after another moment Tollison rushes to fill it. "Listen. The reason I called was, I was wondering if you have anything going in that SurfAir thing."

In an instant, Hawthorne becomes careful and circumspect, donning the protective reticence of his business. "We've got a few files. Twelve, I think. Why?"

"Two women in Altoona lost people in that crash. One—her name is Brenda Farnsworth—lost her sister. She isn't—"

"A sister isn't much of a client in that kind of thing, given the rules on damages."

"I know. I just thought . . ."

Impulsively, Hawthorne makes a commitment that, among other things, will infuriate Martha when she learns of it. "We can take it on. No problem. What's the other one?"

"The woman is Laura Donahue. Her husband, Jack, was one of the survivors. He's in a coma down at San Jose Memorial. Lots of brain damage."

"What'd he do for a living?"

"Real estate. A bit of a hustler, I guess. Started with residential stuff, but was moving up. His big dream is a resort complex—golf, tennis, swimming—something to lure tourists from the wine country and the coast to this part of the state."

"How far off the ground was it?"

"I don't know yet; Jack's affairs are tough to get a handle on. He and I weren't close, though his wife and I have . . . anyway, I've told her she ought to get rolling on this. She's low on funds, and the insurance people are after her to settle but aren't offering anything serious."

Hawthorne is careful. "That one sounds promising."

"I think so, too."

"I'd want to talk to both of them, of course."

"That's why I'm calling. I thought we could set something up."

"Let's see. I'm in Salt Lake the end of the week. Then Chicago the next. Hmmm. Actually, tomorrow would be best if we're going to get it done right away. Afternoon. Do you think you could get them in here on such short notice?"

"I'd have to check."

"Anytime after three."

"Let's shoot for four. That way Brenda doesn't have to miss school."

"She a teacher or a student?" Hawthorne asks.

"Teacher. Altoona High."

"Teachers are good; juries like teachers. Okay. Why don't you see if they can make it, then call me back. Might make it easier if you come along too, if you can. We can finalize the referral arrangement."

"I don't want anything out of this, Alec. They're friends of mine; I'm just seeing they get the best advice available. I just think it would help if they were *doing* something about what's happened."

"I understand. But you're entitled to a referral fee, Keith. We usually go up to thirty percent of our award, after expenses. No use being a martyr about it."

Tollison's response contains the moralistic timbre that Hawthorne remembers as his only flaw. "That isn't necessary, Alec. Thanks anyway."

"Well, it'll be here if you want it. Provided we take the case."

Tollison plunges on as if he hasn't heard. "I should tell you that Brenda—the one with the sister—doesn't want to sue at all, and the other—Laura—she wants *me* to handle it. I've told her I'm not competent in something this complex, but she's insisting. So be ready to persuade them they're in better hands with you than me."

"It sounds like they're pretty close to you."

"They are, I guess. You know small towns—everyone's a friend or an enemy."

"That's all the more reason for you not to be of record in their cases." His unseemly comment is made before Hawthorne becomes aware of its origin, which is the lucrative damage claim of one Jack Donahue.

"Right. That's what I've told them both: I shouldn't be involved."

Hawthorne hurries to amend his avarice. "Not that it's an ethical problem, of course."

"I know. I just don't want the ... responsibility. Not that I could handle it anyway. Hell, I'm lucky to manage a will contest without help."

Hawthorne wonders if his friend can possibly be as professionally inadequate as he implies. Certainly his intellect could have carried him where he wanted to go, and his ambitions had seemed far larger than Altoona. Hawthorne wonders what happened—a booze problem, a woman, a scandal of some kind—or whether Tollison had been felled by something as insidious as his hometown.

"Okay, Keith," Hawthorne says. "See you tomorrow unless I hear otherwise."

"I appreciate it, Alec."

"My pleasure."

"And I just want to say that I think it's great what you've done with your life. You lived up to your potential, as my father used to say. Not many of us did."

"Thanks, Keith," Hawthorne says with feigned humility. "I'm sure you make a difference, too." The sentence sounds as silly as he feels. Then, because his friend seems so deflated, Hawthorne extends the focus. "Hey. Whatever happened to—"

"I'm sorry, Alec," Tollison interrupts.

"For what?"

"For whatever it is I've been doing. I'm not ashamed of my life— I'm pretty much the man I wanted to be, if not the lawyer. All in all I'm more disappointed in the world than in myself." He pauses. "It's good to talk to you, that's all. I'll leave it at that—so who were you going to ask about?"

"That guy—what was his name—Moose? The big guy who wore torn T-shirts and lifted weights at noon?"

"He went to Washington with HEW. Then to South America with AID. Buenos Aires. He's still there. Changed his priorities a bit—they say he's made millions in real estate."

"That suggests a disturbing dichotomy between brains and money. How about Roger Granbrook?"

"Got mixed up in a securities thing and was disbarred. Seems the registration statement he drew up was about as truthful as a Reagan press conference. Stayed out of jail, though. Sells burial insurance. Lives over in Turlock."

Hawthorne laughs. "He might be better off in jail."

As suddenly as he has laughed, Hawthorne is depressed. It's as if the fates of all of them have been a random chance, unearned and undeserved, part of a game that has as its object the destruction of faith and reason.

A second gap develops—even the past is not a sanguine subject for their reunion. Casting about for one that is, Hawthorne blurts, "I had a heart attack three months ago."

"You're kidding."

"Nope."

"Are you okay?"

"They say so. I don't know if they're right or not. What I do know is I can't seem to get my mind off it. I sit here for minutes at a time doing nothing but pressing my fingers to my carotid artery, touching my heartbeat. Of course the longer I monitor it, the more irregular it seems to be. They say that kind of thing is normal and I'll get over it in time, but that doesn't help a whole lot when I'm lying there at three A.M. counting the number of times a minute my heart decides to thump. I'm thinking about retiring," he concludes, as though it is inevitable.

"Really?"

In hock to his final phrase, Hawthorne is uncertain how to respond. "It's funny. That's the first time I've ever said that word and meant it."

"I know what you mean; I've thought about it, too. But what I always wonder is, what the hell would I do after breakfast on Wednesday mornings?"

Hawthorne laughs. "That's the problem, isn't it? Lawyers learn all about how other people live their lives, but we never seem to learn how to live much of a life ourselves."

Tollison is describing how a client fills his time by building miniature mansions out of toothpicks when Martha sticks her head in the door and points at her watch. Hawthorne waits for an opening. "I've got to go, Keith. Nice talking to you. Look forward to seeing you tomorrow."

"Same here."

The instant Hawthorne hangs up, Martha enters the office. She sits down on the couch at the far end of the room, crosses her legs, unfolds her notebook, and prepares to read off his schedule for the rest of the day.

As she opens her mouth, he holds up a hand. "Do you think you could run this place on your own?" he asks casually.

"What do you mean?"

"I mean if I cut my schedule back, do you think you could handle things in my place?"

She fixes him with a glare that says he'd better not be kidding. "I'd say it's up to you."

"You sound like you've thought about it."

"I have."

"Since when?"

"Since your heart took a coffee break."

Her candor is not surprising, but her initial equivocation is contrary to her essential self-assurance. "Why aren't you certain you could take over the practice?"

When Martha decides he really wants to know, she speaks in strident tones. "I didn't say I couldn't, I said I'd need your help. I could handle the legal part; most of it's just shit work and I've been doing that for years. The problem would be the referrals. No one would believe I was in charge unless you made it clear that I was the one they had to deal with."

"Because you're a woman?"

She shrugs. "And because I don't have a track record in big cases. And because people know we sleep together and they think that's the only reason you keep me on. And because unless you were dead, people would assume sooner or later you'd be coming back, so they would never regard me as a permanent replacement." Martha stops and frowns. "Why are we talking about this, anyway? You know lawyers never retire. They go on the bench or they litigate till they drop, and you can't afford to go on the bench."

He inhales and closes his eyes. "I don't know what I'm going to do. It may depend on SurfAir. I'm thinking there's a chance to do something there that's never been done in a crash case before. It will take some luck and some blunders on the part of Hawley Chambers, but if I can pull it off, SurfAir could be something they would remember me for."

Martha is perplexed. "What's this master stroke amount to?"

He shakes his head. "I need to think about it some more. I want to make sure it will work, as sure as you can be in a jury case. If I think it'll fly, we'll talk about it."

Martha hesitates, then shrugs. "Whatever."

As Hawthorne watches, her eyes drift toward the window and her lips spread into an introspective smile, which he reads as a red ripe stripe of satisfaction that her most fervent prayer is one step closer to being answered.

T he ride had seemed interminable. Relieved that it was over, marveling that it had occurred at all, Keith Tollison guided the women through the door, then followed after them himself. Once inside, the three of them stood transfixed. Finally, Brenda spoke: "My God," she muttered sotto voce. "This place must have cost a fortune."

In keeping with the impression radiated by her surroundings, the receptionist seemed posed for Avedon and *Vogue:* her hair a spiral mop that seemed wet enough to drip, her neckline exposing her sternum and suggesting mannish breasts. But when Tollison and his charges approached her desk, she reacted with a cordial smile.

"I'm Keith Tollison," he began, his words laboring to escape his throat as her enamel lips pursed to a thoughtful circle. "I have an appointment with Mr. Hawthorne."

Her glance fell to the leather diary in front of her. "You're a bit early, I'm afraid; Mr. Hawthorne is still at lunch." The blue-black eyes forgave him. "But he should be back momentarily. Perhaps you can take a seat."

She gestured across the foyer. In response, Brenda and Laura eyed each other cautiously, then took seats at opposite ends of the Italian-leather couch, beneath a dangling sculpture that seemed made of rusting steel. Tollison took the chair at their flank. Exhausted from persuading Brenda and Laura to occupy the same room at the same time, he closed his eyes and waited as patiently as a pet.

A stream of people passed them by and was swallowed by the office. Well-dressed and self-absorbed, they were the junior lawyers, Tollison assumed, the court to Alec's golden throne, so many princes and princesses that the question of succession would surely spark a civil war.

Fifteen minutes passed. Brenda smoked, Laura gazed at the aggressive artwork, Tollison glanced furtively at everything but either of them, trying to imagine how the years would have treated his friend. By the time he heard his name, he was hoping Hawthorne looked like Porky Pig.

He turned to see a woman—tall, thin, stainlessly attractive—inspecting them with high-bred disapproval. Tollison acknowledged his name.

"Mr. Hawthorne can see you now," the woman said without inflection.

"Are these? . . ." She glanced quickly at a note. "Ms. Farnsworth and Mrs. Donahue?"

"Yes."

"Good. Alec would like to see the three of you together, then meet with the women individually."

Tollison glanced toward the couch and received a pair of nods. "Sure."

"Fine. Follow me, please."

Younger up close than she dressed or looked from a distance, the woman pushed through the swinging door at the rear of the reception area and led them down a hall that bypassed secretaries pounding word processors and file clerks tending rolling racks of folders. The doors off the hallway revealed persons buried in paper or talking on phones, jackets off, legs on desks, shirtsleeves rolled to broadcloth doughnuts. When they glanced up, each looked eager to be intruded upon and disappointed when the phalanx passed by. Moments later, their guide preceded them into an anteroom at the end of the hall, tossed her notebook onto a table, and turned to face them.

Documents gathered around her desk as though they were mutually magnetic, a computer blinked forth a jaundiced menu, a coffee machine gave off the odor of short circuits. Barring the door behind her as though it led to the spread-sheets from her subconscious, the woman said, "My name is Martha. Would you like a refreshment?"

They shook their heads, as the invitation unquestionably demanded.

"Then I'll introduce you to Alec. I'll be sitting in, but don't mind me, I'm just taking notes. Also, a tape machine will record the conversation. If you have objections you may discuss them with Alec, but he is adamant on the point, given some unfortunate experiences with clients who subsequently managed to forget the rules of the game or deny that they ever knew them. Are we ready?"

They nodded.

Martha pushed open the door. "Alec, I have Mr. Tollison, Ms. Farnsworth, and Mrs. Donahue. This is Alec Hawthorne."

Martha stepped aside. The women entered the office as hesitantly as they would an alley. Tollison followed as quickly as he could.

After the glories of the lobby, the initial impression was disappointing. The motif was aeronautical—propeller, landing gear, yoke, landing light—which Tollison took to be souvenirs of Hawthorne's courtroom triumphs. The remaining accumulation appeared haphazard, none of the furnishings an exact fit with the rest, none so out of place as to be tasteless. The resonance was not of elegance but of rumpled comfort and memories randomly preserved, and Tollison was strangely cheered—the room suggested that Alec was not as removed from the old days as he had feared.

Tollison caught himself staring at a plastic DC-10 and remembering that Hawthorne had built model planes even back in law school, hanging them on strings from the ceiling of his room, creating an air force that had to be grounded whenever Alec threw a party, which was every Friday night. He glanced to his right just in time to see Hawthorne striding toward him, jacket off, tie askew.

"Ladies. Pleased to meet you." Hawthorne stuck out his hand. "Keith. Nice to see you after all these years. You look great."

"So do you."

Hawthorne pumped his hand and slapped him on the back. "Thanks. Sit down. Please."

He gestured toward the grouping of furniture at the end of the room. As the women took the couch and he and Hawthorne the facing wing chairs, Tollison noticed that Martha was already sitting at a small rolltop snuggled against the wall to the right of Hawthorne's massive desk.

"Well." Hawthorne got comfortable in his seat. He wore charcoal pants, white silk shirt, paisley tie, tasseled loafers, and reading glasses that had drooped to the point of his nose over the course of the initial pleasantries. When he sensed the slippage, Hawthorne removed the glasses and let them dangle from a thong around his neck. When he crossed his legs, he displayed a sockless foot.

"I can't get over seeing you after all these years, Keith," he began.

"Me either."

"I had it in my mind you were somewhere back East. But you've been up there in . . ."

"Altoona."

"Right. Altoona, all the while. Well, we're going to have to make up for lost time."

"Right."

Hawthorne glanced to his left. "But not at the moment. Memories are fascinating only to their participants, so we'll take care of that another time."

Tollison nodded, a trifle annoyed at the easy chivalry.

As Hawthorne recrossed his legs, Tollison glanced at Martha. She seemed focused elsewhere, staring out the corner window at the easy undulation of the bay, massaging the back of her neck, looking so thoughtful and at ease Tollison wondered if she and her boss were lovers.

"Well," Hawthorne began. "I'm assuming you're here to consult me professionally. Provisionally, at least. I say this to establish the existence of the attorney-client privilege. After a few introductory remarks, I'll meet with each of you separately, ask some questions I have, and attempt to answer any you have yourselves, then let you meet with Mr. Tollison and discuss how you wish to proceed—whether you wish to engage me to represent you in the SurfAir matter. Satisfactory?"

They exchanged glances, then nodded.

"Very well. First, let me tell you generally what I do, how I do it, and what you can expect if you decide to hire me to file suit on your behalf." Hawthorne leaned back in his chair and clasped his hands behind his neck. "What we are about in this office is torts. Blackstone defines a tort as a violation of duty imposed by law or otherwise upon all persons occupying the relation to each other that is involved in a given transaction. A bit circular to my mind, but then that's lawyers for you."

The women gave him the smile he sought.

"Because torts is a subject of much debate of late, and because if you decide to file suit against SurfAir you may be in for a struggle of several years' duration, it would help you to know how the system works. I'm sure questions will arise as I proceed with my little lecture. To the extent they bear upon your personal circumstances, I hope you'll save them till we meet privately. Disclosures in the presence of persons not your lawyer is arguably a waiver of the attorney-client privilege. Okay so far?"

Three heads nodded, but only after reflection.

"Torts," Hawthorne repeated. "Someone or something screws up, and someone else is hurt and sues the tortfeasor for damages. The problem is, since no one can agree on the philosophical basis for the concept, there's moaning and groaning on all sides.

"Some people say the primary purpose of tort law, other than spreading the risk of loss, is to promote desirable behavior, under the theory that if you collect money from someone because he's injured you, he'll make damn sure to put a stop to the conduct that made him pay. But if that's the purpose, why do we allow folks to insure themselves so it's not them but their carrier that has to pay the judgment? And how can we expect behaviorism to work when for most businesses liability costs are only a tiny fraction of sales? The answer may be that it can't. On the other hand, Pinto gas tanks don't blow up anymore and Firestone tires don't shred and DC-10 doors don't fall off, and all those problems have been the subject of extensive litigation. So to some degree, business behavior *is* affected by what happens in the courtroom."

His students nodded; Hawthorne smiled approvingly.

"There are other problems with behaviorism. In California it's cheaper to kill someone than disable him, because if you're dead your heirs can't recover for the pain and suffering you endured prior to the time you died, and because defendants can't be made to pay punitive damages for wrongfully killing someone, only for wrongfully injuring them. And it's cheaper to kill a child than an adult, because our system is based on monetary loss and the heirs of an adult suffer more significant losses than do the heirs of a child, at least if the adult is a wage earner. So in a sense, the law encourages people to be totally abandoned rather than merely imprudent.

"There are also significant down-side consequences to using lawsuits as a tool of social control—doctors stop entering risky specialties and start practicing defensive medicine, which runs up costs; because they fear punishment, people conceal mistakes rather than report them; improvements aren't made because businesses fear remedial steps will be seen as admissions of fault; tortfeasors fight to the bitter end rather than paying fair settlements; victims exaggerate losses. *Everyone* has gripes with the behavior theory. Even me." Hawthorne grinned. "Am I boring you to death?"

Like a trio of seals, they shook their heads in tandem.

"The other idea," Hawthorne went on, "is that tort law exists to compensate victims of a wrong—to make them whole. The problem with that is the system is riddled with arbitrary considerations—recovery depends on your attractiveness as a plaintiff, the part of the country you live in, the kind of injury you suffer, the quality of the lawyer you have, all kinds of variables. In many ways the whole thing's a crap shoot. Also, of course, it's essentially a fiction. A person who loses a loved one or is badly injured is *never* fully compensated for that loss by a sum of money.

"So the compensation concept is a charade—money damages aren't compensatory, they're a solace for suffering, and because juries don't like big numbers, the system overpays the small claimant and underpays the person who has suffered greatly and is in real need of help. But charade or no, so far there's nothing better. All of which is to say the law in large part stinks, and mostly it's stacked against plaintiffs—

people like you. But in some ways it's stacked against the defendants, much as I hate to say it."

"How?" Brenda asked, enthralled.

Hawthorne looked at Laura. "Assume your husband is totally disabled. Also assume he had the foresight to take out a disability insurance policy beforehand and that the policy pays him fifty percent of the amount he was earning at the time of the accident. That's called a collateral source. You might argue, and the insurance companies certainly do, that such a source of funds should mean that if their insured is found liable for the injury, they should have to pay only the other fifty percent, so your husband receives one hundred percent of his former income but no more. Sounds fair, doesn't it?"

Laura hesitated. "Yes."

"Well, the defendants have to pay it all, no matter *how* much your husband is receiving from other sources. So we don't follow pure compensation theory, either, since some victims get *more* than their economic loss. Which means there's some punishment and revenge mixed in there, too.

"What it comes down to is perspective. Defendants say, Look at what the plaintiffs should collect; plaintiffs say, Look at what the defendants should have to pay. The victim hasn't done anything wrong, after all. One way or another there's a windfall, so why shouldn't it go to the party that's completely innocent?"

"But ..." Laura's brow folded in concentration.

"It seems wrong, I agree. But the so-called reforms are even worse. Eliminating awards for pain and suffering except in the case of permanent disability is licensed cruelty. Requiring proof beyond a reasonable doubt to establish punitive damages will encourage corporate recklessness. The idea that the airlines will offer flight insurance to passengers, with recovery after a crash limited to those policies, well, you can see how ridiculous some of the suggestions can—"

"So there are all these problems," Brenda interrupted, her face flushed with irritation. "How much is it going to cost us to hire you to solve them?"

"Good question." Hawthorne smiled easily. "Probably the most frequently lamented aspect of the tort system is its costs. A study of the asbestos litigation showed that an award of two hundred million to asbestosis victims cost seven hundred million in litigation expenses. And when people think of expense, all they think of is the fees charged by the plaintiffs' attorneys." Hawthorne's smile stayed straight. "That is to say, by people like me. This is despite the fact that of that seven hundred million spent in litigating the asbestos cases, more than six hundred million was *defense* costs; was, in other words, the expense incurred by the asbestos manufacturers to avoid paying compensation to the victims of a disease to which they *knowingly and deliberately* exposed thousands of innocent workers over a period of forty years."

For the first time, Hawthorne's grin contained malevolence. "But you don't read about that, do you? You only read about gunslingers like me, how much money we make, how we feed on injured people, taking money that should rightfully be theirs and putting it in our silk-lined pockets. Well, let me tell you another thing about those asbestos cases. When they were settled before trial, the average amount paid to the asbestosis sufferer was sixty thousand dollars. When they were settled during trial but before judgment, the average amount was ninety thousand dollars. And when they went to a jury verdict—when guys like me did what we were hired to do and an impartial jury was given a chance to decide what was fair and right—the average amount awarded the sick or deceased worker was almost *four hundred thousand dollars*. I don't know what that says to you, but what it says to me is that we gunslingers earn our money."

Hawthorne waited for a response, but got none but startled silence. "You're wondering what I charge in a case like this," he continued. "The first thing to say is that my fee is structured the way it is because even if I win the case for you—even if every claim we make is proved to be true and correct—the jury can't give you one thin dime for attorney's fees. Now if it was your *business* that was injured, under the antitrust laws you could get attorney's fees in addition to three times the actual damages you suffered. And if your civil rights were violated, in some cases you could get attorney's fees as well. But if you or your loved one are killed or maimed, the court can't award you one penny to pay your lawyer with. So I have to be paid out of what I recover for you in damages. Understand?"

Brenda nodded. "That's crazy."

"Yep," Hawthorne agreed. "But that's the system. It's also why the windfall I mentioned earlier isn't really that—the so-called collateral source is really an attorney's fee, not a gift to the victim.

"But back to the point. With a major accident with multiple victims, I charge a contingent fee of twenty percent of any recovery received from inception to trial, twenty-five percent if it goes to trial, and thirty percent if it's appealed, expenses off the top. A contingent fee means, of course, that if you don't win you don't pay.

"Now, I can hear you say, 'But Mr. Hawthorne, you have twelve clients in the case. If each of them gets a million-dollar judgment, you're going to get a three-million-dollar fee.' And what I'm going to say is, that's absolutely right. And I will damn well deserve it. You know why? Because in the last major case I tried, the final judgment was *one hundred and fifty times* the offer my client received from the insurance company the day after the crash, before I got in the picture."

"Wow." Brenda's eyes were the size of baseballs.

"Not many of my cases go to trial anymore," Hawthorne added. "The insurance companies tend to be willing to pay my clients what they deserve without the expense and embarrassment of litigation. But they don't do it until they know I've gotten the goods to nail them. They won't give a fair amount to you, acting on your own, and with all due respect, they most likely won't give a fair amount to Mr. Tollison here either, intelligent and capable though I know him to be, because he's not experienced in this type of law. The insurance companies reach fair settlements with me because I've been trying cases against them for twenty-five years. I know what the airlines do well and I know how they screw up and I know how their lawyers try to hide it when they do. So they tend not to fuck with me anymore, excuse my French, because they know if they do, I'll nail them to the wall."

Hawthorne folded his arms and closed his eyes. "One final thing. If you sign on with me, you're going to end up telling the defendants, by which I mean primarily the insurance lawyers, everything about your life they want to know. That's the way I work—my clients tell the whole truth and nothing but the truth so I can tell the judge that since my clients came clean, the defendants should have to do the same. Most of the time the airlines have a lot more to hide than my clients do, but if you've got any skeletons in your closet, I can't promise they won't come out. I can't promise you'll get a million-dollar judgment, either. I can only promise to do what I've done for everyone I've ever represented—fight as hard as I can, do whatever it takes within the boundaries of the law to get the best possible award for you, given the circumstances."

Hawthorne paused. A quick streak of pain seemed to cross his face. For the first time since entering his office, Tollison remembered his heart attack.

"Any questions before I see you individually?" Hawthorne concluded softly.

One woman shook her head; the other met his eye. "Why did the plane crash?" Brenda asked heavily.

Hawthorne opened his eyes and nodded. "Usually, by this time I'd have an answer, but in SurfAir I don't. It may have to do with the design. The Hastings is a new airplane. Some veteran private pilots won't fly in a commercial airliner until it's been operational for at least two years—they figure it takes that long to get the bugs out."

"Nobody tells the *public* that, do they?" Brenda was irate. "Nobody warns *us* not to get in the damn things."

Hawthorne became paternal. "Building an aircraft involves some two thousand subcontractors, three thousand engineers, and over a decade of planning, construction, and testing. After it's built, the FAA has the responsibility of certifying the new plane as airworthy. But because the FAA has a limited budget—and given its responsibilities, the budget is more limited every year—it doesn't have enough inspectors to certify new planes, let alone inspect the ones already in the air, so the way they certify airworthiness is to have the manufacturers inspect their planes themselves. That sounds like a gigantic conflict of interest, and that's exactly what it is. But that's the system we're stuck with."

Brenda cursed. "Why don't people *know* all this? Why doesn't someone do something *about* it?"

Hawthorne shrugged. "Pressure from airlines and manufacturers and private pilots to keep down expenses, pressure from cities that can't afford to improve their airports, pressure from citizens who buy the nonsense that the government doesn't do anything worthwhile with their tax money." Hawthorne looked at Brenda. "One recent development might interest you."

"What?"

"An Aviation Trust Fund was established back in 1970, to promote aviation safety. It's financed by a tax on plane tickets. Right now that fund has a surplus of close to six *billion* dollars—billions that could be spent on safety but aren't."

"Why the hell not?"

"The Reagan administration is keeping the money to offset the budget deficit."

"You have to be kidding."

Hawthorne only grinned.

Brenda seemed close to ignition. "You mean my sister might have died because some politicians are trying to cover their asses?"

"Maybe."

"You know what the bastards did?" Brenda continued angrily.

"What?"

"They buried Carol without her head."

Hawthorne accepted the non sequitur with equanimity. "It's too bad, but if you've ever seen the wreckage of a commercial airliner, you know how—"

"People have been asking questions about me," Laura interrupted suddenly, as though to perpetuate the tide of outrage. "About me and my husband. All over town. About our marriage, about Jack's business, everything. Who's *doing* it, anyway?"

All eyes flew toward Hawthorne. "It's an investigator hired by Hawley Chambers, the attorney for Federal Airline Underwriters."

"But why?"

"To find evidence to use against you if the case gets to court. To smear you and your husband in any way they can."

"But the airline people were so *nice*."

"The airlines usually *are* nice. And genuinely concerned. Then they turn over the defense of the crash litigation to their insurance carrier. The carrier wants to poison the well—if the victim is a single man, they'll try to show he's gay; if it's a single woman, they'll try to show she's a lesbian or a whore; if it's a married person, they'll try to show the marriage was on the rocks and both spouses were practicing adulterers. All this to convince you to give up the fight or keep a jury from awarding a fair amount in damages."

Tollison locked his eyes in place and prayed that Laura would as well.

"They better not try to show *Carol* was a whore," Brenda spat.

Hawthorne looked at each of them. "What I said about your own lives is true of the victims', too. If they have skeletons in their closets, you can be sure the investigator will dig them out."

"But can't you *do* something?" Laura asked. "It's bad enough that Jack's . . . the way he is. Now they get to smear his name?"

"They take a life, then try to show it wasn't worth living. Is that it?" Brenda's tone was vicious and put her in league with Laura.

"The only thing I can do is try to keep the dirt from being admitted in evidence if the case goes to trial," Hawthorne explained. "Sometimes I can, and sometimes I can't. The law's not clear enough to force the judges to keep it out under all circumstances."

"But—"

Hawthorne held up his hand. "Let's worry about that when the time comes. Of course if they start harassing you, hanging around your house, tapping your phone, searching the place, telling your employer there's some deep dark secret in your past, then I can get a restraining order."

"Bastards," Brenda muttered.

Hawthorne leaned back and looked at the ceiling. "As I said, commercial aviation has problems. As we go along, you're going to learn even more about them. But it's not all bad. Air travel is by far the safest form of transportation. True, in this case the system broke down—the Hastings may not have been fit to fly, the controllers may have screwed up, the pilot may have ignored his radar or violated emergency procedures—and it may take years of litigation to find out what the problem was unless the NTSB comes up with something more than they have already. What I'm telling you is, at this point we don't *know* what the hell happened up there."

Hawthorne paused, then looked at them with the rosy aplomb of an evangelist. "What I'm also telling you is, if things go the way I hope they do, it won't *matter* why flight 617 went down. It won't matter at all."

UNITED STATES DISTRICT COURT
NORTHERN DISTRICT OF ILLINOIS

IN RE SURFAIR DISASTER OF)   MDL DOCKET NO. 498
MARCH 23, 1987   )   ALL CASES

APPLICATION FOR APPOINTMENT OF ALEC HAWTHORNE, ESQ., AS CHAIR OR CO-CHAIR OF THE PLAINTIFFS' COMMITTEE

Alec Hawthorne, Esq., respectfully requests appointment as Chairman of the Plaintiffs' Committee charged with conducting pretrial procedures in the SurfAir litigation.

1. I am the senior partner in the Law Offices of Alec Hawthorne, attorneys for the families of twelve passengers killed in this catastrophe. I commit myself to personally and diligently perform the responsibilities assigned by this Court.
2. I have been an active attorney for twenty-three years, specializing in aviation litigation for most of that time.
3. I have served as lead counsel, liaison counsel, or a member of plaintiffs' committees in the following crash cases:
   - In re Air Crash Disaster at Florida Everglades, 360 F.Supp. 1394 (1973);
   - In re Turkish Airlines DC-10 Air Disaster, Paris, France, 376 F.Supp. 887 (1974);
   - In re Pago Pago Air Disaster, 394 F.Supp. 799 (1975);
   - In re Air Crash Disaster at Tenerife, Canary Islands, 435 F.Supp. 927 (1977);
   - In re Chicago DC-10 Air Crash Disaster, 476 F.Supp. 445 (1979);
   - In re Disaster at Riyadh, Saudi Arabia, 540 F.Supp. 1141 (1981);
   - In re Air Florida B-737 Air Crash Disaster at Washington, D.C., 533 F.Supp. 1350 (1982);
   - In re Air Crash Disaster Near New Orleans, 548 F.Supp. 1268 (1982).
4. I have been retained as counsel, both in this country and abroad, in over one hundred cases arising from air-crash disasters that were not the subject of Multi-District Litigation jurisdiction.
5. I have held leadership positions in and have participated in the

work of numerous bar associations. The positions I have held include:

— president, San Francisco Trial Lawyers Association;
— chairman, Aviation Law Section and Member of the Board of Governors, Association of Trial Lawyers of America;
— chairman, Aviation Law Committee and Member of the Board of Directors, California Trial Lawyers Association;
— member of California Bar Association Society of Medical Jurisprudence and American Bar Association Litigation Section and Insurance, Negligence and Compensation Section;

6. I am co-author of a treatise, Air Law and Litigation Tactics, used in many law schools and continuing legal education programs around the country. I am also Adjunct Professor of Trial Advocacy at the Hastings College of Law.

7. I am a member in good standing of the Bars of the United States Supreme Court and of the states of California and Nevada; the United States Courts of Appeal for the Second, Fifth, Eighth, Ninth, and District of Columbia Circuits; and the United States District Courts of the Northern, Central, and Southern Districts of California, the Southern District of New York, and the District of Columbia District. I have been specially admitted to practice in particular aviation actions in many other District Courts, including those in Alaska, Arizona, Hawaii, Massachusetts, Nevada, and Florida.

WHEREFORE, I respectfully request appointment by this Court as Chair or Co-Chair of the Plaintiffs' Committee in the SurfAir Crash litigation.

DATED: October 9, 1987

Alec Hawthorne, Esq.
Petitioner

EIGHT

Although proceedings have yet to begin, the courtroom swells with swagger. Battles for supremacy rage in every corner of the only room in the building large enough to accommodate both the lawyers and their egos, which is the ceremonial chamber where judges are sworn to uphold the laws of the land and newly naturalized citizens are welcomed to the fold.

The attorneys arrange themselves by avocation—to the left, food and wine aficionados rhapsodize over gastronomic glories. To the right, fitness fanatics relive the delicious agony of marathons and triathlons. Near the bar of the court the airplane nuts, lawyers who not only try aviation cases but are also private pilots, compare prices on the latest advances in avionics. The rest of the troupe passes time by bringing everyone within earshot up to speed on their legal prowess: experts suborned, witnesses impeached, judges bamboozled, juries charmed, verdicts filched. That they are roundly disbelieved by their audience is not a hindrance.

Only a few of the lawyers are under forty, and those are the house counsel for the insurance companies—since today's agenda concerns only the victims, most of the defendants have sent the second team, underlings earning half the rate of their peers in private firms. A few heavy hitters are present nonetheless, because experience has taught that no judge, not even a federal one, can be trusted to stick to a supposedly harmless script.

Although convocations like this one are social as well as professional occasions, Alec Hawthorne has spent the previous evening alone in his room, atop the best hotel in Chicago. An out-of-the-way place of

European ambience, he stays there because it has a view of the lake, because its windows open to admit unconditioned air, and because of the wine list in the adjacent restaurant.

Although the hotel was its usual well-run self, Hawthorne is not. Because it is November and Chicago, after a night of fitful sleep he has ventured outdoors only from the revolving door to the rear of a waiting cab, but the crafty wind has found him nonetheless. Under his cashmere topcoat his muscles are clenched in rigor mortis and his teeth would chatter if he emancipated them by unlocking his jaw.

Lonely as well as chilled, what he lacks is Martha. Usually, she is with him—because he likes her company, because she takes care of the nagging snags of travel, because his colleagues envy her competence and sensuality, speculation about which provides him with yet another edge. Although Martha is never eager to encounter the men with whom he plies his trade—whom she calls maggots when she does not call them worse—she comes if he asks. But this time her presence was not an option: The hearing is a step toward the fulfillment of his plan, and the tactic he is about to employ would cause Martha to commit mayhem.

Hawthorne feels a hand on his shoulder. When he turns he sees Ed Haroldson, ally, idol, friend, the dean of aviation litigators. Haroldson, legend has it, was the first attorney in the nation to turn down a million-dollar settlement offer to take a case to trial. The jury gave him two point six and, in the envious corridors of his profession, Ed Haroldson became a god.

In his seventies, small and stout, bald and battered as a cobblestone, Haroldson moves in mind and body like a colt, unpredictable and spry. "How are you, Alec? You look as cold as a goat on skis."

Hawthorne makes room for Haroldson on the dark oak pew. "I'm okay, Ed. You?"

The old man's eyes are warmer than the room. "One thing about being as old as I am, by the time my toes find out how cold it is, I'll be back in Palm Beach."

Hawthorne laughs at the familiar shuffle. Haroldson winters in Florida and spends the rest of his time in midtown Manhattan in a brownstone that is the envy of even his most successful peers. His less visible fibers had sprouted during the years spent helping his parents raise enough Tennessee okra to keep the mortgage bankers on the far side of the river.

Hawthorne pats his diminutive colleague on the back. "Congratulations on the result in Chicago. What did they give you, twelve?"

Haroldson laughs the quick titter of a child. Of the twoscore people in the room, he is the only one who finds personal promotion unseemly. "Twelve-five, I believe it was. I got lucky."

"You've been lucky for fifty years, you old bastard. What do you hear about the Detroit crash?"

"That was a mean one, wasn't it? Folks are going to have the TV shots of that freeway in their minds for a long time. Hope that little girl pulls through."

"They know anything about cause?"

"They were talking wind shear for a while, but I hear now they think the flaps might not have gotten set."

"Hard to believe the crew could fuck *that* up. That's about as basic as it gets."

Haroldson nods. "There's a scary paradox in the business these days, Alec. On the one hand, what with these mergers and all, you got guys flying planes they barely know how to steer, let alone handle in an emergency. On the other, for an experienced pilot, flying has become routine—what with computers and all, these new babies are as exciting as flying a refrigerator. So there you are, thirty thousand feet in the air with a pilot who's green or a pilot who's bored. Either way, they're too damn likely to screw up. Hard to see how to correct the situation, either, except by banning everything newer than the DC-3." Haroldson's voice slides to a whisper. "Speaking of screwups, I hear your pump had to be primed a few months back."

Hawthorne nods, embarrassed by the concern rumpling the old man's face.

"Bad?"

"They pronounced me dead for a while."

"So tell me. What have I got to look forward to?"

Hawthorne smiles. "On the whole, I'd rather have been in Kenya."

The reference is to a series of depositions he and Haroldson had taken back in 1975, pursuing the reason a 747 had somehow missed the Nairobi runway by a quarter mile.

Haroldson's palm falls onto Hawthorne's left knee. "You look pretty spunky for a dead man, Alec. But from now on, leave the dying to those of us who're ahead of you in line. I'd hate to lose you, boy. You're the only man in the room I enjoy breaking bread with. Or trust when my back is turned."

Haroldson fixes him with his fathomless blue eyes and the twinkle that has charmed juries around the world for more than half a century. Hawthorne feels the surge of affection he always experiences when the old man pays him a compliment. "Coming from the best there ever was, that means at lot."

"Well, it's God's own truth."

Haroldson smiles at a memory. Hawthorne guesses his friend has used the identical phrase before a thousand juries and has persuaded each of them that he and the Lord are on a first-name basis.

"Hear you boys in California are about to solve this here liability crisis we've got ourselves mixed up in," Haroldson continues.

Hawthorne shrugs. "We're giving it a go. Got to keep folks from shooting themselves in the foot by passing another initiative measure."

"Well, I hope you get it done. I swear, these days people would vote to sleep in a swamp if someone promised it would reduce their tax bill."

"We put a deal together in Sacramento last month, but I don't know if it's going to be enough to keep the insurance boys happy. They still want a cap on contingent percentages that will make sure personal injury lawyers earn slightly less than poets."

As Haroldson nods morosely, a gale of laughter rises in the front of the room, from the vicinity of Vic Scallini. Haroldson leans toward Hawthorne so he can be heard above the din. "I expect you'll be made top dog in this thing, Alec. If so, I'll support you any way you want, including keeping my mouth shut. Not much competition out your way except Scallini, and I wouldn't back Scallini for boxing commission. Even in New Jersey."

Hawthorne enjoys the old man's gibe. "You're going to try to get us sent to Florida though, aren't you?"

"Sure. And if I win, I'll put in for co-chair and ask for you to be my running mate. But I expect them to send the whole kit and kaboodle to San Francisco, and if so, I'll let you have the top slot with my blessing. I'm too old to run from coast to coast every other week, plus you know how I feel about Californians."

"Scallini will make a strong pitch for lead counsel," Hawthorne says. "Think he has a shot?"

"Maybe. This panel doesn't know Vic the way we do. He puts together a good application, since he's not encumbered by compunctions against prevarication. As usual, his best chance is that they'll give it to him just to shut him up."

"That could turn SurfAir into a marathon."

"Surely could, especially since the NTSB is still stuck for a proximate cause. That could leave it up to Vic to find one, and Vic couldn't find liability in a crash case with the help of my best bird dog." Haroldson laughs. "Look at him. If his chest expands any further, they'll put him on a platter and serve him at Thanksgiving. Took the East Coast boys to dinner last night, you know, trying to buy some votes."

"I heard."

"All except me, that is. I can't forgive him for the fuckup in St. Louis. He should never have let the airline keep those test documents from the press. Cost us the best chance we've ever had to make crashworthiness a requirement for newly certified aircraft."

"Vic's never been strong on public policy."

Haroldson nods. "Vic's only strong on Vic."

As Haroldson makes a move to leave, Hawthorne puts a hand on his arm to stop him. "You've been around a long time, Ed. Don't you ever think of throwing in the towel?"

Haroldson laughs his customary squeak. "Trying to get me out of your hair so you can take over the whole country instead of just the silly side of the Mississippi?"

"It's just that lately I've been wondering what I'll be doing twenty years from now, and I'm not sure I want it to be this."

"Hell, son. If you're breathing without help and not wearing a diaper you'll be ahead of the game, believe me. But I know what you mean. I swam that ditch after my first wife died. What I finally decided was that I couldn't think of anything I'd rather do in life than go to court to help folks who've been busted up in a plane crash."

"But it's so inefficient."

"So's anything folks do in groups of more than two. It just happens to be the best system anyone's come up with to help right wrongs. When they come up with a better one, then I'll retire."

"You have kids don't you, Ed?"

"I got kids and I got *grand*kids. Come Christmas, it's like a beehive at our place in the Hamptons. I'd throw them out if I didn't love them so damn much. And I love them because they're little bitty scrappers just like me."

"Sounds nice."

"Is nice. But it wouldn't be nice if it happened every day, know what I mean? I go to work because I like to, Alec. And I come home because I like to do that, too. If I did only one or the other, I'm not sure I could say the same." Haroldson paused and looked him in the eye. "You're not thinking of hanging up the briefcase, are you?"

"Naw. Just chatting."

"Well, don't decide one way or another till you get your health back. I know you've had a scare, and the medics are probably telling you it's the job that brought you down. Well, maybe it was and maybe it wasn't. Some guys work their whole life just to retire at sixty-five and a week later they're dead from the decompression." Haroldson leans close. "We're sharks, boy. We feed on this nonsense—not the money so much, but the sport. Some of us couldn't live five minutes if they took it all away."

"I suppose not."

Haroldson's face is worthy of Rushmore. "I do know one thing, son—it'll kill you if it doesn't make you proud, and you can't be proud if you don't give it all you've got. If you can't do that, sell your practice and buy a house down in little old Carmel and watch the waves go back and forth. Ain't nothing we do worth dying over, that's for sure. Though once in a while we do more than we get credit for."

"Sometimes it's hard to keep that in mind."

"We're the best lawyers in the world, Alec. And we work for the folks who need us most. That's what the big boys can't stand, you know, that in our kind of work the poor man has a better lawyer than the corporations. They won't quit till they change that around, Alec; we've got to fight them all the way." Haroldson claps him on the shoulder. "Now I got to go tell some lies to Vic. Hell, the panel might have gone mad and he might end up stud bull in this thing."

Haroldson slides out of the pew. A moment later, a door opens beyond the jury box and the judicial panel files into the courtroom. The three robed arbiters glance with disapproval at what amounts to a pin-striped mob, then take their places atop the elevated bench. The chief judge bangs the gavel and the lawyers reluctantly drift toward seats.

The gavel bangs again. "We are here pursuant to a motion to consolidate the SurfAir litigation for the purpose of pretrial proceedings, to choose the proper forum for those proceedings, and to select a plaintiffs' committee to coordinate all motion and discovery practice in the case."

As the chief judge fumbles with his papers, the lawyers eye each other like quiz contestants five minutes before the show. The selection of the plaintiffs' committee is in the nature of an all-star vote. Because the prize is less money than renown, it is particularly coveted; each pursues the job not for the doing but for being asked. As in most varieties of law practice, the actual labor—the preparation of papers and reviewing of documents and digesting of depositions—will be done by people like Martha, up to the eve of trial.

"We have reviewed the file in the matter," the judge continues, "and are prepared to rule on the consolidation and transfer issue. Are there any additions to the papers previously presented on the point?"

Vic Scallini hops to his feet clutching a snarl of documents. His unbuttoned vest flaps around his watch fob like a blue serge sheet hung to dry on a golden line. Behind him, several heads shake, slowly and sarcastically. Scallini is an exemplar of one of the most dispiriting axioms of modern life—that noise becomes believed.

"Victor Scallini of Los Angeles, Your Honor. Counsel for the families and loved ones of twenty-one crash victims. With all due respect, I would like to urge the court to transfer these cases to the great state of California. Even though, as usual, the majority of the lawyers in this room are from the East Coast, that should not be of significance. Flight 617 was a West Coast plane crashing at a West Coast location while flying the colors of a West Coast airline. The appropriate forum is obvious, for the convenience of both plaintiffs and defendants. Moreover, I—"

The judge's brow furls. "We have read your moving papers, Mr. Scallini. Have you anything new to add?"

"Only that since the papers were filed, my office has been engaged by the mournful heirs of three additional victims, and we will be filing wrongful death claims on their behalf within the week. *California* heirs, I might add, Your Honor. The number of plaintiffs represented by my office now exceeds the number represented by any other counsel in the room. I therefore—"

"Thank you, Mr. Scallini. Your comments are duly noted. Anyone else?"

"Ed Haroldson, Your Honor. Counsel in the Brooks, Hoskitt, and Shadburne cases."

"Yes, Mr. Haroldson?"

"I rise only to point out that the proximate cause of this crash is still in dispute. The NTSB has not yet issued its report, and until it does so, the possibility exists that the engines on the aircraft failed in some respect. Since the engines were manufactured in Florida, I submit that to discount that forum at this stage of the litigation would be premature. Thank you, Your Honor. That's all I have."

"Thank you, Mr. Haroldson. Anyone else?"

When no one moves, Hawthorne gets to his feet, feeling a momentary lightness in his head, a prickle in his hands. "Are you considering only the forum issue, Your Honor?"

"At this point, yes."

"Then I have nothing to add. Sorry to interrupt."

The chief judge glances at his colleagues and receives two nods. "If there is nothing further, the panel is prepared to rule. We hereby order all cases in the SurfAir disaster litigation, heretofore or hereafter filed, consolidated for pretrial proceedings and transferred to the Honorable Hugh V. Powell, Judge of the United States District Court for the Northern District of California."

The audience grumbles, but no one rises to object. It has been a foregone conclusion. Ammunition is saved till later.

"Now then. We are also here to select the lead counsel of the plaintiffs' committee and the membership of the committee itself. The panel has reviewed the petitions and accompanying affidavits and finds itself duly impressed with the qualifications and experience of the applicants. We are also cognizant of the objections filed by at least two counsel of record, claiming that the appointment of a plaintiffs' committee deprives litigants whose counsel are not on the committee of their right to be represented by the attorney of their choice. As it has done many times before, the panel rejects that argument, pointing out the delay and expense, to say nothing of the duplication and consequent burden on the defendants, of allowing these actions to proceed separately. The panel also observes that the consolidation of cases and the actions of the plaintiffs' committee apply only to pretrial proceedings, not to trial of the cause itself. The right to a trial attorney of choice is thus preserved inviolate. At this time—"

Scallini lumbers toward the vertical once again. "Your Honor, may I point out that of the victims in this case, seventy-two percent are from California, and of those seventy-two percent, my office represents thirty-six percent. Therefore, it seems only equitable, particularly in light of the historic favoritism shown to *East* Coast attorneys in these matters, that I be—"

"We have duly noted that point in your petition, Mr. Scallini. Thank you. Now, at this time—"

"One more matter, Your Honor. If you please."

"Yes, Mr. Scallini?"

"Since filing my application, it has been my pleasure to acquire a new partner in my practice. He—"

"How is that relevant, sir?"

"I'm happy to suggest an answer. My new partner is Daniel Griffin, Esquire. Mr. Griffin is known to the men in this room as a skilled and experienced aviation attorney. He was formerly with the law office of Mr. Alec Hawthorne, but some weeks ago Mr. Griffin chose to join me in litigating the SurfAir matter, as well as the many other major cases that I have been engaged to pursue all over the world. Even as we speak, Mr. Griffin is in my offices in Los Angeles preparing a discovery schedule to include all possible sources of admissible evidence, as well as—"

"Thank you, Mr. Scallini. Your point is noted."

"Your Honor?"

"Yes, Mr. Hawthorne?"

Eyes crawl over him like lice. Unprepared for the revelation of Dan Griffin's new allegiance, Hawthorne finds Scallini's coup both painful and embarrassing, but at the moment there is nothing to be done but endure his colleagues' slimy speculations. He clears his throat and speaks from a hidden script.

"Since filing for appointment as lead counsel, I have been informed by my doctors that I should not assume such a stressful undertaking at this time. Therefore, I respectfully withdraw my application."

Amid the murmurs of his colleagues, the chief judge peers over his tortoiseshell glasses. "Does that mean you do not wish to serve on the committee at all, Mr. Hawthorne?"

"It does, Your Honor."

"Well. This changes things. Quite frankly, we had been prepared to appoint you committee chairman, Mr. Hawthorne. Perhaps my colleagues and I can confer for a moment."

The judges engage in whispered colloquy. The other eyes in the room turn back toward Hawthorne. Ed Haroldson frowns in puzzlement; Vic Scallini beams victoriously. The others could normally be expected to look on with glee, but in this case the villain is the heart, and not one man in the room has failed to fear that his will one day bring him down.

The chief judge bangs his gavel. "We have reevaluated the matter in light of Mr. Hawthorne's unexpected withdrawal. Lead counsel for the plaintiffs' committee will be Victor A. Scallini. The committee itself will be composed of Edward Haroldson, Esquire, Stanford Rosen, Esquire, and David Lively, Esquire."

Several hands thrust skyward, several voices demand attention, but the chief judge hurries on, speaking above a rising tide of protest. "Since the docket today is long and difficult, these proceedings are adjourned."

The gavel bangs a final time and the judges file from the courtroom as though they fear a stoning. Sullenly, the lawyers gather their papers, stuff them in briefcases, and file toward the door. A few pat Hawthorne on the shoulder as they pass, whether out of gratitude or sympathy he isn't sure.

When he reaches Hawthorne's side, Scallini stops with the grace of an eighteen-wheeler. "Smart move, Alec," he proclaims, making sure everyone in the room can hear him. "Don't take chances with the ticker. If you want out of it entirely, I'll give you an equal split on the referrals."

Hawthorne smiles. The sun still shines; Vic remains Vic. "I think I'll stick around and see how it goes."

"It'll go like gangbusters; I'll have this baby wrapped up in nine months."

"What's your liability theory?"

Scallini's eyes shift left and right. "I can't get into details, but it's no exaggeration to say that this case could blow the lid off the airframe industry. We have reason to believe certain design decisions on the H-11 were ... well, let's just say this could be as big as the Electra scandal. When I get the feds to move their ass into a settlement structure, we're on the way to the bank." Vic abruptly consults his diamond-dialed Rolex. "I got to go. Hell of a thing about your heart. Better try some preventive medicine."

"Like what?"

"Fish oil and fucking women half your age."

Hawthorne laughs despite himself. A moment later, Ed Haroldson replaces Scallini at Hawthorne's side. "I thought you said you were up to speed, son."

Hawthorne smiles. "As Einstein observed, that's a relative term."

Haroldson inclines his head and squints. "What the hell are you up to, boy?"

"What makes you ask?"

"You're enough like me to be my son. And there's never been a time I didn't know when Little Ed had a shenanigan up his sleeve."

Keith Tollison crossed his arms and tried to suppress a smile. "I couldn't agree with you more, Mr. Tiggle. November first *is* too early. The problem is, I don't know of a law that governs the proper time to put up Christmas decorations."

"How about the laws against blasphemy? How about the laws against avarice? How about the laws against offending public decency?"

"I don't think we have laws against those things anymore."

"Well, if we don't, we damn well should."

"Maybe so. And maybe if we did, someone would say it's blasphemy not to keep the decorations up all year."

"Nonsense. Clyde Winnett's the one behind it, Tollison. Using city property to herd people into his luggage shop before Thanksgiving, is what it amounts to. If I have *my* way, Clyde's served his last term on the council."

"That's the spirit, Henry. Vote the bastards out. It's the American way."

"The problem with *that* is, the American way don't seem to be working so good anymore."

Keith Tollison was pondering Henry Tiggle's own brand of blasphemy when Sandy appeared in the doorway. "Mrs. Donahue on two. She sounds . . . excited."

Tollison stood up. "I've got to go, Henry. I'm afraid you'll have to grin and bear it with the decorations unless you can get Clyde Winnett impeached."

"Maybe I'll just tear the damn things down. A little guerilla warfare may be called for in this situation."

"Now, Henry."

"What are they going to do, shoot me? I'm half dead already. Lucky for that young lady who just peeked in here, the dead half is below the waist."

The old man cackled his way out of the office and Keith Tollison accepted the first phone call he'd received from Laura Donahue in a week. "Hi. How's it going?"

"The hospital called. There's been some change in Jack."

"Good or bad?" As if her fervor hadn't told him.

"Good, but I don't know what that means yet. They want me down there right away, so I can't make our meeting. Maybe next week, but if Jack is conscious, I don't know if I'll be able to—"

Tollison glanced at his calendar. "Why don't I go with you?"

"There's no need for that."

"Not for you, obviously. But I happen to have quite a *large* need for that."

"I can't deal with anything but Jack right now, Keith."

"Come on," he urged. "You can use the company and I can use a change of scene."

"Promise not to grill me?"

"About the case?"

"About us." She hesitated. "Don't you see? If you and I kept on the way we were, we'd be ganging up on him. It wouldn't be fair, and I have this overwhelming need to be *fair* to him. It's the only way I can get through this, I think."

He could only beg a crumb. "Will you tell me you love me?"

Her voice thickened. "Of course I love you. I'm just not sure what to *do* about it anymore."

"Thanks," he said. "I guess."

She failed to submit to irony. "I'll be at your office in five minutes."

Tollison replaced the phone. According to the Sunday morning tenets of his youth, Laura's distance was precisely what he deserved, the Calvinist consequence of breaking the seventh commandment. But whatever its truth, the assessment produced only a consuming ache.

Tollison was about to tell Sandy he was leaving when she buzzed him. "Mr. Winton on two."

"Finally." Tollison pushed a button. "Harold. What's the verdict?"

"Hi, Keith. You sound frazzled."

"That's an understatement."

"You should take more time out for your friends. Martin Knoller tells me you haven't made Rotary in months."

"You know how it is, Harold."

"Actually, I don't, Keith. I've *always* made time for civic matters."

Damned from all directions, Tollison could only beg reprieve. "I'll try to do better, Harold."

"That's the spirit. Altoona has been good to you, Keith, considering what your father . . . that is, I didn't mean to sound like I blame *you* for what he—"

"I know what you meant, Harold."

"Good. Well, back to business. We'll approve the refinancing, Keith. Nine and a quarter, thirty-year fixed."

"How about the principal?"

He heard the rattle of papers. "Let's see. Your current balance is at eighty. I'm afraid we can only go to a hundred."

"You told me at least one twenty-five."

"I know I did, but with the new tax law, everyone in town is coming in to reduce their equity, so we're having to proceed very carefully. Yours is an old place, Keith, and not that well maintained, if you don't mind my saying so. Not a big market for that type of home around here; most folks come up to Altoona to build a place of their own, you know that. The appraisal was only one-thirty, after all."

"You're kidding."

"You need a new roof, a furnace, and you've got some dry rot in the bathroom and beetle damage in the back. If it were up to me personally, of course, I'd approve you in a minute, but the board ..."

"I understand, Harold."

"Of course you're free to try elsewhere."

"Go ahead with the hundred. When can I get the surplus?"

"Should be about three weeks."

"Fine. Thanks, Harold."

"Anytime, Keith. And can we count on you to man a table at Founders' Day this fall?"

"I'll get back to you."

Tollison hung up and hurried out to the street. Laura pulled up a minute later, driving the Mercedes with the FOR SALE sign still languishing in the window. She looked frantic yet jubilant, in a mix with a dozen equally ecstatic emotions.

Tollison waited for her to buzz down the window. "Why don't you let me drive? You're too hyped to keep your mind on anything but Jack."

She nodded, then slid to the opposite side of the car. He got in beside her, adjusted the seat, wrapped himself in the belt, and pulled away from the curb.

As they crept toward Highway 101 between a UPS truck and a minibus still bedizened in psychedelic hues, Tollison glanced at his companion. Her face was flushed, her hair awry, her hands a blur of pointless motion. Though he tried for a while to share it, her excitement made him feel a trifle mean.

"What did you think of Hawthorne?" he asked.

"I think he's very slick." Her lips wrinkled, then compressed. "Slick and smart."

"By which you mean corrupt, I suppose."

"Not corrupt. Just lawyerish."

In defense of himself as much as his friend, Tollison lashed back. "You're going to need all the lawyering you can get before this is over, Laura."

She looked toward the orchard that stretched beyond the window. "I didn't mean to insult you, Keith."

He was unable to respond before she changed the subject. "Mr. Chambers called again last night."

"And?"

"He says I should accept his offer. He claims there's no evidence the plane was defective or the pilot was negligent or the controllers fouled up or that anything else went wrong. He says that even if there *was* such evidence, we're not entitled to damages since Jack was bankrupt before the crash and they can prove it. He says they're only offering to settle to avoid the expense of a trial, and if they have to go to court, they won't offer anything at all. He says juries are getting tired of people like me begging for outrageous sums. He says—"

"That's *bullshit*, Laura," Tollison said, breaking the chain of rhetoric. "Your case is worth a million dollars."

He sensed a weary smile. "Your friend Alec told me five. If Jack is permanently disabled." The qualification prompted a morbid laugh. "See how he has me talking? I'll get a ton of money if Jack has to spend the rest of his life as a pillow. And I got the impression from your friend that somehow this is supposed to make me happy."

"Come on, Laura. That's not fair."

"What's not *fair* is having our future depend on your slippery Mr. Hawthorne, to whom this is just another headline."

"*Our* future?" Tollison mimicked miserably, and recklessly looked her way.

She reddened. "You know what I mean."

"I guess I finally do."

The silence cowed them both. "Sometimes I think you've been hurt by this more than anyone," Laura said at last, but only after he was driving faster than was safe, passing a van in a cloud of dust and an angry blast from his horn. Luckily for both of them, the bridge above the bay was too dangerous for him to give her anything more essential than a glance.

After weaving through the city and climbing toward the freeway once again, Tollison glanced at his passenger. "So how are you, Laura?" he asked. "I mean *really*."

She shrugged. "I'm surviving, I guess. People are being nice, all of a sudden. *Too* nice, actually. It's quite amazing," she added. "People see me on the street or come by the house to drop off food or flowers or something, and they express such outlandish condolences that I find myself starting to believe Jack and I really *were* happy because so many people keep *telling* me we were."

"That's nonsense."

She didn't affirm or deny the label. "On the other hand, there're Jack's shirttail relatives who keep calling to ask how much *flight* insurance he took out that night; they're convinced there's a million-dollar policy floating around somewhere. Then there're his poker buddies, calling to chat, supposedly, but really calling to see whether Jack wants to sell his real estate office or his country club membership or his bowling ball. A few of them even imply Jack might want to sell his *wife*." Her laugh was sour. "Then there was the local seer, who claimed Jack had spoken to her in the night, and for a modest fee she'd be happy to tell me what he'd said."

"Hang up on them," Tollison retorted, angry that he had left her vulnerable. "If they keep bothering you, let me know. How's your money situation?"

She shrugged. "Luckily there are a few souls left in Altoona who don't think Jack stiffed them some time or other. The Main Street Market lets me buy on credit, and the gasoline man fills my tank though he knows I'm lying when I say I've forgotten my wallet. The garbage company is the only one who's cancelled—I spend Saturday mornings at the dump. You meet the most amazing people at the dump—one of our illustrious city fathers spends every Saturday out there, complete with hospital mask and metal detector, trying to find his fortune. But otherwise life is wonderful. The hospital is reminding me how much we owe them, Blue Cross has decided it's never heard of us, the bank is going to foreclose on the house, and I'm working for the visiting nurses to try to make ends meet. I have the night shift. Tuesday I comforted an Alzheimer's case from midnight to four A.M. The poor woman thought I was her daughter. And she *despises* her daughter."

"I'm sorry," he said, struggling for more.

"So is everyone. Except maybe Mr. Chambers."

"I wish you'd let me loan you some—"

"I won't borrow money from you, Keith. Things always fall apart when money's involved."

It's *already* fallen apart, was what he wanted to say, but instead he established a charade. "I've found you some funds."

She looked at him suspiciously. "From where?"

"I came across an insurance policy that pays off in Jack's situation."

"But you told me he didn't have any—"

"I only found it the other day, when I was down at his office on the conservatorship thing. It's not much, but it'll help a little."

"How much is a little?"

"Twenty thousand. It should be available in about three weeks, when the papers are processed."

Her sigh made harmony with the road noise. "I can keep the house. Thank God. I was afraid the first thing I was going to have to tell him when he came to was that—"

"House or not, you still have to sue the bastards, Laura," Tollison interrupted. "They won't negotiate until you do."

Her spirits slumped. "Fred Fitch called today."

"What for?"

"To remind me that he's been handling Jack's business affairs for the past five years."

"And?"

"That Jack always had the utmost faith in his professional competence."

"And?"

"That since that was the case, I was honor bound to engage him to pursue Jack's claim against the airline."

"And?"

"That if I didn't retain him within a week, he would be forced to consider having me removed as Jack's conservator. He said I would be particularly interested in the grounds for removal."

"Which would be?"

"Moral turpitude."

"What the hell is he talking about?"

"I assumed he was talking about you and me."

She waited for him to speak, but he was imagining the reception their secret would receive as it spread throughout Altoona. "Can he do what he says?" she asked after a moment.

"I don't think so."

"But maybe?"

He shrugged. "Do you think he really knows about us?"

"I think everyone who wants to know about us knows about us," she said cavalierly. "Fred offered a deal."

"What?"

"He said he could be persuaded to withhold his objections if you would associate him with you in the case. As 'of counsel' or something like that. With a split of the fee."

"Fuck him," Tollison blurted. "It's just a bluff, like all Fred's threats."

"I also got a call from Channel Eight. They want to do a feature on Jack and me. The SurfAir crash—six months later."

"No."

"Why not?"

"Because they'll get you all smiling and stalwart and show their little clip on the nightly news, then a year from now the insurance company will show the tape to a jury and claim it proves how nicely you've recovered from what happened to your husband."

Laura shrugged. "I also got a letter from Larchmont Productions."

"Who the hell is that?"

"TV people. They want to buy my story. *Our* story."

"Yours and mine?"

By the time he knew his question was absurd, Laura was laughing at him. "Mine and Jack's. For a movie of the week. They're offering twenty-five thousand."

"It sounds uncouth."

"Uncouth or no, back when everyone was hounding me for money, I'd have done it in a minute. But since they've eased up lately, I—" She frowned. "Why do you think that is, by the way?"

He concocted a lie that would cover the deep depletion of his funds that had resulted from acting as a surety for Laura Donahue. "I told them your case is in litigation and that you'd eventually recover a large sum and would pay them off completely."

"Some of them didn't seem the sympathetic type," Laura said dubiously. "Oh well. We can discuss the movie later. They may not want me, anyway. Apparently there was a super saleswoman on the plane as well, a legend in her field or something. If her parents agree to sell *her* story . . ."

"This is fluff, Laura. What's important is that you get your lawsuit on file."

When she didn't respond, he glanced her way. Her jaw was set in a level line. "I don't want that Hawthorne man to represent me."

"Why not?"

"Because he *wants* things from me."

"Like what?"

"I don't know, I guess what I feel is that he wants me to surrender, somehow. He wants me small and helpless, so he can play the white knight and gallop in to rescue me."

"Well, that's sort of the way it is, isn't it?"

Her anger filled the car. "No, it *isn't*. If I never get a *dime* from the airline people, I can deal with it. I don't *need* your Mr. Hawthorne. And I don't want him to think I do."

"You talk like he's a shyster, Laura. He's not."

"I know he's not a shyster. That man Scallini. *He's* a shyster. But I don't want *either* of them; I want you."

Moved by her tribute, Tollison blurted a commitment he had sworn to never make. "I suppose I can give your case a try. If you really want me to."

She nodded wearily. "Then it's settled."

As quickly as that, he had jumped to another league, one he had aspired to for thirty years. Sweating from the ramifications, Tollison guided the Mercedes off the freeway and followed the labyrinthine route to the hospital. When he was finally parked in the lot, he put his hand on Laura's shoulder to prevent her from getting out. "You need to tell me something."

"What?"

"If Jack is better, if he's even approximately normal, will you divorce him?"

She avoided his eye. "I don't know."

"In other words, you're going to give him another chance."

"God's given him one, Keith. I keep thinking maybe I should, too."

Laura asked for the keys, then got out of the car and opened the trunk. By the time he joined her, she was holding a cardboard box filled with odds and ends. "I'll carry it," he offered, then asked her what it was.

"Stuff," she said.

"What kind of stuff?"

"For Jack."

He took a sniff. "Vinegar?"

She nodded. "We decided to go for broke to bring him out of it. Some doctors claim it doesn't work, but I thought it was worth a try. Reticular activity formation, it's called."

"Which means?"

"I bombard him with sensation. I put vinegar under his nose, ice on his neck, peanut butter on his tongue. I blow a whistle in his ear, prick his finger with a pin, wear as much perfume as I can stand. I even tape open his eyelids and show him pictures of naked women."

He had to laugh. "Has it worked?"

She looked at him. "I think we'll know in a minute."

She led him through a rear door, up the fire stairs, down narrow corridors and mammoth wings through the door marked NEUROLOGY to the door to 414. This time, Laura pushed through without slowing down.

There were two beds in the room. One was empty and stripped; three white coats were huddled above the other. For the first time since entering the building, Laura hesitated, as though her husband's health would be imperiled by the slightest sound. "Dr. Ryan?" she whispered finally.

The tallest figure turned. When he saw who it was, he smiled. "Laura. Good. Come here."

Uninvited and ignored, Tollison remained in the doorway, his view of the patient obscured but for the lower extremities, which were bare and slick from salve.

"See?" Ryan spoke again as Laura edged beside him at the bed.

"See what? I—*my God.* Is he really? . . . *Jack?* Can he hear me, Dr. Ryan?"

"I don't know yet. We just hooked up an EKG and some other monitors, and they should tell us whether he's responding to verbal stimuli. So far he doesn't appear to be, but—" The doctor shrugged. "That's why we wanted you to come down. If he responds to anyone, he'll respond to you."

The truth of the statement made Tollison retreat to a corner of the room, where he kept company with an IV rack and a blood pressure cuff.

"Jack?" Laura said again. "It's me. Laura. Hi, Jack. I—" She turned to Ryan once again. "Is it okay if I talk to him like this?"

He nodded. "That's what we want you to do. We'll leave you for a few minutes, then come back and check out our machines. They may tell us something and they may not. If not, we'll do a scan. In the meantime, we'll hope for the best."

Laura placed her hand on the doctor's arm. "This is a good sign, isn't it?"

"Of course." The doctor paused. "You look dubious."

"It's . . . I guess I expected something more dramatic."

"I'm sorry if you're disappointed. Perhaps I should have given you more details on the phone. Progress in these situations is invariably slow."

"But this *is* what we've been waiting for, isn't it?"

"It's too soon to say for certain. Even if it's a definite event, it doesn't mean all the problems are solved; it just means we're closer to finding out what they are."

"But—"

After a glance at Tollison, Dr. Ryan crossed his arms. "As I've told you before, I believe your husband can come out of this, Laura. But he can't do it on his own. Someone will have to help him, night and day, directing his therapy over what will probably amount to many years. I suggest you start thinking about whether that someone will be you." He paused, then patted her shoulder. "Come on, troops. Let's leave the Donahues alone for a minute. If he responds in any way, be sure to let us know exactly how. Blinks, nods, tears, twitches, anything."

"Of course. I . . . thank you, Doctor."

"Hey. This is what we get paid for."

After another glance at Tollison, Ryan and his entourage vacated the room. When they were gone, Laura bent over the bed and began to whisper in her husband's ear. Since she had not indicated otherwise, Tollison stayed where he was, gripped by emotions that were mostly inappropriate.

"Jack? Honey? I'm here, Jack. Right beside you. You're *okay* now, Jack. Everything's going to be fine. You've been hurt very badly, and you've been unconscious for a long time, but now you're back. You're back and everything's going to be *wonderful* again. You can smile if you want to, you know. You can even *talk* to me. Here. Feel my hand? We've been poking and pricking you for months, haven't we? And you just lay there, didn't you? But now you can *feel* it. I know you can. There. That felt good, didn't it? How about that? You must be so *sore*, lying there all that time. Oh, Jack. I love you, Jack. I love you very much. Please tell me you can hear me say that."

At her back, Tollison put his face in his hands and his fingers in his ears. As though she could sense his anguish, Laura suddenly fell silent. After a long minute she backed away from the bed and closed her eyes and rubbed them, her body slumped in a tired parabola. When she opened them again, her look was trained on Tollison. "I didn't mean ... I was just trying to do whatever—"

"It's all right," he lied.

"Come here. Please. Come look at him."

Tollison joined her at the bed. Mouth open, cheeks sunken, flesh flat and ashen, skull a peeled potato sliced at its crown, someone—far more a gargoyle than anyone he knew—stared up at them from behind a marble mask. Breaths rasping as a crone's, eyes as recessed as the dregs in teacups, Jack Donahue stared at the ceiling with utter desolation, as though a patron saint had broken a promise to appear above the bed.

"See?"

The cheery query startled Tollison out of his astonishment. "See what?"

"His eyes. They're *open*. They were never *open* before."

Tollison gulped, glanced, then looked away from their dumb fixation. "Great."

She sought his hand. "I've prayed for so long. For *something*. Now at least there's this. I think I'll stay down here for a few days. To watch him come back." She handed him her keys. "There's a motel across from the hospital. I'll call you when Jack's ready, and you can drive down and pick us up. Would that be all right?"

191

He nodded.

"I'm going to get Dr. Ryan," she continued quickly, "so they can complete their tests." She took Tollison's hand and squeezed it, then left him with her husband.

A minute passed, then another. Machines ticked and clicked and whistled softly. Tubes ran from them into Jack Donahue's throat and nose and arm; others disappeared below the bedclothes. Tollison crossed his arms and uncrossed them, shifted from one foot to another, moved to where he could inspect the intravenous contraption more closely. As he did so, something happened—two frozen eyes thawed, then moved in the direction he did.

Tollison took another step and then another, watching closely, but this time the darkly dotted spheres failed to track him. He backed up, then stepped forward once again. The eyes stared back, then blinked, then closed.

Tollison looked around to see if there was anyone to call to, but the room was empty. When he looked back, it was in time to see the mouth make its rigid ring a softer oval, then form the framework of a word.

"Hwwah waawaa."

The shock of sound was a fist against his heart. "Hey. Jack. What was that? Say it again."

Jack Donahue lay inert, oblivious, as though the moment had been but a frame from Laura's dream.

Tollison hurried across the room, shoved open the door, and found Laura and the doctors huddling right outside. "He said something," he blurted into their whispered conference. "I don't know what it was, but he definitely said it."

Laura's hands pressed against her lips, as though a word would silence Jack forever.

"Let's take a look," Ryan said, and hurried into the room.

Tollison waited until the rest had followed, then walked to the nurses' station and waited for one to look at him.

"My name is Tollison," he explained to a pert young woman with a pencil behind her ear. "I'm going home now. When Mrs. Donahue comes out, please tell her I'll come back for her whenever she wants. She can give me a call anytime, day or night. Okay? She's busy, or I'd tell her myself. Her husband seems to be coming out of it."

"Really? How wonderful."

"Yes," he said, and by the time he was home, he believed he believed just that.

Although it was not yet five when he reached Altoona, Tollison shunned the office for his house. Sunk deep within the club chair in his living room, shoes off, coat and tie draped over a faded lampshade, he placed a call to the city.

"Law offices. May I help you?"

"Mr. Hawthorne, please."

"Just a moment."

"Martha."

"Martha, this is Keith Tollison."

"What can we do for you?"

"Is Alec free? I need to talk to him a minute."

"I'll check."

"Keith? What's up?"

"I just wanted to touch base about the SurfAir people I brought in."

"Of course."

"The first one, Brenda, I'm still not sure what she's going to do, so maybe you should call her and—"

"She's already retained me, Keith. She signed on last week."

"Oh. I didn't know. Good. That's great. So the only problem is Laura. She still wants *me* to take her case."

Hawthorne's pause was indecipherable. "I see."

"I'm trying to convince her otherwise, but I just wanted to ask, for one thing, how much will I have to advance in costs if I decide to take it on myself?"

"That's hard to say. Expenses in a big case can run to six figures. In the Paris crash, the lawyers advanced two and a half million out of their own pockets, and I've had experts that cost me fifty grand. On the other hand, no one has to go it alone. A plaintiffs' committee has been picked, and at some point the committee will assess a fee from the other plaintiffs, to defray discovery costs."

"How much of a fee?"

"Several thousand per plaintiff, probably. Five, maybe. Ten."

"Will I have to put up anything else?"

"Probably not. Except for whatever damage experts you hire."

"You think experts are the way to go?"

"Saves you a lot of trouble, and if you pick an experienced man, the defense can't mug him on cross-examination the way they can with amateurs."

"What one do you use?"

"Depends on who's available and how complex the problem is. Litigation Economists is probably the best."

193

"How much do they charge?"

"Three twenty-five an hour."

"You're kidding."

Hawthorne laughed. "If they get you a million-dollar verdict they're worth it, right?"

"I suppose so. Jesus. The CPA I use charges a hundred bucks a day."

"I've found in this business you get what you pay for, Keith. But it's up to you."

"I suppose they'll want money up front."

"With a new kid on the block like you, probably."

"The other thing I was going to ask was, What's the chance of me piggybacking along on this thing? Letting you pros do the work on the liability side. It's not so much that I'm lazy, but—"

"I understand. It's a lot to learn for a one-shot deal."

Hawthorne hesitated for so long Tollison thought he might be laughing at him. But when he spoke, his words contained a mild encouragement. "I don't see why you couldn't tag along. You'd have to prepare your own damage case, though."

"Sure. No problem."

"Then why don't you give it a go? If you find yourself in over your head, I can bail you out by substituting as her counsel. I sure didn't charm the lady, though, did I? And her case is such a laydown, especially the loss of consortium."

"Her husband seems to be coming out of his coma."

"Yeah? Well, that can go either way. On the plus side, it preserves the pain and suffering. On the minus, the jury may decide that eventually he'll recover completely." Hawthorne paused again. "She say what it was that turned her off about me? Mrs. Donahue, that is?"

Tollison felt himself redden, somehow responsible for the rebuff since he had made himself the beneficiary of it. "I think the problem is she's been hounded by the insurance lawyer to settle, then she ran into Vic Scallini in the hospital, and between the two of them they convinced her that all lawyers were scum, and—"

Hawthorne laughed with obvious entendre. "All lawyers but you, you mean."

"Laura and I are—"

"I saw how Laura and you were. Just keep it zipped till after the trial, counselor. She's going to have to convince a jury she's devastated by the loss of her husband's care and comfort. It won't help if Hawley Chambers's private eye tells them she's spending her nights getting care and comfort from her lawyer."

KARNEY, BRUNSON, McCAULEY & WILLIAMS
ONE MARKET PLAZA
SAN FRANCISCO, CA 94105
ATTORNEYS FOR DEFENDANT HASTINGS AIRCRAFT
CORPORATION

UNITED STATES DISTRICT COURT
NORTHERN DISTRICT OF
CALIFORNIA

WALTER J. WARREN, Plaintiff,	)	
vs.	)	NO. MDL 498
SURFAIR COASTAL AIRWAYS INC.,	)	
et al., Defendants.	)	

INTERROGATORIES TO PLAINTIFF

    Pursuant to Rules 26 and 34 of the Federal Rules of Civil Procedure, defendant Hastings Aircraft Corporation (hereinafter "defendant") requests plaintiff to answer under oath the following interrogatories within 30 days of service. Each interrogatory calls for not only your knowledge, but information available to you by reasonable inquiry and due diligence, including inquiry by your agents and attorneys.

Interrogatory No. 1:

    (a) Do you claim that any component system, part, or equipment of the aircraft manufactured by defendant was defectively designed, assembled, or manufactured in any manner which caused or contributed to causing the crash or the death of Rhonda J. Warren and/or Randolph F. Warren (hereinafter known as the decedents)? If so, please answer the following:

    (b) Describe each part or component which you claim was defective.

    (c) Describe the nature of each claimed defect.

    (d) If a claimed defect was one of design, describe each alternative design which you contend was technically feasible at the time the aircraft was manufactured.

    (e) Describe the manner in which you claim each defect caused or contributed to causing the crash.

(f) Identify each document which you contend supports your claim that such defect(s) existed and/or caused or contributed to the crash, and identify each person believed by you to have knowledge of such defects, causes or contributions.

Interrogatory No. 2:

(a) Do you contend that any defects in the design, manufacture, assembly, construction, testing, labeling, instructions, warnings, failure to warn, maintenance, inspection, and servicing of the aircraft which allegedly caused the crash or the death of the decedents were created, in whole or in part, by the negligence of defendant? If so, please answer for each such defect the following subparts.

(b) Describe the defect which you contend was negligently created, in whole or in part, by defendant.

(c) Describe the act or omission by defendant which you contend was negligent.

(d) Describe the manner in which you claim the act or omission created the defect.

(e) Identify each document which you contend supports your claim that such act or omission by defendant occurred and/or that such act or omission by defendant was negligent, and identify each person believed by you to have knowledge of such act or omission, and/or that such act or omission was negligent.

Interrogatory No 3:

(a) Do you contend that any component system, part, or equipment of the aircraft which was manufactured by defendant was defective in a manner which caused or contributed to causing the crash as the result of missing, inadequate, incomplete, and/or incorrect instructions, warnings, or failures to warn of risks or dangers in any manual or other writing? If so, please answer the following subparts.

(b) Describe each such missing instruction or warning, identifying the flight manual, maintenance manual, technical manual, or other writing where you claim each such missing instruction or warning should have been, describing where in such writing the missing instruction or warning should have been, and describing the manner in which you claim the absence of an instruction or warning caused or contributed to causing the crash.

(c) State the language of each instruction or warning which you claim was inadequate or incomplete or incorrect, identifying the paragraph(s) of the manual or other writing in which such inadequate or incomplete or incorrect instruction or warning was contained, describing the way in which you claim the instruction or warning should have been written to make it complete, adequate, and correct, and describing the manner in which you claim the inadequate or incomplete or incorrect instruction or warning caused or contributed to causing the crash.

(d) Separately describe all information available to defendant at the time of manufacture of the component system, part or equipment, and subsequent to that time, which did indicate or should have indicated to defendant that written instructions or warnings contained in the manuals and other writing were inadequate, incomplete, and/or incorrect, or that appropriate instructions or warnings were missing.

(e) Identify each person believed by you to have knowledge that warnings or instructions were missing, inadequate, incomplete, and/or incorrect, and/or that the absence of adequate, complete, and correct warnings and instructions caused or contributed to causing the crash, and identify each document you contend supports your claims concerning the adequacy, completeness, correctness, or absence of the warnings or instructions.

DATED: December 4, 1987

Karney, Brunson, McCauley & Williams
by _____
Gerhard X. Williams
Attorneys for Hastings Aircraft Corporation

NINE

Alec Hawthorne glances at a clock set into the hub of a propeller that had fallen off a Cessna at five thousand feet, doffs his coat, loosens his tie, and sits behind his desk. As always, Martha is waiting at the rolltop.

"Good morning," he says.

Her look is truculent. "I wouldn't know; I've been here all night."

"Doing what?"

"The pretrial brief in the dog case."

"Why the marathon?"

"Because I had last week set aside for it, but you sent me to LA to badger the NTSB on Aeromexico."

"You didn't say anything about—"

"My job is to do what you need me to do when you need me to do it. Which is what I did."

Hawthorne sighs. In the interval since his heart attack, as he has struggled to determine which of the depressions and inspirations that occur within him are real and which are byproducts of his medication, Martha has taken on a raw and grasping air, as though she is scrambling to salvage something off the deck of a sinking ship.

He has seen her infrequently in recent months, and not at all outside the office, so he does not know the source of the ballooning desperation that seems to have at its core the sense that her decision to invest her personal assets entirely in the stock of Alec Hawthorne has been a big mistake. He knows only that he misses the old Martha the way he would miss a pair of comfortable loafers that can no longer be resoled. His guess is that she is finding solace elsewhere, in forms more reliable than the ontologic musings that of late provide his own.

In the meantime, it is disconcerting that even within the autocratic confines of his law firm, he no longer knows what to expect when he walks through the door.

"The transcript of the controller deposition came in," Martha reports, her current claim on him only that he do his duty.

"How'd it go?"

"As expected."

"That bad?"

"At least."

When Martha makes no move to leave or to engage in small talk, Hawthorne glances at the current *Wall Street Journal*, which lies at the center of his desk as always, headline up. Nothing above the fold seems to bear upon his job, except to the extent that the market crash of two months before—which reduced his net worth and raised his blood pressure by equally alarming percentages—suggests that he will never manage to stay rich no matter how hard he works or how long he lives.

Martha stirs at the fringe of his consciousness, so he asks her what's on tap for the day. "Nothing much," she replies tonelessly, then pauses for effect. "Dan Griffin called yesterday."

He swivels to face her fully. "Returning the SurfAir client, I trust."

She shakes her head. "He wants me to come work for him."

"I thought he went with Vic."

Martha nods. "He and Vic are reorganizing. Getting rid of the drones, hiring fresh troops. Dan says Vic's cut his schedule way back, bought a place in La Jolla, and will spend half the year down there while Dan runs the LA office. They're offering me my own branch up here, plus a senior partnership and my name in the title once Vic is out of the picture completely."

Hawthorne is sweating. "Are you going to take it?"

She shrugs. "The door will still have Vic's name on it. To say nothing of his reputation."

As Martha lapses into melancholy, Hawthorne cannot form a reply that encompasses the jeopardy he feels. "So are you going to?" he blurts finally. "Go to work for Vic, I mean?"

"That rather depends on you."

His optimism fades. "How me?"

She looks toward the storm that stirs the bay. "For one thing, are you planning to propose to me anytime soon?"

The question surprises him into aphonia.

She swivels in her chair, which makes a squeak that mimics the mouse he has become. "I take it that panic-stricken look on your face means you aren't."

He stammers. "I've been burned a few times, you know; I'm a little gun-shy. I guess I thought—"

Her eyes begin to broil him. "What? That I was a clever advance in robotics? Or merely an inflatable doll?"

"Come on, Martha," he blurts into the evidence that his skill at misreading women remains immaculate. "You spring this on me out of the blue and expect me to decide in two minutes whether I'm ready for *marriage* again? That's not quite fair, is it?"

"Fair? Like in how fair it was of you to make me abandon any semblance of a personal life for the past ten years to keep both your mood and your law practice afloat?"

"You talk like I've been *using* you."

"You don't like *using*? Try *exploiting*."

His guilt is quickly enameled with righteousness. "I think I'd be a bit more sympathetic if I hadn't been paying you a hundred thousand a year for most of that time. Maybe you've been using me as much as the other way around."

She leaps to her feet and looms over him. "What the hell do you mean by that?"

Unable to prevent what they are doing to each other, he taunts her with the truth. "You know what I mean—you came out of law school with your eye on a place you wanted to get, and decided I was the quickest way to get there. You kept me fit and trim and full of fight and rode me to the top like I was Alysheba and you were Chris McCarron. I benefited from the arrangement, sure. But so did you."

"That's all it was, huh? Tit for tat. Well, that's just *bullshit*." She storms across the room and back. "I'm tempted to sign on with Vic right now."

As desperate as she, Hawthorne tries a mean diversion. "I get it— you want a raise. Okay, ten thousand a year. Make it twenty." He opens the *Journal* with feigned indifference. "Does that take care of it?"

Martha casts the shadow of an obelisk, its point advancing on his heart. "That's not what this is about, and you know it. But I accept the money. If I stay. In the meantime, I've got another proposition for you."

"What?"

"I want to try SurfAir myself. I've never tried a commercial crash, as you well know. All I get are the goddamn *dog* cases."

The reference is to their suit on behalf of a woman who took her pet with her on a flight to Denver. The dog rode in a carrying case in the baggage compartment, but a heating system failed en route and it died from exposure. The baggage handler put the case on the conveyor anyway, and the lady learned of her dog's demise as Scotty's little corpse went round and round on the carousel. Hawthorne expects the jury to award at least a quarter million.

"The way I see it," she is saying, "until you let me try a major case, I'll always be a horse holder."

"SurfAir was only twenty miles from here," he protests. "People will think it's weird if I don't handle it myself."

"Tell them you're still recovering. Or breaking in the next generation. Better yet, tell them it's none of their fucking business."

"But people retain this firm because they assume I'll—"

"The firm," she interrupts. "They hire the *firm*—no more, no less. All they're entitled to is the services of someone in the office, which includes me. For now."

"You can't seriously be thinking of going with Scallini. He's everything that's wrong with this business."

"And you're everything that's wrong with me. What about retirement?"

Gladdened by the opportunity to flaunt his generosity, he answers happily. "Our profit-sharing plan is more than adequate to provide you with—"

"Not *my* retirement," she snarls unexpectedly. "When is retirement in *your* plans?"

His shrug is slow and truthful. "I'm not sure yet. I'm thinking about it," he adds when he sees she wants much more.

"If you did retire, who would take over the firm? Would you bring someone in from outside? Merge with another office? Sell the practice? How would you handle it?"

Flustered by her persistence, Hawthorne can only stammer. "I don't know; I haven't gotten that far. I guess I'm still not certain retirement would be healthy for me."

Her upper lip curls into a gutter. "Right. You were so healthy eight months ago they pronounced you dead."

A pall seems to flood the room. Hawthorne is desperate to drain it. "You don't understand as much as you think you do, because I don't understand that much of it myself."

"I understand you better than anyone in this room."

Belatedly, he realizes that she has insulted him. Their stares collide and threaten further warfare, but in the next moment they mutually abandon the fray. He is sorry he has hurt her, sorry that what they had seems lost. Martha seems equally chagrined, for reasons of her own. As always when he has endured some stress these days, Hawthorne listens to the signals from his heart. This time the message is incoherent.

"The Farnsworth woman is coming in an hour," Martha reminds him finally.

"Then let me see the deposition."

She leaves the office and returns with a volume fat with onion skin. "Read it and weep," she says, and drops it on his desk and leaves the room.

"Go home and get some sleep," he calls after her. When she doesn't answer, he debates saying whatever she needs to have him say in order to keep her happy, but in the end decides to let her go; her needs have flown so far beyond his ability to meet them they are no longer negotiable.

Relieved to be back to business, Hawthorne leans back in his chair and imagines the deposition setting—Vic Scallini flashing his pinky ring and black pearl cuff links, clutching his silk lapels, circling the witness like a toreador around a stricken bull, his toupee flapping as though a crow is trying to land atop his head.

Although obvious and rudimentary, the deposition isn't entirely useless. Vic establishes the drastic reduction in the number of controllers after the PATCO strike, the resulting increase in near misses and runway incursions, the pressures to push trainees through the controller academy to the extent that instructors systematically overgrade and students systematically cheat on the exams, the fact that the San Francisco facility is handling 25 percent more traffic with 25 percent fewer personnel. But as usual, Vic has done more research in *Time* than in the regulations of the FAA. Because he doesn't know the manuals and regulations, he can't document mistakes by going step by step through the procedures the night of the crash, letting the facts speak loudly for themselves. Instead, Vic relies on the Perry Mason approach, badgering the witness in the hope that he will crumble and confess. The problem is, in real life nobody confesses to anything.

Hawthorne keeps reading, until Vic is about to wrap it up:

Q—by Mr. Scallini: Much of the computer and radar equipment currently in use in the traffic control system is quite ancient, is it not, Mr. McCaskell?

A—I guess so. Some of it.

—Twenty years old, some of the computers, is that not correct?

—The ASR-4's are that old, I think.

—They frequently break down?

—Once in a while.

—Last year the Washington, D.C., control center lost all radar and computers for over twenty minutes, did it not?

—Yes.

—Anything like that ever happen to you?

—Nothing that severe.

—What has happened to you in the way of equipment failure?

—A few glitches, is all. Once in a while the MSAW—Minimum Safe Altitude Warning—acts up.

—Isn't it true your system had a glitch on the night of March 23 that caused you to lose track of the general aviation plane that struck the SurfAir flight?

—No. And I'm still not convinced another plane did strike that flight.

—That's exactly my point, sir. You didn't see the other aircraft because you turned off at least one channel of the decoder that evening, did you not? To reduce screen clutter?

—No.

—In fact you do that every evening during peak periods, don't you?

—No. Never. I—

—Come now, Mr. McCaskell. We're going to get to the bottom of this sooner or later. You'll be better off if you come clean.

—I have nothing to come clean about. If the tapes show pop-up traffic at the time of the crash, it doesn't mean I was responsible.

—Are you telling me that the radar data entering the system computer and shown on the tapes does not necessarily show up on the controller screens?

—Yes. Absolutely.

—What causes this variation, sir?

—Atmospherics, basically.

—So the system sometimes loses altitude data entirely?

—Yes. That's what happened in Aeromexico. And the Wings West midair in San Luis Obispo, too. The system doesn't always—

—But on the evening in question—the evening of March 23, of this year—you took liberties with that system, did you not?

—No. And I resent your suggestion that I did.

—Your resentment is not material, sir. What is material is the griev-

ous harm suffered by the families of the loved ones who met their tragic deaths in the crash of the plane you were sworn and duty bound to guide safely to the ground.

—Why you phony son of a . . .

It was stipulated by all parties that the remaining remarks of counsel and the witness would be off the record.

Hawthorne laughs and closes the transcript. He is estimating the chances that Martha could go to work for a rooster like Scallini when the door opens and Brenda Farnsworth enters the office. Hawthorne nods a greeting, then looks beyond her for an instant, but Martha is nowhere to be seen.

His newest client is dressed in short tan skirt and top of yellow fleece. Her boots are soft brown leather; her hair is a dark derby atop her head. Her look is simultaneously dubious and daunting. It occurs to Hawthorne that she would make a wonderful lawyer.

Clasping his hands behind his head, he dons the insouciant mask he presents to women who intrigue him. "So," he begins, "are your students going to survive a day without their beloved teacher?"

A corner of her mouth moves leftward. "The most useful emotion to foster in students is fear, not fondness."

"How's our friend Mr. Tollison?"

Her voice betrays nothing. "I wouldn't know; I haven't seen him since I was here the last time. Why?"

He shrugs. "I'm just wondering if I need to know the status of your relationship with him."

"Why would you need to know that?"

Hawthorne smiles. "He and I may work together on this. At some point I may need to know how objective he is about your claim."

She thinks it over and shrugs. "Keith and I go way back. From time to time familiarity has bred both contempt and something we treat as passion." She pauses to gauge his interest in the subject. "The situation is currently in flux," she concludes gruffly.

Hawthorne finds himself aroused. She is one of those women who are alluring primarily because they believe themselves impregnable.

When he says nothing further, she continues. "But I'm not the one to ask about Keith's well-being these days."

"Who is?"

"Mrs. Donahue would be a good place to start."

"How's her husband doing, by the way?"

"Well enough to come home."

"Really? Since when?"

"A week ago."

"Has he recovered?"

She shrugs again. "Apparently they're applying all kinds of therapies that are designed to bring him back to normal. *My* question is, why would anyone *want* him back to normal?"

"A difficult situation."

"For all concerned." The pause drips hostility. "Poor Laura. There. I've saved you the trouble."

"I take it you and she have little in common beyond your mutual admiration of Mr. Tollison."

"Let me put it this way," she concludes with a burst of venom. "Only one of us admires Mr. Tollison enough to hire him as our lawyer."

Hawthorne shakes his head. Brenda Farnsworth reminds him of his third wife. Which is fine, potentially even fascinating, as long as he remembers not to marry her. "Well. Down to business," he intones.

As he glances at her file, she arranges herself along his couch. It occurs to him that the women most confident of their remoteness from romance often become the most blatant initiators of it. "I'm not your enemy, Ms. Farnsworth," he begins.

"I know enough about lawyers to know that remains to be seen, Mr. Hawthorne."

"Are you always this combative?"

"When there's money on the line, I am. You should see me dicker with the school board. Their last negotiator threw coffee in my face. Luckily, he took cream."

They pause to let things simmer. He asks if she wants anything to drink. When she shakes her head, he becomes official. "I asked you here because, as you know, we filed a complaint on your behalf in the SurfAir matter. The defendants have noticed your deposition, which they have set for December ... tenth."

"Where?"

"One Market Plaza. Hawley Chambers's office."

"The guy who says my sister's worth twenty thousand dollars. Do you suppose that's for all of her or only the part they put in the casket?"

Hawthorne ignores the sarcasm. "Have you ever been deposed before?"

She shakes her head. "Am I on my own, or what?"

"A witness has a right to counsel anywhere but in a grand jury proceeding—Martha will be with you every minute."

She freezes. "I hired you, not your maid."

"You hired whoever and whatever I feel will most effectively advance your interests."

"The second team for Brenda, huh? Well, it won't be the first time." She makes a hatchet of her jaw. "So what happens at these depositions? They throw darts at me or what?"

He shakes his head. "Martha will meet you at Chambers's office. Some defense lawyers will be there, and a member of the plaintiffs' committee as well. A court reporter will put you under oath, take down what you say on her machine, type it up a few days later, and give you the transcript to review so you can alter anything that came out wrong or you want to change your mind about. When you sign it, it's filed with the court and can be used to perpetuate your testimony if you die or impeach you if you say something different at trial than you said in the deposition. Martha can object to the form of the questions to the extent they're confusing or vague, but objections such as relevance or hearsay are deferred till time of trial."

"How long will it take?"

"Impossible to tell. I've had some I thought would go a day last a month, and vice versa. If you were a sole plaintiff they might string it out, make you miss work, delve into every corner of your private life until you start thinking maybe it's not worth the aggravation to go through a lawsuit after all, but since getting rid of you wouldn't do them that much good, I imagine they'll make it brief. On the other hand, if Vic Scallini shows up, there's no telling what will happen. Vic likes to hear himself talk, especially in the presence of attractive women."

She digests the compliment without comment. "I've got a decade of sick leave coming anyway. So why am I here?"

"I thought we'd talk about what you're going to say."

She recrosses her legs, causing her skirt to slide midway up her thigh. Her stockings are tan, with filigreed imprinting. Although they seem half the length of Martha's, her legs are nice enough to linger over. "So what *am* I going to say, counselor?" she asks with stale amusement.

"I never put words in people's mouths, Ms. Farnsworth; I just advise them to tell the truth. But I like to learn what the truth sounds like, so I can play the right accompaniment." He smiles. "And jazz it up if it needs it."

Her mouth tilts. "Like I said. What am I supposed to say about my sister?"

He maintains his smile despite her slander. "As I told you at our first meeting, your deposition will cover only the damages you have suffered as a result of your sister's death. As I also told you, those damages don't amount to much according to the letter of the law."

"I remember. Believe me."

"The usual claim—economic loss, or loss of income—is pretty much out in your case. Except for gifts to you and to your son, you didn't receive any payments from your sister when she was alive. Right?"

"Right. Though I could always lie about it."

He shakes his head a single time. "No one's suggesting you do that. When your sister died, under California law her pain and suffering died with her. So that's out, as well."

"Great. What about these punitive damages I hear so much about?"

"That depends on the conduct of the defendants—whether they were grossly or willfully negligent and by being otherwise could have prevented the crash. That's a possibility, but at this point a remote one. So we're stuck with a single claim—the loss of society of your sister. Okay so far?"

Her nod is minuscule. "This isn't exactly quantum mechanics."

He swallows his reply and continues. "In talking with you before, it seemed clear that Carol was very close to you—your best friend, in fact. You lived in the same town, saw each other regularly, and so forth."

"Correct."

He nods. "Good, but it's not enough. The friendship was real and important, but it doesn't have that special something we can count on to capture the sympathies of the jury and make them want to reward you beyond the strict entitlements of the law."

"Sure. No big deal. They kill your sister, it shouldn't cost them anything."

"Unfortunately, that sometimes is the case. What *might* turn into some significant dollars is the situation between Carol and your son. Spitter? Is that what you call him?"

She nods, wary of revelation.

"Why do you call him that?"

"Why the hell do you think?"

Her look defies his grin. Hawthorne folds his arms and proceeds with care. The subject of her son is the one delicacy he has unearthed about the woman.

"I understand Spitter is ... mentally disabled to a degree," he continues.

She closes her eyes and speaks with suffering. "When he was little,

I took him to doctors every other week. Some said he was retarded, others said he was autistic, others that he was emotionally disturbed —the old what-have-you-done-to-this-poor-child group—and a few said he was just weird and scary and I should dump him in the nearest home."

"What did *you* think?"

"I thought it was the wrath of God." Surprisingly, she smiles. "But that was back when I thought there was a *plan* behind it all, that things happened for *reasons*. Now that I know it's only a comic strip, I hardly think about it at all."

Her nihilism spurs him to count the paltry blessings that beflower his relationship with Jason. "Could Spitter testify at the trial?" he asks finally.

She shrugs. "He's not an idiot or anything. What he'd testify *to*, I don't know. And neither will you. The thing about Spitter is that every minute is a brand new toy."

"So it would be a risk to use him?"

"It would be a risk to have him in this room."

He conceals a shudder. "You mean he's violent?"

"Only with me."

"Has he hurt you?"

Her face is as empty as ice. "You mean physically, I presume."

"Yes."

"Not for a while."

"Has he become more violent since Carol died?"

She hesitates. "It would help if I said yes, wouldn't it?"

Her question flushes anger. "Please don't keep implying that I asked you here to suborn perjury, Ms. Farnsworth. Would you be willing to tell a jury exactly how things have changed between you and Spitter since your sister's death?"

"I could tell them he quit his job and camps out on Carol's grave. I could tell them he sneaks into the house in the middle of the night and scares me half to death. I could tell them all *kinds* of things, Mr. Attorney-at-Law."

"Could you make them believe you?"

She crosses her arms in the mode of wrestlers being interviewed about their trade. "I'm a teacher. It's my *job* to make people believe me. Even when they shouldn't."

Her look reminds him of the earliest days of his practice, when he confronted corporate criminals who took delight in falsehood. "Would Spitter talk to a psychotherapist?"

Her eyes mist with memory. "At one point he talked to them till they didn't want to talk to *him* anymore. Why?"

"I'd like to have you and Spitter meet with a psychologist I know and talk about your relationship with each other and about Spitter's relationship with Carol, particularly about how things have changed since she died. If it goes well, the psychologist can testify that Spitter and Carol were symbiotic, that she was his emotional rock—his security blanket, if you will—and that your life has become much more difficult since Spitter lost that source of . . . serenity. That would pretty much be true, wouldn't it?"

She looks at him furiously. "You've *already* talked to him, haven't you?"

He considers but discards denial. "It's a her. And yes, I have."

"You know *exactly* what she's going to tell the jury, and she hasn't even laid *eyes* on me or Spitter yet. And you preach to *me* about perjury."

"You're pretty cynical, Ms. Farnsworth."

"And each time I think I'm too cynical, I run into guys like you." She thrusts her chest. "So tell me this. You know what *I'm* going to say and you know what the *psychologist* is going to say, so what's the fucking *jury* going to say?"

"How do you mean?"

"I mean what are they going to *give* me. How much is it going to cost that airline to have killed my sister?"

Their stares meet head-on. "Not enough, I'm afraid."

"How much is not enough?"

"If we get a hundred thousand we'll be lucky."

"What about those million-dollar verdicts I've heard so much about?"

"Those are for widows whose husbands make a hundred thousand a year and ten times that much in performance bonuses. Those are for people who have to live in pain every minute of the day and whose lawyer convinces a jury to award them a dollar an hour to compensate for it. You know what a dollar an hour amounts to for a thirty-five-year-old woman over the course of her lifespan?"

"What?"

"Almost four hundred thousand dollars. Would you take that amount of money to let someone expose a nerve in your tooth and leave it that way the rest of your life? Well, that's why people who do get a million deserve it. But that's not you and that's not Carol. So put the million out of your mind."

Hawthorne looks at his watch. When she notices, Brenda Farnsworth laughs bitterly. "My hour is up, huh?" Tugging at her skirt, she starts to stand, then doesn't. "Is there time for one more question before you keep your lunch date?"

He shrugs. "Sure."

"How much will Laura Donahue get out of this plane crash thing?"

"Laura? Or her husband?"

"Since he's a vegetable it's going to be all hers, right? So how much for the pair? A million?"

"More, if Tollison is any good."

"Why would anyone give her a million dollars? I'd like for you to explain that to me."

He shrugs. "Well, there's pain and suffering."

"The man is paralyzed, for God's sake. He couldn't feel it if they cut his leg off with a saw."

Hawthorne shrugs. "Tollison may dig up a doctor to say it's possible Donahue can feel pain anyway, even though he might not be able to express his feelings verbally. If the jury believes him, you've got a quarter million right there."

"I'm sure you'll dig up a doctor that will say anything he wants. What else will he have up his sleeve?"

"Donahue worked in real estate, so Keith will send his records to an expert in evaluating businesses. The expert will project Donahue's future earnings over his work expectancy, which, since Donahue was forty-five when he got hurt, would be close to twenty years. Projecting real estate commissions that far in the future gives you a pretty big number if you consider population growth and inflation."

"Inflation's next to nothing."

"Inflation over the past thirty years has been about six percent as measured by the Consumer Price Index. But the expert will want to come out with as large a number as possible, so he'll look at real estate inflation instead of general inflation, and lately that's been more than fifteen percent per year in northern California. Population growth up around Altoona has been at least ten percent per year as well, and multiplying that out gets you close to a million dollars of lost commissions, even if Donahue couldn't sell a doghouse to a dog catcher."

"So that's what Laura gets."

He shakes his head. "The expert will discount the future earnings to present value. This time, the smaller the percentage the bigger the award, so the expert will say the discount rate should be something like four percent. That discounted sum will be what Keith will ask the jury to award for Donahue's lost earnings."

"But—"

"Then there's his resort project. Keith will bring in someone to say it's the greatest idea since Disneyland, and if the jury buys it, we're over two million without even trying. Then there's Mrs. Donahue's loss of her husband's society—of his care, comfort, and companionship—which a good lawyer will make seem more delightful than Tracy and Hepburn in *Desk Set,* and that will be *another* half million easy, not to mention punitive damages or the expense of Donahue's medical care and rigging the house for a quadriplegic. There's your multimillion-dollar verdict. Simple. And appropriate. I wish to hell the case were mine."

Brenda looks insulted. "But it's all a *guess.* It's hocus-pocus. It's—"

"It's not Donahue's fault no one can know for certain what he'll earn over the next twenty years. He just took a plane ride. Why should the airline take advantage of its misconduct by claiming this kind of projection is too speculative for a jury to consider? What should we do, say he gets nothing?"

"That's *exactly* what you should say, since that's exactly what she deserves."

Hawthorne grins. "I thought we were talking about the husband."

"Sounds to me like we're talking about the goddamn lottery. Jack Donahue isn't worth a million dollars to his *mother.*"

Hawthorne smiles. "Maybe he won't get that much. When it's his turn, Hawley Chambers will say Donahue wasn't a good businessman, the resort thing is pie-in-the-sky, the boom is over and real estate won't appreciate at anything like fifteen percent in the future, and that Donahue's share of commissions would inevitably decline because the increased population will bring an increased number of realtors into the area, which means more competition. Then he'll attack the numbers—that the CPI inflation rate is too high, since inflation for the past few years has been more like three percent; that the discount rate should be more like eight percent, which is what triple A bonds with a twenty-year maturity are bringing. Fighting over the numbers can reduce the bottom line to less than half of what Tollison's asking for."

Brenda swears. "You guys are practicing law with crystal balls. What it comes down to is how much the jury likes little Laura. Right?"

Hawthorne waits for the vituperation to fade. "You hate her, don't you?"

"Who I hate is none of your business," Brenda growls. "I just don't like to see people get away with murder."

"The *airline* is the one trying to get away with murder, Ms. Farnsworth."

In the silence, she wars with what she has just heard. Hawthorne watches her, hesitates, then speaks casually. "I keep an apartment near here—for clients from out of town and for when I get too drunk to drive the bridge. I keep some nice wines up there. And I could scrounge up something for lunch. Want to join me?"

Her smile is more knowing than he is prepared for. "And I'm the dessert. Right, counselor?"

He remains impassive.

She waits long enough for him to color. "I don't think so, thanks all the same. I'm not hanging on to Keith by much, but I'm still hanging on. Maybe if I lose my grip, I'll take you up on it." She blinks. "Lunch, I mean."

He bows to her decision. "If you're insulted, I apologize."

"When I'm insulted, you'll know about it."

He nods briskly, and they both stand up. They are walking to the door when she stops. "What if this Chambers guy shows the Donahue marriage was a joke, that they were both adulterers and were about to get a divorce? Laura wouldn't get anything, would she?"

"With the lost earnings, it doesn't matter. That kind of evidence isn't admissible in court."

"You're kidding."

He shakes his head. "Judges don't want defendants concocting seamy testimony that suggests the surviving spouse couldn't count on being supported for much longer even had the husband not been hurt. The court won't assume a couple will eventually divorce—if they were married when the plane went down, they're considered married for life. Even if she divorces him and remarries before the trial, the result's the same—the jury never gets told."

"That's asinine."

"That's smart. Otherwise, every personal-injury case would turn into a divorce action. But with loss of consortium it might be a different matter. If the defense can show she was about to leave her husband or that she had a lover, that might be admissible to show her claim of lost comfort and companionship was bogus. But the law's not entirely clear, and a smear-the-victim defense could backfire if the jury sympathized with the wife anyway. On the other hand, if the defense *is* allowed to present that kind of evidence, it could color the way the jury looks at the other claims, and the wife could end up with zip."

He tries and fails to assess the machinations that roil behind Brenda

Farnsworth's eyes. "Okay," she says abruptly, as though her suspicions are confirmed. "What if someone stands up in court and says Jack was nothing but a hustler, that his resort idea was a joke, that he was basically a shiftless bum?"

"Then it depends on who the jury believes." Hawthorne opens the office door and waits for her to exit. "And let me tell you something that's true, Ms. Farnsworth. Who the jury believes depends on who has the best lawyer in the courtroom. And that, my dear," he proclaims with unfettered conceit, "is almost always me."

"But you're not Laura's lawyer; Keith is."

"That's her problem."

She shakes her head. "Not entirely."

At the corners of her eyes, her flesh crinkles with resolve.

Keith Tollison fumbled for the phone with inebriated imprecision as he struggled to focus on the numbers branded into the face of his alarm clock. Three-fifteen. God. It *felt* like three-fifteen, which meant it felt like a riot in the basement of hell.

Why was he so . . . The *bar* meeting. The monthly cocktail of bluff and bluster, lawyers overindulging with their peers, a roomful of reeling drunks.

Propping himself against a pillow, Tollison picked up the receiver, dropped it, picked it up again, listened, and reversed it, while his skull shrank inexorably around his brain. ". . . Hello?"

"Keith?"

"Um-hummm. Who's this?"

"Brenda."

"Brenda. Uh . . . just a minute, let me get a light on. Jesus. Is it really three o'clock?"

"I need help, Keith. I didn't know what else to do."

As best he could, Tollison massaged a throbbing temple. "What's happened?"

Her voice was flat with fear. "It's Spitter. He's been arrested."

"What for?"

"Disturbing the peace. Resisting arrest. Everything short of murder, it sounded like."

"Who called you?"

"A man named Yancey. I think he's a policeman."

"He's the night-shift sergeant at the county jail. Is he the one Spitter assaulted?"

"I don't know. Why?"

"Abe Yancey weighs three hundred pounds. If Spitter took a swing at Abe, he'll be lucky if he's compos in a month."

"They wouldn't—"

"They would if he gave them half a reason to. Is Spitter in jail or in the hospital?"

"Jail. I . . . can you get him out of there, Keith? Please?"

He sought therapy in a breath of air. "I'll check it out, Bren. Don't worry."

"Thanks." The word lingered long enough for him to know she meant it. "Call me when I can pick him up, okay?"

"There may not be much I can do till morning. A judge will have to set bail, and both of them were at a bar meeting tonight, so they're probably making sure no one can reach them till noon. I'll do my best to spring him, Bren; that's all I can say. How much bond could you post?"

"How much is it likely to be?"

"Ten percent of the bail, which could go as high as fifty thousand. Judges tend to come down hard on people taking a swing at a cop, under the theory that if they don't protect the cops, the cops won't protect them. Courtrooms are scary places these days."

"I think I could come up with five thousand."

"Okay. I'd put up some myself if I had it, but I'm tapped out at the moment. Where's Spitter living? With you?"

"He's got a room on Jackson. Above the carpet store."

"He have a job?"

"No."

"How's he eat?"

"He . . . I gave him some of Carol's things left over from the sale—some appliances, her car. He fixed them up and sold them." She paused. "And sometimes he steals from me."

The phrase shimmered with helplessness. Tollison felt a surge of sympathy reminiscent of the days before his sympathies had strayed to Laura Donahue. "You can't let him get away with that, Brenda. If he steals from you, he'll start stealing elsewhere."

"I know, but he's so . . ." The label remained imprisoned in her throat. "Just get him out. Please? We'll figure out what to do about him later."

"I will if I can," he promised. "How's your case going?" he asked idly as he reached for the slacks draped over the chair beside his bed.

Brenda paused. "Fine, I guess. There's a hearing next month, I think. A settlement conference?"

"Right."

"I'm hoping that will lead to something that will make things easier. I've heard about a school in Davis that has had success with kids who ... with kids like Spitter. But it's expensive, so—" The sentence vanished in an unexpressed contingency.

"How'd your deposition go?"

"Alec said I did fine, but I don't think I did. A man named Chambers kept laughing at things that weren't funny. I could have slapped him. In fact I *tried* to slap him."

Despite the racket inside his head, Tollison grinned at the vision of Brenda Farnsworth lunging for her adversary's throat across a ring of lawyers. "Good for you."

"How about Laura? How's Jack doing?"

He listened for bile but heard only a weary inquiry. "He's getting better, I guess. But Laura's having to sell off assets to pay for nursing help and rehabilitation therapy. And she's doing too much herself. If she keeps it up, she's going to fall apart." He hesitated. "She could use someone to talk to, Bren. She's not a bad person, you know."

"I suppose not," she said softly. "I suppose you wouldn't love her if she were."

"I—"

"You don't have to explain anything; I know what's been going on, and I know there's not much I can do to stop it. But I also know I'll always be here if you want me, Keith. I'm not proud of it, especially, but I know myself well enough to know it's true."

"You shouldn't count on me, Brenda. Not that way."

Her laugh was heavy with resignation. "That's life, right? If it was a piece of cake we'd all have a weight problem. I should never have ..."

"Never should have what?"

"Who knows? If I hadn't made the mistakes I made, I'd have made some other ones. And maybe the new batch would have been worse." After a moment she again waxed firm. "Help my son, Keith. Call me after you talk to him."

It took him ten minutes to reach the jail. Inside the squat block building the fluorescent atmosphere was the color of cheap chablis, as diluted and depressing as the men who lounged beyond the scrim of a white wire cage. Tollison walked to the desk and rang the bell.

Moments later, a uniform emerged from behind a curtain. Though it was the size of a hot-air balloon, it was still too tiny to fit the man who wore it. "Howdy, Keith," the giant said jovially. "Thought you might show up tonight."

"Hi, Abe. I need to see the Farnsworth boy."

"Sure. Got him down in intake. Be just a minute."

"Many customers tonight?"

The jailer smiled. "A couple of the regulars. Plus one of your esteemed colleagues."

"Who?"

"Joseph Dungan, Esquire. Seems he was driving drunk this evening. Allegedly, of course."

"Every lawyer in town was driving drunk this evening," Tollison murmured.

"Well, Joe was the only one to do it in front of a squad car. Got him for driving backwards down Battery Street. Claimed he was looking for a hubcap, which seemed strange since his vehicle had four already."

"I'll post his bail if it's the usual, Abe."

"Maybe you best let him stay. Last time someone took Joe home before he sobered up, his wife beat him half to death with a skillet while he was still sleeping it off."

Tollison shrugged and nodded. "Anyone been able to raise a judge tonight?"

Abe shook his head. "A couple have tried, too."

"What's the boy charged with?"

Yancey consulted a clipboard and repeated the list Brenda uttered on the phone. "Trying to move him out of the graveyard was all it amounted to. Guess he didn't want to go."

Tollison nodded. "I'll try to raise Judge Bloomfield. After that, I want to see the boy."

The jailer disappeared behind a curtain. Tollison went to the phone on the wall and called the judge's number. After it rang a dozen times, he tried Altoona's only other judge but got the same result. As he hung up, Abe Yancey emerged from behind the door at the far end of the reception area.

"I put the kid in Interrogation Two. Now, that cut on his head, he already had that when he come in here, Keith, so don't be thinking I took a whack at him."

"Who made the collar?"

"Olson."

"How'd Olson look?"

"Okay."

"You know what I mean, Abe."

"Like I said; Olson looked okay."

Yancey opened the door and let Tollison precede him down the narrow hall. Disembodied voices made gruff intrusions into the lengthy box of space, but they were ballads of longing rather than protests of confinement. When they reached room 2, Yancey unlocked the door.

Spitter sat in the center of the overlighted space, head lowered onto arms that were crossed atop a metal desk. A tail of hair dangled against his neck, revealing a silver earring. His field jacket bore the smears of long neglect.

Tollison sat in the only other chair and scooted it closer to the desk. "Spitter? It's me, Keith Tollison. Your mom asked me to come see you."

Spitter made no move.

"So how're you doing? Are you hurt?"

The grunt was more epithet than answer.

"What happened, Spitter? Why were you busted?"

Spitter raised his head. Squinting at the light, his eyes were wholly black, as though the milky sclerotic had drained dry. A cheek was dark and swelling, a lip had puffed to twice its size, his forehead was laced with webs of blood. The T-shirt beneath his jacket formed a dingy backdrop to the words HEAD CASE.

"How are you?" Tollison said again, this time to the boy-man's slack regard.

"Fuck you."

"Your mother's worried about you, Spitter."

"Fuck *her*."

"If you're hurt, I want to make them take you to the hospital. Did you lose consciousness? Are you dizzy? Headache? Anything like that?"

"Get *out* of here, why don't you?"

"I'd like to get *you* out of here, Spitter, but I can't do that till I get hold of a judge and I can't do that till morning, so you'll have to spend the night. I'll ask them to put you in an empty, but I don't know if they have any."

"I don't need no favors."

As he examined the boy, Tollison felt a burgeoning need to help him, to compensate for the pain he had so casually inflicted on his mother.

217

"If you spend the night in the tank, I want you to be careful," Tollison said easily. "Don't make trouble; don't say anything that will make anyone mad. If someone tries to hurt you or get you to do something you don't want to do, call for the guard. His name is Abe. He's okay, even if he is a cop. Call him, and he'll come."

Spitter sang the anthem of adolescence: "Why can't you just leave me alone?"

Tollison put a hand on Spitter's shoulder, but it was quickly shrugged off. "Did you hit the cop or did he hit you first?"

"I didn't hit *no* one. They been after me since she died, and now they got me. They're going to kill me, wait and see. They're going to beat me till they kill me. What they don't know is, I don't give a shit if I die or not."

The fervor of the declaration was chilling. "Why do they want to kill you?" Tollison asked softly.

In a twist of emotion, Spitter seemed about to cry. "Because I wouldn't do what they want."

"What did they want you to do?"

"Tell them about Aunt Carol."

"What did they want to know about her?"

"Everything."

"Who's *them*, Spitter? Who wants you to talk about Carol? The police?"

He shook his head.

"If you tell me who they are, maybe I can help you. Maybe I can get them to stop."

Spitter blinked. "The man."

"What man?"

Frowning, Spitter called upon his only area of expertise. "The one in the Taurus with the CB unit."

Remembering the encounter on the road to Laura's, Tollison asked, "A curly-haired man with a beard? A gray car?"

Spitter's nod was vigorous. "He came to the graveyard and asked me about Aunt Carol. Over and over."

"What did he want you to say?"

Suddenly flustered, Spitter looked away.

"Tell me, Spitter. I need to know."

The recollection was clearly agony. "He wanted to know if we did it."

"Did what?"

"You know. *It.* He claimed me and Carol used to sneak off all the time together. He offered to pay me a hundred dollars to sign a paper that said so." Spitter shook his head so violently Tollison was afraid he would hurt himself. "I *hate* that guy. I hope he dies and they bury him without his head and nobody guards his grave."

Tollison suppressed an urge to embrace the boy. "I'll try to get him to stop bothering you. Okay?"

Spitter wiped his nose on his sleeve, then nodded.

"Good. I have to leave now, Spitter, but I'll be back in the morning. I'll get you out of here and take you home."

"I don't want to go home."

"Where do you want to go?"

"The graveyard."

"Why there?"

"She talks to me out there."

"What about?"

"Things."

"What things?"

"What it looks like where she is."

"Where is she?"

Spitter blinked again. "In Heaven Above. Don't you know *that* much, Mr. Tollison? I thought you were her friend."

"When you get out of here, I want you to see someone," Tollison said finally.

"Who? A doctor?"

His tone made the profession seem despicable. "A woman named Laura. She was Aunt Carol's friend, and she needs help because her husband was hurt in the crash that killed Aunt Carol. If you like her, maybe you could help her around the house, clean up the yard, maybe even help take care of her husband. What do you think?"

Spitter frowned. "I don't know. I got things to do."

"She's got a car you could work on."

"What kind?"

"Mercedes."

"Yeah? What year?"

"'Seventy-nine, I think."

"You think she'd let me drive it?"

"Probably, if you can get it fixed."

"What's wrong with it?"

"Why don't I take you out to see her, and you can decide if you want to help while you check the car out, too?"

Spitter nodded reluctantly, then lowered his head to the desk and began to breathe in sleepy sighs. Tollison patted him on the back, then went to the door and pressed the buzzer and waited to be let out.

Five minutes later he was driving aimlessly, winding through the back streets of the sleeping town, climbing into the wooded hills, his thoughts a stew of past and present as he looked for a place from which to watch the sunrise. As dawn threatened to inflict him with another day, he realized the Donahue house was one road over from the one he traveled.

After a left and a right, he cruised slowly past the lane. Surprisingly, the lights were on, golden rectangles that easily outstripped the pink spilling over the hill behind him. Too tired to think, Tollison turned into the drive and, regardless of hour and etiquette, went to the door and rang the bell.

Sooner than it should have, the door opened. "Keith. What on earth are you doing here at this hour?"

"I was in the neighborhood so I thought I'd stop by."

"You must be joking."

He leaned against the door frame. "Actually, I'm not. I don't suppose you have any coffee on the stove."

"I don't, but I can make some."

"Were you awake or did I wake you?"

"Awake."

"Why?"

"Why not?" Laura Donahue countered, the question hinting of equal exhaustion and a mild hysteria.

He followed her to the living room and waited in front of the emerging view while she disappeared into the kitchen. When she joined him in the light of the new day, her face was smudged and blurred, its outlines rearranged as though she had labored to erase whatever messages it contained.

When she felt his glance, an apology edged through her lagging smile. "If I'd known you were coming I'd have done something about ... this."

Her gesture encompassed every inch of her, from the paint-spattered Levi's to the sweatshirt from Sonoma State to the battered shell around her soul.

"What are you doing up at this hour?" he asked again.

"Things."

"Like what?"

She shrugged. "Reading. Thinking. Crying," she added after an awkward pause.

"Crying over what?"

"Jack. You. Life." She exhaled a distant whistle. "Sometimes there just seems to be a lot to cry about."

Her reached for her hand. "Has he gotten worse?"

Her smile was crooked. "I'm afraid not. But then you wouldn't know, would you?"

He reddened. "I'm sorry I haven't been out to see him, but I just couldn't . . ."

"Couldn't what?"

He looked at the treetops rising through the morning mist and tried to tell the truth. "I've hated Jack for forty years—once I was so mad at him I tried to shoot him with my BB gun. And now he's my client, so I have to stop. But I was afraid if I came out here and saw you nursing him back to health, I wouldn't be able to. Watching you at the hospital that day, hearing what you said and the way you said it, almost drove me crazy."

"I suppose I understand. And I suppose you don't have to see him if you don't want to." Her words curled. "You can just send a video crew, the way you did last month."

"You know that's for the lawsuit."

"But *video*? My God. It was so . . . mercenary."

"It's been proved time and time again that visual aids are indispensable in showing the consequences of disability," he intoned officiously, then went to her side and took her hand. "It wasn't so bad, was it? I told them just to film a typical day in your lives. Nothing cute, nothing phony. It's why I didn't come along, so Chambers couldn't say I staged it." He paused. "They have to come back, you know."

"Why?"

"Because you didn't let them film everything."

"I don't have to."

"Yes you do." As she pulled away from him, his temper echoed through the house. "Don't *fight* me on this, goddamnit. You got me into the case, now let me do what has to be done to *win* it. I'm going to send them out again, and this time I want every nasty bit of your life *on that tape*."

It was long seconds before she could bring herself to speak. "Maybe by the time the trial starts he'll be back to normal and the freak show won't be necessary."

He closed his eyes. "My job is tough enough without you implying there's something perverted about it."

"I beg your pardon. I thought *Jack* was the one who had it tough." She crossed her arms in clear disdain. "Since you're not making another horror film, how come you're here?"

He was beside her with a step, embracing her gingerly at first, then roughly, his apologies muffled by her soft shoulder. When at long last he paused to give her a chance to stop him, her arms locked at the base of his spine. Her tongue probed lips, parted teeth, entered a grateful mouth; his hand slid like a serpent around her ribs, advancing on her breast.

When she sensed his purpose, she pulled away. "I can't."

"Then why did you—"

She shivered. "I don't know. Maybe because it reminded me that there was something to live for outside these walls. But I shouldn't have teased you like that. I'm sorry." Tears returned, then flowed toward a plucky grin. "You're not the only one who's frustrated, you know. I can't do what I want, either."

"What *do* you want, Laura?"

She feigned an awkward gaiety. "For Christmas, you mean? I want all kinds of things. A new dishwasher, a new bra; mostly, a new husband." Her laugh was manic. "But Jack is like the Mercedes—I can't get rid of him until I fix him up."

Shamed by the brief burlesque, she turned toward the window that looked onto her husband's lapsed ambitions. "I want to feel *normal* again, Keith. I want things back the way they were. Sins and all."

He couldn't suppress a glance toward the bedroom in the rear. "What we did wasn't sin, Laura."

"Not then, maybe," she murmured. "But it would be now."

He tried to make himself dispute her, but his only response was a digression: "I need to use your phone."

Her eyes widened. "Who will be awake at this hour?"

"Every client I've ever had."

He went to the kitchen and dialed the number. Brenda answered after the second ring. "I've seen Spitter," he said.

"How is he? Is he hurt?"

"He got beat around a little, but nothing serious."

"The bastards. Can I go get him?"

"Not till ten or so. I couldn't get hold of a judge, so I'll have to make bail at the arraignment. But he'll be all right. The jailer's watching out for him."

"Did you talk to him, Keith? How did he get in trouble?"

"The cops rousted him from the cemetery. But what's messing up his mind is that insurance investigator who's been prowling around town since the crash. He's been grilling Spitter about Carol. He seems to be trying to get Spitter to admit there was something sexual between them."

"You must be kidding."

"You'd better warn Alec about this, Brenda. If they're suborning Spitter, God knows what else they're up to. At least Alec's got plenty of time to counter whatever lie they're trying to establish."

"There's not *that* much time; Alec says we could go to trial in March."

Tollison labored to persuade himself that the forecast must be false.

"Thanks for helping, Keith," Brenda was saying. "I know you don't have any reason to do me favors these days."

"Anytime."

"I do try to do right by him, you know. It's just, I don't always know what right is. I was jealous of Carol for a long time, angry and hurt that Spitter liked her better than he liked me. Now I just wish she was here to give him whatever it is he needs." She sighed. "Where are you, by the way? At the office?"

"Home."

"No you're not, I just called there. . . . You're with *her*, aren't you? Jesus, don't you ever get *enough*? I'll bet you didn't see Spitter at all. I'll bet he's rotting away in that goddamn *jail* because you couldn't keep your hands off her long enough to get him *out*."

"No. I was just down there, Brenda. I—"

"You'll regret this, you bastard. You can do what you want to *me*, but to leave Spitter in that hellhole while you . . . well, you're going to wish you hadn't. *Believe* me. You and that bitch will wish this day had never *happened*."

Before he could object again, Brenda hung up.

Her tirade still ringing in his ear, Tollison trudged back to the living room. "Who was that?" Laura asked.

He told her.

"How is she?"

He shrugged. "Mad at me."

"I'm sorry."

He looked at her.

Discomfited by his distress, Laura switched subjects. "Brenda hired Hawthorne, didn't she?"

He nodded. "It would be wise if you'd follow her example."

"We've been all through that, Keith."

"What if I lose, Laura? What if you come out of the lawsuit without a dime?"

For the first time that morning, he sensed some purpose in her. "I can *deal* with it, Keith. I told you that before. Why are you going back on your promise to help me?"

"There's quite a large conflict of interest here, for one reason. If I lose, people will say I went in the tank deliberately, so Jack would have to be institutionalized and you'd be free to ride off into the setting sun with me."

"You don't lose other cases, so why would you lose this one? Besides, Mr. Hawthorne's going to help you, isn't he?"

"So he says. But talk is cheap with lawyers, especially with lawyers who are supposed to be your friends."

Her eyes were falsely bright. "Well, the way I see it, I've got two lawyers instead of one. So I don't want to hear about this anymore. Let me get you some coffee. Then we'll go see Jack. If you want to."

"Sure," he lied.

Moments later she was waiting at the head of the hallway, extending a grin and a cup. "Shall we?"

He accepted both the coffee and her silent toast.

"He's really not that bad," she said after a sip. "You get used to the situation quite quickly."

After a second sip of coffee, she started down the hall, giving him no alternative but to follow. At the bedroom door she took his hand. "Ready?"

"Is he . . . can he understand what I say?"

"It's hard to tell what he grasps and doesn't grasp. He's not glib, but he makes sense sometimes, at least to me. They're working him like crazy now—cognitive rehabilitation, they call it."

"So he's getting better."

She frowned. "In a sense. But he's a stranger, Keith. If I'm going to help him, I have to find out who he is." She refused to meet his eye.

"You think he won't make it without you, don't you?"

"In the beginning I did, but I'm not sure I do anymore. I'm not sure I'm up to the job."

"Of course you are. If you want to be."

She sighed. "After a while I started assuming Jack would never change, would never be anything more than what he was right after the crash. A 'persistent vegetative state,' they called it. I got used to the life I led while he was in the hospital—the solitude, the freedom, the simplicity. Now that he's conscious, I'm not sure I know what to do. That sounds funny, doesn't it?"

He gave her a quick hug. "You'll be fine."

"But what if I'm not? Do you know what a *defeat* that would be for me?"

"I'm beginning to," he said, and was doleful in her silence.

"So how is he physically?" he asked after a moment. "Can he move his legs yet?"

"He's still paralyzed on the right side. And generally unsteady. But most of it's mental. He's . . . strange. He loses track of what he's saying and can't remember much of anything. They say that's normal with brain damage, that memory takes a long time to return, but I don't think they're telling me everything."

"That's probably because they don't know everything."

"True." She hesitated. "Do you mind if he's naked? I've been rubbing him with lotion and—" She reddened. "That was stupid of me, wasn't it? Wait here a minute."

She opened the door and disappeared. Too soon, she was back. Grasping his hand, she towed him toward her husband.

The room was dim—shades pulled, curtains drawn, lights focused toward the ceiling and corners. Tollison took two steps, then freed his hand and stopped. Nothing moved but Laura, who continued to the bed and stood beside it like a shopkeeper next to a bin of bananas, urging him to admire her wares.

Beside the bed were two chairs, one suitable for a lengthy vigil, the other stiff and temporary. He started to sit on the latter, but a glance at Laura stopped him. Leaning over her husband's high-tech pallet, she murmured incantations as though Jack's brain could be healed by conjuring and magic. Watching anything but the body on the bed, Tollison waited for her to stop.

When Tollison coughed at the vapors in the room, Laura turned. "Well," she began, her compassion now extended to encompass him, "what do you think?"

So he had to look, at the man who had unknowingly been his rival for his wife's affections and was now unknowingly his client. His vision caught the details—sunken eyes, foggy pallor, chiseled cheeks, arid lips, stubby beard, skull as bare and faceted as a peeled potato. But bad as it was, the sheet stretched parallel over his legs and torso implied that the worst was out of sight.

A moment later the eyes below him blinked. Convinced the flutter was not a mindless tic, Tollison held his breath and waited. When nothing happened, he glanced at Laura, then did what seemed to be her bidding. "Hi, Jack. Uh . . . how's it going?"

"He's doing well today," Laura interjected into the void beyond his question.

"Great."

"He's had a nice nap."

"Good."

"And he's watched some television. A show about fishing. Jack loves to fish."

"I know. I went with him once. Up at Lake Berryessa. We caught some nice bass, didn't we, Jack?"

From within the mire of illness, Jack Donahue's eyes might have belonged to the species just evoked. When they closed once again, this time to provide a rest, Tollison backed away from the bed and waited for Laura to join him. "Do they say he'll recover fully?" he whispered.

"No."

"Do they say he'll get worse?"

"They say I should be ready for anything."

He glanced at the bed again. Jack's eyes were open, his head conceivably inclined his way. Tollison took a further step beyond his range. "How long do you stay with him every day?"

"My shift is eight hours. Right now, it's two till ten." She smiled. "A.M."

"Are you sure he wouldn't be better off in a hospital?"

She shook her head. "The hospital wasn't doing anything but waiting for something to happen, so I insisted they discharge him. I had this huge fight with Dr. Ryan—he refused to consider it until I told him I'd been an LPN. That made him agree to release him, but only after they drew up a chronic-care program for me to administer." She thrust her chest like a soldier. "So that's what I'm doing. I've become quite expert on the latest techniques."

"Who's helping you?"

She frowned. "*That's* been an experience, let me tell you. The first nurse I interviewed took one look at Jack and informed me that if I just let him lie there—didn't turn him or anything—he'd drown in his own fluids and that would be best for all of us."

"Can't the Altoona hospital find you good people?"

"Oh, they have. I've got a nice team now. We rotate shifts. I have the graveyard this week." She gestured toward the corner of the room.

A lumpy rectangle spread across the floor beneath the window, a narrow mattress covered with a thermal blanket and an uncased pillow, evocative of jails and monasteries.

She heard his question before he asked it. "I want to do it, Keith. I *need* to do it." Her smile bore vague traces of the enthusiasm she had previously bestowed on him. "My normal life wasn't all that fulfilling, as you may remember. I think the first thing I ever said to you was, 'God, I'm sick of cleaning this swimming pool.' Well, now I'm Florence Nightingale." Her face was sweet and sour. "It's a much better job than being his wife."

He reached for her hand, but she avoided his grasp.

"At least I have something to do." She glanced at her husband. "It's a lot like tending a victory garden, I imagine." She reddened. "Isn't that terrible? I've learned why battlefields and emergency rooms are such fertile grounds for humor."

When he looked away from her, he noticed that the walls were laden with pictures of Jack—Jack with local celebrities and Little League teams, Jack beside the entrance to his subdivision, Jack in uniform with a softball team. Beneath the pictures was a row of pegs. On them hung a sportcoat, golf bag, fishing creel, and what looked like lingerie. He looked at Laura and raised a brow.

"Dr. Ryan says the sight of familiar things might help bring back his memory," she said. "I play tapes, too; his favorite songs—Beatles, Beach Boys, things like that. Right now it's sleep music."

"What's with the lingerie?"

She blinked. "It's what I wore the first time we made love."

He could not resist. "If you want to *really* shock him out of it, why don't you put *my* picture up there?"

Laura was transfixed by his outburst. Tollison gestured with detachment. "The video people should get another shot of all this."

"Why?"

He shrugged. "Better safe than sorry."

"I'm afraid the best I can do these days is be safe *and* sorry."

They drifted to a hush.

"Lau . . . ra?"

The call came from beyond, an ancient urge rising from the speaker's core. "Lau . . . ra?" Jack Donahue repeated, his voice a drunken drawl.

She hurried to his side. Tollison followed until he was looking down on a figure who, if not precisely the person he'd known nine months before, was once again a man. Laura began massaging her husband's chest, rubbing him with oil, murmuring soft assurances, regressed to a level of healing and hospice where the rules were prehistoric and obscure.

The eyes suddenly rolled his way. "Whooo . . . yooo?"

The voice was raw and anxious, but the eyes stayed with Tollison until he squirmed. "I'm Keith, Jack. Keith Tollison. The lawyer. Remember?"

"I . . . Keeeith."

"How are you, Jack? It's great to see you getting better."

"Whaaat . . . done . . . meeee . . . Keeeeith?"

Uncertain whether the brooding inquiry addressed Jack's marriage or his flesh, Tollison stood frozen in confusion. When he glanced at Laura, he thought she urged him to respond.

"You were in an accident, Jack. A plane crash. You were injured very badly."

There was nothing resembling comprehension in the eyes, only a narrowing that reflected the effort it had taken to make those few beseeching words. In the next moment they closed in a languid blink, then looked up through a cellophane of tears. "Helllppp . . . meee . . . Laurrr . . . ra."

Of the hundred possible responses to that pitiable cry, Keith Tollison's was that Jack Donahue's statement of pain and suffering, if documented and preserved and presented to a jury, was worth a million dollars.

The eyes closed once again, and Laura backed away from the bed until she reached the open door. "We need to talk about some things," Tollison said when he joined her.

"What kind of things?"

"How to prove the damages you've suffered."

"You mean if I just *tell* them what happened they won't believe me? I have to draw pictures? I know—let's hire an actress to play my part. Meryl Streep would be wonderful. I'm sure she could live my life *much* more believably than I do."

He persevered. "You can't ignore the lawsuit, Laura, much as you'd like to. *You're* the central part of the case, not Jack—loss of consortium is the strongest claim we have. I've been reviewing Jack's business records, and frankly, he was a disaster as a—"

Her eyes were flint that sparked against his thesis. "I know you think he can't understand," she hissed angrily. "But I'm positive he can. So if you have something *insulting* to say, let's go in the other room."

"It's not insulting, it's just the truth."

"*Please.* I have to finish with the lotion, then I'll join you. Go. Leave. Now."

She shoved him toward the door. When he glanced back, it was to watch her place an apologetic kiss on her husband's clammy forehead and begin to rub his chest.

In a stiff pique, Tollison retreated to the living room and looked out the window to the driveway. Beyond his Cutlass and her Mercedes a line of oleander bushes circled the yard. Beyond them a vehicle was parked at the side of the road—the gray Taurus he'd seen on his last visit, the one Spitter had recalled at the jail.

He watched from the shadows until Laura returned. "So tell me," she said. "How are we going to win our case besides show the home movies?"

He met her look. "You have to dig out your mementos. Go to the closets and the attic or wherever you keep photo albums and things like that and pull out the best stuff."

"I take it the tactic is to prove the crash has made me insane."

He refused to yield. "Make up a folder, a collection of items that describes your life with Jack. Photographs, letters, souvenirs, anything you have around the house that shows how you felt for each other. If he wrote you poems, put them in it. If he sent you flowers, put the cards in it. If you knit him sweaters, put pictures of them in the folder. I want the jury to see how strongly you and Jack cared for each other, how much you miss not ... doing what you used to do together."

"Shall I put in my diaphragm? How about my baby-doll pajamas?"

He closed his eyes against what he had done to her and what, with far more justification, she had just done to him. "This is hard for me too, you know. I don't want to think you *ever* had a decent life with Jack. But you did, and we have to show what it was like."

"What it was like, or what I *wished* it was like?"

Because his answer would demean him, he plunged ahead. "I also want you to start keeping a journal of what you do each day, particularly what you do for Jack. It's very important, Laura. I think Alec is going to try to separate our cases from the rest and get an early trial."

"I'm all for that."

"Then we have to be ready. When the time comes, we have to be ready to go."

She turned toward the window. "Every time I come across that stuff, I keep thinking there should be a child in there someplace. Baby pictures and locks of hair and bronzed booties and the like. I never realized how important all that would seem one day. It hurts that I'll never ..."

That she did not suggest that he could fill the void wounded him more than anything she had ever done. "That's not what hurts *me* the most," he retorted angrily.

"What is?"

"That you keep saying you still love me but doing things that say you don't. That in the process of being his nurse, you're falling in love with Jack all over again."

She joined him in the shadows and reached for his hand and squeezed it to her cheek. A moment later a tear splashed onto a knuckle, then trickled toward his wrist. "We're being watched, you know," he murmured. "That car beyond the bushes is the detective working for Chambers. He's out there digging up dirt."

"Is that what we've become?"

Her question dissolved into a quiet mystery that neither of them could solve. Huddled out of sight of the intruder, his arm draped across her shoulders, her head nestled against his chest, they endured the morning side by side, lives in the lurch, sin under siege.

**Litigation Economists
555 Van Ness Avenue
San Francisco, CA 94103**

January 18, 1988

Keith A. Tollison, Esq.
450 Main Street
Altoona, California 95555

Re: Disability of John C. ("Jack") Donahue

Dear Mr. Tollison:

Enclosed please find our Economic Loss Analysis for the disability suffered by Jack Donahue in the SurfAir crash of March 23, 1987, along with the supporting Background Report, and Business Market and Industry Profile. We have used the market-share approach for valuing lost future profits. This method yields results which appear to us to be reasonable for Mr. Donahue's real estate sales and development enterprises.

We will be pleased to discuss our findings in greater depth should you so desire.

Very truly yours,

William T. Daters, Financial Analyst

Arthur W. Ely, President

SUMMARY

This report assesses the economic loss to the Donahue family resulting from Mr. Donahue's total physical disability. Analysis is based on federal tax returns, financial statements from Mr. Donahue's former business, market research obtained from banks and from the County Board of Realtors, and interviews with Mr. Donahue's business associates and spouse. For additional background information, the reader should refer to our accompanying report: "Business Market and Industry Profile."

We find the present cash value of the net economic loss to be in a range from $210,000 to $1,055,000. The lower figure results from a detailed analysis of the case using conservative assumptions. The higher figure results from a more simplified approach, which relaxes our more stringent assumptions.

Our model is a market-share approach. Damages are measured by the share of total market sales Mr. Donahue could have been expected to have attained had he not become disabled. The basic equation of this model is: Average Value of New Single-Family Residence in Altoona County multiplied by Average Market Share equals Predicted Sales. Predicted Sales is then multiplied by Mr. Donahue's Average Return to Sales Ratio. Return is defined as salaries plus cash distributions plus share of changes in equity. All figures have been adjusted to constant 1986 dollars.

Exhibit 3 calculates the Average Value of New Single-Family Residence in Altoona County for the years 1975 through 1986. This period includes several market cycles.

Exhibit 4 calculates the aggregate market share of the real estate development business operated by Mr. Donahue.

Exhibit 5 Calculates Mr. Donahue's average adjusted return to average adjusted sales ratio.

Exhibit 6 calculates Mr. Donahue's yearly earnings lost as a result of disability. We have assumed that Mr. Donahue's market share will increase over a period of five years and remain constant thereafter. This is based upon our judgment of Mr. Donahue's likely prospects for the future.

Exhibit 7 discounts Mr. Donahue's lost earnings to a present value.

Exhibit 8 breaks out Mr. Donahue's lost earnings into an executive salary and a return from entrepreneurial activity. The executive salary is Mr. Donahue's fair-market salary and is discounted at a rate of 3 percent, which is consistent with wrongful-death cases of an employed decedent. The entrepreneurial return is discounted at a higher rate of 25 percent in order to take into account its greater riskiness.

Exhibit 9 calculates the present cash value of Mr. Donahue's lost earnings from his proposed resort complex—Nirvana West. Because this project was not yet in start-up mode, we have predicted this amount based on assessments of similar projects in the state and on interviews with informed parties.

Simplified Alternative: After considerable research and analysis, we have concluded that Mr. Donahue would have an earning capacity of between $25,000 and $125,000 per year, depending upon assumptions.

In addition to the normal discount rate of 3 percent, because real estate is a risky business we would add another 10 percent. Assuming a remaining 18.375-year work life, the calculation yields a present cash value of between $210,000 and $1,055,000—once again, depending on the assumptions utilized.

It should be pointed out that Mr. Donahue's business experienced rather dramatic fluctuations in profitability over the past few years, making projections of his future income more problematical than those for more stable businesses. This report makes no judgment as to the preferred basis for evaluating Mr. Donahue's circumstances. However, we do note that in the period in question, virtually everyone who entered the real estate market as a broker in this section of Northern California made a significant income from that business.

TEN

As Martha guides the Rolls to the curb, Alec Hawthorne opens the door and steps out. "Put it in the garage, then wait for me in the courtroom," he instructs through the open window.

Martha raises a brow in an unasked question. When he remains silent as to his purpose, she wrests the burgundy chariot back into the stream of traffic, leaving him to complete his scheme.

Hawthorne glances up and down the block, then inspects the entrance to the Federal Building. Seeing no one who might recognize him, he crosses Turk Street and, after a veronica with a streaking cab, pushes through the door to the restaurant on the opposite corner and descends to the dining room in the basement. The dark and mysterious establishment is perfect for what he has in mind.

He waves away the approach of Ernst, the unctuous maître d', who bears a menu the size of a tabloid, and takes a seat at the bar. Using the mirror that runs the length of the room, Hawthorne confirms that his quarry is where he is supposed to be, which is where he is every noon from Monday through Thursday, lunching with his wife.

Raising a hand, Hawthorne hides the side of his face visible to the couple in the rear, the ones flirting with each other as unashamedly as if this were their first date instead of their fifth decade of marriage. After confirming that his presence is unremarked, he orders a brandy, glances at his watch, takes a healthy gulp, glances at his watch again, then eyes the reflection of the man he is waiting for a chance to approach in private.

Five minutes later the target busses his wife on the cheek, stands, tosses two bills on the table, helps his wife to her feet, hands her a coal-black cane, and guides her toward the exit. Along the way he waves to various diners and red-jacketed attendants, nods briskly to the bartender, pats Ernst on the shoulder as he leaves the dining area. At the checkroom in the foyer he helps his wife on with her wrap, then strolls toward the men's room. As the lacquered door swings open, Hawthorne downs his brandy, tosses a bill on the bar, and hurries to join his quarry. As Hawthorne has anticipated, the two of them are alone, and must share adjoining urinals.

"Good afternoon, Judge," Hawthorne says as he begins his business.

Judge Powell dares a sidelong glance. When he recognizes his co-reliever, he smiles. "Alec. Good afternoon. How are you?"

"Fine."

"Ticker back on track again?"

"Right as rain."

"I suppose you're down for the SurfAir business."

"Yep."

The judge hesitates, confirms that they remain alone, then opts for candor. "I was sorry to hear you weren't made lead counsel, Alec. Mr. Scallini is a ... hindrance, I'm afraid. Off the record, of course."

"Of course. I'm sorry I wasn't able to help you out on this one, Your Honor."

"Well, I miss you, I don't mind saying. I don't have any official word on how things are going, but rumor has it the case has bogged down in discovery."

"I'm afraid that may be true."

"Apparently, Mr. Scallini has some outlandish theory of liability that will take years to establish, if one of the more bizarre stories floating around my chambers proves true."

"I've heard something like that as well, I'm afraid," Hawthorne admits, zipping his pants and stepping back, allowing the judge a final shake in private.

When the old man completes one of the many processes that with age becomes unwieldy, he moves to the washbasin. As he wipes his hands on a roll of paper toweling, Hawthorne begins his pitch.

"I've never backdoored you on a case before, Your Honor, but I'm afraid I didn't meet you here by accident."

The judge finds him in the mirror. "No?"

"I wanted to let you know ahead of time that even though I'm not on the plaintiffs' committee, I'm going to make a motion this afternoon."

Powell's brows soar like matching gulls. "You're not withdrawing from the case entirely, are you?" The old man's expression betrays a real concern.

Hawthorne shakes his head. "You may think it odd when you hear it. Out of order, perhaps."

"Oh?" For the first time, the old man's eyes take on a protective slant, as though he suspects something untoward may be occurring.

Hawthorne hastens to disabuse him. "I've never asked a special favor in all the years I've practiced in your court."

The judge nods. "I don't remember any, certainly."

"And I'm not asking for special privilege now. All I'm asking is that you give my motion more careful consideration than you might originally be inclined to."

"Well, I . . ." The judge trails into an uncomfortable silence.

Hawthorne looks away, at the crack in the window that exposes rusting reinforcing wires, at the mildew on the ceiling, at anything but the judge he admires more than any other on the bench. "SurfAir is my last case, Judge Powell."

The old man stops wiping his hands, as though the towel has sprung to life. "What do you mean 'last,' Alec?"

"I mean, after this one I'm retiring."

The judge joins his fingers in a steeple that would pass for prayer. "Surely not. You have *years* ahead of you . . . oh." He colors with embarrassment. "Is it because of your coronary?"

"That. Other things as well. I've just decided I've done enough. And had enough done to me."

The judge nods. "Aviation practice is exhausting, I'm certainly aware of that. And I know that much of your exhaustion has come in helping me get several of my cases processed faster than they probably should have been. Don't think I haven't appreciated it, Alec, because I have. So of course I'll give your motion every possible consideration."

Hawthorne finally meets the old man's kindly eyes. "Thank you, sir. If this conversation is improper in any way, I apologize for it. It was just something I felt I had to do."

Judge Powell pats him on the back and strides briskly toward the door. "What conversation? I'm just here to take a piss. Can I help it if these days it takes me twenty minutes?"

Hawthorne allows time for the judge to leave both the restroom and the restaurant, then does so himself. Without another stop, he returns to the Federal Building, passes the AIDS vigil and the Vietnam veterans and the street people seeking sun, squeezes through the metal detector, and takes the elevator to the eleventh floor.

The hearing is in the largest room in the Federal Building, which is still not large enough to seat all the people interested in the proceedings. These include the regular courtroom denizens—the retired and unemployed who find more drama in these chambers than in those on TV or in the movies—as well as several of the plaintiffs themselves, who need not be in attendance but who want to see what's going on and why things are taking so damn long. And the lawyers, of course, many of the more than one hundred of them already of record in SurfAir, as well as their regular retinue in the form of younger associates and, more commonly these days, paralegal assistants.

Hawthorne surveys the scene from the doorway. He sees Vic Scallini ensconced at the table reserved for the plaintiffs' committee and defense counsel; sees Keith Tollison looking bemused and out of place and vulnerable to the surprise that Hawthorne has in store for him; sees Martha conversing with Dan Griffin in the row of seats behind the counsel table; and sees Ed Haroldson just as Ed sees him. They exchange affable waves, and Hawthorne moves to a seat near the front of the room. His goal is to be close enough to be heard by Judge Powell when the time comes to make his motion, and to avoid conversation until that moment.

The cacophony that surrounds him is particularly shrill this afternoon, because a plane has just crashed near Paso Robles, evidently the consequence of a defect not in the aircraft but in the security system. Vengeance in the skies; fourscore victims. Six lawsuits have already been filed.

Hawthorne closes his eyes. He waits for the noise to blot out both his reservations and his better judgment, but the din is not that potent. He is about to risk his clients' welfare more drastically than ever, is about to put his own needs before theirs for the first time in his career. Although he has persuaded himself that he is doing it for a cause that has beneficiaries far in excess of the dozen he represents in the case, he is uneasy with the rationale—when he has indulged in similar justifications in the past, he has invariably regretted it.

Five minutes later, Judge Powell strides onto the stage, accompanied by two law clerks and the clerk of the court. As the four take their seats, the clamor subsides and the crowd scrambles for its places. Because of its size, five minutes later it is still scrambling.

Judge Powell bangs his gavel. Silence slowly finds the room. "This hearing has been denominated a status and settlement conference," he begins. "Let me take up the last matter first. Have any of these cases been settled. Any at all?"

Scallini and Chambers rise simultaneously. "They have not, Your Honor," Scallini booms, "except for those instances where the defendants' tactics of threat and intimidation have persuaded a few misguided individuals to believe they would enjoy fair treatment without engaging an attorney to represent them. Five unfortunate families of crash victims have—without benefit of counsel—executed releases, abandoning their right to fair and full compensation in return for the most minuscule of sums. Efforts are under way to set those settlements aside, but the labor may well be unavailing.

"Except for such instances of coercion, Your Honor, I am loath to report that our settlement discussions have been hampered by the unwarranted recalcitrance of the defendants in the face of *massive* evidence of their—"

"Excuse me, Mr. Scallini," Judge Powell interrupts. "I think I would like to hear from Mr. Chambers at this point. You are representing the airline, are you not, Mr. Chambers?"

"I am, Your Honor."

"Have you settled with any of the plaintiffs in the case?"

"No."

"If there is a simple reason for that, perhaps you will enlighten me."

Chambers bows his head. "We have not settled because we believe the demands of the plaintiffs are excessive if not outrageous in their overreaching, given the absence of anything resembling misfeasance on the part of SurfAir or the other defendants."

The judge's sigh is audible in the tenth row. "I take it you are not prepared to confess liability in this matter."

"Not only are we not prepared to confess liability, we are prepared to strenuously resist its imposition. This was an accident in every sense of the word, Your Honor. No one is at fault. Nothing was defective. Ergo, no one should have to pay."

"There are more than a hundred families and loved ones who *are* paying, Your Honor," Vic Scallini intones, "paying for this tragedy every day of their lives in pain and in sorrow and in the involuntary penury imposed on them by the defendants, who writhe and wriggle like vipers to escape their responsibility to those who trusted SurfAir to transport them without incident from the great city in the south to the great city in which we meet today. The conduct of the defense in the face of this avalanche of human misery is intolerable, and as I have for forty years, I pledge to do my *utmost* to—"

The judge waves for silence and adopts a weary smile. He has seen and heard it all before, seen and heard enough. He looks at Hawley Chambers. "You have served a cross claim in this matter, have you not, Mr. Chambers? A suit by SurfAir against both Hastings and the government for contribution and for loss of the aircraft? That indicates that SurfAir believes fault was involved, does it not?"

Chambers bows his head. "The claim is on file, Your Honor. For strategic reasons."

"Well, I am going to separate those matters from the passenger cases in any event, so we need not get bogged down in such questions now. What I want to do is what I always do in these cases, which is to get relief to the victims as quickly and as economically as possible. Your vociferous denial of liability suggests my wish for an early solution may go abegging. However, I am an optimist. Mr. Scallini, as chairman of the plaintiffs' committee, I assume you dispute Mr. Chambers's statement."

Scallini grasps his lapels and swells his chest. "I most certainly do, Your Honor. I not only *dispute* it, in a very short period of time I will be prepared to lay it waste."

"Which leads us to the next point. What is the status of discovery? How close are we to trial?"

"Close, Your Honor. In spite of the determined, not to say maniacal, resistance of the defendants—including the federal government, to its eternal shame, I might note—I am proud to say that definite lines of liability are developing. We are hampered, of course, by the continued lack of a National Transportation Safety Board report in the case."

"When is the report due? Does anyone know?"

A portly gentleman rises from the end of the counsel table. "Bert Askwith, Your Honor. FAA staff attorney. The report will appear within three months. One series of hearings remains to be completed, after which the report will be prepared and published in due course."

"Is there some difficulty that was unexpected?"

"Well, Your Honor, as you know, usually in these matters the problem is obvious. However, in this instance the proximate cause was not readily apparent. We naturally do not want to suggest blame where none properly attaches, so as always, we are proceeding with care and with thoroughness."

The judge nods. "Of course. Mr. Scallini, what is the precise status of your discovery?"

"We have completed the first wave of liability discovery in the form of depositions, Your Honor. They have revealed *fascinating* threads.

As fascinating as they are deplorable. It appears likely that the wing and tail assemblies of the H-11, which were manufactured by Air Technologies of Japan, were designed so that in the event of an attempted recovery from a stall condition, the aircraft would become unresponsive to both elevator and aileron controls due to matters of lift interruption and air-wash diversion. Upon closer examination of this phenomenon, I feel certain that—"

"How much *longer*, Mr. Scallini?" the judge interrupts again, this time with zest. "That is what we are concerned with here."

"Six months, Your Honor. At most."

Several chuckles can be heard. Everyone in the room knows the schedule Vic has in mind will take two years to complete. So far, Vic's "first wave" has barely scratched the surface of the evidence. The deposition of the traffic controllers alone took four weeks by the time each member of plaintiffs' committee got his shot and the schedules of the defense lawyers were accommodated. Which threw the rest of the schedule out of whack, which meant—

As the judge prods Vic for more specific information, Hawthorne loses the thread of the debate and closes his eyes. Vaguely, he senses more heated argument, demands emanating from the bench and denials following from the table below. When he tunes back in, the judge is saying, "I won't have this matter drag on for two more years, Mr. Scallini. If you can't get it to trial before then, I'll remove you as chief counsel and appoint someone who can."

"We'd be ready for trial *now* if the defense had shown any degree of—"

Judge Powell bangs a fist on the table. "I'm through with charge and countercharge, gentlemen. As far as I'm concerned, it's the fault of everyone in this room that this matter isn't farther along. At the next sign of delay, I'm going to impose monetary sanctions on the attorneys responsible. Those of you who have been in my court before know that I mean what I say. Now. Is there any further business?"

Hawthorne waits for two minor matters to be discussed, then rises to his feet. The judge finally catches his eye and smiles. "Yes, Mr. Hawthorne?"

"Your Honor, I am counsel for plaintiff in twelve death cases, collectively known as Warren versus SurfAir. All were originally filed here in the Northern District and all involve California plaintiffs. The applicability of California law in these cases is, I believe, indisputable." He hesitates, and finds solace in his objectives one last time.

"Yes, Mr. Hawthorne?" Judge Powell prods.

"Your Honor, at this time I move that those cases—plus the case of Donahue versus SurfAir, a single survivor action in which the plaintiff is represented by Keith Tollison, Esquire, of Altoona, California, who is present this afternoon—I move that those thirteen matters be set for trial no later than one month from today."

Vic Scallini leaps to his feet, only to be shoved aside by Hawley Chambers. "Your *Honor*," Chambers explodes. "This is entirely outside the guidelines of multidistrict proceedings. Mr. Hawthorne apparently intends to go forward on his own, duplicating the discovery of the rest of the plaintiffs, making the defense endure needless repetition of a host of procedures, causing untold delay and expense that will—"

"Our discovery is *complete*, Your Honor," Hawthorne interrupts loudly. "And the same should be true for the defense, since the depositions of the named plaintiffs have been taken to the extent that notice has been filed. We're ready for trial. I'm prepared to file plaintiffs' proposed pretrial statement on liability issues and a list of proposed witnesses and to issue subpoenas to various agents and employees of the defendants who are in the room today. Further delay is unconscionable. My clients have suffered enough."

Chambers is fumbling through a stack of pleadings as thick as a brick. "Mr. Hawthorne's complaint contains some *eighteen* causes of action, Your Honor," he pleads, his voice catching on the final word, making the sound of a startled goose. "Are we to conclude that he intends to proceed with them *all*? There has been *no* narrowing of the issues in this case, no theory of liability offered by Mr. Hawthorne, no . . . *nothing*. This grandstand play is unexpected from a man of Mr. Hawthorne's reputation."

Hawthorne's smile is his most avuncular. "I can take care of Mr. Chambers's problem right now."

The judge hides a smile behind his palm. "How is that, Mr. Hawthorne?"

He crosses his arms, determined to appear more confident than he feels. "If this case is set for trial within the next two months, my clients agree to dismiss with prejudice all claims against the defendants except for the fourth and twelfth causes of action set forth in their respective complaints."

"Four and twelve?" Chambers intones as he pages madly through his file. "What the hell are? . . . Here. Why that's . . . crashworthy? You're going to trial on *crashworthiness*? Good God, man. No one's ever won a crashworthy case in the history of commercial aviation. No one's seriously argued that a modern airliner is not fit for—"

"Maybe it's time they did." The judge's paternal inflection has been replaced by a mastiff's bark.

"Your Honor, the schedule Mr. Hawthorne suggests is totally prejudicial to the rights of the defense. This is nothing short of a denial of due *process*. You can't—"

The gavel bangs. "The motion is taken under advisement. I will issue my ruling within a week. In the meantime, if the defense wants to be heard on the point, submit argument to me in writing no later than Friday. Anything else? Fine. Hearing is adjourned."

The gavel bangs again. A hundred eyes turn Hawthorne's way, trying to assess his sanity. Beyond the faceless mob is Martha's grudging nod of tribute to his gamble and, at the rear of the room, Keith Tollison's astonished comprehension of the implications of the moment. Ed Haroldson wears a gremlin's grin; Vic Scallini, an angry scowl. Above them all, the glow of Judge Powell's thoughtful frown floats across the fluorescent sky.

"Mr. Tollison? Art Ely. Of Litigation Economists."

"Yes, Mr. Ely. How are you?"

"Well, thank you. I'm sorry to bother you at home."

"No problem."

"I'm calling to ask if you received our report on the Donahue matter."

"I just got it today. Which is good, because the case may go to trial next month."

"Really? Frankly, we believed there would be more time than that."

"So did I, but Alec has made a motion for the Donahue matter and several others to proceed on their own. If Judge Powell agrees, I'm going to be out of my mind trying to get ready. Fortunately, your report is one less thing I have to worry about."

"I wouldn't put it quite that way, Mr. Tollison."

The beers he'd just imbibed began to seep from behind his brow. "Oh?"

"We were not able to be as ... encouraging as we originally supposed."

"Really? The report looked pretty solid to me."

"Yes, well, appearances can be deceiving, can't they?"

"Like how?"

"Suffice it to say, Mr. Donahue was not the most scrupulous record keeper we've ever come across. Nor the most accomplished businessman. Nor the most honest taxpayer."

"But can't you—"

"We've done everything we can, and then some. This report has caused more conflict between my partner and myself than any we've ever prepared."

"Why is that?"

Ely cleared his throat. "As you know, if this matter goes to trial we will be called upon to defend our analysis in court. Frankly, even with the drastically reduced estimate of earnings I insisted upon, this is the most indefensible document our firm has ever issued."

"I don't want you to do anything you can't live with, Mr. Ely."

"I would never go that far, you may rest assured. It's not as though you're an important . . . that is to say, we have done the best we can —I'll leave it at that. But there is a great deal of ammunition for the defense in this case. A jury could easily find that if Jack Donahue had not been injured, it is much more likely that he would have become a bankrupt than a millionaire."

"I was afraid that might be the case."

Ely warmed to the subject. "For instance, his resort project? Nirvana West? You advised us that the trip to Los Angeles had been to secure financing for that project and that his trip had been successful—tha. financing had been secured."

"Isn't it true?"

"Only in outline, I'm afraid. Further investigation has revealed that the individual who promised to underwrite the venture is well known to law enforcement agencies in Los Angeles, including the Organized Crime Task Force. In past projects he has been a joint venturer with the Central States' Pension Fund of the Teamsters Union; other associates have included two Las Vegas casino owners currently under indictment for skimming violations. Which in my opinion makes the venture of questionable utility in a litigation context."

"I'm afraid I agree."

"Mr. Donahue was not much more successful in his more conventional operations. For example, he built two spec houses back in 1979 but was unable to move them when the market was at its strongest, because inadequate soils analyses caused them to start sliding down the hill even before the subs were paid. He was forced to carry them until foreclosure, back when rates were at sixteen percent, which undermined his cash flow, which caused the Oakwood Acres project to become stillborn after significant architectural and engineering costs were incurred, some of which form the bases for outstanding and uncollected judgments against Mr. Donahue."

"I see."

"I tell you this because I'm sure that when he recommended us, Alec told you our studies are often accepted at face value in court. But we've never had a case that was this ... what I'm saying, I'm afraid, is that if it weren't for Alec Hawthorne, we would have declined the commission once the facts were known. Declined it with dispatch."

"I understand, Mr. Ely."

"Resist the temptation to believe our report is as favorable as it appears on the surface, Mr. Tollison. That's all I have to say."

"I appreciate your candor."

"I hope you remain appreciative when you get our bill."

Tollison replaced the phone, got himself another beer, and sank into his chair. Within the nearby tube of his Trinitron, Gifford handed off to Dierdorf, but Tollison had become oblivious, his mood so soured by the phone call that he could no longer take pleasure even in a Monday night.

The case was becoming a nightmare—the trial approaching like a runaway train while his proof collapsed like the trade of arms for hostages. His nights restless stretches of gloomy forecasts, long hours of every day were spent doing nothing more productive than seeking a way out of the mess he had made. But he could find no exit that would not so erode the elements he had hoped the case would enhance—his trial skills, his financial security, his grasp on Laura's heart—that surrender would make him even more miserable than he was already.

Ambition had lured him beyond his depths. In the spell of a dozen venalities he had persuaded himself that the SurfAir case was no different from any other—that, with Hawthorne handling the liability evidence, it was merely an airborne fender bender. Hire some experts, charm the jury, show your client in a sympathetic light, then watch the fees roll in. Fueled initially by fancy, now he confronted only truth—the heart of his case was as insubstantial as cream cheese: Jack Donahue, as Art Ely had confirmed and as Tollison had known for forty years, was worthless.

As he was getting his third beer, he heard the doorbell. He was expecting no one, so he sat and sipped and hoped they'd go away. The bell rang a second time. A Witness with the *Watchtower*, or possibly his mother. Neither a welcome interruption. Irritated, he yanked open the door, prepared to be as inhospitable as necessary.

"Laura. I'll be damned."

"Hi, Keith."

"I . . . you've never been here before."

"I know."

"Has something happened?"

In the dusk her eyes were queerly hooded, as though her purpose were nefarious. "I'm giving myself a treat."

He glanced past her at the street, then behind him at the mess. When he looked at her, she was laughing. "Why are you so *nervous*? I'm just visiting my lawyer. What's wrong with that?"

He thickened with embarrassment. "Come on in. The place is essentially filthy, but . . ."

She followed him into a gloom appropriate to the evening he had planned. After he brushed *Sports Illustrated* and *Newsweek* off the couch she took a seat, but only after brushing at the thin velour herself, this time to scatter Cheetos.

He broached the only subject that still linked them. "How's Jack?"

"He's back in San Jose. They're running more tests. Trying to revive another square inch of his brain, I guess," she added, casually enough to disturb him.

He sat on the ottoman across from her. "Is he still making progress?"

She shrugged, her eyes taking in as much of the room as was visible in the dusk. "He's better physically—he can move his left side now, pretty much, but his right side is still paralyzed."

"How about mentally?"

"Most of the time his mind is still somewhere I can't reach. And lately I've been too tired to try." She looked around. "Do you always keep it this dark in here? I feel like I'm at the bottom of a well."

He turned on a light and opened the curtains. As he apologized again for the state of the house, he wondered why she had come. They had always made love on neutral territory, and though he tried to see her arrival as a sign that their relationship had not only revived but had become flagrant, he was unable to see the visit except as a relapse to when their meetings didn't matter.

He asked if she wanted a drink. She shook her head. He motioned to the chips and the gangrenous dip. She shook her head again. Al Michaels cackled over a tackle. Tollison turned him down.

"I . . . was I interrupting something?"

"Just a game."

"Monday night. Of course. I shouldn't have—"

"There are plenty of games," he interrupted. "This one was going to be boring."

"How do you know?"

"They're all boring these days—everyone you want to watch is always hurt."

"But you were going to watch anyway?"

"Sure."

"Why?"

"Because I like the things I think about when I watch sports. And I love bloodshed."

Her look of censure made him sad. "I was kidding about the blood, Laura. You look like you haven't been kidded for a while."

She looked toward the TV, at the silent slammings of the game. "I suppose I haven't."

In the space vacated by their conversation, she seemed uncertain of how to proceed. "Where'd you get your drapes?"

"My mother gave them to me."

"She lives down the block, doesn't she?"

He nodded.

"Does that mean she knows I'm here?"

He nodded again.

"Do you mind?"

"Are we going to do something that would upset her?"

She shook her head.

"Shucks."

She grinned ruefully, but changed course. "Spitter's been a real help around the house, did I tell you? He's a nice boy, underneath his anger. We get along pretty well, though I think he comes mostly because it makes his mother mad. And because he likes my car."

"He hasn't gotten violent, has he?"

"Not at all."

"You don't have trouble communicating with him?"

"Well, he keeps calling me Carol. But if I don't dispute him, things move along just fine."

"Spitter loved Carol."

She nodded. "We talked about her once. He started to cry and, after he told me about standing guard on her grave, so did I."

A second silence swelled. "Do you need anything, Laura? Money? Anything?"

She shook her head. "I'm getting by. But I never realized how *exhausting* poverty is. How much is that? Can I afford this? Which is the cheapest brand? It's like doing algebra all day long." She sighed. "The walls were closing in on me, so I thought I'd stop and see if you'd heard when the trial was going to be. Dr. Ryan said you talked with him about being a witness, and he wanted to know how soon he would be called."

Tollison shrugged. "Alec's motion hasn't been decided, so I can't tell you exactly. But I want to make sure you're getting the stuff together we talked about. I need to get it to a printer so he can make up a brochure on you and Jack that I can give the jury to take with them when they deliberate."

Her hesitation spawned a sigh. "I'm not going to do it, Keith."

"Why not?"

"Because I have to live with myself after the trial is over and I'm left with ..." The smile was gone before it registered. "I'm not sure what that will be, but it will probably include my conscience, don't you think?"

"What's the problem, Laura?"

She opened her purse, took out an envelope, and handed it to him. Inside were several sheets of paper, edges irregular and oddly shaded, handwritten in a woman's round precision, photocopied, stapled, folded with care. He flipped through them quickly but found no title, no salutation, no signature at the end. After a glance at Laura, he began to read.

We fucked the first time I let him in the house, the first time I let him touch me. He wouldn't stop, and after a while I begged him not to. He took me places I've never been, did things to me no one's ever done, made me do the same to him. It would be nice to say he hypnotized me, diary, but of course I hypnotized myself. He came along at the right time, I guess, because I was ready to be his mistress from the moment he bought me a drink.

As you know, I've done things that were silly before, diary, things that were dumb, dangerous, even immoral in most people's sense of the word, but this is the first time I've done something even *I* believe is wrong. There's no good end to this—I'll be hurt, and so will others. I should put a stop to it, tell him I can't see him again, make him stay away. But I won't. I'm getting too old to be safe, too old to be good, too old to let a chance like this go by, too old to consider other people's feelings more than my own.

Sweating, he stopped reading. "What the hell *is* this?"

She shrugged. "Some woman writing about Jack."

247

"How do you know?"

"Read the rest."

He turned a page and continued.

He's like no man I've ever known. He's so *sure* of himself, so certain he is right no matter what the issue, so confident he can get away with anything he decides to do, which I guess explains why some people think he's a crook and why he kept coming on to me despite my cold shoulder the first time he made a pass. But who am I to judge? I gave in, after all—and I got what I wanted, so far, at least. When I'm with Jack I share his vision; I become what he wants me to be, which is more than I have ever been before.

He says he loves me. He doesn't, I don't think, not for anything other than the sex, but somehow that doesn't matter. He's expecting big things to happen soon, and when they do he expects me to enjoy them with him. And I *want* to. I want to be *someone* before I die, if only for a moment. I guess what I'm saying is that I'm with him for as long as he wants me to be, no matter what the consequences, no matter how badly it's going to hurt, or who.

He says it's over between them, that I'm not breaking anything that isn't already broken. I don't know if that's true, but I don't care if it is or not. At this point all I know is that I'm going along for the ride, wherever the ride will take me. Maybe after next week, and the ride has taken me to La La Land and back, maybe then I'll know what I want to do. I just hope—

The final page appeared to have been ripped in half, the bottom missing. Tollison gathered the papers together, put them in his lap, and contemplated the medium and the message. "I'll be back in a minute," he said, then hurried to his bedroom and closed the door.

It took three calls for him to track her down. When she was on the line, he spoke with a blunt insistence that was prompted by his duty to the woman in the other room. "You sent some papers to Laura, didn't you?"

"I . . ."

"Didn't you, Brenda?"

Her voice summoned a familiar bluster. "Maybe I did. So what?"

"It's supposed to be Carol's diary, isn't it? But I didn't find a diary when I searched her house."

"It's hers, all right."

"Where'd you get it?"

"Someone sent it to me."

"Someone from the airline?"

"Some guy from Portola Valley. He found it while he was out riding his horse. It may have blown over there in the crash, or he may have stolen it, who knows?" Brenda paused. "I know what you're thinking, but I don't care *what* you think. I told you you'd be sorry for what you did to Spitter. I want you two to hurt the way *I* hurt, Keith."

"If anyone was hurting more than Laura, they'd be in a mental ward. And the only thing I did to Spitter was get him out of jail. Have you shown this to anyone else?"

"Not yet."

"Well, don't. Especially not the insurance company."

"I'll do whatever I want."

He gripped the receiver until his hand hurt. "That diary could ruin Laura's lawsuit, Brenda. I know you think that's what you want, but if we don't win this case, Jack Donahue will never get better than he is right now, which is pretty damn pathetic. Therapy could bring him back to normal, at least partway, but he has to be able to pay for it. You'd have a hard time living with yourself if you took away that chance away from him."

Her voice was raw and cavalier. "I've always had a hard time living with myself. That's why I used to hope I could live with you."

"If you try to testify against us, I'll cut you up the way I would any other hostile witness. I *mean* it, Brenda."

She hung up in the middle of his warning. His trepidation unrestrained, Tollison returned to the living room.

Laura wore a thin, expectant smile. "Brenda?"

He nodded.

"I never got along with her very well, but I always liked Carol."

He stared at her. "How did you know?"

"There were hints, even before the crash. I just didn't want to deal with them."

He gestured toward the papers. "It doesn't make a difference, you know. Not to the case."

"It makes all the difference in the world," she rebuffed softly. "I'm glad this happened, in a way."

"What do you mean?"

"We were going to go to court and say I had a wonderful marriage that was destroyed by the plane crash. And it wasn't true."

"It used to be."

"I'm not a lawyer, but I don't think that's the point. The point is what was the marriage like when Jack was hurt, and when his plane went down, I'd been sleeping with you for over a year and Jack had been with Carol Farnsworth for I don't know how long."

He was shaking his head before she finished. "You don't know what would have happened, Laura. People have affairs all the time. That doesn't mean their marriage falls apart. Besides, that diary was Carol's, not Jack's. Just because she thought he loved her doesn't mean he did."

"It's not that he loved her, it's that he didn't love me."

"That's not necessarily true. And even if it was, you might have patched things up."

Her look was bright and damning. "That's a rather strange argument coming from *you*, isn't it?"

"Of course it is. That's why representing you in this case is insane."

Her smile refused to release him from any of the many contracts he had entered into with her. Face red, sweating from the beer and the debate, he tried once more to circumvent her principles. "I understand that you don't want to lie in court, Laura. And I promise not to ask you to say anything but what you see as the truth. But you don't have any obligation to make the airline's case for them. Unless you say something, it's possible neither our affair nor Jack's will even come up. Hawley Chambers thought I was such a pushover he didn't bother to schedule your deposition, and I doubt if he will take a chance on going into your love life at trial, since he runs the risk of alienating the jury if there's nothing to show for it. Of course that means we can't put Jack on the stand. He might spill the beans about us."

"You don't need to worry about that."

"Why not?"

She turned away, looking around the room. "You need some pictures on the walls."

The remark was so unexpected he started to laugh. "Pictures of who? You? Brenda? My dad? Jack? Who the hell am I supposed to *put* up there?"

He had done what he intended, which was to add his own plight to her burden. "I'm sorry, Keith. I want to win the case, I really do, but you have to understand one thing. The insurance company may not know about Carol and Jack and the jury may not know about Carol and Jack, but *I* know about them. And I know about us. I won't ask the court for money I'm not entitled to."

"But—"

"I mean it, Keith. I won't ask for consortium, or whatever you call it. Not if it means claiming my marriage was a splendid jewel that was worth a million dollars."

He knew her well enough to believe her. "Based on what I learned today from my expert, I have to tell you that loss of consortium is the strongest claim we have. If you give it up, you may get nothing."

"I won't ransom my dignity, Keith. If you don't know that, you don't know me at all."

He lost his grip on all but longing. "How can you *care* for him night and day like that? How the hell can you devote your *life* to the guy, knowing what he was doing behind your back?"

Her lips tightened and her eyes became small stones. "He's my husband. He can't move and he can barely speak. I can't leave him while he's like that. And besides, he wouldn't understand."

"What do *you* care what he understands?"

She looked at him with gray despair. "He thinks we're still happy, don't you see? *He doesn't remember we were ever anything else.*"

Reeling, Tollison resisted one last time. "How about after the trial? What are you going to do then?"

She met his look. "I don't know."

He could do nothing but mimic Brenda. "I imagine I'm going to spend the rest of my life waiting for you to find out."

The phone rang before either of them could respond to what seemed to be a pledge. He answered it in the bedroom.

"Keith? Alec Hawthorne."

"How's it going?"

"You sound depressed."

"That's putting it mildly."

"What's the problem?"

"I just heard from Art Ely. The report on Donahue's future earnings is less than sterling. He said it was the most vulnerable analysis they'd ever done. He also said if it weren't for you, they would have bailed out."

"That's too bad, but it's not fatal. You've got the perfect plaintiff in Mrs. Donahue, remember. The jury will want to give her something no matter *what* the law says about her right to it. Loss of consortium alone should yield a million."

"Mrs. Donahue has decided not to pursue that particular claim."

"You're kidding. Because of her husband's affair?"

Tollison paused. "I take it you talked to Brenda."

"She just called. She wants to cross-claim against Laura on the basis that the real loss in the case was suffered by her sister, not Mrs. Donahue."

Tollison completed the point: "Because Jack was about to divorce his wife and marry Carol, any future earnings would have gone to her, not Laura."

"That's the argument."

"She can't do it, can she?"

"She won't, let's put it that way." Hawthorne laughed easily. "So Laura has decided it would be unethical to sue for the destruction of a relationship that was already in ruins before the crash. My, my. A client with standards. I thought they were an endangered species."

"It's not funny, Alec. The ship is sinking fast. And why do I have the feeling you're about to add to the load?"

Hawthorne chuckled. "I have good news and bad news."

"What's the good?"

"The clerk called this morning. Judge Powell's going to grant my motion. The order will go out as soon as he can get it typed. Trial date is March twenty-third."

"Exactly a year after the crash."

"Right. Pretrial conference on March first. All discovery to be completed by then."

"Is that a problem for you?"

"I guess that brings me to the other news."

"Why do I feel the sky's about to fall?"

"Depends on how you look at it."

"I've always looked at it from the bottom," Tollison said sourly. "What's happened?"

"The clerk called Hawley Chambers right after he called me, to tell him about the order. Then Hawley called and asked if he could come by the office. I just finished a four-hour session with him."

"And?" Tollison could barely manage the conjunction.

"To make a long story short, he made me an offer I couldn't refuse. My cases are settled. All twelve of them."

"Jesus Christ, Alec. How in the hell could you—"

"I didn't *want* to, Keith. Hell, I wanted SurfAir to be my last hurrah. But I have an obligation to my clients. I tried like hell to stretch it as thin as it would go, but I guess Chambers didn't think he was ready to go up against me this soon. His people are willing to pay a nice premium to get me out of their hair."

"How do you mean, a premium?"

"Back in July, I made what I thought was an outrageous demand for settlement in a letter I sent the day the complaint was filed. Well, this afternoon Chambers accepted it. He gave me every penny I asked for, Keith. I couldn't say no, on any front whatever."

Tollison's laughed uneasily. "Well, hell. You can take over from me in Laura's case and—"

"They don't want me in there, Keith; I thought I made that clear. As part of the settlement, I had to agree not to appear on behalf of anyone else in the matter. I didn't want to do it, but I had to. Your friend Brenda, for instance, got a quarter million in the deal. That's more than I could have gotten her at trial if the jury were made up of my immediate family. Or hers."

"Jesus Christ, Alec."

"Sorry to bail out on you, pal."

"Wait a minute. What's Chambers going to offer the Donahues? Hell, maybe the whole *thing* will settle."

Hawthorne paused. "He's not going to offer the Donahues anything."

"But Laura's been—"

"Sure she has. So has her husband. But since you've never tried a crash case before, Chambers thinks he can beat you on the liability side. At least he's willing to take the chance."

"So we go to trial in a month."

"Not we, old buddy."

"But I can't *do* it, Alec. I have to find Laura another lawyer. Hell, *Scallini* would be better for her than I would in this thing."

"Don't panic. This aviation stuff isn't that different from what you do every day."

"Like hell it isn't."

Hawthorne laughed. "Okay. So I'll help you. It has to be on the sly, is all. You can do it. Hell, man. You'll be a *hero*. See, I've got this theory."

"What theory?"

Hawthorne paused. "What are you doing this weekend?"

"Drinking myself senseless sounds attractive at the moment."

"You don't have time. Can you be at my place at Tahoe Friday night?"

He glanced at the woman on the couch. "I suppose."

"Can you stay up there till the trial?"

"I don't know."

"Check your calendar. Get rid of everything you can. I'll have Martha send you a map, and she'll meet you at my place Friday. She'll bring everything you need to know to establish the liability of the airline.

I'll join you on Monday, and stay till we've done what has to be done."

"This is ridiculous, Alec. You make it sound like a Mickey Rooney movie."

"We've got a month. If you're willing to pay the price, by the time we go to trial, I can make you the second best aviation attorney on the West Coast. No sweat."

"No sweat for *you*, you bastard."

"I really am sorry, Keith; I tried a gamble and it didn't work. Or did work, depending on how you look at it. But it's not the end of the world. And anyway, I'm the only chance you've got."

"That's for sure."

"See you next week?"

Keith Tollison said the only thing he could possibly say. "One last question," he added.

"What?"

"I've got no economic loss and no loss of consortium. Even if I prove them liable, what the hell will they be liable for?"

Alec Hawthorne giggled. "Punitive damages, of course. And maybe a little pain and suffering."

PART III

PART II

Keith A. Tollison, Esq.
450 Main Street
Altoona, CA 95555
Attorney for Plaintiff

UNITED STATES DISTRICT COURT
NORTHERN DISTRICT OF
CALIFORNIA

John C. Donahue, Plaintiff,	)	
vs.	)	No. MDL 498
SurfAir Coastal Airways Inc.,	)	
et al., Defendants	)	
————————————————	)	

PLAINTIFF'S VOIR DIRE INTERROGATORIES:

Plaintiff requests the following interrogatories be addressed to prospective jurors in the above-entitled action. By this request, plaintiff does not waive the right to propound additional inquiries in written or oral form.

Interrogatories

1. Are you afraid of flying?
2. Have you ever flown on a commercial aircraft?
3. Have you ever worked in the aviation, travel, or insurance industries?
4. Have you ever studied law, medicine, accounting, or engineering of any type?
5. Have you ever been in a crash, including a crash in an automobile?
6. Do you understand that this is a civil case, not a criminal case, that no one will be found "guilty" of anything in this proceeding, and that the plaintiff will be required to prove his case by a preponderance of the evidence, not beyond a reasonable doubt?
7. Do you believe it is fair to compensate someone with money damages for both the psychological and physical harm they suffered as the result of the actions of another? Do you believe it is as fair to compensate for damage done to the plaintiff's mind and body caused by the conduct of another as it is to compensate for damage done to the plaintiff's property which was caused by that conduct?

8. Do you believe in fate, that sometimes accidents happen without cause, or are the result of acts of God?

9. Do you believe that no matter what the circumstances, a million dollars would be too much to pay someone for their losses as a result of a plane crash, no matter how badly they were injured? If a million dollars is not too much, do you believe there is some amount beyond which damages would be unwarranted no matter what the facts show?

10. Are you aware that money is the only form of compensation for injury that a person can seek under our system of justice? Though money may not be capable of restoring a physical or emotional loss, would you feel justified in determining an amount of money to be paid to a person who has suffered a loss?

11. Is there anything in your education, background, experience, or belief system that makes you feel that a person cannot be compensated with money for pain and suffering? Would you feel this way even if the court instructed you that the plaintiff has the right, under law, to be compensated for all pain and suffering he has felt or will continue to feel as a result of the defendants' conduct?

12. Once you have reached the sum of the reasonable amount to which the plaintiff is entitled as compensation, will you award the total amount rather than "knocking a little off the top" so the verdict won't seem too high?

13. You will be asked to decide whether punitive damages should be assessed against one or more defendants for their behavior in this matter. If you decide punitive damages are warranted, is there anything in your education, background, experience, or belief system that will prevent you from awarding an amount that will punish the company for its behavior and discourage it from repeating that conduct in the future?

14. Do you promise to follow the law applicable to this case as given to you by the judge at the end of the trial, no matter whether you agree with the law or not?

15. If you were a party to this lawsuit, do you know of any reason you would not want someone like yourself to serve as a juror in the case?

Respectfully submitted,

_____

Keith Tollison
Attorney for Plaintiff

ELEVEN

On the nineteenth floor of the Philip Burton Federal Building, on a rock-hard bench in the crowded arena of Courtroom 12, Alec Hawthorne allowed himself a grin: In a den of people who knew him best—lawyers, court personnel, marshals, news reporters—he had managed to become invisible.

Crossing his legs, he felt the scrape of denim rather than the itch of worsted wool. In response to a sudden tickle, he scratched his cheek, burying his fingers in an unfamiliar beard. Strange sensations all, in keeping with the unclipped hair, the dimestore eyeglasses, and the flannel-and-Levi's combination he had donned that morning in furtherance of his disguise. But the acid test lay beyond the bar of the court, in the person of Hawley Chambers.

Seated at the defense table, whispering terse directions to his young assistant as Judge Powell addressed the freshly impaneled jury, Chambers was simultaneously taking the measure of the courtroom. Alert for the lawyer's bane—a surprise, an unexpected presence, a thrust from his inevitably unscrupulous opponent—Chambers was also, Hawthorne knew, devoting a crease of his mind to searching the room for him.

In the settlement that excised his clients from the SurfAir suit, Hawthorne had promised not to appear in the action in any capacity and not to provide materials obtained in the litigation to attorneys for other plaintiffs. Technically, he had observed the caveat. What he had provided was not evidence but advice—suggestions, counsel, tips— the amorpha of litigation that had never been encompassed in any writing, not even those published by the many enterprises that promised to teach what had always seemed to Hawthorne essentially unteachable—how to be good in court. Such abstract aids had not been foreclosed by the artless verbiage of the settlement agreement, or so Hawthorne was prepared to argue, but his position was so far from solid that Martha had prepared a brief on the subject, in case he was found out.

The more tangible assistance he had proffered—the records, reports, and analyses Martha had carted to Tahoe a month ago and back the night before—had been amassed long before the Hastings had gone down, as part of the data Hawthorne accumulated to keep current with the technology whose eccentricities rendered him his living. Such assistance lay outside the settlement bounds as well, he believed, though with regard to a few documents the argument stank of sophistry. Whatever the legalities, were Chambers to learn of his presence he would quickly cry "contempt" and throw the proceedings into an uproar. Still, Hawthorne was uncommonly tranquil. It was nice to be in a courtroom without the weight of a client on his back.

From the bench, Judge Powell was reading his opening instructions to the jurors, outlining their duties, recalling their oath, briefing the case. Courtly, polite, bordering on the unctuous, in both intonation and demeanor Powell suggested that the task the jurors and their alternates were about to undertake was as vital as any they had ever done. Unless they had led lives more remarkable than the voir dire had revealed, the suggestion was unquestionably correct.

Below the bench, the portly clerk returned a handful of numbered balls to the cylinder from which they'd been extracted to randomly select the jury. At his flank, a court reporter kneaded her Stenorette in obeisance to the judge's words, the breathy ripple to her scarlet lips perhaps revelatory of a lascivious train of thought primary to the autonomic output of her job. Opposite the jury, half a dozen newspeople splayed across the tables set out for their convenience, looking more like entries on the bankruptcy docket than members of the fourth estate. To the rear, Powell's law clerk tilted his chair against the wall, implying he had seen it all before.

Meanwhile, the audience settled in for the show. A few were lawyers on their way to other venues, stopping by to look in on the first trial to come out of the SurfAir crash. Others had more specific interests. Vic Scallini had dispatched a lissome young associate to monitor the proceedings. Legal pad poised atop her slender lap, she would pass along anything that might advance the claims of other victims or save her boss some work. An assistant U.S. Attorney was present for similar reasons. The remaining onlookers consisted of what Hawthorne called "the float," regulars who moved from courtroom to courtroom enjoying the fruits of vicarious existence—the absence of consequence and the immunity from mistake. Like Hawthorne, they were eager for the trial to begin, having no stake in the outcome beyond what their sense of justice and fair play would conclude as the proceedings moved toward judgment. What was unsettling to Hawthorne was how often the collective ethic of the bedraggled mob exactly matched his own.

Seated at the table closest to the jury, dressed in the boots, suspenders, and wide-wale corduroys that fit his chosen court persona, Keith Tollison was at that moment tilted toward a question posed by the most pivotal player in the game, who looked in both dress and decorum to be present as an ambassador from God. Hawthorne sighed with envy. Never in twenty years of practice had he been the attorney for an angel.

While his charges conversed in careful whispers, Hawthorne's nervous knot unraveled. If he had passed the test of anonymity, Tollison had passed his threshold test as well: The jury that listened to Judge Powell's homilies was the one he would have chosen had he been trying the case himself.

Four women and two men. Not perfect, of course—Chambers was too good a lawyer to allow an unabashedly plaintiff's panel to sit in judgment of his cause—but most signs were encouraging. According to the profession's enduring bigotry, the Italian was the right temperament, the cook the right class, the jeweler the right faith. The female majority was also a plus, as long as Laura was careful not to alienate them by challenging the definitions of their gender. Juror number one was perhaps too dominant in word and body language to admit to much compassion, but juror number two—a black construction worker—could surely be counted on to compensate Jack Donahue to the full latitude of the law, unless the pathway to the middle class had burdened him with conservatism's least defensible belief—that misfortune is the fault of the unfortunate.

Conversely, the widow was the wrong age and tax bracket, the bookkeeper might think herself too slick with numbers to accept expert projections at face value, and the veteran might have endured such prolonged terror near Da Nang that Jack Donahue's instantly inflicted trauma would seem trivial in comparison. It was, as usual, a crap shoot. The most that could be hoped for was what Tollison had apparently achieved—the dice were not, as far as anyone could tell, loaded against his client.

That his friend had selected a jury of promise was not surprising to Hawthorne. During their weeks in the mountains, it became evident that Tollison had picked more than a hundred juries in his career and had tried cases of factual complexity if not of monetary gleam. Previously beset by demented jurists, forgetful witnesses, vanishing exhibits, deceitful counsel, and eerily ungrateful clients, Tollison was sufficiently alert to litigation's pitfalls to endure the preparatory tedium that was the only antidote to disaster.

At least up to a point. At 3 A.M. three nights before, Tollison had protested that if he didn't know it now, he couldn't possibly absorb it in the hours they had remaining, that at this point the best use of time was sleep. Hawthorne disagreed, and Martha sided with her boss. Tollison damned them both, only to have his commitment to the cause denounced by Martha. Eventually the point was mooted—Tollison fell asleep in his chair and could not be roused. Belying her earlier accusation, Martha draped him with a comforter and kissed him on the cheek. But that was the only lapse. By the eve of trial, Hawthorne found himself looking forward to watching his friend perform.

In the process of picking his jury, Tollison had accomplished the crucial corollaries—he had begun to sell his case and to sell himself as well. More important, as legitimately as he could, Tollison directed attention to the woman sitting next to him. The result would not be known for days, but it was their collective wisdom—the only point Hawthorne, Tollison, and Martha had united behind—that the key to the case was Laura. As he watched the jurors repeatedly glance her way, Hawthorne decided the bargain was halfway made.

His welcome concluded, Judge Powell looked expectantly at the plaintiff's table. On what was obviously his second try, Tollison managed to stand, stagger to the podium, and begin his opening statement.

He was nervous. Hawthorne saw it from where he sat, and the jury saw it vividly. Although veteran lawyers occasionally feigned jitters to foster sympathy for the underdog, such ploys often backfired—a lawyer succeeded not by tricks or artifice but by making the courtroom a world in which he was the sole teller of the truth. But Tollison's parched words and inelegant gestures were so surely symptomatic of his state they could actually prove endearing, especially compared to the pomp and polish of Hawley Chambers.

The opening continued as planned: simple, to the point, void of cant or emotionalism. Tollison described the Donahues' lives, noted the trip to Los Angeles, and mentioned the crash, all in neutral phrases. Because all but one of the jurors had seen or read accounts of the disaster, he urged them to suspend judgment until all the evidence was introduced, so he would not plead his case to persons who knew even before the first witness was sworn how they were going to vote after they ostensibly retired to deliberate.

As the opening neared its end, Tollison seemed to become convinced by his own rhetoric. Mentioning Jack's injury in its barest guise, he listed the compensatory sums he would ask the jury to award. Then, because he knew they expected it of him, he returned to the crux of the case.

"There is a big question in your minds at this point, I would guess," he said as he approached the jury box closely enough to suggest candor. "You're wondering what happened that night; you're wondering why the airplane crashed."

The lure in place, Tollison stepped back. "I'm afraid I have bad news for you, ladies and gentlemen," he admitted amid their full attention. "The answer is, I don't know. To my knowledge, *no one in this courtroom* knows why flight 617 crashed that night, not even Mr. Chambers over there, and he's the lawyer for the people who flew it. So I hope you will put that out of your minds for the next few days because, as important as it is, that question will not be answered in this trial. We're not going to be talking about the *first* collision that occurred that evening, ladies and gentlemen; we're going to be talking about the *second*."

Tollison paused for effect. When the murmurs of disappointment subsided, he continued. "The question that *will* be answered in this trial is a simple one," he said softly, making his audience work to hear and thus remember. "And that question is—why was Jack Donahue so badly injured in the crash of flight 617?"

Tollison folded his arms across his chest. "I *can* answer that one for you. Our evidence will show that the Hastings H-11 aircraft that crashed on the evening of March twenty-third of last year, as manufactured, sold, operated, and maintained by the defendants, was *not a crashworthy vehicle*. Had it *been* crashworthy—had the defendants been careful and prudent in building it and flying it, had they exercised due care in the decisions they made about the design and conformation of that airplane—Jack Donahue's brain would not have been damaged in the crash. Had the airplane been built the way it *could* have been and *should* have been, Jack would have walked away without a scratch because, as our witnesses will demonstrate, *the crash of flight 617 was survivable*.

"What's true is this: The defendants' failure to build and operate a crashworthy aircraft, in face of their duties under the law and the availability of alternate technology, was so willful and reckless in its disregard for the safety of the passengers on flight 617, that you will be justified—indeed you will be compelled by your collective sense of right and justice—to award Jack Donahue the amounts I have mentioned, plus punitive damages against these defendants in the aggregate amount of two and one half million dollars."

With a gulp of unburdened breath, a last look at the jury, and a quick glance toward the man in the rear of the room who had crafted the position he just set forth, Keith Tollison took his seat.

Hawley Chambers is deeply into his opening before Keith Tollison begins to sense its substance. Opposed by a tableful of lawyers and their data-laden advisers, his own beginning a glossary of terms he incompletely understands, Tollison can't believe the event he has dreaded for a month is actually upon him. There is so much to remember, to anticipate, to beware, that he is, for several minutes, unable to do any of it.

On the bench above, Judge Powell seems deep in meditation. At his side, Laura Donahue makes notes on a yellow pad. Somewhere behind him, Alec Hawthorne lolls like a jaded critic, passing judgment on his every move. At the podium, Hawley Chambers declares that what the jury has just heard from Tollison is a flight of febrile fancy— the word *nonsense* is used, as are *baseless* and *absurd*.

The charges sting. Anger swells, heated by a flame of rectitude. As if from a photographer's bath, Tollison's senses reappear. If he is as able in this venue as in Altoona, before the trial is over, they will reach a state of near omniscience.

Chambers continues, his rhetoric precise, his expertise a gloss on every phrase. Tollison suspects he has used the exact wording countless times before, but this is something the jury cannot know. To them as to Tollison, SurfAir is unique.

As he watches SurfAir personnel exchange approving nods at one of Chambers's sarcastic sallies, Tollison feels sorry, for the merest moment, for his adversary. Vic Scallini's digression into Oriental manufacturing techniques, coupled with Hawthorne's private plea to Judge Powell, let the Donahue case exceed the normal pace of discovery, so Chambers knows far less than usual about the plaintiff's case. Also, in a sense, the trial will likely be without profit for him. If the Donahues receive nothing, Chambers will have done no more than meet his clients' expectations. Even if the verdict is for Jack, the amount will most probably be small, still no great achievement. But the threat of punitive damages, which are uninsurable and thus potentially disastrous, looms large until the trial is done. Though such a judgment is, quite obviously, seen by the defense as less likely than world disarmament, an award of millions to the Donahues could end Chambers's career as a leading defense counsel. It is permissible to lose—indeed, Alec Hawthorne claims you should not make the Trial Lawyers' Hall of Fame until you have both won *and lost* a million-dollar judgment —but it is not permissible to take a bath so deep that it jeopardizes the client's existence. If insolvency is a possibility, you settle out of court.

Listening to Chambers's bombast, Tollison scans the room. In contrast to Altoona, where he performs before folks who are easily impressed, this crowd seems impatient, as though it has a right to a tour de force. The single friendly face belongs to Hawthorne. Tollison barely subdues a smile. The beard invokes their Berkeley days and the hippies Hawthorne disparaged in everything from their dress to their indulgences. Now, in furtherance of hallucinations of his own, Hawthorne has come to look like Ram Dass.

He wishes he knew what Hawthorne really thought about the case. "There are some problems," is as pessimistic as he has ever been when asked to assess their chances, "but also opportunities." Despite the easy optimism, Tollison knows they are on the horns of a dilemma.

Because Laura has steadfastly refused to press a loss of consortium, he has dismissed that claim, leaving Laura in the case only as Jack's conservator and as witness to his pain and suffering. The development would not have been disastrous had not the basic case—Jack's loss of earnings—been even weaker than Art Ely had suggested. As the airline's witness list made clear, Chambers's detective had tracked down every soul in Altoona who ever dealt with Jack and felt skinned in the process. The list is long and menacing—Tollison knows at least three people on it whose hatred of Jack Donahue had prompted threats of violence.

But Hawthorne and Martha are convinced they have the perfect counter—the case will be won, they predict with confidence, when Laura takes the stand to describe her husband's suffering and reveals her own ordeal as well. Barred from rewarding her directly, the jury will multiply its allotment to her husband, rogue though he may be.

Given the decision to base the case on Laura, argument on the best approach has ebbed and flowed. How should she appear—lovely and vibrant, or reduced to misery by the crash? Intelligent and capable, or dependent on a substantial judgment for a decent life? Coolly professional, or a hapless housewife unhinged at what has become of the man she married? As baldly stated, the spectrum hints of sham and artifice, but at one time or another Tollison has seen Laura exhibit each and every posture they discussed.

They have decided to defer Laura's testimony until the liability evidence is in. In the interim, they hope to catch a glimpse of Chambers's hand, to learn how much he knows about the Donahues, meaning how much damage he can do to Jack. Tollison and Hawthorne are experienced enough to know that the only safe assumption is that their opponent knows everything that they do. But what only Tollison knows, and what he has not yet been able to reveal to his partners in the enterprise, is that Laura's testimony entails great risk—if she takes the stand, Chambers may impeach her by revealing her romance with her lawyer.

Tollison shakes his head, curses both his predicament and his inattention. Chambers is denying his clients' culpability with an amplitude that makes it impossible that the plane crashed for reasons other than an act of kamikaze madness by the pilot. Slick enough to slide him onto a skewer at any stage of the proceedings, Chambers's every word must be weighed and heeded. The pressure is immense and unrelenting, and comes from all directions. Tollison is on trial as surely as anyone in the courtroom.

Chambers shifts to firmer ground. Gingerly but unmistakably, he begins to attack Jack Donahue. With the blows of a velvet hammer, he denounces Jack as a reckless plunger, an unscrupulous adventurer to whom an award for lost earnings would be tantamount to a prize for a pickpocket. The decision to damn a man whose brain has been pulverized by his clients is either brave or foolish, typical of the decisions a trial requires; only time will tell if Chambers has erred in attempting to shift stigma from the tortfeasor by smearing the victim of the tort. An injury trial is a quintessentially subjective decision for a jury, of the type that drives insurance companies and their lawyers to drink or to the legislature, often depending in large part on their measure of Donahue the man. In the final analysis, Tollison believes, the judgment may depend on whether it is Donahue or his wife who reveals the pathos of his condition. And that particular decision is not Chambers's but his own.

During the first days at Tahoe, Tollison and Hawthorne had assumed Jack would be unavailable as a witness. But their regular calls to Laura revealed that her husband had begun to progress at a startling rate—according to her, Jack was increasingly aware and verbal, occasionally even charming. But improvement was erratic and haphazard; Laura described black moods and vacant trances that came and went like zephyrs. One day, milk and cookies would be just the thing; the next, the tray would be thrown across the room. One day Jack would enjoy being manipulated and massaged; the next he would order his nurse to vacate not only his sickroom but his house, even when his nurse also happened to be his wife.

A similar fickleness stamped Jack's memory. On the first of four visits Tollison and Hawthorne made from Tahoe to his bedside, Jack remembered Tollison clearly, including the rules of engagement in the chilly war they had waged for forty years. On the next, he seemed never to have seen Tollison before. On a third, he seemed to think they were fast friends, to the extent that he wept when Tollison said goodbye. The pattern was so perverse that Tollison began to think Jack was having them on, as a method of amusing himself during the dull routine of convalescence.

As for the crash itself, Jack never varied. He remembered nothing, not the trip to LA, not the financing arrangements he negotiated while there, not the return on flight 617. On his final visit, when Laura had left the room, Tollison had mentioned Carol Farnsworth. Not that she was dead or had been in the crash as well, just her name. But it evoked no reaction beyond mild curiosity about a slight acquaintance. The same was true of the other ventures Jack was pursuing at the time of the crash. It was as though the hole in his head had never closed and all memory of the past few years had leaked into the mattress. For her part, Laura seemed incapable of looking further than the next item on the rehabilitation schedule.

A juror coughs. Beyond Tollison's reverie, Chambers again maligns the victim. At his side, Laura clenches a fist and mutters. When he realizes she has asked a question, he shakes his head. There is nothing he can do—Chambers can say anything he wants, there is no rule of court to stop him, there is only proof to the contrary. If they can marshal it. When the time comes.

Belittling the claim to punitive damages as the product of irrational minds and avaricious advocates, Chambers begins to close. An unfortunate accident, is his assessment. Tragic, to be sure, but the fault and responsibility of no one. To find otherwise would be to make mockery of the concepts of duty and justice. The defendants did all they could to bring the flight in safely, obeyed each and every regulation regarding the safety of passengers in the event of a crash landing. There is no reason in law or equity for making SurfAir or Hastings pay a single dollar to the Donahues, let alone the millions Tollison is asking for, no basis beyond notions of revenge or sympathy that have no foundation in the law. By the time Chambers has finished, Tollison is sure that at least two members of the jury believe he and the Donahues are scoundrels.

Chambers takes his seat. Judge Powell looks at Tollison. "If there is nothing further at this point, I believe we should read the stipulations."

The lawyers nod. The judge clears his throat and informs the jury that the matters he is about to elucidate have been agreed by the parties and are to be taken as proven for purposes of the case. "The crash occurred on March 23, 1987, at approximately 6:35 P.M., in the vicinity of Woodside, California. The aircraft in question, a Hastings model H-11, was manufactured by defendant Hastings Aircraft Corporation in April of 1985.

"At the time of the crash, the plane was owned by defendant SurfAir Coastal Airways and operated by that company through its authorized agents and employees. At the time of the crash, plaintiff John Charles Donahue was a ticketed passenger on SurfAir flight 617.

"In fiscal 1987, defendant Hastings Aircraft Corporation had net earnings after taxes of twenty million dollars; in fiscal 1987, defendant SurfAir Coastal Airways had net earnings after taxes of five million dollars."

Finished, the judge regards the courtroom. When he is certain all is in readiness, his eyes fall like a guillotine. "Call your first witness, Mr. Tollison."

BASIC JURY INSTRUCTIONS
RESPECTIVE DUTIES OF JUDGE
AND JURY

Ladies and Gentlemen of the jury: It is my duty to instruct you in the law that applies to this case. It is your duty to follow the law. As jurors, it is your duty to determine the effect and value of the evidence and to decide all questions of fact. You must not be influenced by sympathy, prejudice, or passion.

BELIEVABILITY OF WITNESS

You are the sole and exclusive judges of the believability of the witnesses. In determining the believability of a witness, you may consider any matter that has a tendency in reason to prove or disprove the truthfulness of the testimony, including but not limited to the following:
- the demeanor of the witness while testifying;
- the character of that testimony;
- the extent of the capacity of the witness to perceive, recollect, or communicate any matter about which the witness testified and the opportunity of the witness to perceive any matter about which the witness has testified;
- the character of the witness for honesty or veracity or their opposite;
- the existence of a bias, interest, or other motive.

CONCERNING INSURANCE AND
INSURANCE COMPANIES

There is no evidence before you that the defendants have or do not have insurance against the plaintiff's claim. Whether or not such insurance exists has no bearing upon any issue in this case and you must refrain from any inference, speculation, or discussion upon that subject.

STATEMENTS OF COUNSEL—EVIDENCE STRICKEN—INSINUATIONS

Statements of counsel are not evidence; however, if counsel have stipulated or admitted a fact, you must treat that fact as having been conclusively proved.

You may not speculate as to the answers to questions to which objections were sustained or as to the reasons for the objections. You may not consider evidence that was stricken; that evidence must be treated as though you had never known of it.

A question is not evidence. You may consider it only to the extent it is adopted by the answer.

INDEPENDENT INVESTIGATION FORBIDDEN

You must decide all questions of fact in this case from evidence received in the trial and not from any other source. You must not make any independent investigation of the facts or the law, or consider or discuss facts as to which there is no evidence. This means, for example, that you must not on your own visit the scene of the crash, conduct experiments, or consult reference works for additional information.

TWELVE

From his perch on the back row, Alec Hawthorne stifled a snicker. For the first time since he had known him, Ray Livingood seemed unsure of himself as he took the witness stand—hesitant, perhaps even a touch alarmed. Ironically, had Hawthorne been handling the case himself, he would not have used Livingood at all, would have relied instead on the report of the NTSB investigators, under the theory that the findings of government servants are immune to impeachment. But such evidence cannot be given live—it must be read from transcripts—and Hawthorne feared that Tollison's brand-new expertise might not hold up without the aid of a friendly face on the witness stand. So in the final days of pretrial preparations he had summoned Ray Livingood to the lake, only to discover that he had promoted a fight.

Irked at the demands of the preceding weeks, edgy from a month of sleeping a third of his normal diet, within minutes of Livingood's arrival, Tollison bridled at what he perceived to be the expert's accusation that he had not done his homework. For his part, Livingood responded with ill-concealed contempt and, as he estimated the effect a feeble showing in the SurfAir trial would have on his consulting business, became increasingly churlish. Like cats in a cage, the men snarled and snapped for hours, until Hawthorne called a halt by sending Livingood back to the city. Which was why, in the moment before Tollison began to question what was supposed to be his safest witness, the men were eyeing each other with crystal glints of insolence.

Garbed in a fresh-pressed suit that lacked only a row of ribbons to

271

pass for a colonel's greens, Livingood adjusted his body to the witness seat and his mind to the man who was about to interrogate him. Poised at the podium, Keith Tollison uttered what was supposed to be a brilliant fanfare but was more a croak than a call to arms.

"What is your job, Mr. Livingood?"

The question was routine and the answer would be perfunctory, which made Tollison's swollen smile seem forced and false. Hawthorne cringed: Such patent artifice could alienate the jury for the duration.

"I'm the founder and chief investigator of Aviation Investigations, Incorporated," Livingood intoned, his practiced importance still unbowed.

"What business does that company engage in?" Tollison asked.

"Precisely as it sounds—we investigate plane crashes."

"Are you a government agency?"

Livingood shook his head. "Totally private."

"There is an agency that investigates plane crashes, is there not? So why not let the government do the job?"

Livingood's look implied a bureaucracy less competent than Inspector Clouseau. "Sometimes they miss things, sometimes they take too long to reach a decision, sometimes they're too eager to pin the problem on the pilot instead of on the airlines and manufacturers. And sometimes they're just plain wrong."

Hawley Chambers pushed himself to his feet and clutched at his lapels with a gravity he clearly hoped was Lincolnesque. "Objection, Your Honor. Move to strike as argumentative."

Judge Powell tugged his ear in a gesture familiar to Hawthorne, indicative of irritation. "It's the reason he went in business for himself. The jury can accept it for whatever they think it's worth."

"Thank you, Your Honor." Tollison smiled and, on the strength of the minor victory, Livingood seemed to relax. "Let me direct your attention to the evening of March twenty-third, 1987," Tollison continued. "Did you have occasion to visit the site of the crash of SurfAir flight 617 on that occasion?"

"I did."

"Why did you go to the site?"

"I was asked to. And paid to."

"By whom?"

"An attorney named Daniel Griffin."

"Who is Mr. Griffin?"

"At that time, he was an attorney in the law office of Alec Hawthorne."

At the mention of the name, Livingood probed the courtroom, clearly hoping Hawthorne's warning that he would not be in attendance would prove false and the audience would include someone who could save the day if matters took a disturbing turn. That his search ended in disappointment was evident from the distinctly civilian sag to Livingood's broad shoulders.

"Who is Alec Hawthorne?" Tollison continued.

"An attorney here in San Francisco. He's probably the foremost aviation attorney in America."

Hawthorne basked in the compliment until a curl to Judge Powell's upper lip made him wonder if his machinations weren't an open book that would soon be thrown at him in the wrappers of a contempt citation.

"What did Mr. Griffin ask you to do at the scene of the crash, Mr. Livingood?"

Chambers spoke from his seat. "Hearsay."

Powell consulted the ceiling. "I'll allow it. It goes to his state of mind."

Livingood nodded his concurrence. "Mr. Griffin told me he'd just heard about the crash on the news and that I should get there as soon as I could and go through the usual routine."

"You had previously performed similar services for Mr. Griffin?"

"Several times. For the Hawthorne law firm, actually."

"What did your routine involve?"

"Inspecting the site, examining the wreckage, taking statements, getting still photos and videotape, talking to federal investigators— basically, learning all I could about what happened."

This time it was Tollison who chose to scan the courtroom, his glance sweeping the crowd until, like a searchlight atop a prison wall, it zeroed on its target. When Hawthorne nodded an imperceptible encouragement, the light moved on.

"I'd like to go more specifically into your qualifications for this undertaking, Mr. Livingood."

"Fine."

"Please tell us about your educational background."

"I received a B.S. from Iowa State University in 1960, a master's in electrical engineering from Purdue in 1962, and a Ph.D. in aeronautical engineering from the University of Washington in 1966. I was an army aviator from 1966 to 1970, flying a variety of propeller-driven aircraft during two tours in Vietnam, mostly on recon missions. I hold both a commercial and instructor's rating for single- and twin-engine aircraft and rotocraft. I own my own plane and fly it frequently."

"Did you organize Aviation Investigations, Inc. right after you left the service?"

"No, after the military I was hired by the National Transportation Safety Board as an air safety investigator specializing in aircraft structures."

"The NTSB is an arm of the government?"

"The NTSB is given the mandate, in Title 49 of the United States Code, to investigate the facts, conditions, and circumstances of civil aviation accidents."

"So your job with the government was to do what you do today—determine the cause of plane crashes."

"That's correct."

"Approximately how many crashes did you investigate while you were with the NTSB?"

"Over one hundred."

"And how many have you investigated since you founded your company, Aviation Investigations, Inc.?"

"Over fifty."

"While you were with the NTSB, did you receive any training in accident investigation?"

"I attended the six-week course in basic investigation at the board school in Oklahoma, and later the two-week advanced course. I also attended numerous seminars on investigative techniques."

"How long were you with the NTSB, Mr. Livingood?"

"From 1971 through 1976."

"Why did you leave?"

"Objection, irrelevant."

"Sustained."

Tollison frowned and consulted his notes. "What is the relationship between the NTSB and the Federal Aviation Administration?"

"The NTSB makes recommendations to the FAA as to what new or amended regulations it deems advisable, primarily in the area of safety. The FAA propounds the federal regulations that control both general and commercial aviation in this country."

Chambers clambered to his feet, his forehead rippled with disgust. "Have I stumbled into a political-science class, Your Honor? The relevance of this is sufficiently obscure as to be invisible."

"Yes, Mr. Tollison. Let's move ahead, please."

Reddening from his chastisement, Tollison grew flustered. In the silence following the ruling, his glance again swiveled to the rear. When it reached its target, Hawthorne began to fidget. It would take only a few more sorties before Chambers would cry foul.

As Chambers was queried by an assistant, Hawthorne slid to where he could signal Tollison that he was doing just fine. When he received the message, Tollison blinked and asked a question. "What time did you arrive at the crash site on the night of March twenty-third, Mr. Livingood?"

"Approximately eight-fifteen."

"Please tell us what you saw that indicated what happened to the aircraft from the moment it struck the ground."

"Objection—irrelevant."

"Overruled."

Having apparently concluded that Tollison's inexperience was not so vast that it was a threat to his livelihood, Livingood turned to the jurors as though they had waited in long lines to hear him. "Amazingly enough, considering the topography of the region, the Hastings touched down in a reasonably level area. There was slight upslope at the point of impact—maybe two degrees—but nothing like the bluffs and falloffs that mark much of the terrain in that area. Though visibility wasn't good that night—less than a thousand feet—by luck or skill, the pilot found a decent place to set her down."

"Do you conclude that the pilot attempted to make an emergency landing?"

Chambers was up again. "Objection. No foundation."

"Sustained."

Chastened, Tollison closed his eyes and nodded. "Your Honor, at this time I wish to tender Mr. Livingood as an expert witness."

Judge Powell smiled a grandfatherly approbation. "Do you wish to voir dire his qualifications, Mr. Chambers?"

Chambers stood up. "I do, Your Honor. Mr. Livingood, isn't it true that your primary experience both at the NTSB and in your private business has been in determining the proximate cause of plane crashes?"

"I'd say that's true."

"Yet you've been told by Mr. Tollison, have you not, that the cause of *this* crash is not at issue in this trial."

"I have."

"So whatever you are about to say here is not within the purview of your past experience."

Livingood's jaw set and his chest expanded. "I wouldn't say that at all."

Chambers pivoted from the protest. "Move to strike the testimony and to excuse the witness, Your Honor."

Before Tollison could rebut, Powell addressed the jury. "Ladies and gentlemen, I am overruling Mr. Chambers's objection and allowing Mr. Livingood to testify as an expert in this case. I do so because he has certain knowledge, experience, and training that enable him to give opinions that may assist you in your task. In determining what weight to give such opinions, you should consider the qualifications and believability of the witness, the materials upon which his opinions are based, and the reasons for each opinion. You are not bound by any opinion given in this case, by this witness or any other. An opinion is only as good as the facts and reasons on which it is based. If you find that any such fact has not been proved or has been disproved, you must consider that in determining the value of the opinion." Pausing to assure himself that the jury had understood the admonition, he pointed a finger. "Proceed, Mr. Tollison."

Looking hugely pleased, Tollison nodded. "Please answer the question, Mr. Livingood. Do you feel the pilot of flight 617 was attempting an emergency landing?"

"Based upon my estimation of the angle and speed of descent, the place of impact, and the direction of travel once the aircraft touched down, plus the absence of any failure in the cockpit controls, I feel certain the pilot was attempting to land the aircraft safely."

"Upon what do you base the estimate of speed?"

"Upon the length of the gouge in the earth made by the aircraft after impact, the angle of upslope, and the weight of the aircraft. I estimate that the speed at impact was between one hundred and one hundred forty miles per hour."

"Is there any other fact that indicates to you that the pilot was attempting a safe landing?"

Livingood nodded. "The Hastings touched down in an open area. Some two hundred feet east-northeast of that point is a small stand of conifers that are some forty feet opposite a stone outcropping. The pilot, in my judgment, attempted to steer between those obstacles. Unfortunately, there was not adequate clearance. The wings struck the obstacles virtually simultaneously, causing the aircraft to break apart."

"In other words, the—"

"Objection, leading."

"Sustained."

Tollison changed course. "Can you be more specific?"

Despite their truce, Livingood seemed to enjoy Tollison's come-uppance. "Basically, the plane attempted to scoot between some trees and the rocks, and it didn't make it. The wings hit, and the plane stopped dead except for the forward portion—that is, the portion of the fuselage in front of the wings. That section broke away and continued some fifty feet up the hill, where it hit another rock formation and was badly smashed. The rear two thirds of the fuselage remained at the point where the wings struck the trees and the rocks."

Tollison approached the witness box. "Mr. Livingood, I show you an item marked Plaintiff's Exhibit One, which purports to be a model of a Hastings H-11 fan-jet like the one that crashed on March twenty-third. To your knowledge, is this model similar to that aircraft?"

"It is. Except for this place where the model has been cut in two."

"Right. Now, would you show the jury approximately where that plane broke apart when the wings struck the trees and rocks."

"Objection, Your Honor. No foundation."

"This is illustrative only, Your Honor. A visual aid."

Powell nodded. "Overruled. The jury will give the demonstration whatever weight they feel it is worth."

"There." Livingood divided the plane at the point where the wings attached to the fuselage.

"Addressing your attention to the rear portion of the fuselage at the point where it broke away from the forward portion, can you describe what you saw in that area when you inspected it at the site?"

"Yes. First, there was a fire burning in and around the area; it obviously had been ablaze for some time."

"What caused the fire, if you know?"

"The wing tanks had ruptured, and the spilled fuel had ignited."

"Was there fire both inside and outside the cabin?"

"Yes."

"What else?"

Livingood donned a mask of sympathy. "As is typical of a major crash, there was a mass of mangled metal, a web of wiring and hydraulic hose, scraps of baggage and clothing. Human remains, of course. And fortunately, some survivors."

"Had any passengers been thrown free of their seats?"

"Some, but the majority were still strapped in."

"How about the seats themselves?"

"Virtually all the seats had come loose from the airframe and been thrown against the forward bulkhead."

"Along with the passengers strapped in them."

"Yes."

"So that they endured a second impact."

"Yes."

"How about the overhead compartments?"

"They had broken open as well; baggage was scattered all over."

"In the area of the front bulkhead?"

"Most of it. Yes."

"Would you indicate the position of the bulkhead on the model? Thank you. The bulkhead is, among other things, the partition which divides first class from tourist class in the plane, is that correct?"

"Yes."

Tollison nodded and looked at his notes. "In your work as an expert in this area, have you had occasion to define the term *survivable accident*, Mr. Livingood?"

"We utilized such a concept at the NTSB and I've employed it since, as a working definition."

"What is that definition?"

"May I read from my notes?"

"Yes."

"At the NTSB, we considered a survivable accident to be one in which the forces transmitted to the occupant through his seat and restraint system do not exceed the limits of human tolerance to abrupt decelerations and in which the structure of the occupant's immediate environment remains substantially intact to the extent that a livable volume is provided for the occupant through the crash sequence."

"Are there any other definitions of a survivable accident that you're aware of?"

"NASA uses a three-part test: if a survivable volume of the airframe is maintained during impact and at least one occupant did not die from trauma and the passenger had the potential for egress, then the crash is considered by NASA to be survivable."

"Thank you." Tollison glanced at Laura. Buoyed by her smile, he read from his notes. "Mr. Livingood, based upon your education, training, and experience, and upon what you observed at the crash site, do you have an opinion whether the crash of flight 617 was survivable under either or both of the definitions you have just enunciated?"

"Yes, I do."

"What is that opinion?"

Chambers had been on his feet for seconds. "Inadequate foundation, calls for a conclusion, invades the province of the jury, and is grossly speculative, Your Honor."

Powell was shaking his head before the litany was complete. "Overruled, Mr. Chambers."

Tollison was suddenly colossal. "What *is* your opinion, Mr. Livingood? Was this crash survivable for a passenger sitting in the tourist portion of that airplane?"

Chambers was apoplectic. "May I be heard, Your Honor? This man has never rendered an opinion on survivability in his *life*. This is not proximate cause, this is idle speculation. There is no detail as to the basis for the opinion, nothing on which the jury can assess the value of the statement. *Please*, Your Honor. This is inappropriate."

The judge shook his head. "I'm going to allow the opinion, Mr. Chambers. If you want to assail it, do so on cross-examination."

"Thank you, Your Honor," Tollison said. "Again, Mr. Livingood. Was this crash survivable?"

Livingood's nod was adamant. "For passengers sitting anywhere behind the forward bulkhead—that is, for anyone in the so-called economy class in that airplane—the crash was definitely survivable. Under both definitions I gave."

As though a wire had been unplugged, Tollison became affable. "Thank you, Mr. Livingood. Your Honor, I have another area to develop at this point, but perhaps it would be a good time to break for lunch."

Judge Powell glanced at his watch and nodded.

By prearrangement, they meet for lunch at a table behind the staircase of a North Beach restaurant purchased out of the proceeds from the wrongful-death suit filed after the demise of the owner's wife in the San Diego midair. "Every time he sees me, he starts to cry," Hawthorne warned as he told Tollison of the meeting place, "but the food is worthy of the sentiment."

The prediction has proved true. As he awaits their orders beneath the creaking staircase, the proprietor dotes on Hawthorne like a toady. "This man," he effuses in a gush that dragoons all four persons at the table into a pep club, "is a saint. Without him I am a prune, a raisin, a pile of dust." Blotting his eyes with the corner of his apron, he gestures toward the noisy tables to their front, invisible from the nook behind the stairs. "It is Alec who gave me this—a reason to live until I am united with my Loretta in the life that follows this one. So eat. We serve only Carmine's best."

Keith Tollison and Laura Donahue exchange commiserating glances above antipasto and Chianti. Though it is their first intimate moment in weeks, Tollison is unable to take advantage. In a delirium of duty, his mind springing back to the morning's session and ahead to the afternoon's, he cannot abandon his anxiety long enough to frame a sentence that will express what he wants the occasion to produce. From her rapt appraisal of the food that emerges from the kitchen on a squadron of flying saucers, Laura is less essentially preoccupied. Tollison sighs. How far his life has strayed from what he thought it had finally become.

He leaves Laura to her meal and asks Hawthorne to evaluate the morning. "We got in what we need to make a good summation," Hawthorne responds. "Which is what direct examination is all about."

"But?" Tollison prompts, alert to the implicit reservation.

Hawthorne lowers his voice, as though they were joined in conspiracy. "You need to relax. You're making the jury nervous and making Powell doubt his decision to do me a favor. You have to prove you're not going to embarrass him in this thing, Keith, and the way to do it is take charge. You don't have to know what you're doing, you just have to *act* like you do. Otherwise, you won't keep Powell on your side. And that's your most important job."

"I thought he threw some rulings my way that he didn't have to."

"Sure he did; that's his style. He'll do the same for Chambers when *he's* offering the evidence."

"Why?"

"Powell worships juries. He believes they develop a collective genius that lets them wade through hip-deep bullshit and come out with something approximating perfection. So he lets the bullshit flow."

"Is he ever reversed?"

Hawthorne shakes his head. "Not often. The system can barely digest a crash case once. A retrial would clog things up for years."

"I still don't see why we had to dismiss against the FAA," Tollison complains, out of a sense that the more targets there are, the better his chance of hitting one.

Hawthorne sips his wine and, amid the newly complex maneuver, soaks his beard. "The government can be sued for administering its rules improperly, but it can't be sued for failing to have any rules at all, so the fact that the FAA hasn't adopted adequate crashworthy standards—hasn't even included the term *crashworthy* in its regulations—isn't anything we can nail them for. It's called the discretionary function exception to the Federal Tort Claims Act."

"Seems unfair."

"It wasn't long ago you couldn't sue the government for anything: sovereign immunity and all that medieval nonsense. So when it comes to the feds, we count our paltry blessings."

Hawthorne turns to Livingood and begins to discuss a point about his coming testimony. When the men are absorbed with each other, Tollison returns to Laura.

His ego revived by Hawthorne's easy self-assurance, he places his arm across the back of her chair.

She is ethereal in a jersey skirt and sky-blue blouse. Her fuzzy focus—sediment of Chianti and exhaustion—makes her as appealing as a drowsy child who is fighting to stay awake. "How are you holding up?"

Her attempt to smile is ponderous. "Okay, I guess. How about you?"

"You've been watching the jury—you tell me."

For a moment the eyes throw off their strain. "They like you, I think."

Pleased that she has bothered to be extravagant, Tollison leans to whisper. "Do they like Livingood as well?"

"That's asking a bit much, isn't it?"

Partners prospering in the joke, they look slyly at its object and share a giggle. The moment is so similar to many they shared when their secret was an exclusive toy, he forgets they no longer have a secret to enjoy. "Are you keeping up with the testimony okay?"

"I think so."

"Good. When you think I'm making a mistake, let me know, particularly if it's something the jury seems upset about. I can get overbearing sometimes."

She raises a sardonic brow. "Really?"

He regrets supposing he can portray himself in guises she hasn't seen already. "I wish we could go someplace and watch old movies," he whispers slyly, teasing her, and testing.

He is grateful when she nods. "I need this to be over, too. I keep remembering high school—I had a bit part in the senior play. The waiting was such torture, by the time I heard my cue I'd forgotten my lines. I'm afraid by the time I have to testify I won't know my name."

"The jury will love you," he predicts, then is dismayed when her mouth hardens as though he has betrayed her.

"They don't have to *love* me," she mimics, "they just have to do what's right." She closes her eyes and shakes her head. "Chambers made it sound like I'm a thief. And your girlfriend makes me *feel* like one."

Tollison frowns at the reference. "Brenda?"

Laura nods. "Didn't you see her come in the courtroom at the end? What's she *doing*, in heaven's name? She's hovering over us like a vulture."

"I guess she wants to make sure we stick to the script."

"What script?"

"The one that omits any reference to your marriage."

Laura twists her napkin into the semblance of a noose. "Nothing is what it seems—I'm not a good wife, Jack's not a successful business-man, you're not merely my lawyer. We're in the Twilight Zone, aren't we, Keith?"

Tollison shakes his head. "We're just in court." A moment later he places his palm over her hand. "What will you do after it's over? Have you decided?"

"It depends on the jury."

"Don't base anything on that. Even if you win, it could be years before Jack gets his money."

She pulls her hand away. "Time seems to have lost a lot of signif-icance lately."

Although it is likely that she has just declared there is no room for him in her life, now or ever, Tollison is strangely calm, as if what each of them is saying comes from a clever melodrama rather than their real lives. "*I've* decided something," he announces impulsively.

"What?"

"I'm going to leave Altoona. Start over somewhere else."

"Where?" she blurts, her look suddenly wild and eager. "Where are you going *to*?"

Though the question throbs with urgency, he can't tell whether its source is concern or merely gossip. "I'm not sure," he answers lamely.

He is waiting for her reaction when a hand touches his shoulder. "Show time," Hawthorne announces.

Tollison looks at his watch. They are due in court in fifteen minutes. When he looks at Laura she is nibbling lukewarm tortellini, no trace of emotion in her face. Tollison hurries to the street to call a cab.

The proceedings are under way on time. Livingood is on the stand; Hawthorne is hidden behind a broad-beamed matron and her hive of hair. Judge Powell gavels the room to order.

"Mr. Livingood, is the name of Colonel John Paul Stapp familiar to you?" Tollison begins, relieved to focus on exploits more noble than his own.

"Yes, indeed."

"How do you know Colonel Stapp?"

"I don't know him, I know *of* him. He is famous for a series of experiments having to do with the capacity of the human body to survive great physical stresses."

"Are his calculations accepted by specialists in the field of biomedical research, as well as in various engineering disciplines?"

"They are."

"This morning, in defining a survivable crash, you used the phrase 'within the limits of human tolerances to abrupt deceleration.' Do Colonel Stapp's experiments bear upon those tolerances?"

"They certainly do. They define the outer limits."

Chambers is again irate. "Your Honor, I object to this line of questioning. Mr. Stapp, whoever he is, is not on plaintiff's witness list."

For the first time, Tollison experiences a whiff of victory—Chambers is reacting from a genuine sense of danger rather than a calculated ploy. Buoyed, he gets to his feet. "Counsel is well aware of Colonel Stapp's importance, Your Honor. If I may be allowed to continue, I will demonstrate that the colonel's experiments have a crucial bearing on this case."

The judge nods. "You may proceed. Subject to a motion to strike if relevance is not shown."

"Thank you, Your Honor. Mr. Livingood? Tell us about Mr. Stapp."

Livingood crosses his arms with obvious satisfaction. "In 1954, when Stapp was in the air force, he built a sled and placed it on a track, sort of a car frame on a railroad. The sled was powered by nine rockets, each capable of forty-five hundred pounds of thrust. Not just once but several times, Stapp would strap himself to the sled, wrap himself with safety belts, clamp his teeth onto a block of rubber, and fire the rockets. In the final test in the series, the sled reached a speed of six hundred thirty-two miles per hour, faster than any man had ever traveled on land up to that time."

From his look, Hawley Chambers has become impossibly weary, though Tollison knows he dreads the jury's rapt attention. The objection warbles with sarcasm. "I didn't realize this was story hour, Your Honor."

Judge Powell scratches his ear. "I'm not aware of the inclusion of that objection in the code, Mr. Chambers."

"Then I object that this tale—more accurately, this *fairy* tale—is hearsay."

"Overruled."

Tollison prompts his witness. "So Colonel Stapp went fast in a sled. What does that have to do with flight 617?"

"It wasn't the speed that was important; it was the stop. The experiment was arranged so that water brakes near the end of the track brought the sled from top speed to zero in just over one second. In other words, the experiment came as close as possible to running into a brick wall at the speed of sound."

The crowd murmurs in wonder; the jurors exchange blinks of incredulity; Tollison expands the moment. "Let me see if I understand. The man sitting on this sled is going six hundred miles an hour. A second later he's stopped cold."

"Right."

"Did he survive?"

Livingood nods. "Thanks to the safety belts, Stapp suffered only repairable eye damage and some aches and pains."

"What was the practical result of his experiments?"

"There were two. Because Stapp proved that, contrary to the belief of many, seat belts wouldn't cut a person in half in a high-speed accident, the mandatory auto seat belt law of 1966 was passed. More important for our purposes, Stapp proved humans could withstand deceleration stresses in excess of forty times the force of gravity."

"Tell the jury how such forces apply to the crash of flight 617."

"Gravity force, or g force, is a measurement often used to determine structural strength. Seats in commercial aircraft, for example, are required by regulation to be attached to the airframe in a manner that will withstand a certain level of g forces forward and sideward in the event of a crash. That is, they are to remain in place if the forces applied to them don't exceed the designated g number."

"So seats in an airplane must be built to stay attached to the airplane in the event of a sudden stop as long as the forward momentum of the seat and its passenger doesn't exceed the specified times the force of gravity."

"Yes. Essentially, that's it."

"And Colonel Stapp proved that humans could withstand g forces of forty or more."

"Yes."

"Do other experiments confirm the capacity of humans to withstand high levels of impact?"

"It's not accurate to call them experiments, but various falls have been recorded that indicate we humans are extremely resilient. A Russian stewardess fell out of a plane at three thousand feet and survived. A Russian pilot supposedly fell from *twenty-nine* thousand feet and lived to tell the tale."

"Some of the jurors might regard tales of Soviet exploits with some suspicion. How about Americans?"

"A navy parachute rigger jumped out at sixteen thousand feet and survived, even though his parachute never opened."

Tollison's eyes oscillate in amazement. "So we can assume the FAA requires airline seats to be attached securely enough to withstand a pretty high degree of force. On the order of forty g's or so."

Livingood shakes his head at the feigned naïveté. "I'm afraid you can't assume that at all."

Tollison's frown is as broad as burlesque. "I don't understand."

Ever the expert, Livingood assures himself that the jury is paying appropriate attention. "The Federal Aviation Regulations require seats in commercial aircraft to withstand forces of nine g's forward and one point five g's sideward."

"Nine, did you say?"

"That's correct."

"Even though humans can survive a force *five times* that great?"

"I'm afraid so."

"Are you telling me people were killed in the SurfAir crash not by the sudden stop but by their seats breaking away and hurtling forward, with helpless passengers strapped to them, at the velocity of the plane as it struck the rocks?"

"*Please*, Your Honor," Hawley Chambers wails. "Argumentative, immaterial, leading, speculative, and absurd."

Judge Powell seems to be smiling. "Sustained on more than one but less than all of those grounds. Control yourself, Mr. Tollison."

Tollison bows his head. "Sorry, Your Honor," he says, but continues to milk the moment. "I'm shocked, Mr. Livingood. But I suppose the explanation is that the nine-g requirement is difficult to meet."

Wallowing in the jurors' fascination, Livingood shakes his head. "It's no big deal to make seat anchors stronger; the military does it all the time."

"Please explain."

"The air force requires its seats to withstand seventeen g's, and the navy requires forty. *Car* seats have to withstand more than twenty g's, and most cars crash at relatively slow speeds."

"I see." Tollison pauses for effect, though he knows the jury has understood every word. "You've testified that the H-11 touched down at approximately a hundred and forty miles an hour, then skidded along the ground and stopped abruptly when it struck the trees and rocks. What is your estimate of how fast the plane was traveling at that point?"

"I estimate just over one hundred miles per hour."

"What g force would be exerted on the seats at that speed, assuming a stop of the type made by the H-11."

"Between ten and fifteen. Give or take a couple."

"Nothing the human body couldn't tolerate, according to Colonel Stapp's experiments."

"Correct."

"You also testified that during your observation of the wreckage, you saw several seats from the rear portion of the plane that had come loose from their anchors, causing the occupants to be thrown forward into the forward bulkhead. Causing them to endure a *second* crash, in other words."

"Definitely."

"The phenomenon of seat failure is not unique to the SurfAir crash, is it?"

"No. Forty percent of passenger injuries are caused by seat failure."

"Is that fact well known in the industry?"

"Yes."

"How?"

"In 1981 the FAA published a study of seventy-seven survivable crashes. In those cases, the seats failed eighty-four percent of the time; the overhead compartments failed seventy-eight percent of the time, and the galleys failed sixty-two percent of the time. The study is called 'Cabin Safety in Large Transport Aircraft.'"

"Yet the FAA still maintains only minimal standards of seat and cabin strength."

Livingood nods. "In 1969 they tried to increase the seat requirement from nine to twenty g's, but they withdrew the proposal."

"Why?"

Livingood hurries to beat the objection. "Pressure from the manufacturers. The metal benders figure if it's cheaper to kill you than fix it, they'd just as soon kill you."

As his clients fume at his side, Chambers is volcanic. "Your Honor, I insist on a mistrial. Such statements are totally beyond the bounds of ... of *morality*, to say nothing of admissible evidence. I urge the court to end this farce immediately. I—"

Powell's voice is stern. "The motion for mistrial is denied, but your objection is sustained. The jury is instructed to disregard the answer. And I mean *completely*. The witness will cease such hyperbole immediately."

For the first time Tollison regards his witness with admiration. Then, to hide his pleasure, he turns to check his notes. "When you arrived at the crash scene did you take any pictures, Mr. Livingood?" he asks after the tempers in the room have cooled.

"I videotaped the scene as best I could, given the conditions."

"This was some two hours after the crash occurred?"

"Yes."

"Do you have a copy of that tape with you?"

"I do."

"You took the tape yourself?"

"With a Panasonic PV 30 VHS camera and an HGX cartridge, using available light."

"Your Honor, I ask that Mr. Livingood be allowed to show his tape."

Chambers advances on the bench. "Counsel's purpose is both clear and inappropriate, Your Honor. Tapes of the scene will be grossly prejudicial to my clients, of no probative value whatever. No one enjoys what happened that evening—it was a tragedy of immense proportions. But nothing on that tape will add to the jury's ability to decide the issues of fact in this case. I urge that it be rejected."

Judge Powell squints at his assailant. "I've previewed the evidence in my chambers, counsel, and I'm afraid you're overruled. Mr. Tollison may show his tape."

As Chambers sputters to silence, the room darkens at a signal. A rear projection receiver Tollison appropriated from Hawthorne's cabin is rolled to a position from which it can be seen by all concerned. Tollison inserts the cartridge into the VCR.

The jury views in silence, except for a collective gasp at the glimpse of what appears to be a human torso burning like a yule log near the wreckage. Although Livingood assures them it is only a duffel bag, they remain stunned by the possibility. Moments later, a murmur of approval greets a priest as he leads a woman from the wreckage, and another issues as a fireman douses what everyone hopes is a rag doll with foam as white as milk. The remainder is expressionistic—scraps, ruin, litter, junk—limitless and devastating. Tollison wonders whether anyone who sees it will ever fly again.

When the lights come on, the entire room is thankful.

"That's all I have, Your Honor. Thank you, Mr. Livingood."

"Your witness, Mr. Chambers."

Chambers is on his feet immediately. "Your Honor, at this point I move to strike the testimony in its entirety, for lack of a foundation for the conclusions offered and, more importantly, on the ground that it is immaterial—there is no evidence Mr. Donahue had a problem with his seat or with any of the other aspects touched on by the witness."

"Mr. Tollison?"

Tollison is sweating. Before the first witness has left the stand, Chambers has spotted the vulnerable portion of the case, a defect Tollison has sensed for weeks. He reacts as best he can, which for the moment is to feign indifference, to delay and hope Hawthorne can provide him with a witness who will shore up the proof of proximate cause.

"We can only do one thing at a time, Your Honor," he argues, as though the rupture is nonexistent. "I know of no rule that allows Mr. Chambers to dictate our order of proof. If at the close of our case he believes it suffers from the defect he suggests, I'm sure he can frame the appropriate motion."

The judge nods. "Ruling is reserved. Cross-examine, Mr. Chambers."

Chambers abandons his colleagues and his clients and strides to a position directly opposite the witness. "You're getting paid for this, aren't you, Mr. Livingood?"

"Naturally."

"What's your rate?"

"Two hundred dollars an hour for investigation; two fifty for court time."

"How much more do you get if your side wins?"

"Not a penny."

Chambers's brow decrees the denial preposterous. "You've testified in other crash cases, I believe you said."

"Correct."

"Isn't it true that in every one of those cases you have appeared for the plaintiff?"

"I believe so. Yes."

"And on each of those occasions the person who hired you was a lawyer named Alec Hawthorne, right? The same man who engaged you to investigate the SurfAir crash?"

"Not *every* case has been for Mr. Hawthorne. But most."

"Mr. Hawthorne represents *only* plaintiffs, does he not? Persons injured in plane crashes?"

"I believe so."

"Mr. Hawthorne wouldn't use you if you didn't testify exactly the way he wanted you to, would he?"

Tollison interrupts. "Objection—calls for speculation."

"Overruled. You may answer if you know it."

"Mr. Hawthorne never tells me what he wants. He hires me to investigate, and I tell him what I believe happened."

"You always come up with something helpful for him, though, don't you?"

Livingood preens with righteousness. "What I come up with is the truth."

Chambers shakes his head. "Your *truth* always finds fault with the airline or the manufacturer, doesn't it?"

"It's true I seldom find your side of a crash case tenable, Mr. Chambers. If you want reasons, I would be happy to give them."

"Move to strike, Your Honor."

"I believe you asked for that one, counsel. Continue."

Chambers regards the ceiling. "Let me put it this way, Mr. Livingood. What portion of your income last year was derived from services you performed for Alec Hawthorne?"

"I'm not sure. Sixty or seventy percent, probably."

Chambers bows theatrically. "We'll let the *jury* decide how far you would be willing to stretch the truth to preserve the largess of a man whose entire career is devoted to suing airlines such as SurfAir. Let's move on. You've made various statements about what you believe happened during and after the crash of flight 617. Frankly, quite a few of them seem incredible. For example, you say the plane was going a hundred miles an hour when it hit the tree. But it's possible it was going faster, right?"

"Twenty miles an hour faster, at most. It's also possible it was going slower."

"If it *was* going faster, the g forces exerted on the seat anchors would be greater than you estimated, would they not?"

"Some. Not much."

"And if the angle of upslope at the point of touchdown was *less* than you calculated, then the speed at impact would have also been greater, right?"

"Right."

In like manner, Chambers moves through the testimony with a fine-tooth comb, stretching calculations, undermining certitudes, casting doubt anywhere he can. But Livingood holds up, at least as far as Tollison can tell. What the jury thinks is far less clear.

At the end of the afternoon, Chambers folds his arms. "Isn't it true, Mr. Livingood, that as the videotape showed, you made your investigation of the crash site in the dark?"

"It was dusk. Yes. But fires were burning, and some of the rescue personnel had arc lights to help them search for bodies. Car lights were trained on the wreckage as well."

"Dusk, and lots of smoke from the fires, right?"

"Yes."

"Because of the flames, you couldn't actually enter the wreckage?"

"Correct."

"How close to the bulkhead were you able to get?"

"Maybe twenty feet."

"Yet through the fire and smoke at dusk you're able to tell us all about broken seats and storage compartments and everything else."

Livingood's lips stretch in a smug retort. "I'm glad you brought that up; Mr. Tollison should have mentioned it, but he didn't. I not only examined the wreckage at the crash site, I examined it at the mock-up area some three weeks afterward. On that occasion I paid particular attention to the seats. By my calculation, eighty percent of the seats in the aft cabin, or tourist class, came loose during the crash. Both overhead compartments had broken off as well, which means much of the luggage in tourist class impacted against the bulkhead, too, pummeling those passengers *also* thrown to that location."

Chambers reddens at the riposte and for the first time makes use of his assistant, who whispers an urgent tip. "Regardless of that, Mr. Livingood," Chambers continues, "it's true, is it not, that at no time did you see the plaintiff in this case, Mr. Donahue, at the crash scene."

"That's correct."

"So you don't know whether his seat came loose or not."

"Not specifically."

"One last point. You mentioned, in your definition of a survivable accident, that for a crash to be survivable the passenger in question should have a means of egress from the wreckage. Isn't that your testimony?"

"Yes."

"Isn't it true that the wing exits were rendered inoperative in the crash? Weren't those two doors so mangled they wouldn't open, so neither Mr. Donahue nor anyone else could use them?"

"That's true. But had the plane been designed properly, there would have been two *additional* doors in mid-fuselage of the H-11, in areas that experienced far less stress."

"You're not saying the failure to add those doors was a violation of federal regulations, are you?"

Livingood is equal to the challenge. "I'm saying that anyone with a reasonable regard for safety would have put them in."

Chambers gestures grandly toward the jury. "Fortunately, what is or is not reasonable is for *these* good people to decide."

"If Hastings and SurfAir had done their jobs properly, these good people wouldn't have to *be* here today."

"Move to strike, Your Honor."

"Sustained. The jury will disregard it."

"I . . . no more questions."

"Redirect, Mr. Tollison?" the judge inquires as Hawley Chambers sits down amid a retinue of nervous frowns.

Tollison stands. "One item, Your Honor. Is it your understanding, Mr. Livingood, that the Hastings H-11 *can* be built with two additional exit doors?"

"Definitely. In fact it has been. All-Europe Airways ordered a dozen H-11s last year, each with two exits in the fuselage as well as the two wing exits and the exits in the front and rear."

"And SurfAir could have ordered that version as well."

"Certainly."

"That's all I have, Your Honor."

Judge Powell addresses the jury. "Ladies and gentlemen, court is in recess till nine A.M. You are not to discuss the case among yourselves or with anyone during that time."

DUTY OF COMMON CARRIER

A common carrier of persons for hire must use the utmost care and diligence for their safe carriage and must exercise a reasonable degree of skill to provide everything necessary for that purpose. A common carrier is bound to provide a vehicle which is safe and fit for the purpose to which it is put, and is not excused for default in this respect by any degree of care. The care required of a common carrier is the highest that reasonably can be exercised consistent with the mode of transportation used and the practical operation of its business as a carrier. This requirement must be measured in the light of the best precautions which, at the time of the accident in question, were in common, practical use in the same business and had been proved to be effective. Failure on the part of such carrier to meet the foregoing standard of conduct is negligence.

A common carrier does not guarantee the safety of its passengers. Its responsibility is not to use the most effective methods for safety that the human mind can imagine or that the best scientific skill might suggest. However, a common carrier and an aircraft manufacturer must take accidents into consideration as reasonably foreseeable occurrences involving their aircraft. They must evaluate the crashworthiness of the product and take such steps as may be reasonable and practical to avoid crash injuries and to minimize their seriousness.

THIRTEEN

Sprinting out of the building before the courtroom emptied of anyone who knew him, Alec Hawthorne hailed a cab to Martha's, where he had arranged to change into something he could wear home to Belvedere without being booked as a vagrant. Mired in the rush hour, the cab inched its way along Van Ness and through the early-evening revelers on Union until it finally deposited him beneath Martha's austere flat.

As he prepared to use his key, Martha opened the door. Obviously awakened from a nap and furious at being caught, she buttoned her blouse over her bare chest and backed away to let him enter. He considered but withheld a comment on her somnolence. Martha brooked no jests about her efficiency—she would have Hawthorne believe she never closed her eyes.

"Any luck down south?" he asked instead.

She shook her head. "I located the crew that hauled him to the hospital, but all they remember is that someone brought Donahue to their unit and they hit the siren and took off. I talked to the first deputy on the scene, and he said there were at least twenty people out there rescuing survivors—claimed it was the first time he'd ever been in a situation where there were too many heroes. The deputy, by the way, is still in therapy because of what he saw that night."

Hawthorne frowned. "After all this work, I'd hate to see Tollison get bounced on proximate cause. Let's put an ad in the papers— *Chronicle, Mercury-News*, whatever else they read down there—asking people to call us if they pulled victims from the crash. Offer a grand —we don't have much time."

"What if you don't find him?"

Hawthorne shrugged. "Then we try Donahue."

"His wife says he can't remember."

Hawthorne winked. "Maybe we teach him to fib. Apparently, he did it rather well before the crash."

They exchanged dark looks. Martha did not like jokes that implied her profession was akin to selling door-to-door. "Have you told Tollison about the proximate-cause thing yet?"

Hawthorne shook his head. "He has enough to do without worrying about getting nonsuited."

"He might come up with an answer, you know. He's not stupid."

From Martha, the comment was a ringing testimonial. Because as usual she knew what he was thinking, she stuck out her tongue.

He bent to kiss her. "Drink?" she asked when he was finished. He nodded.

To the tune of rattled ice, Hawthorne went to the guest room and changed into a sport coat and slacks. By the time he returned, there was a tumbler of Scotch beside his favorite chair. "What's on tap tonight?" Martha asked after a sip of vodka-rocks, her feet in ankle boots, her legs in leather slacks, her blouse a shimmering bib.

"Tollison's coming to the office at eight to go over the evacuation tests and the Mistite evidence."

"How'd our boy do today?"

"Not bad," he said. "He's still nervous, so the jury's nervous, too; they're not quite sure they can trust him not to lie to them. But he's getting there. Chambers is doing us a favor by being as pompous as a law professor, but we could use some breaks, like finding the guy who hauled Donahue from the wreck and getting the treatment tape admitted."

"How's the Mrs. holding up?"

He shrugged. "She looks good enough to put in Gumps' at Christmas, but she and Tollison are going through some kind of psychodrama, it looks like. He's in love with her or used to be, but I'm not sure it's reciprocated."

Martha's look was pained. "When is it ever?"

Because he was no longer current with the sources of her anguish, Hawthorne evaded meekly. "Want to come check it out in the morning? Maybe you'll see something I've missed."

She shook her head. "Mike and I are doing the response in the Reno crash tonight, then I'm going back down the peninsula in the morning. But if I don't come up with Donahue's savior tomorrow, I'll have to hire an investigator to take over—things are stacking up."

"Get Tanner if you can—he's the only one we don't have to double-check." Hawthorne looked at his watch, then asked what she was doing for supper.

"Turning on the microwave."

"Enough for me?"

"I'll do two."

"Two what?"

She shrugged. "I buy them by the gross and take off the wrappers and stuff them in the freezer. When I get home, I close my eyes and grab one. It's a real rush to see what comes out that little door."

"Tomorrow we eat out."

"Unless I get a better offer," she said sourly, and brought him a second drink.

"Have you bothered to tell Tollison that your leap at immortality has made his job impossible?" she asked when she returned.

"What do you mean?"

"You know damn well what I mean. There's no need to get into crashworthiness at all in this case; he could win on common-carrier liability by itself."

Hawthorne eyed the arch of her brow. "Like I said, Keith's got enough to worry about. And I've got ways to keep him too busy to find out on his own."

Martha smiled enigmatically. "I can think of a few myself." She paused. "You don't think you may have jeopardized a few too many people to get your reputation cast in gold?"

"You mean is the wrong lawyer trying the wrong case under the wrong theory of recovery?" Hawthorne's look was barren. "No. That hasn't occurred to me at all."

By the time the gavel banged the room to order the following morning, Hawthorne was convinced not only that Martha was no longer in love with him, but that the evaporation of her affections was causing her to reconsider her decision not to jump to another firm.

"Plaintiff calls Charles Bledsoe," Tollison announced, the tug of glumness in his face a byproduct of the drudgery of the night before. Meeting at the office at 8, they had not knocked off till 3 A.M., when Tollison took Hawthorne's ten-page outline of the next day's testimony back to the hotel to study. Hawthorne frowned as Tollison rubbed his eyes. Exhaustion had felled more than one lawyer in this business.

An officer of SurfAir, Charles Bledsoe was from the enemy camp and would thus be Tollison's first test. Although some attorneys hesitate to use the opposition to make their case, Hawthorne liked to call as many as he could, because in his experience the corporate types seldom helped their cause. More often than not, they came across as arrogant and unimaginative, so fearful of losing their jobs they hewed to the party line no matter how powerfully the evidence suggested the party line was crooked.

"What is your job, Mr. Bledsoe?" Tollison asked easily.

Bledsoe leaned forward. His power tie swung away from his stomach and his hands were clasped loosely on the rail guarding the witness chair. Chambers's clients always assumed a pious pose, until the shooting started.

"I'm vice-president of operations for SurfAir Coastal Airways," Bledsoe intoned.

"SurfAir is one of the defendants in this case?"

His smile was briefly homicidal. "Unfortunately, yes."

"What are your duties, Mr. Bledsoe?"

"I'm in charge of acquiring aircraft for SurfAir from various airframe manufacturers."

"Do your responsibilities include overseeing the specifications of the purchase orders for those aircraft?"

"Yes, they do."

"Did you in fact prepare the order for the H-11 that is the subject of this lawsuit?"

"I supervised the preparation, yes."

"That plane was ordered by SurfAir in early 1985, was it not?"

"Yes."

"And it was delivered in April of that year?"

"Yes."

"Directing your attention to the actual order for that aircraft, which has been marked as Plaintiff's Exhibit Six, can you tell me what exit configuration was specified?"

"The order specified model H-11A2, which included exits over both wings, as well as the main exit in the front and an emergency exit in the rear."

"At that time was it possible for you to order a plane with two *additional* exits, located in mid-fuselage, approximately halfway between the wing exits and the rear exit?"

"Yes. That was model H-11A4. We chose not to order that model."

"Why?"

His answer ready, Bledsoe blossomed with good will. "It cost four hundred thousand dollars more per unit."

Pleased with himself, Bledsoe looked at Hawley Chambers, who frowned a caution that made his client squirm. "Also," he amended quickly, "our testing indicated there was no need for it—we could comply with federal regulations without the additional exits."

"Thank you, Mr. Bledsoe. No more questions."

"Mr. Chambers?"

Chambers shook his head.

Tollison nodded. "Plaintiff calls Polly Janklow."

The courtroom stirred as a woman in a bright blue suit rose from the third row, pushed her way through the bar of the court, and stood behind the witness chair on heels as long as fingers. After swearing to tell the truth she took her seat, set her jaw, crossed her legs, and trained her ornamented eyes on Tollison, impatient to assert her truth.

"What is your current employment, Miss Janklow?"

"I'm a face model for a line of cosmetics."

"Locally?"

She nodded. "I work primarily at a department store downtown. At this point it's only part-time."

"Have you ever been employed by SurfAir?"

"From June of '82 to January of '87."

"In what capacity were you employed?"

"Flight attendant. Ultimately, *senior* attendant."

"As a stewardess for—"

"Flight attendant," she corrected quickly.

"Sorry. As a *flight attendant* for SurfAir, did you ever have occasion to fly in a Hastings H-11 aircraft?"

"Many times."

"I show you a model marked Plaintiff's Exhibit One and ask you if that represents a model of the aircraft you know as the H-11 as flown by SurfAir at the time you worked for them."

"It appears to."

"Can you tell me where the exits are located on that aircraft?"

She pawed at her hair and offered a grimace. "I should hope so— I used to point them out six times a day, not that anyone paid attention. There's one here, just behind the flight deck. One in the rear. And one over each wing."

"Did SurfAir ever conduct tests to determine whether the number of exits in the H-11 was adequate to meet the needs of passengers in a crash landing or other emergency situation?"

She nodded. "Twice, that I know of."

"What was the purpose of those tests, if you know?"

"They told us regulations required that in the event of an emergency, all passengers had to be able to escape through fifty percent of the exits in ninety seconds or less."

"There are a hundred twenty passengers on that plane when full?"

"Yes."

"And fifty percent of the exits is two exits?"

"Right. In the version we flew."

"So to comply with regulations, sixty passengers had to move through each of those exits in ninety seconds. If my math's correct, that's one and a half seconds per passenger."

"Right."

"So tell us. Did SurfAir pass the tests?"

Her mouth wrinkled. "They're still flying them, aren't they?"

Tollison waited for a titter from the audience to fade. "Can you tell us *how* SurfAir managed to pass those tests?"

Polly Janklow turned full front toward the panel. "The first test was run even before we had the planes."

"How is it possible to test a plane you don't have?"

"They made a pattern on the floor in the maintenance hangar—laid out tape to show the cabin walls, put in folding chairs for seats, built little wood frames where the exits were, that kind of thing. See, they were trying to decide which model they were going to buy, and they were worried about the evacuation rules, so they—"

"Objection," Chambers shouted. "*She* has no knowledge of what SurfAir was worried about or whether it was worried about anything at all. Move to strike as hearsay."

"Sustained. The jury will disregard the statements about the company's concerns."

Tollison waved away the irritant. "After they had acquired the aircraft, did they run a second test?"

"Yes. That was sometime in the fall of '85. This time they used a real airplane," she added briskly.

"Tell me about the second test. Do you feel it was a fair test of the emergency evacuation?"

"Objection—speculation."

"Sustained."

"Your Honor, this woman has been trained in emergency procedures. She should have a good idea whether—"

"Continue, Mr. Tollison," Powell instructed.

His fatigue fed by his defeat, Tollison rubbed his eyes again. "Tell us how the second test was done, Miss Janklow."

"First of all, they used the best-trained crews in the system to play the passengers, including people who'd done these tests before."

"Hardly the typical air traveler."

"Not even close. And of course no one thought it was a *real* emergency—we all knew it was a test. The whole thing was a joke, basically. I mean—"

"Objection. Move to strike the word joke."

"Sustained," Judge Powell ruled. "The jury will disregard the characterization. Please confine your testimony to the facts, Ms. Janklow. Leave the editorializing to the lawyers—they're getting paid for it."

The room chuckled above Polly Janklow's terse apology. "What I meant was, there wasn't any *effort* to make it an emergency condition. The lights were on the whole time. There was no smoke or fire or anything else that threatened anyone. It was more a party type of thing, to tell the truth about it."

"Is there any reason a true emergency environment couldn't be created?"

"Only money. Japan Airlines uses a crash simulator in their tests and training both—it turns out smoke, fire, noise, the whole works."

"Did anything else ease the difficulty of evacuating the aircraft rapidly?"

She nodded disgustedly. "The fifty-percent requirement is so you can assume two of the exits malfunction for some reason, right? But in a real crash, you won't know which exits aren't available until you *try* them. Then the people who find the door blocked have to turn around and go to another one, and there'd be a traffic jam and a lot of confusion that would use up a *lot* of those ninety seconds, it seems to me. But none of that could happen in the tests."

"Why not?"

"Because we knew which exits were going to be blocked."

"Before the test began?"

"Definitely. We knew the forward door and the starboard wing exit were the ones that didn't work."

"How?"

"Because there were two video cameras in the plane and they were trained on the *other* exits, which meant those were obviously the 'go' doors."

Tollison crossed his arms. "Let me see if I have this right. A group of healthy young SurfAir employees is sitting around in a plane that's parked securely on the ground, the lights are on and the exits are marked, then someone blows a whistle and everyone runs for doors they've picked out ahead of time. The plane is empty in ninety seconds, and the company tells the FAA it passed the emergency test with flying colors. Is that the way it worked?"

Chambers's objection was a snarl. "The question is argumentative and counsel knows it."

"Sustained. You know better, Mr. Tollison."

Tollison grinned so only Laura and the jurors could see him. "Tell me, Miss Janklow. Based on the tests you have described, did you regard the exit configuration in the H-11s flown by SurfAir as adequate in an emergency situation?"

Before she could respond, Chambers was on his feet. "There is no foundation for such testimony from this witness."

"Sustained."

Tollison shrugged. "Apparently the jury will have to decide how adequate they were; I have no more questions."

"Mr. Chambers?"

Halfway to his seat, Tollison muttered to himself and shook his head, and Hawthorne knew the reason. Caught up in the wrangle over the tests, Tollison had forgotten to show that Polly Janklow was a biased witness. By bringing the details out himself, Tollison would suggest they were nothing that needed suppressing, no big deal, nothing for the jury to be concerned with. Now Chambers would make the revelation, which could cost them momentum and, worse, suggest to the jury that Tollison was not trying to produce the truth but to shield them from it.

"Thank you, Your Honor," Chambers was saying. "Miss Janklow, you were fired by SurfAir, weren't you?"

She arched her back. "I was terminated."

"If you prefer the euphemism, fine. And you're suing SurfAir because of that dismissal, aren't you?"

"Yes, I am."

"You're suing in federal court for wrongful termination, you're alleging sexual harassment, and you're asking for a million dollars in damages, isn't that right?"

"If you knew what that bastard *said* to me, you'd know a million wasn't nearly enough to—"

"Objection," Chambers shouted. "Nonresponsive."

"Answer the question put to you and only the question put to you, Ms. Janklow. Please."

"But—"

"*Do* it, Ms. Janklow."

"I'm sorry, Your Honor."

Chambers retreated to his table. "It's fair to say that you'd do *any-thing* to get back at SurfAir for firing you, isn't it?"

"I wouldn't lie. Not under oath."

Chambers's smile was a stainless doubt. "By the way, you don't know for a fact that SurfAir didn't conduct evacuation tests that you had no part in, do you?"

"I guess not."

"Or conduct tests after you were terminated by the company for insubordination?"

"I don't know about that. And I wasn't insubordinate until my operations superintendent tried to get me to make it with him in the middle of the goddamn—"

"Move to *strike*, Your Honor."

"Sustained. Behave yourself, Ms. Janklow. You can consider that a warning."

Chambers regarded Polly Janklow the way he regarded the transients who loitered about the building. "That's all I have, Your Honor."

"Rebuttal, Mr. Tollison?"

Under the guise of looking at the clock, Tollison glanced at Hawthorne, who turned his head an inch. "No, Your Honor," Tollison said.

"The witness is excused. Next?"

Still shaken by his mistake, Tollison sounded hesitant. "Plaintiff calls Bryan Udall."

The clerk disappeared in the direction of the witness room. A moment later a sunny, stocky man dressed in a camel blazer and tartan slacks took the stand and awaited a question with what looked very much like glee. "Please state your current employment, if any, Mr. Udall," Tollison began.

"I have the pleasure to be retired."

"Where did you work before you retired?"

"West Pacific Oil Company; Long Beach, California. For forty years."

"What was your job at West Pacific at the time you left the company?"

"I was vice-president in charge of special fuels."

"Was one of your projects the development of a safer aviation gasoline?"

The witness puffed with pride. "Yes, indeed. I nursed that baby on and off for more than a decade."

"Tell us about it."

Udall nodded briskly. "Well, in a plane crash one of the worst problems is fire. In fact, in survivable accidents fire kills twice as many passengers as the crash itself. Now, one of the factors that contributes to fire is the fuel tank—when it ruptures, chances of fire increases tenfold. At West Pacific we don't have anything to do with fuel tanks —Robertson Aviation and others make them, and we look them over from time to time, to keep current. The latest are made out of rubber. Indy cars use them and the army put them in its helicopters—cut deaths by fire back to almost nothing in the airmobile units. Problem is, no one at the *airlines* seems to want to buy them. I guess they figure—"

Chambers cut off the digression. "Move to strike the portion about the airlines not wanting the fuel tanks, Your Honor," he grumbled. "Hearsay."

"Sustained. The jury will disregard the portion of the statement regarding the tanks. Proceed."

"Tell us about your aviation fuel, Mr. Udall."

Undeterred, the witness nodded happily. "Well, sir, what you usually get after a crash landing is a vapor in the cabin as a result of the rupture of the fuel tanks. Because of a high ratio of surface area to mass, gasoline vapor is highly flammable, much more so than the fuel in its liquid state."

"What does it take to ignite that type of vapor, Mr. Udall?"

"Just a spark will do it."

"Are sparks easy to come by in a plane crash?"

"You bet. What with metal scraping along the ground and engines breaking apart, you get all *kinds* of sparks. The vapor could ignite in contact with a piece of hot metal—the combustion chambers, say— or even a heating element in the galley."

"I take it at West Pacific you tried to improve the situation."

"You bet your buttons we did. What we came up with was an additive we called Mistite—basically, it's a long-chain polymer I cooked up with the help of some work the British had done along those lines. It's an antimisting kerosene; when it's added to the tanks, it prevents jet fuel from vaporizing."

"Doesn't jet fuel have to be vaporized for it to burn?"

"That's a fact; what you have to do with Mistite is add a degrader that converts the fuel back to a more volatile form just before it's squirted at the engines."

"Did you run any tests on Mistite, Mr. Udall? To see if it worked to reduce the danger of a post-crash fire?"

"Hell, yes. We had excellent results in the lab and so did the FAA. They had studies that showed over a hundred lives a year might be saved if the carriers started using it. And I personally think that was on the low side."

Tollison faced the jury. "When did the airlines start using your additive, Mr. Udall?"

For the first time since he took the stand, Udall's face grew dreary. "They never did."

"Why not?"

"Because of this *test* they ran—one single solitary test—back in 1984."

"Tell us about it."

Udall shook his head, as though what he was about to say was too bizarre to be believed. "Basically, what they did was load Mistite in the tanks of a 720B and crash it out in the desert. Remote-controlled, of course."

"What happened?"

Udall shook his head. "Sucker burned like she was built of balsa."

Tollison shrugged. "So why *should* the airlines use Mistite? It didn't work, did it?"

"The *hell it didn't*. What happened was, they screwed up the crash. The remote-control operator got the plane off course and she smacked into these cutters that were supposed to rip open the wing tanks to generate a fuel spill that would create the vapor they were testing. But the plane hit them head-on, so the thing turned into a firebomb. This was supposed to be a *survivable* crash, but the way *that* airplane crashed the Lord Himself wouldn't have survived, Mistite or no Mistite."

"What happened after that?"

Udall muttered an oath. "I tried to convince the FAA to run more tests, but they wouldn't. Claimed Mistite was a failure. But hell, even though there *was* a fire, the burn was cleaner and cooler than with ordinary fuel, which meant the fuselage wasn't penetrated, which is damn important if you're inside trying to get out. But they wouldn't listen to reason. When I got tired of boxing with them, I retired."

"So SurfAir doesn't use an antifire additive in its jet fuel."

"Nope. Neither does anyone else."

"And the FAA doesn't require it."

"No, sir. They don't even fund any research in the field."

"Thank you, Mr. Udall. No further questions."

"Mr. Chambers?"

Chambers remained seated. "Do you own stock in West Pacific Oil, Mr. Udall?"

"Sure do."

"How much?"

"None of your business, is it?"

Judge Powell leaned to his right. "Please answer the question, Mr. Udall."

Udall frowned. "Sorry, Judge. They didn't tell me I'd have to strip to my skivvies when I came down here. I got twenty thousand shares of my own and another thirty from the profit sharing."

"So if West Pacific were able to peddle the additive to the airlines, you'd stand to make a lot of money, wouldn't you?"

"I suppose I would. I don't know how much."

Chambers nodded. "Incidentally, Mr. Udall. In that test you mentioned, didn't the FAA estimate that only nineteen of the fifty-three passengers aboard the plane would have gotten out of that crash alive?"

"They claimed it was something like that."

"Yes they did, didn't they?"

Hawthorne is around the corner ordering a case of wine, leaving Keith Tollison and Laura Donahue momentarily alone in the restaurant. Once again isolated beneath the stairs, their eyes flick on and off each other as though they would like to be introduced but have no idea if they share an interest that would sustain a conversation. Fortified with the morning's progress, feeling for the first time capable of winning what he finally has come to consider his case, Tollison decides to tell her what has been bothering him all week. "We've got a little problem," he begins.

Laura raises a brow. "Really? I think it's going wonderfully. The jury seemed very upset at what you brought out about those tests."

"The problem's down the road."

Laura's eyes sparkle for him like in the old days. For a moment he is reminded how little loveliness there is in his life without her.

"Are you afraid I'll make a spectacle of myself?" she asks merrily.

He grins. "You're too honest to be a *great* witness, but I'll beat that out of you when the time comes. The problem is with our proof. We're trying to show the plane wasn't crashworthy, and so far that evidence looks pretty good. But we still haven't connected Jack to the defects."

"I don't know what you mean."

"Take the seats. We've offered proof that they were inadequately fastened to the frame and that most of them came loose at impact, but we haven't showed *Jack's* seat came loose. That's called proximate cause, and if we don't connect up our proof, we'll be thrown out of court."

"But the doctor—"

He nods. "Ryan can give circumstantial evidence of how Jack got hurt and say he was damaged by the fire. But I don't know if it's going to be enough. What was it that stuck into Jack's head, anyway?"

She closes her eyes and shakes her head. "A piece of metal of some kind. That's all I know."

"The next time you talk to Ryan ask him, okay? If they still have it at the hospital, ask him to bring it to court the day he testifies."

Laura nods absently, as if his worries and tactics are too trivial to entertain.

He takes her hand. "I may have to put Jack on, Laura. Just to make sure I'm doing everything possible."

Her composure vanishes. "You *can't*. He's not ready for that. Not *nearly*."

"I won't unless I have to, but it may be our only chance. What I need you to do is go home and see if you can dig up any memory at all of what happened that night. Where he was sitting on the plane; where he ended up. Anything."

She shakes her head. "That's gone, Keith. Every bit of it."

"You have to try, Laura. It's important."

"Not to me."

As he reels from yet another belittling of his effort, Laura grabs his arm. "I'm sorry. I didn't mean that."

When he doesn't excuse her, she asks a question: "Did you see Brenda this morning?"

He nods.

"She called me last night."

"What on earth for?"

"She said she was checking on Spitter, because she hadn't seen him for several days. But I know he went home last weekend, so I think it's just the trial."

"How do you mean?"

Laura shrugs. "She shows up every day, and hears people talk about everyone but her sister, and it's starting to drive her crazy."

Tollison swears. "If she gets crazy enough, she can ruin it."

Laura seems about to comment when Hawthorne returns with his wine and hauls them off to court. By the time they are seated at their table, Laura has almost persuaded Tollison that it would be suicidal to use her husband as a witness no matter how badly the case needs buttressing. For his part, Tollison wonders what he can offer Brenda Farnsworth that will persuade her to give them peace.

"Plaintiff calls John Stacy," Tollison declares after Powell gavels them to order. "Mr. Stacy, will you state your current employment?"

The wizened man adjusts his rimless glasses, blinks at his interrogator, and fingers his bow tie. "I'm a combustibles expert. I work at the FAA tech center in Atlantic City."

"Please tell the jury what your job entails."

"I test foam cushioning and upholstery materials to determine suitability for use in aircraft interiors. My tests primarily involve the combustibility of such materials—how they react to fire."

"Is it part of your job to recommend changes in the federal regulations based on your findings in the laboratory?"

"Yes, indeed."

"What percentage of your recommendations eventually become incorporated in the federal regulations, if you know?"

Chambers pounds the table. "Objection, irrelevant."

Tollison's voice is ringing. "Since the defense intends to rebut the claim of negligence with evidence that they were in full compliance with the FARs, I'm entitled to show those regulations were and are inadequate."

"I agree, Mr. Tollison. Overruled."

"What percentage of the recommendations from your office have been adopted by the FAA over the years, Mr. Stacy?" Tollison repeats.

Stacy presses his glasses to his forehead. "The last figures I saw showed an adoption rate of sixty-five percent with regard to recommendations by the NTSB, and I'd guess our shop has about the same result."

Tollison moves ahead. "Before we get to the materials used *inside* the H-11, Mr. Stacy, it's true, is it not, that neither the aluminum skin nor the plastic windows offer much protection in the event of a fire outside the aircraft."

He shrugs. "The windows melt rather rapidly, but it takes a pretty good blaze to penetrate the skin."

"Aren't there are instances of a fire penetrating the skin of a commercial aircraft in less than thirty seconds?"

"I believe that was the finding in the 737 fire in England back in '85. Such events are rare, but they happen."

"The skin could be made more impervious to fire than it is, could it not?"

Stacy nods. "We've done tests where we've painted the underbelly of an aircraft with an intumescent paint. What it does is swell up and form an insulating layer when it makes contact with a heat source. Our tests did not persuade us that the paint is invariably effective."

"When was the last such test you performed?"

"Seventy-six, I think."

"You've done nothing since?"

"No. Not with the paints."

"Intumescent paint is not required on airliners?"

"No."

"But it's available, is it not?"

"Yes."

"Does SurfAir coat its planes with such a material?"

"I've seen no evidence of it."

"Thank you." Tollison consults his outline. "Are there other means of increasing the protection of passengers from fires outside the aircraft?"

"Goodyear sent us a fire-resistant polycarbonate window to look at, but we don't have the money to test it, so it's just collecting dust."

"Have *any* fire-resistant measures been utilized on the outside of a commercial aircraft?"

"Well, McDonnell Douglas puts a phenolic resin insulation in the walls of the DC-10."

"What does that do?"

"Provides additional resistance to heat."

"Did the government require that insulation?"

"No. Douglas did it on their own."

Tollison nods. "Did you have occasion to examine the wreckage of flight 617, Mr. Stacy?"

"Yes I did."

"Where did you do that?"

"At the mock-up at Moffett Field."

"So when I ask you about the flight 617, your response includes what you observed during that inspection."

"Yes."

"On that basis, I ask you this—did Hastings Aircraft Corporation put an insulating resin into the walls of the H-11 that crashed on March twenty-third?"

"Objection, hearsay."

"Overruled."

"Answer the question, please," Tollison instructs.

Stacy shakes his head. "I saw no indication that they put anything in there that would insulate from fire."

Tollison nods briskly. He is on a roll, and he tries to prolong it. "Aviation history is littered with the bodies of passengers who were otherwise unhurt but who perished in flames after an emergency landing, isn't it?"

"Well, I wouldn't put it quite that—"

Chambers ejects from his chair. "Argumentative and irrelevant, Your Honor. Counsel continues to be outrageous."

Judge Powell does not seem perturbed. "Rephrase the question, counselor."

Tollison nods. "Let's get specific, Mr. Stacy. In the 727 crash near Salt Lake City in 1965, more than forty people died from the effects of toxic inhalants, isn't that correct?"

"Objection, irrelevant."

Tollison's fists clench and his face flushes. "I'm trying to show a pattern of knowledge in the industry, Your Honor. So the jury can judge whether the defendants' conduct in building and operating the H-11 was reasonable under the circumstances."

Judge Powell nods. "Overruled."

Chambers murmurs an angry aside to his assistant, who seems to shoulder blame for the ruling personally.

"Mr. Stacy?"

"I believe that's true—most of the deaths in the Salt Lake crash were from poison gases."

"And in the Varig in-flight lavatory fire over Paris in 1973, more than three fourths of the deaths were from fire-related carbon monoxide inhalation, true?"

"I believe it was something like that."

"That plane landed only eight minutes after the fire broke out, didn't it?"

"Yes."

"Yet over one hundred people died."

"I'm afraid so."

"In response to that fire, the NTSB recommended that regulations be amended to require smoke detectors in aircraft lavatories and that portable oxygen bottles be provided for flight attendants, correct?"

"Yes. It also recommended that automatic discharge fire extinguishers be installed in the lavatories and full-face smoke masks be available for the crew as well."

"Yes. But it's true, is it not, that *not one* of those recommendations was adopted at that time, that the *sole response* of the FAA was to order NO SMOKING and NO CIGARETTE DISPOSAL signs placed in the lavatories on commercial flights?"

Stacy wriggles within his clothing, as though it has combusted in sympathy with the subject. "That's correct."

Tollison surges forward. "Ten years later, on an Air Canada flight in 1983, twenty-three people died because of a lavatory fire, a fire that smoke detectors and automatic extinguishers would have prevented, correct?"

"I—"

"Objection. Speculation."

"Sustained."

Tollison ignores the interruption. "After this fire, the NTSB made eighteen *more* recommendations for improved fire safety?"

"Yes."

"And *still* none were immediately adopted by the FAA, except for the addition of some emergency lighting in the floors."

"Right."

Because he wants a jury inundated with disaster and incensed at the failures to prevent them, Tollison hurries to proceed. "A crash similar to flight 617 occurred in Portland a few years back, did it not?"

"True. An aircraft approaching the Portland, Oregon, airport was forced to land in a wooded area."

"What was the speed at the time of touchdown?"

"Right at a hundred twenty knots per hour."

"Only eight of the one hundred eighty-one passengers on that flight were killed, isn't that right?"

"Yes."

"Because there was no fire aboard the aircraft."

"Objection. Speculation."

"Sustained."

"*Was* there a fire aboard that aircraft after it crashed?"

"No."

"Why not?"

"Because there was no fuel left in the tanks—they ran out of gas."

"Yet in a similar accident in Atlanta, when there *was* fuel on board a plane that crash-landed in an area similar to Portland, sixty-two of eighty-nine people died, the majority from fire."

"Correct."

"In fact, there are over six hundred instances of fire, smoke, fumes, and explosions aboard U.S. aircraft *each year*, are there not?"

"Something like that."

"So it would be fair to say the danger of fire has been known to the FAA and to the industry for a long time."

"No question about it. We spend a lot of time on the subject."

"In fact, in 1978 the FAA recommended that new flammability standards be adopted regarding smoke and toxic emissions from cabin materials, didn't it?"

"Yes."

"Were the new standards in effect when the Hastings H-11 was manufactured six years later?"

"They were not."

"Are they in effect today?"

"No. The agency withdrew those proposals. We are recommending new standards, however, and—"

"In fact, the flammability standards in effect—not proposed, but *in effect*—both in 1985 and today were adopted *forty years* ago, were they not?"

"I'm afraid so."

"And over this period of FAA inaction, over a thousand people have been killed by fire in survivable accidents, isn't that right?"

"I . . . if you say so."

Chambers renews his objection of relevance, but it is too late. Tollison has done his duty, Hawthorne's script has prevailed, and the point has been made indelibly.

When the objection is overruled, Tollison continues quickly. "Isn't it true, Mr. Stacy, that the fabrics used in airplane interiors are synthetics rather than natural fibers?"

"Most of them."

"There's approximately a ton of plastic in the average airliner, right?"

"Just about."

"When synthetics burn they create toxic gases, don't they?"

"Yes."

"The accumulation of such gases creates a danger of synergism, does it not?"

"At times."

"Can you tell the jury what synergism is?"

Stacy turns their way. "It's the combination of toxic gases from various sources to form a substance of even *higher* toxicity and the corresponding reduction in the oxygen level that results in the process."

"Synergism is what happens when the interior of an airliner catches fire, is it not? The cabin becomes a gas chamber?"

"Not always, of course. But it's certainly possible."

"Have you examined the pathologists' reports on the victims of the SurfAir crash?"

"Many of them, yes."

"A significant number of those victims showed signs of toxic poisoning that are consistent with the existence of synergism, did they not?"

"Yes. Cyanide and carbon monoxide were present far in excess of toxic levels. Up to five micrograms per milliliter in the case of cyanide, which is toxic at a tenth of that."

"Fine. Now, the other thing that frequently happens in a crash situation is flashover, correct?"

Stacy's smile is tolerant. "A lot of things happen in a crash, sir. Flashover is only one of them."

"What is flashover?"

"Basically, it's a burst of fire at the ceiling of the aircraft from the ignition of gases that have collected there."

"Flashover can cause burns and damage to the pulmonary system and a host of other medical problems, can it not?"

"I'm not a medical man, but those would seem to be the consequence of any fire."

"A flashover is a particularly *intense* fire, though."

"Yes. The temperature at the ceiling can exceed two thousand degrees."

"In fact, flashover killed all three hundred people in the Saudi Arabian cargo fire in 1980, didn't it? Killed them even though the plane was on the ground when the fire started. Killed them before they could get the doors open and get out?"

"Objection," Chambers thunders. "Irrelevant."

"Overruled."

"Mr. Stacy?"

"Yes. The Saudi fire was a particularly virulent example of flashover."

"Did your examination of the SurfAir wreckage indicate flashover had occurred in the rear cabin following the crash?"

"Yes."

Tollison pauses so the jury can catch up. "What are the padded portions of the seats—the cushions—in the H-11 made from, Mr. Stacy?"

"They're made from urethane."

"Did many of the seats catch fire in the crash?"

"Yes. Most of them."

"When urethane burns, does it gives off gases?"

"Yes."

"Name them."

"Well, there's acrolein, hydrogen cyanide, carbon monoxide, sulphuric acid ..."

"Phosgene?"

"That, too."

"Phosgene is so toxic it's used in chemical-warfare weapons, is it not?"

"I wouldn't know."

"Well, there's no question that each of those gases is toxic to humans, is there?"

"Yes they are, depending on the density."

"And the *combination* of those gases is *highly* toxic?"

"Yes."

"The cushions and cabin materials aren't the only things that give off toxic fumes in a cabin fire, are they?"

"No, many of the materials the passengers bring on board contribute as well. For example, a burning wool overcoat can emit enough cyanide to kill seven people."

"Thank you. Let's get back to the seats. One answer to the toxic-emission problem would be to wrap the urethane cushion in fire-blocking material, isn't that so?"

"Yes."

"Is such a material available?"

"Yes. Kevlar is one. There are others, including some that are fire-resistant and also self-extinguishing. NASA has developed a polymide material that is smokeless when it burns."

"Did Hastings wrap the H-11 seat cushions in Kevlar or other fire-blocking material, Mr. Stacy?"

"No."

"Even if they didn't use a fire block, they could have used an alternative to urethane for the cushions, could they not? An alternative that was less flammable?"

Stacy nods. "Du Pont makes a neoprene called Vonar that they've tried to sell for that purpose, I believe. Other brands, such as Celiox and Norfab, are available as well."

"But Hastings didn't use them."

"No."

"And SurfAir didn't require them."

"Apparently not."

"I have no more questions, Your Honor."

"Cross-examine, Mr. Chambers."

Chambers advances on the witness like a panther. "Mr. Stacy, you examined the wreckage of flight 617 carefully, did you not?"

"Yes."

"Did you find, as regards the interior of the aircraft, that federal regulations had been violated in any way?"

"I did not."

"No violation that would contribute to a fire aboard the plane?"

"No."

"In fact, did you see *anything* that did not conform to the custom and practice in the industry?"

"No."

"Fine. It isn't true, is it, that the FAA has done nothing about the fire hazard aboard commercial airplanes?"

"No, it isn't. We made a rule requiring fire-blocking material to be incorporated in seat cushions just last year. The requirement went into effect this November. Also, we have noticed a rulemaking procedure for an increase in flammability standards, though they won't go into effect until next year."

"So the impression of FAA inactivity that Mr. Tollison was trying to create is essentially incorrect?"

"Objection," Tollison intones. "Argumentative."

"Sustained."

Chambers mutters to himself. "It's certainly true, isn't it, Mr. Stacy, that the various changes suggested by Mr. Tollison would cost a lot of money?"

"Certainly."

"Which would raise the cost of travel to consumers?"

"I imagine so."

"Most of the so-called improvements Mr. Tollison spoke about would also add weight to the plane, correct?"

"Yes. Some of them."

"Which would create additional safety concerns, in terms of lift-off speeds and runway lengths and the like?"

"Well, that's not really my—"

Chambers nods with satisfaction. "No more questions, Your Honor."

"Mr. Tollison? Rebuttal?"

"Just briefly, Your Honor. None of the new regulations you mentioned applied to the H-11 that crashed with Mr. Donahue on board, did they?"

"No."

"In fact, at the time the H-11 was built, there had been no upgrading of the flammability standards governing cabin furnishings in commercial aircraft since 1947, right?"

"I'm afraid so."

"Knowing this, neither Hastings nor SurfAir took steps to improve the situation themselves."

"No. Not that I could see from the mock-up."

"Thank you." Tollison pauses, then decides to pursue another point. "Since Mr. Chambers repeatedly deferred to the mighty FAA, I'd like to review that agency's regulatory process with you for a moment, if I may. The FAA is only just *now* requiring smoke detectors inside aircraft lavatories, is it not? Fifteen years after the NTSB recommended them?"

"Yes. We've issued a notice of rulemaking on that, so it should happen soon. We do move slowly at times, I admit."

"Neither SurfAir nor Hastings *voluntarily* installed smoke detectors on the H-11, did they?"

"No."

"The *French* require smoke detectors in all their planes, don't they?"

"I believe so. Yes."

Tollison nods. "The FAA has required smoke detectors to be placed in the *cargo* bays of commercial planes for years, have they not?"

"I ... yes."

"But not where the people are."

"No."

The audience murmurs, and Tollison waits for the fact to be absorbed. "You mentioned some new rules that are in the works, Mr. Stacy. The FAA also filed a notice of rulemaking to improve flammability standards and lessen the toxicity of cabin materials back in 1978, did it not?"

"Yes."

"What happened?"

"We withdrew the notice."

"So even though a rulemaking procedure has been filed, at this point there is no certainty that the new flammability standards will actually go into effect."

"No, I suppose not."

The audience rumbles again.

"The rear door fell off a DC-10 in a flight over Windsor, Canada, back in 1969, did it not, Mr. Stacy?"

"I believe so."

"How long did it take for the FAA to require a correction in the design of those doors?"

"I'm not sure, I—"

"It took four years, didn't it?"

"I guess that's right."

"In the meantime, a DC-10 crashed in Paris because a rear door fell off, and three hundred and forty people died."

"Unfortunately, yes."

"How long did it take after a pilot accidentally deployed the spoilers on an airborne DC-8 for the FAA to make spoiler locks mandatory?"

"Four years, I believe. There's a bit of a disaster-response mentality in the agency."

"Let's look at midair collisions. The midair over the Grand Canyon in 1958 led to the establishment of the FAA in the first place, correct? So there has been concern about midair collisions for thirty years."

"Yes."

"And the government set out to come up with a technological means to avoid them."

"That was one approach. Yes."

"But by the time of the San Diego midair some twenty years later, there was *still* no collision-avoidance technology aboard commercial aircraft, even though the FAA had considered that its primary mission since 1958."

"No, but—"

"And the technology that has been available for years—the so-called ACAS system—is *still* not required in commercial aircraft, is it, even after the Aeromexico midair took almost a hundred lives in 1986?"

"No, but a rule has been proposed, and—"

"*Today*, sir. The system is still not required *today*."

"No it isn't."

Puffed with satisfaction, Tollison glances back at Hawthorne. Blessed with an infinitesimal nod, he looks to the bench. "No more questions," he announces, then strikes a formal pose. "This completes the liability phase of our evidence, Your Honor. Unless the court prefers otherwise, we will begin the damage portion tomorrow morning."

Powell nods. "Court stands adjourned until nine A.M."

Depleted by the day, Tollison is about to return to the table when he sees Brenda Farnsworth edging toward the door at the back of the room. He shoulders through the crowd and grabs her arm. "We need to talk."

"No, we don't," she hisses, and tries to wrench away.

"Just for a minute."

She allows him to tug her out of the stream of traffic and onto a back pew.

"What is it?" she demands sullenly.

"I just want to know why you're torturing yourself like this. Carol's name isn't going to come up in this trial. No one's going to say bad things about her. Why don't you go home and forget about it? You've got some money now, so spend it. Fix up the house. Take a trip. Do something other than sit here day after day and rehash the crash."

Her lips flatten. "You just want me to make it easier for you."

He is genuinely baffled. "Easier to do what?"

"Tell lies."

"About what? Laura isn't going to claim she and Jack were lovebirds. We threw that out."

"It's not enough."

He sighs. "I know you have a reason to be mad at her. Because of me, I mean. But that's over. And Laura's not asking for anything for herself out of this; the money will go to Jack. So why don't you just—"

Brenda looks toward the table in the front. "I did a lot of reading after the crash, Keith. Law books, mostly. And I came across something about the 'but for' rule. Do you remember that one? It says you legally cause a thing to happen if 'but for' your act it wouldn't have occurred."

Tollison closes his eyes. "So?"

"So 'but for' Jack Donahue, Carol would still be alive. He *killed* her, Keith. He made her go to LA, which means he put her on that plane, which means he *killed* her."

"Carol got on that plane because she wanted to, Brenda."

She shakes her head. "Men like Jack Donahue are *devils*—they work on women their whole lives, study them like scientists until they learn how to make them see things that aren't there, believe things that are false, feel things they shouldn't feel. *You* read her diary—Jack swooped down on Carol and turned on the charm until she couldn't say no to him. And so she's dead. Well, I won't sit here and watch you convince that jury they should give Jack Donahue a *prize*."

"Jesus Christ, Brenda. Jack's a *basket* case. Even if his therapy works wonders, he'll suffer every day of his life. Don't you think that's enough?"

Her eyes beam her heartache toward his soul. "It hasn't been for me; why should it be for him?"

COMPENSATORY DAMAGES—PERSONAL INJURY

If, under the court's instructions, you find that the plaintiff is entitled to a verdict against the defendants, or either of them, you must then award plaintiff damages in an amount that will reasonably compensate him for each of the following elements of claimed damage, provided that you find that such harm or loss was suffered by him and proximately caused by the act or omission upon which you base your finding of liability. The amount of such award shall include:

The reasonable value of medical care, services, and supplies reasonably required and actually given in the treatment of the plaintiff to the present time and the present cash value of the reasonable value of similar items reasonably certain to be required and given in the future.

Reasonable compensation for any pain, discomfort, fears, anxiety, and other mental and emotional distress suffered by the plaintiff and of which his injury was a proximate cause, and for similar suffering reasonably certain to be experienced in the future from the same cause.

No definite standard is prescribed by which to fix the reasonable compensation for pain and suffering, nor is the opinion of any witness required as to the amount of such compensation. In making an award for pain and suffering, you shall exercise your authority with calm and reasonable judgment and the damages you fix shall be just and reasonable in the light of the evidence.

PUNITIVE DAMAGES—RECOVERY OF AND MEASURE

If you find that plaintiff suffered damages as a proximate result of the conduct of a defendant on which you base a finding of liability, you may then consider whether you should award punitive damages against defendants, or either of them, for the sake of example and by way of punishment. You may in your discretion award such damages, if, but only if, you find by a preponderance of the evidence that said defendant was guilty of malice in the conduct on which you base your finding of liability.

Malice means conduct with a conscious disregard for the safety of others. A corporation acts with conscious disregard of the safety of others when it is aware of the probable dangerous consequences of its conduct and willfully and deliberately fails to avoid those consequences.

The law provides no fixed standards as to the amount of punitive damages, but leaves the amount to the jury's sound discretion, exercised without passion or prejudice.

In arriving at an award of punitive damages, you are to consider the following:

(1) the reprehensibility of the conduct,

(2) the amount which will have a deterrent effect on the defendant in the light of defendant's financial condition,

(3) that the punitive damages must bear a reasonable relation to the actual damages.

FOURTEEN

"Caught you, counselor."

Just when Alec Hawthorne had decided he was safe for the duration, the greeting attacked him from the rear.

From beneath her yellow rain hat, Brenda Farnsworth inspected him from head to toe. "I like the beard," she said offhandedly, "but the outfit carries Ralph Lauren a bit too far."

His chin sank with resignation. "How'd you spot me?"

She pointed. "The watch. It's far too fancy for a tramp. You've been a naughty boy, Mr. Hawthorne."

"How?" Without trying, he thought of a dozen ways.

"You're not supposed to be there."

He watched her tongue swab her upper lip. "So you and Hawley are intimates these days."

"We keep in touch. In case we need each other." Brenda crossed her arms. "So how's it going, anyway?"

He shrugged. "Your guess is as good as mine."

"Keith's better than I expected, I have to admit. But it won't be enough—Chambers is holding too many cards."

"Are you one of them?"

She raised a shoulder, then let it drop.

"I still can't figure your interest," he said. "Why are you here every day? What are you doing on their witness list?"

She rolled her eyes in a burlesque swoon. "That nasty crash injured one of Altoona's leading citizens. Naturally, I'm concerned about it."

"Bullshit."

The word cancelled her performance. "I lost a sister, remember?"

320

"The trial isn't going to change that."

"I also lost a lover."

"It won't change that, either."

"Prick."

He laughed. "So tell me—how's Hawley going to use you when he puts on his defense?"

"He thinks I'm going to say bad things about Jack."

"Are you?"

"Only if I have to."

"What would make you have to?"

Her look was crafty. "If I thought Laura and Keith were about to get their hands on a big hunk of money, I'd try to put a stop to it."

"How?"

"By blowing the whistle on the lovebirds."

"Are you so sure Keith and Mrs. Donahue are lovers?"

"Sure enough to say so to the jury."

Her intent was clearly independent of truth or falsity. "What if I asked you not to?"

"Since you got a nice settlement for Carol, I'd think it over. And then I'd do it anyway."

From a sudden impulse, he took her hand. "What can I do to convince you to stay out of the Donahue case?"

Angered, she pulled away. "I'll do what I have to do," she retorted hotly, then seemed to cool. "If they don't try to make Laura and Jack like Ozzie and Harriet, maybe I'll keep quiet. But if they do, I tell what I know." She stuffed her hands in her pockets, as if to preserve them from contamination. "When's she on, by the way? I want to be sure I catch the show "

"Monday, probably. The doctor goes tomorrow." He pointed to the hotel that surveyed them from the other side of Market Street. "Can I buy you a drink? I hear vengeance works up quite a thirst."

Although he expected her to refuse, she glanced up and down the street, then examined him long enough to make him wish he hadn't issued the invitation. "Why not?" she said finally, and took his arm and strolled with him to the hotel bar.

"What have you done with your settlement money?" he asked as she sipped her stinger.

"Bought a car. Had the house painted. Put my son in therapy. You know—the basics."

"How's he doing?"

"Better, I guess. At least he's out of the graveyard."

"Is he back with you?"

She shook her head. "With Laura. He sleeps in her garage."

"How do you feel about that?"

For the first time since confronting him, she softened. "When you've spent twenty-five years dealing with someone like Spitter, you get used to mixed blessings."

Hawthorne watched her stir her drink, then glanced at the clock on the wall. "Got any plans this evening?"

Her lip twitched. "I thought I'd sit home alone, down a six pack of Bud, and watch *L.A. Law* to see how Keith measures up."

"Would you like to have dinner together?"

She looked around. "Here?"

"It's not the Fairmont, but I expect it has a steak."

She hesitated. "I noticed you sneaking into one of those side rooms with that woman who works for you. What's the deal there, anyway?"

He looked out at Market Street, once grand, then tawdry, now rebounding. Rather like himself. "We used to be close, but now we're not."

"When's the last time you slept with her?"

"The night before my heart attack."

"When's the last time you tried?"

He laughed. "The night before my heart attack."

"Why not since?"

"She's afraid I'm going to drop dead in the middle of the festivities. I'm a little afraid of that myself," he added with false flippancy. "So how about it? Shall we adjourn to the dining room?"

She looked at him until he squirmed. "I've got a better idea."

"What?"

"Let's try that apartment of yours. The one with all the wine."

"I take it you're willing to take your chances," he said as he threw money on the table.

"I grew up in my daddy's bar. There's nothing you could do, in the middle of the festivities or otherwise, that I haven't seen before, including drawing your last breath."

They left the hotel and took a cab to Vallejo Street, to a point just behind the blare of Broadway. He unlocked the gate that guarded the unprepossessing walk-up, allowed her to precede him to the entrance, then ushered her inside. "Somehow I don't see you conducting your love life in a place like this," she whispered.

"That's the idea," he replied. "And you can be as loud as you like

—I'm the only tenant who speaks English."

They took the stairs to the second floor. The apartment was small—pullman kitchen, sitting room, with a narrow view of the bay and the looming undercarriage of the bridge that spanned it toward the east. Hawthorne helped Brenda off with her coat and motioned for her to take a seat on the couch, then left her for the kitchen.

The refrigerator was not as he had left it last; he suspected Martha had entertained a new friend since the last time they had entertained each other. "Chenin blanc or champagne?" he called.

"Champagne. Maybe if we pretend it's an occasion it'll turn out to be one."

He delivered her Veuve Clicquot in a stem glass that had a bluish cast. She sipped and smiled. "This isn't Cold Duck."

"Nope." He sat in a club chair and regarded her as he imbibed his own accomplice, which was Scotch.

"You look surprised we're here," she said.

He shrugged. "I am, a bit. I figured you were still hung up on Keith."

"I'll always be hung up on Keith, but the equation has gotten too unbalanced lately—this may even things up. Besides, I haven't had an adventure in twenty years." She raised a brow. "You're not diseased or anything, I trust?"

He considered his heart. "Nothing catching."

She upended her glass, then raised it in the universal gesture for another round. "If we're going to be naughty, I better be drunk enough to enjoy it."

From the kitchen he watched as she strolled around the room, examining the furnishings, the art, the books, the view. "Not that it's relevant, but are you married at the present time?" she asked as he brought the bottle to the sitting room and refilled her glass.

Her look told him she knew enough of his past to be mischievous. "Not at the moment."

"You've been to the altar an obscene amount."

"It would appear that way to anyone but a Moslem, I suppose."

"Have you been faithful to any of them?"

Since honesty is the most seductive line of all, he said, "One."

"The first?"

"The third."

"Why her?"

"I decided to try the only thing I could think of that I'd done wrong the first two times."

"Did it work?"

He shook his head.

"Why not?"

"She didn't choose to reciprocate."

"You mean she had other men."

The bitterness of his response surprised him. "If she confined herself to men, it was the only taboo she observed."

Brenda's smile was sloppy. "Let's hear it for our side." She lofted the stem glass once again. "If I get drunk, can I stay here all night?"

"Be my guest."

He refilled her glass and she emptied it in successive swallows. "Ready as I'll ever be," she said, blinking with her buzz. "Just remember, I live in Altoona so I've only screwed in the minor leagues." She banged her glass onto the coffee table hard enough to spill its dregs. "But I'm working on my game."

"Will Mr. Tollison be bothered if he finds out about this?" he asked, uncertain of the answer he preferred.

Her lush smile vanished. "I sure as hell hope so."

As manipulated as she, he tugged her to her feet, then led her toward the bedroom. By the time he was out of his clothes she was naked on the bed, her arms grasping the rods of the headboard, her legs spread for him to admire their confluence. "The last time I fucked a stranger, I got pregnant," she observed lazily.

"I'm not a stranger; I'm your lawyer."

"I'll probably have twins."

He stood over her and read her flesh. Unlike Martha, she was excited to be the subject of a dissertation. As she arced her back, his cock elongated to intersect his gaze. A moment later she grasped it like a fry pan and tugged him to her side.

They wallowed in flesh for long minutes that were in turn yielding and belligerent, trying proven combinations and invited variations, exhibiting the skills each hoped would spur the other on. Brenda writhed in increasingly spastic throes, to the point that Hawthorne considered whether she wanted to be punished, then decided she was content to be punishing herself. Her ministrations were both insistent and defiant, as though done primarily to prove her courage, a French frill on the theme of Russian roulette. As a result, he was quickly on the brink.

He arranged their torsos and entered her conventionally. She quickly holstered him to his hilt, then slid hands between their bellies and monitored the redundant progress of his prick with nails that were sharp enough to circumcise him. When he was confident she wished him no harm, he glanced at his watch, then hurried toward the close; he was supposed to meet Tollison at eight.

He was spent in a dozen convulsive writhes. After wiping himself with a Kleenex, he stood to dress. She turned toward the telltale sound, stretched, scraped semen off her thigh with a forefinger, licked, and finally swallowed it. "Lots of calories in this stuff. Guess I better go back on my diet."

Her look was bothersome. "How do you feel? Booze-wise?"

"Sober enough to get out of your hair, if that's what you're worried about."

"You're free to stay," he offered.

She eyed him skeptically. "Will you want an encore?"

He shook his head. "Not tonight."

"The old wham-bam, huh? Well, it's not the first time."

She dressed reluctantly, as though she would prefer to remain naked. When she was finished, she went to the other room and waited while he cleaned himself and the apartment. Though he felt a need to reveal that she had excited the first orgasm since his heart attack and that he was indebted to her for proving he was back to normal, at least below the belt, he didn't because he couldn't be sure what she would do with the information.

"Does Hawley have any tricks up his sleeve?" he asked as he was washing out the glassware.

Her laugh was bitter. "Why, Mr. Hawthorne. I believe you're asking me to betray my cause."

He laughed. "So does he?"

"I certainly hope so."

When he entered the courtroom some sixteen hours later, Alec Hawthorne was far less fearful of his future than he had been in a dozen months. But despite his powers of persuasion, Brenda still seemed determined to defeat the trial. Indeed, he wasn't at all sure he hadn't revealed to her more than he should have about the problems with the plaintiff's case, while learning nothing about what Hawley Chambers had in store for Brenda Farnsworth's former lover.

"Plaintiff calls Dr. Arthur Ryan," Tollison was saying as Hawthorne took his seat.

The top of Ryan's head glowed in the fluorescent ether like a baseball just out of the box. His rumpled suit gave him an air of ascetic authority; his height made him seem too large to lie. Hawthorne smiled—he could not imagine anyone disbelieving the man.

The doctor swore to his oath while fingering his necktie like a rosary.

Waiting for the formalities to conclude, Tollison seemed relaxed and personable. Out of the world of aviation, of which he knew little, into the world of medicine, where he had trod before, Tollison for the first time looked at home in federal court.

"What is your profession, Doctor?"

"I'm a physician," Ryan answered.

"What is your specialty?"

"Neurosurgery."

"Do you have hospital privileges?"

"I'm chief of surgery at San Jose Memorial Hospital."

"How long have you held that position?"

"Six years as chief. I've held staff privileges for eighteen."

"Are you a board-certified neurosurgeon?"

"Yes."

"Do you hold any other professional honors?"

"I've been elected to the Congress of Neurological Surgeons and to the Harvey Cushing Society. I'm also a fellow in both the American and International College of Surgeons."

"These are professional honors conferred by specialists in your field?"

"Yes."

"Very impressive, Doctor."

Chambers's voice dripped vinegar. "May we dispense with the editorials, Your Honor?"

Tollison apologized before the ruling. "Please tell the jury about your educational background."

Chambers did not bother to stand. "In order to speed things along, we stipulate to Dr. Ryan's credentials."

Tollison bent in a mock bow. "Your acknowledgment of the doctor's eminence is appreciated, counsel. But I believe the jury would like to hear his record for themselves."

Hawthorne smiled—Tollison had avoided another trap. Chambers never yielded anything unless—sometime, somewhere—it would work to his advantage. By offering his stipulation, Chambers hoped to avoid the jury's being overwhelmed by the doctor's pedigree.

"I have a B.S. in zoology from Yale," Ryan said easily, "and a medical degree from Tufts."

"Where did you have your hospital training?"

"I interned and was a surgical resident at Sloan-Kettering in New York. After that I was a resident in neurosurgery at Stanford Medical Center. Eventually, I was chief neurosurgical resident at Stanford."

"How long was your residency at Stanford?"

"Five years."

"And since then you've specialized in treating injuries to the brain, have you not?"

"Yes I have."

"How many brain surgeries have you conducted in the last eighteen years, Doctor? Just roughly."

"More than a thousand."

Pleased, Tollison nodded. Who could not be impressed with a thousand visits to the brain? "Have you had occasion to treat Jack Donahue, the plaintiff in this case?"

"Yes."

"How did that occasion arise?"

Ryan crossed his legs. "Last March, when news of the SurfAir crash began coming in, the administrator at Memorial thought it possible that if there were many survivors, some would likely be transported to our shop, since next to the Stanford center we are the largest tertiary-care facility in the vicinity. After someone gave me a call, I went to the hospital immediately, both to see if I could be of help and to observe our emergency procedures in action. We believe we're prepared for a mass disaster, but you never know till it happens."

"Were you at the hospital when they brought Jack Donahue in?"

"Yes."

"What time was that?"

"May I consult my chart?"

"Was it made contemporaneously with the events it records?"

"Yes."

"Do you rely on it in the course of your work?"

"Of course."

"Please consult it."

Ryan flipped a page of the sheaf in his hand. "I first saw Jack Donahue in the emergency room at eight forty-five that evening. March twenty-third."

"Have you been in charge of his treatment ever since?"

"Yes."

"Is that treatment continuing to this day?"

"Yes, it is."

Tollison nodded. "What exactly was wrong with Mr. Donahue when they brought him to the hospital?"

Ryan recrossed his legs. "I'll start with the easy ones. He had broken each arm—the left in the deltoid area of the humerus, the right at the radius and ulna of the forearm, near the styloid process. His left foot was badly crushed—the metatarsals were fractured, as were other major bones, and damage to the ligature was severe as well. He had lacerations and contusions front and back, first- and second-degree burns over his upper body, and significant pulmonary impairment. And that doesn't even get us to his main problem."

"Which was?"

Ryan looked at the jury. "Brain damage, to put it simply."

Tollison left time for the image to become as concrete as the imaginations in the jury box could make it. "Let's leave the brain for the moment and get back to the other injuries. Which of them, if any, will result in permanent disability?"

Ryan frowned, doubtlessly remembering the preparation session with the lawyers and his irritation at Hawthorne's suggestion that he answer the question with unalloyed assurance. "Aside from his neurological impairment, the arms are fine except for minor scarring. There may be residual restriction in his foot as a result of the fractures and dislocations. But the primary chronic condition—again, aside from his intracranial injury—is pulmonary."

"What is that condition, exactly?"

"Mr. Donahue suffers from adult respiratory distress syndrome. His bronchial and lung passages were damaged from inhaling toxic substances, to the extent that his respiratory capacity will be impaired for life."

"By how much?"

"I'd say between forty and sixty percent."

"What does that mean to Mr. Donahue as a practical matter?"

"His physical activity will be limited because of his reduced capacity to absorb oxygen, and he will be more vulnerable to environmental irritants such as air pollution and the like, and hence to respiratory disease."

Tollison nodded. "Thank you. Now if you will, Dr. Ryan, please tell us about Mr. Donahue's head injury."

Ryan looked toward the ceiling, as though Jack Donahue floated like a satellite amid the lights and tiles. "When he was brought to Memorial, Mr. Donahue was unconscious. His head had swollen and was purplish-black in color. Blood and brain tissue were oozing from a wound in his skull. His blood pressure was two-fifty over two hundred, his pupils were dilated, and he was not responsive to stimulus, at least initially. But we didn't need to diagnose symptomatically—it was obvious his skull had been pierced by a foreign object."

Tollison nodded. "At this point I'd like to take Mr. Donahue's initial treatment step by step, if we may. When he reached the hospital and you recognized the symptoms of brain injury, what exactly did you do?"

Dr. Ryan flipped some pages. "First, we performed general emergency procedures. We gave him primary ventilatory assistance—a mask and air bag. We sandbagged his head and neck as a precaution against spinal jeopardy. We put him on cardiac and blood-pressure monitors to watch for Cushing's Triad, which is indicative of subdural hematoma. We put him on a Mannitol IV to counteract cerebral edema and to shrink brain tissue to relieve intracranial pressure. We cross-matched blood for surgery and ran a blood count and blood-chemistry profile to get a line on the toxins."

"What was your general assessment of his condition?"

"He was in bad shape. Death was certainly a possibility. Painful stimuli—sticking him with a pin—resulted in bilateral decerebrate posturing—the extension of arms and legs while the body arcs at the torso, indicative of deep cerebral dysfunction. Our initial evaluation placed him at level five on the Glasgow Coma Scale."

Tollison nodded. "We'll return to that in a minute. What did you do next, Doctor?"

"We administered drugs to control the posturing and broad-spectrum antibiotics to guard against infection, and gave him a tetanus shot. We suctioned his airway to remove secretions. We administered Lasix and dopamine to counter supraventricular tachycardia and atrial fibrillation caused by the stress to his heart. I also administered Pavulon, a curare derivative, in order to facilitate an intubation that would allow us to administer pure oxygen to reduce BP. It was at this point we decided to go in to relieve the intracranial pressure and extract the invasive object, so I administered sodium pentathol to anesthetize him and reduce his brain metabolism, and performed an emergency craniotomy."

"All this time Mr. Donahue was unconscious?"

"Yes."

"How long did he remain unconscious?"

Dr. Ryan looked at the jury once again. "Mr. Donahue remained unconscious for almost six months."

"In a coma."

"In a coma. Correct."

"Please describe the surgery, Doctor."

"Objection, irrelevant and prejudicial." Chambers's interruption was clearly an irritant to the jury.

"I can understand counsel not wanting the jury to know the ordeal his clients' conduct put Mr. Donahue through," Tollison argued, "but it is proof of what he has suffered."

Judge Powell nodded. "Overruled."

"Doctor?"

"As I said, we opted for surgery to relieve the subdural hematomas and to remove the object that had pierced the skull. We shaved the head and made an incision in the scalp so it could be peeled back to expose the portion of skull we needed to remove. In this case that portion was approximately the left forehead, about here." Ryan pointed. "Once the skull was exposed, we drilled four small holes at the corners of the portion we wanted to remove, then cut out the rectangle with a cranial saw. In Mr. Donahue's case, we removed a section of bone the size of a playing card."

The room was hushed, as if the surgery were still in progress. "Then what?" Tollison asked.

"I cut through the dura—the protective membrane around the brain—to see what was going on. There was a great deal of bleeding, so I cauterized as many of the bleeders as I could, then sucked out the clotted blood that was causing pressure, being careful to extract as little brain tissue as possible.

"After we relieved the hematomas and stopped the obvious sources of bleeding, I extracted the foreign object, then waited to see if further bleeding would result. When it did, I blocked as many bleeders as I could find and removed such skull fragments and other debris as I could without doing further damage. At that point, I did nothing further beyond an exploratory peek at the invasive injury, because we had not yet run tests showing the extent of the problems in there, and because you don't invade the mid-brain unless you have to. Since it was quite possible I would have to go back in once the tests were run, we put a temporary cover over the portion of the brain we had exposed, replaced the flap of scalp, and bandaged him up, doing everything possible to avoid infection."

Tollison reached into his briefcase. "I show you an object marked Plaintiff's Exhibit Two. Can you identify it?"

"That's the object that pierced Mr. Donahue's skull."

"What is it, if you know?"

A slight smile stretched his lips. "A knitting needle. With accompanying fibers of bright red yarn."

"Thank you. Move that it be admitted."

Judge Powell nodded.

"Is the damage to Mr. Donahue's brain still causing him problems, Doctor?"

Ryan nodded. "A great many of them."

"Will some of these problems persist for the rest of his life?"

"Very definitely."

Tollison glanced at the jury. When they seemed suitably entranced, he moved on. "After the emergency craniotomy, did you make a further examination of the injury?"

"Yes. We performed both a CAT scan and a PET scan."

"Those are methods of assessing brain damage?"

"Yes. The PET scan—positron emission tomography—measures glucose metabolism to indicate which portions of the brain are most active. A radioactive isotope—usually, fluorine eighteen—is administered intravenously and tracked by a machine, which detects the gamma rays emitted as the isotope decays. Emission reflects activity at that point, and lack of emission indicates damage of some sort. The CAT scan, or computerized axial tomography, is a more static reading, a rotating X ray that generates a picture based on the varying rates of absorption of radiation by portions of the brain with different densities."

"These tests are the basis for your testimony as to what damage was done to Mr. Donahue's brain in the SurfAir crash?"

"Yes."

"Thank you, Doctor. So tell us. What exactly *did* happen to Mr. Donahue's brain in the crash? And please keep in mind that none of us are physicians, so we're going to need some explanation of the fancy terms."

Ryan nodded. "I'll be as clear as I can. Three things happened to Mr. Donahue. First, he received a blow to the head severe enough to cause brain shift, that is, movement of the brain within its protective membranes and the cerebralspinal fluid. A portion of the frontal lobes became crushed against the skull, causing lesions and hemorrhaging."

"What was the long-term result of that event, if any, Doctor?"

"There are two. Damage to the cerebral cortex has resulted in a degree of physical impairment, particularly on his right side. For a time Mr. Donahue couldn't move *any* of his limbs without assistance. Now he can use his left arm and leg and rotate his torso to some extent."

"Is he confined to a wheelchair?"

"Yes."

"Will he be so confined forever?"

"Possibly. The most optimistic forecast is that he will have to employ crutches and leg braces for life."

"What is the second product of the damage to the frontal lobes?"

"That is more ephemeral. Through studies of the effects of stimulating or damaging various sections of animal brains, it has been learned that certain personality traits are governed, at least in part, by the frontal lobes. When damage occurs in that area, a person experiences what we call 'frontal lobishness'—his behavior may be drastically altered, although the specific symptoms vary from injury to injury."

"Does Jack Donahue display any such symptoms?"

The doctor nodded. "He is unmotivated and lacking in initiation, which is to say he doesn't start things on his own; he waits to be told to do something. He speaks only when spoken to. He is generally apathetic and prone to drowsiness, but he is also occasionally euphoric."

"How do you mean?"

"He tends to overestimate his well-being. He also demonstrates a lack of inhibition from time to time. He perseverates, that is he tends to repeat what people have said to him; similarly, he suffers from echolalia—he repeats the last thing he heard. Also, he has emotional lability—mood swings, if you will—and there is always a chance that he will experience a catastrophe reaction, that is, a severe depression brought on by his realization of the dimensions of his disability. This is very common with head injuries."

Ryan shifted in his chair. "At this point I should say that nothing about the brain is simple, which means diagnosis cannot be precise. Often the full consequences of a head injury are not apparent for many years. Brain functions are complex and interrelated, so the conditions Mr. Donahue has experienced may also result, in whole or in part, not from the damage to the frontal lobes but from the more permanent damage that was done to his brain."

"Which was?"

"As I mentioned, Mr. Donahue's skull was pierced by a knitting needle, which passed through the frontal lobe and penetrated to the portions of the limbic system known as the hippocampus and the amygdala."

"That's in the interior of the brain."

"Yes. About three inches from here, in the direction my finger is pointing." Dr. Ryan pressed a finger against his head.

"What is the consequence of that injury?"

"The primary consequence is that Mr. Donahue suffers from global anterograde amnesia. That is, he has lost the ability to store and recall newly acquired information for any length of time. The technical term is postencoding consolidation deficit. In practical terms, it means that Mr. Donahue's ability to form long-term memories has been destroyed."

"You mean he can't remember anything at all? Who he is? Where he is? Nothing?"

"That's not quite it. He simply can't remember anything that occurred after the crash. I should note that he suffers a slight retrograde amnesia as well—his memories of approximately two years before the crash have disappeared, too. Basically, anything that happened before 1985, Mr. Donahue remembers. He knows his wife, his old friends, his address, things like that; but anything that happened to him after that year has vanished. And anything that happens to him now, he retains no memory of for even as long as an hour."

"Will this condition last forever?"

"I'm afraid so. The damage to those portions of the brain was extreme. All cases on record of similar injuries show them being permanent."

"You mentioned a third result from the crash."

"Yes. Because of the fire that broke out in the cabin, Mr. Donahue was deprived of a requisite amount of oxygen for a time. That anoxia very likely contributed to both his memory and emotional problems, by damaging the hippocampus. As I said, the brain is vastly complex, and our understanding of it is partial, at best. I could talk for days about what I think has happened to Mr. Donahue, but it wouldn't be particularly helpful. All his problems are interrelated. And all of them are a result of the crash."

"You say, Doctor, that Mr. Donahue has lost his memory. That has psychological aspects as well, does it not?"

"Indeed. Anterograde amnesia makes the victim in some respects like a ghost. He has consciousness without content—he can't remember what he has just done, who he has just seen, why he is where he is, what he was doing five minutes earlier. He can't watch TV, because he forgets the plot before the show is over. He can't make new friends, because he never remembers having seen the people before. Victims of this dysfunction often lapse into a leaden state, to the point that they do virtually nothing without stimulus."

"It seems impossible that a person like that could hold a job. *Any* job."

"I think that would be fair to say."

"It also seems it would be very painful to look on someone you love who was put in that state."

"I would agree. Unquestionably."

As Tollison nodded and consulted his notes, Hawthorne looked at Brenda. The last comment had been noted and filed for future reference.

"Earlier you mentioned the Glasgow Coma Scale," Tollison went on, unaware of the fury at his back. "Please tell us about that."

"The Glasgow scale is a standard tool of neurological evaluation. It measures the level of unconsciousness based on stimulus and response."

"What was Mr. Donahue's score on the scale?"

"When he arrived at the hospital, we put him at five—he failed to open his eyes, exhibited decerebrate posturing, and uttered incomprehensible speech."

"What's the significance of that finding?"

"A GCS of less than six carries a high likelihood, over sixty percent, of early death. In that respect, Mr. Donahue beat the odds. However, a GCS of less than nine carries a similarly high risk of long-term cognitive sequelae."

"He will suffer long-term impairment to his mental capacities?"

"Yes."

"Are there no therapies available to help him?"

"Fortunately, there are. He has already begun speech and physical therapy and has undergone preliminary levels of evaluation such as the Galveston Orientation and Amnesia Test, the Wechsler Memory Scale, the Purdue Pegboard, and the Peabody Individual Achievement Test. Mr. Donahue will improve from his current levels of cognition, undoubtedly. With new computer programs such as the Einstein Memory Trainer and REACT—which stimulate basic skills such as visual tracking, information processing, and pattern recognition—he can be expected to advance further. But it will be a slow process at best and will not be accomplished without a great deal of sacrifice and effort by Mr. Donahue and by those who love him."

With the final phrase, all eyes turned to Laura. From his place in the crowd, Hawthorne winced. Laura's love for her husband was best unmentioned, yet Tollison and his witness had just done so for a second time.

"What is Jack's current level of development, Doctor?" Tollison asked.

"On the Levels of Cognitive Functioning Scale, I put Jack at level five—confused/inappropriate/nonagitated."

"Can you define that more specifically?"

"Yes. Mr. Donahue responds to simple commands, but in nonstructured environments he is random and fragmented. He is easily distracted and lacks ability to focus. Verbalization is often inappropriate and confabulatory, his memory is severely impaired, and he can't learn new information."

"Thank you, Doctor. I have one last point." Tollison drew himself to full height. "I ask you now what you believe, to a reasonable medical certainty, was the cause of the injury to Jack Donahue's brain."

Chambers hurtled to his feet, objecting as he unbent. "We offered to stipulate to the doctor's medical prowess, Your Honor, but we did not stipulate to his powers of clairvoyance. Dr. Ryan was not on the plane and he was not at the crash site. There is no foundation for such testimony from this witness."

Tollison approached the witness box. "If I may, Your Honor, perhaps I can provide a basis for the testimony."

Judge Powell nodded.

"Dr. Ryan, you are called upon in your work to assess the etiology of injury all the time, are you not? The cause of a medical problem?"

"Of course."

"The genesis of an injury is one of the considerations that goes into the formulation of a program to *treat* that injury, is it not?"

"Often. Yes."

"Your Honor, I submit Dr. Ryan's testimony is within the bounds of professional diagnosis and treatment."

Judge Powell nodded. "I concur."

Hawthorne suppressed a grin. Chambers hated to lose such exchanges. When he did he got mad, and when he got mad he made mistakes. What had bought Hawthorne his mansion in Belvedere was the fact that in aviation litigation, mistakes can cost millions.

Tollison clasped his hands at his waist. "Dr. Ryan, what caused Mr. Donahue's brain injury? If you know."

"As I mentioned, my examination indicated that Mr. Donahue had been subject to severe stresses, substantial forces impacting his body both front and back. That is, his head and shoulders seemed to have both struck and been struck by solid objects, with tremendous force. The arms were extended to cushion the blow, as though he knew it was coming, but the momentum was so strong the bones fractured in the effort. His foot was crushed. Consistent with this pattern, I conclude that in the course of the crash Mr. Donahue was thrown into an immovable mass, that he both struck and was struck by various solid objects, and that among the objects he struck was the knitting needle, which, because of the forces involved and the angle of the needle at impact, was able to pierce his skull."

Tollison nodded. "Is your interpretation of the cause of Mr. Donahue's injuries consistent with the suggestion that his seat came loose from its anchors at the time the plane struck the trees, and he was hurtled forward like a missile at a speed of one hundred miles an hour until he struck and was struck by other seats and baggage and debris that were simultaneously being flung against the forward bulkhead of the plane?"

Chambers was livid. "Your Honor, this is the purest fantasy, quite obviously a vain attempt to fill the gaps in the plaintiff's crumbling case."

Judge Powell seemed to think this one over. Tollison held his breath. "I'm going to allow it, counsel, though it's close," Powell concluded finally. "Once again, I remind the jury that they are not bound by any opinion given in this case and are free to give opinions what weight they deem they deserve. You may answer, Doctor."

When Ryan hesitated, Tollison prompted him. "I ask again, Doctor. Were your observations and diagnosis consistent with the event I just described?"

"Yes."

Tollison did not quite suppress a smile. "Thank you, Doctor. No further questions."

Judge Powell glanced at his watch, then peered across the bench. "Cross-examine, Mr. Chambers."

As Hawthorne smiled inwardly, Tollison sagged into his seat, clearly exhausted by his effort and relieved that he had established all he'd hoped. In the next instant, Hawley Chambers donned a carnivorous smile and marched to the center of the courtroom. "Doctor, you've given a rather apocalyptic view of Mr. Donahue's condition. But it's really not that bad, is it? For example, you said there would be no residual harm from the broken arms, but there might be residual disability from the broken foot. It's possible, isn't it, that all Mr. Donahue might have is a limp?"

"It's possible."

"And even that—with the help of exercises to strengthen and retrain certain muscles—might disappear in time?"

"Perhaps."

"As for the lungs, Mr. Donahue won't be able to run a marathon, right?"

"Right."

"Has he *ever* run a marathon, to your knowledge?"

"Not to my knowledge."

"Is there *anything* he did on a regular basis prior to the crash that he won't be able to do now because of the damage to his lungs?"

"I'm not that familiar with his former routine. He will be more prone to pulmonary stress, certainly."

"Did Mr. Donahue smoke prior to the crash?"

"I believe he did."

"So his lungs were already less than perfect."

"Yes, but there's no doubt there was damage beyond any existing disease."

"Let's get to the brain, Doctor," Chambers continued. "It's quite an amazing organ, is it not?"

"That's putting it mildly."

"You've devoted your professional life to its study and repair, if that's the right word."

"Yes, I have."

"Tell me, Doctor. There are instances on record, are there not, where extensive brain damage has occurred and the victim has gone on to lead a perfectly normal life?"

"That depends on what you mean by extensive. And normal."

"Let me be more precise. There are cases on record where a hemispherectomy has been performed—*half the brain was removed*—yet the victim lived and functioned. Is that not correct?"

Ryan nodded slowly. "Thanks to the new lumbar puncture and shunting techniques, hemispherectomies are starting to be performed to relieve progressive seizure disorders. But this is done only on younger persons, whose powers of recovery are substantial. Adults who suffer strokes that destroy half their brain invariably die or are impaired significantly."

"How much brain tissue did Mr. Donahue actually lose?"

"Less than twenty grams."

"What size?"

"Smaller than a marble."

"Lost from the left side of the brain."

"Yes."

"There is of record a woman, age twenty, whose entire left frontal, occipital *and* temporal lobes were surgically removed, yet she remains able to walk and talk and hold a job outside the home. Is that not right?"

"I know of that case. To my knowledge, it is unique."

"The reason such recoveries are possible is that the brain has been found to be blessed with a curious plasticity, has it not? After injury such as this, brain functions often migrate from the portion that no longer works to a portion that is not injured."

"In *some* cases and with *some* functions. In most cases, no migration takes place. When it does, significant migration occurs only in younger persons."

Chambers raised a skeptic's brow. "To a degree, some migration has *already* happened with regard to Mr. Donahue's motor functions, has it not?"

"It may be migration or it may be another phenomenon."

"But there has been improvement."

"Yes."

"And nothing *approaching* half of Mr. Donahue's brain was damaged in the crash, was it?"

"No."

"He has emerged from his coma?"

"Yes."

"He's fully conscious?"

"Yes."

"He is recovering his motor skills?"

"Some of them. Yes."

"He can feed himself?"

"Yes."

"He can sit in a chair without help?"

"Yes."

"Three months ago he couldn't do any of that, could he?"

"No."

"It's entirely possible, is it not, Dr. Ryan, that Mr. Donahue will recover the *entire* range of motor function, given time and a rigorous program of physical therapy?"

Ryan frowned. "Very little of the brain's recuperative powers can be said to be impossible, but I believe it highly unlikely that Mr. Donahue will achieve total motor recovery."

Chambers licked his lips. "I believe I know some experts who will disagree with you, Doctor. Now, as for the retrograde amnesia, that is improving, is it not?"

"I'm afraid I see no sign of it."

"The loss of memory of the past few years may be permanent?"

"Yes."

"Do you regard that as a significant disability?"

"Yes."

"Tell me what Mr. Donahue will be deprived of because he is unable to remember the last three years of his life—can't remember who won the last World Series, for example."

For the first time, the doctor seemed nonplussed. "The effects of memory loss are as much psychological as practical, Mr. Chambers. As I mentioned earlier, people without self-memory often become confused, listless, sleep-prone, unable to decide how they fit into the scheme of things. Studies show that a person with traumatic head injury, who has been in a coma for as long as Jack Donahue was, has only an eight percent chance of returning to his normal job."

"His normal job; not *any* job."

"Yes."

"Other studies have shown that thirty percent of persons suffering prolonged coma progress to a point of moderate disability or complete recovery, isn't that true?"

"Which means most of them don't make it that far."

"Have you administered intelligence tests to Mr. Donahue, Doctor?"

"Yes. Basic ones."

"Do they indicate Mr. Donahue's IQ has drastically lessened because of the accident?"

"Not drastically, no."

"So aside from memory problems, he remains an intelligent man?"

"I suppose you could say that."

"Have you administered the Zung Self-Rating Depression Scale to Mr. Donahue, Doctor?"

"Yes. And the Beck Depression Inventory as well."

"And?"

"He shows no significant depressive states."

Chambers's smile was angelic. "Are you saying Mr. Donahue is a happy man?"

"He appears to be."

"He's in no pain?"

"He says not."

"He has never experienced a moment of pain since the accident occurred, isn't that right?"

"Yes. Subjectively."

"Let's be clear, Doctor. Mr. Donahue is, but for physical disabilities that are diminishing all the time, a healthy, happy individual, is he not?"

Ryan's voice rose angrily. "That's putting it far too strongly. One who cannot retain a long-term memory cannot be called healthy. As for his mood, what I believe happened is, the crash stimulated production of the brain's natural opiates. The endorphins, as some of them are called, neuropeptides that exist naturally in the brain and work to increase pleasure or decrease unpleasantness."

"Mr. Donahue is on a natural high, is that what you're saying?"

"It's much more complex than that."

"You're not implying Mr. Donahue can't do *anything*, are you, Doctor?"

"No. He can perform tasks he remembers from before—typing, for instance. He can also learn simple skills—procedural learning, we call it—which means he can solve puzzles and perform basic tasks. But the kicker is he can never remember having *done* those things before. If he builds a toy house ten times, each time is the first for him. And each time, he's afraid he can't do it."

"Are you saying it's impossible to train him to perform a job?"

"No. I *am* saying it would be very risky to—"

"In your direct testimony you mentioned some computer programs that aid cognitive functioning," Chambers interrupted. "Dramatic strides are being seen in this area, aren't there, Doctor?"

"There are success stories. Yes."

"Mr. Donahue is only in the initial stages of cognitive retraining, is he not?"

"Yes."

"There are many programs that he has yet to try. Correct?"

"Yes."

"At this point you can't say these rehabilitative techniques will be ineffective, can you?"

"I can say they will not bring back the full range of his cognitive processes."

Chambers paused. "There are new drugs on the market that stimulate memory, aren't there?"

"Yes. Vasopressin is one. There are others. They are experimental and have not been proven on persons suffering from head injuries such as Mr. Donahue's."

"Have you *tried* any of them on Mr. Donahue?"

"Not yet."

"Do you plan to?"

"Perhaps. I doubt there will be any effect."

"But perhaps?"

"Perhaps."

"Recent experiments in Sweden indicate that a so-called nerve growth factor can reverse the shriveling of brain cells that results from age, do they not?"

"Those experiments are in the very early stages. I don't envision such medications being prescribed in this case."

"But advances in brain science are rapid, are they not?"

"Some are; some aren't."

Chambers turned toward the jury. "It seems as though you hope your patient *won't* recover, Doctor."

Ryan pounded a fist on the fence that surrounded him as Chambers retreated to his table and took his seat. Tollison's objection was drowned in the hubbub. "No more of that, Mr. Chambers," Judge Powell cautioned sternly.

Chambers only nodded, his lip curled cruelly. "I have no more questions for this man, Your Honor."

For the first time since the case was set for trial and he went to Lake Tahoe to prepare for the ordeal, Keith Tollison has slept in his own bed. His homecoming has not been popular—Alec Hawthorne urged him to remain in the city to prepare to cross-examine the defense witnesses, and Laura Donahue rebuffed his suggestion that they get together at his hotel to rehearse her testimony. Only after he insisted to the point of tyranny that they review at least the portion that would accompany the videotape of her husband's treatment did she finally acquiesce. But because she refused to desert Jack for even a single night, Tollison had to return to Altoona.

As he drove through the sleeping town in the moonlight of the night before, it seemed a foreign land. Even his bed felt alien—sleep came sometime after four and departed again by six, vanquished by his rehash of the trial. Hounded by failings both real and imagined, his mind a tub of clumsy phrases, witless ripostes, missed opportunities, and inadvertent idiocies, he awoke sweating with the fear that all was lost.

Truth ultimately crystallizes over his Raisin Bran: The trial is off the track. As awful as it is to admit it, their strategy has been wrong—the focus can't be Laura; the focus must be Jack. Dr. Ryan's description of his patient's piteous ordeal has left the jury thirsting to see this man whose scalp has been shaved and skull sawed through and brain sliced like a peach by the neurosurgeon's knife.

Tollison swirls cool coffee in his mug as he plots his new tack. Assuming Jack does testify, what will he say? What *can* he say about what has become of him? The last time they spoke, his words ranged from trenchant comments to rambling nonsense. What does he know that will help? Not much, if the memory of the crash is lost. What does he know that could hurt? A lot, if only the memory of the crash is irretrievable. Teetering on a razor's edge, Tollison's task will be to let the jury see and hear his client, not to learn what's in his brain, but only what is out of it.

He looks at his watch. He is meeting Laura at ten. Jack will have just awakened, will be as lucid as he gets. Tollison is about to leave when the phone rings.

"Just checking to make sure you didn't pull a Judge Crater and keep driving," Hawthorne jokes.

"It's that bad?"

"As a matter of fact, you're doing fine. Even Martha thinks so."

"Where's she been, anyway?"

"Here and there. I just thought I'd tell you the game's still on the table as far as I can see, which means Laura will be the difference. Make sure you cover everything with her—not just what she'll say, but also what she won't."

For some reason Tollison does not disclose the stratagem he has just devised. "Check."

"You came pretty close to opening the door to the marriage, you know."

"I'm afraid I've left the door wide open."

Hawthorne doesn't seem concerned. "It can go either way at this point. Powell's a bit of a prude, so he'll be inclined to keep out the sleaze. But you have to keep Laura on the straight and narrow."

"Right."

"How are you doing otherwise? I expected you to come by Martha's for a drink."

"Liquor depresses me, and I was far enough down that road already. But don't worry—I'm awake, I'm sober, and I'm off to Laura's in two minutes."

"When are you coming back to the city?"

Tollison hesitates under the realization that given his imminent departure from the script, he can no longer huddle with Alec at every stage of the proceedings, that from here on he must make his way the way he has made it in Altoona. "Monday morning, I guess."

"Be better if you came in Sunday. We need to go over some things."

"I'm exhausted, Alec—I need two more nights in my own bed. I'll be in early Monday. Did Martha get the jury instructions ready?"

"Yes, but you need to—"

"*I* know what I need, Alec." Before his friend can digest his outburst, Tollison hurries on. "What's the deal on Chambers? Does he always try cases the same way, or does he take some chances?"

The response is wary. "What kind of chances?"

"Like resting his case without calling any witnesses."

"Not in my experience; Hawley pretty much plays it by the book." Hawthorne pauses. "You sound like you have something cute in mind."

Tollison laughs as easily as he can. "Just looking for an edge, as you call it."

Hawthorne becomes distant. "Do you want to discuss it?"

"I don't think so."

"You're not the only one who has a stake in this, Keith," Hawthorne observes quietly.

"I know that, Alec."

"So what do you think you're doing?"

"The same thing you'd be doing in my shoes."

"When I was in your shoes, I made mistakes I regretted for a long time."

"Maybe that's the difference between us—regret's something I live with every day."

Tollison hangs up and leaves the house before he can reverse the deed. In response to his ring at her bell, Laura answers the door. When she meets his eye she seems to recoil, as though she senses she has reason to be afraid of him.

In robe and slippers, she leads him to the living room. "Jack's still sleeping," she says. "I'll wake him if he doesn't come around in a minute."

"There's no hurry; I've got all day."

A familiar look passes across her face, one that includes both affection and desire, but it passes quickly. "You look exhausted, Keith."

"Battle fatigue."

"How are we doing, do you think?"

So she does not regard him as an enemy after all. Not yet. "Good, but not great."

"I thought Dr. Ryan was excellent."

"He was. But I don't think the jury's ready to do what we want them to."

"Which is what?"

"Give us a million dollars."

She gasps and colors, as if she appreciates the scale of their undertaking for the first time. "I don't know if they *should* want to do that."

"If they don't, it's possible that all you'll get, even if they find for us on liability, is the value of Jack's medical bills. When I take a third of that as my fee, you'll still be in hock to the hospital for two hundred thousand dollars. And they'll try to collect it from you—don't think they won't. Is that really the way you want this to end?"

She is as stiff as if he had slapped her. "Of course not."

Still angry, he walks to the window and looks out. No one lurks beyond the hedge to spy on them. The liberation somehow makes him sad.

"I didn't want to take this case, you'll remember," he says without turning back.

From behind him she murmurs, "I know."

"But I did, which means I contracted to do anything within my ethics and the law to let Jack win."

She doesn't answer.

He turns to face her. "I'm going to call Jack as a witness."

Mute but resolute, she shakes her head.

"I have to."

"You can't, Keith. They'll make him look like a fool."

"That's not the worst thing in the world, Laura. It's not nearly as bad as being a pauper."

They exchange accusations that range far beyond the threat to her husband's dignity. "If he's close to cogent," Tollison persists, "I'm going to put him on the stand."

"I can't let you do that, Keith."

"The only way you're going to stop me is if you've got a court order saying he's not well enough to testify. Which is going to be hard to do, since I'm supposed to be his lawyer."

He has frightened her. "Keith, I . . . what's gotten into you? Why are you *doing* this?"

"Because I'm going to try like hell to win this thing for Jack, and at the same time I'm going to do something for you."

"What?"

His answer hurts so much he winces. "Give you a reason not to see me again. A good one. One even I can understand."

"I don't know what you're talking about."

"You will next week."

"You sound like you're planning something horrible."

The charge makes him giddy. "I'm just going to do what any lawyer does—I'm going to sell my client. At first I was going to sell *you*, but you decided not to claim a loss of consortium, so selling you wouldn't get me much. For a while I thought I would sell you anyway, that the jury would help you by helping Jack, but it's not working. They're only thinking about Jack, wondering if his brain is a mangled mess or if all he's got is an Excedrin headache, the way Chambers made it sound. So I have to give him to them, but it's a problem. The product didn't used to be all that great, if you remember."

Her breaths are cavalcades of noise. "So what are you going to do?"

"I'm not going to sell them what he was, I'm going to sell them what he is."

"That sounds so . . . callous."

His words are cold. "It's not *your* job to say what's moral in that courtroom; it's Judge Powell's, and he's doing fine at it. He's doing so well that when Chambers trots in his SurfAir people, the jury may buy the entire bag of bullshit unless Jack convinces them he needs their help more than the airline does."

She shakes her head. "You're so *angry*, Keith."

"Sure I'm angry. I'm angry at what I'm having to do to give you what you want in the world, and that what you want in the world no longer includes me."

"I—"

He shakes his head. "Forget it, Laura—we've got work to do." He brings his briefcase to his lap. "I brought the videotape with me. Both sessions, edited together. I want to go over your comments, just the way you'll give them on Monday."

"If you think it's necessary."

He motions for her to take a seat in front of the TV set, then extracts the cartridge. "There are a couple of things to keep in mind. Don't exaggerate—Jack's situation is dramatic enough without the jury thinking you're trying to pump it up. If you use technical terms, be sure to explain them. And if you need me to stop the tape to give you time, just say so."

"Okay."

"Look at the fireplace and pretend that's the jury. Talk to them. *Persuade* them. That's what trials are all about."

He stands as she swivels to do his bidding. "I'm going to be just like I'll be in court, so I'll start by asking you how long you and your husband have been married."

"Since 1972."

"Any children?"

"No." She hesitates, then foresakes the sooty jury and looks at him. "I can't have any."

He is off course already. "I didn't know that."

"I was waiting for when you needed to."

"Jesus, I—" It is all he can do to stay on track. "At the time you got married, what was your occupation?" He looks at her. "The *jury*, Laura. Remember the fucking jury."

Astonished by his outburst, she turns quickly to the fireplace. "I was a practical nurse working in various clinics in the San Francisco Bay area."

"What training did you have?"

"Two years nurses' study at San Francisco State."

"How many years of practical experience had you had?"

"Six, but only two full-time."

"Prior to March twenty-third 1987, was your husband in good health?"

"Yes."

"No physical or mental problems of any kind?"

"No."

"Good. Where were you when you first learned of the SurfAir crash?"

She looks back at him with the gentleness of memory. "I was getting ready to attend a benefit ball."

He takes her through the night and the morning after, what she learned and when, where she went, what she saw. She covers the essentials and re-creates her first glimpse of her husband in the hospital with more drama than he'd hoped. As he guides her through the days when her husband's life hung in the balance, and the long wait for him to return to consciousness, she becomes the spinner of a legend.

"During the time your husband was in a coma, was he treated at home or in the hospital?"

"At the hospital for three months, then I insisted they send him home."

"After he came home, did you participate in his care yourself?"

"Yes. Because of my nursing background, the doctors felt that with training I could become Jack's primary caregiver. And I wanted to, of course."

"Can you give me a general idea of the kind of care your husband received?"

She hesitates, nods, closes her eyes. "The early stages of his treatment, while he was still comatose, were dictated by the effects of prolonged bed rest on the body. For example, the heart of a supine individual works thirty percent harder than the heart of an active person. Its blood volume also increases, causing a drop in pressure, which may cause thrombus, or blood clots. Bed rest interferes with chest expansion, so respiration is reduced, which can lead to pooling of secretions and pneumonia. Bone and muscle strength are reduced significantly—muscles begin to atrophy from the third to the seventh day in bed; without therapy, three percent of muscle strength is lost daily. Inactivity also causes loss of bone matrix and calcium, which can lead to osteoporosis. Fibrosis can form in connective tissues, leading to contracture that can permanently limit movement. Kidney stones may form from increased urinary calcium. Decubitus ulcers—bedsores —begin to form within twenty-four hours, particularly on bony prominences." She opens her eyes, then inhales to fuel the exposition. "These are just a few of the difficulties facing a person confined to bed rest for a lengthy period. Naturally, we undertook various treatments to combat them."

Mesmerized, he claps his hands. "Great. That was perfect. I'm going to start the tape."

He walks to the TV set and inserts the cassette into the recorder. After a moment of snow, a title appears, hand lettered, crude: JOHN CHARLES DONAHUE ... AT HOME ... AUGUST 15 & DECEMBER 29, 1987. After another moment, the words dissolve into the room where Jack Donahue now spends his life.

"Do you remember when this was taken?"

"Yes."

"Were you present each time?"

"Yes."

"Did both sessions depict a typical period of time in the care and treatment of your husband?"

"Yes."

"Were any extraordinary measures undertaken just for the taping, or were you engaged in routine activity?"

"Only routine activity."

"Was your husband conscious or unconscious?"

"Unconscious, the first time. He didn't come out of the coma for another month."

He presses a button. "Please tell us what you see."

Images materialize. Jack flat on the bed, draped with a thin sheet, body lax, eyes taped shut, muscles thin and wasted. Two people hovering over him. Laura. A husky nurse.

"Why are his eyes taped closed like that?"

"To keep them from drying out."

"Okay, what are you doing here?"

"To prevent pooling of secretions, we turned Jack on a regular basis."

The tape spins on.

"These movements combat fibrosis in the connective tissues. Range-of-motion exercises, they're called—moving the joints on a systematic basis, *every* joint, down to the little fingers. . . . Here the nurse is adducting the hips while I dorsiflect and plantarflex the foot. . . . As you see, when we find bedsores developing, we clean the threatened areas, then protect the prominences with a soft cloth and remove external pressure."

Tollison glances at the screen. "Now what?"

For the first time, Laura turns away. "I don't want to do this part."

"You have to."

"You said you'd edit it out if you could."

"I know. But I can't."

"You never intended to, did you?"

He shakes his head.

She covers her eyes and trembles. "Are you sure you're not doing this to humiliate him, Keith? I couldn't stand it if I thought you were doing that."

"I'm doing this because this is what Alec would do in the same situation."

She turns back to the screen and her voice becomes a drone. "I'm preparing him for a bowel movement. This is after he recovered consciousness, but barely. He's turned to his right side because the descending colon is on the left. There's an incontinence pad beneath him. I usually did this about thirty minutes after his meal, to take advantage of the gastrocolic and duodenocolic reflexes. I'm stimulating his natural reflexes through massaging the anal sphincter. At times this was sufficient; when it wasn't, I used a glycerine suppository. As you see, I use rubber gloves and lubrication."

"Did the nurses perform this as well?"

She shakes her head. "Just me. I didn't think Jack would want anyone else to . . . use him like that." She glares at him. "You can't have him in court when you show this, Keith."

"He won't be," he says gruffly, then returns to the screen. "What's this?"

"The equipment for urination. Initially, Jack was on a Foley catheter to relieve his bladder—that's a needle inserted into the urinary canal in the penis to allow his urine to drain continuously—but prolonged use of a catheter can lead to renal failure, so at this point we were applying an external appliance. It's rather like a condom, as you can see; it remains in place by virtue of a facing cement that avoids skin irritation. It's essential that both the catheter and the appliance be cleaned frequently, and that's what I'm doing here. Now I'm putting the appliance back on his penis. At one point, I thought we were going to have to go to a bladder pacemaker, but fortunately Jack regained consciousness before that became necessary."

"Does he still use this . . . appliance?"

She shakes her head. "He *hates* it. Which is sort of a problem, because he's still incontinent fairly often, and he hates that, too." She shrugs. "We get by, I guess."

Her words are gentle, as though she is back in the days of the coma, reciting prayers that had sustained her then. "What's that?" he asks.

"We're supporting his feet to prevent foot-drop and putting antiembolism stockings on to minimize the risk of deep vein thrombosis. There we're applying head and neck supports, and supports for the hand and hip to prevent rotation."

"And this?"

"We recorded his temperature hourly, because infection in a comatose patient can be lethal. Of course we advised the hospital when unusual symptoms developed, such as diarrhea from the antibiotics or tube feedings, or signs of infection, which are also common."

"Did Jack develop any of these problems?"

"He had diarrhea many times, a urinary infection twice, bedsores on countless occasions. We did the best we could, but he was unconscious for so long that . . . there I'm brushing his teeth, flossing, combing his hair, shaving him. I cut him badly once because he had a seizure while I . . . I'm bathing him here—a sponge bath. We do that after evacuations and exercises; it's important that the skin be kept clean, and we have to apply a moisturizer since his natural oils are not secreting normally. The bath was nice. I always felt he knew who I was when I did it. . . . It reminded me of when we used to . . ."

Her voice trails. Tollison presses a button that stops the tape. When her hands have fallen to her lap, he speaks with laughable formality. "Has this therapy we've just observed, which you employed when Jack was comatose, changed to a significant degree now that he's regained consciousness?"

Laura looks at him as though she had been expecting a more personal question. "Somewhat, but not completely. He still can't move his right side, so we do the ROM, range-of-motion, exercises. A therapist has started putting him through a whole battery of strength modalities. And we've only just begun a range of exercises to stimulate his intellectual capacities."

"These therapies are done every day?"

"Yes."

"How many aides do you employ?"

"Two. We take eight-hour shifts." She looks at him. "And I have a young man who helps with the heavy work, moving Jack from bed to his chair, to the bathroom, things like that."

"Jack's able to use the bathroom himself?"

"With difficulty. As I said, he's incontinent from time to time. At night I usually put on his catheter."

"What would you do differently if you had more money?"

She smiles. "He should go to a rehabilitation facility soon. That costs five thousand a month, and we don't have it. There's some equipment that would be nice—software for his computer, Nautilus machines for physical therapy, and . . . there's just a lot of stuff that would help, I think. And you have to try, you know? You can't live with yourself if you don't try as hard as you can."

The videotape grinds to a halt. He rewinds it, removes it from the recorder, and returns it to his briefcase. He finds he cannot look her in the eye. "You'll be up first thing on Monday. You'll do fine."

Her look is rigid. "I'm glad you think so."

"Any questions?"

She shakes her head.

"Do you need anything?"

"No."

"I should talk to Jack," he says finally.

"I'll see if he's awake."

She hurries down the hall, glad to be rid of him. He wanders to the window and looks out. In the corner of his eye he sees Spitter riding up the drive on a bicycle. He goes to the door and asks him how it's going.

Spitter drops his bike to the ground. "Okay."

"Do you like your job?"

"It's all right."

"Mr. Donahue is going to go to San Francisco late next week, to testify in court. I'll be sending an ambulance here to pick him up, and I'd like you to go along with him and help, if it's okay with you."

"Sure."

"And Spitter?"

"Yes, Mr. Tollison?"

It is the first time he can remember that Spitter has said his name. "Two things. Be sure to put his wheelchair in the ambulance. And be sure he has plenty of exercise that morning. He may have to sit in his chair for a long time, and we don't want him stiffening up, so get him up early and really give him a workout. Can you remember that?"

"Sure, Mr. Tollison."

As he closes the door and turns toward his client's bedroom, Keith Tollison wonders if, after his long ordeal is done, he will ever subdue his conscience.

JURORS TO DELIBERATE

In the jury room it is your duty to discuss the case in order to reach an agreement if you can. Each of you must decide the case for yourself, but you should do so only after considering the views of each juror.

You should not hesitate to change an opinion if you are convinced it is wrong. However, you should not be influenced to decide any question in a particular way simply because a majority of the jurors, or any of them, favors such a decision.

HOW JURORS SHOULD APPROACH THEIR TASK

The attitude and conduct of jurors at the beginning of their deliberations are very important. It is rarely helpful for a juror, on entering the jury room, to express an emphatic opinion on the case or to announce a determination to stand for a certain verdict. When one does that at the outset, a sense of pride may be aroused, and one may hesitate to change a position even if shown that it is wrong. Remember, you are not partisans or advocates in this matter. You must be impartial judges of the facts.

CHANCE OR QUOTIENT VERDICT PROHIBITED

The law forbids you to determine any issue in this case by chance such as the flip of a coin, the drawing of lots, or by any other chance determination. For example, if you determine that a party is entitled to recover, you must not arrive at the amount of damages to be awarded by agreeing in advance to determine an average and to make that your verdict, without further exercise of your independent consideration, judgment, and decision.

CONCLUDING INSTRUCTION

You shall now retire and select one of your number to act as foreperson who will preside over your deliberations.

You will return a verdict first on the issue of liability. Only if five or more of you find that one or both of the defendants are liable to the plaintiff are you to proceed to determine the amount of damages to be awarded the plaintiff under the instructions previously given.

As soon as five or more of you have agreed upon a verdict on the issues of both liability and damages, you shall have it signed and dated by your foreperson and shall return with it to this room.

FIFTEEN

Dressed in his disreputable best, Alec Hawthorne fumed on first one and then another corner of Market Street, in a futile effort to flag a cab. Finally, he was forced to walk. As he cursed Keith Tollison for leaving him to wait in vain for their meeting to chart the balance of the trial, the homeless horde regarded him as one of its own.

By the time Hawthorne squeezed into the throng that filled Court-room 12 to capacity, court had reconvened and Laura Donahue was on the stand. As attracted by her tidy figure as by the tale she had to tell, the admiring faces in the audience glowed like a convocation of full moons. Clearly, the crowd expected nothing less than soap opera.

As the lights dimmed, the congregation wriggled toward a better view. A moment later Keith Tollison produced what to Hawthorne was the most potent evidence he had. As the tape began its crawl, Hawley Chambers was still laboring to block its use.

Enhanced by the visual aid, Laura Donahue was riveting. Her mute labors over the body of her husband were an immaculate blend of the pitiable and heroic and made her worthy of beatification. The jurors were rapt; two were soon in tears. By the time Jack Donahue emerged from his stupor and spoke some therapeutic mumblings from within the holy glow of the TV screen, it seemed a resurrection.

When the tape had run its course, Judge Powell called a break. As the crowd murmured its analysis, Hawthorne sidled toward the room in which he and Tollison normally held their rendezvous. Five minutes later, only Martha had showed up.

"I have good news and bad news," she said as she closed the door behind her.

"What's the good?"

"I know who pulled Donahue out of the plane."

"Who was it?"

"A priest. The guy was a real John the Baptist out there—waded into the wreckage at least a dozen times, fishing out survivors."

Despite the news, her expression did not spark optimism. "I take it there's a problem."

Her grin was twisted. "Turns out the guy isn't a priest at all, he's a paralegal for Scallini. A plane goes down, he puts on his cassock, rushes to the site, and steals ID from as many victims as he can so Vic's people can get hold of the family and sign them up as clients."

"Jesus. Do you know where this character is?"

"No. But I can probably find out."

Idly, Hawthorne wondered how, then remembered Dan Griffin's efforts to recruit Martha for his partnership with Vic. "We don't dare use him though, do we?"

Martha shook her head. "But how important is he? We've got Ryan's version of what caused the injuries. Seems to me the lung problems give you the fire and fabric testimony. And we know his head got bounced around by *something*."

"But we don't know his seat came loose. That's the best evidence of recklessness we have, but the link is only circumstantial. Powell could still nonsuit us."

"So what do you want me to do?"

"Talk to the survivors. See if any of them saw a woman knitting with red thread. If they did, find out where she was sitting, who she was, what happened to her. It won't nail the seat problem, but it might help."

She made a face. "The survivors are pretty messed up. I don't think the families are going to want me grilling them about knitting needles, for Christ's sake."

"Haroldson says his stewardess came out of it okay. Talk to her."

Martha shouldered her purse. "I saw Art Ely out in the hall," she said as she walked to the door. "He didn't look happy."

"That's because Hawley's going to tear him to shreds."

"What happens to Donahue's lost earnings if Ely gets blasted?"

"Down the tubes, along with the rest of the case. I should never have let him *near* the courtroom."

"Art?"

"Tollison."

Marth a raised a brow. "He had a client. How could you have kept him out?"

"If I hadn't agreed to be his tutor, he wouldn't have *dared* take this on."

"I'm not too sure of that." Her face was a mix of pride and irony. "Why are you so angry, anyway?"

"My old pal Keith has staged a coup d'état."

"What does *that* mean?"

"He's taken over. I couldn't reach him all weekend, and he didn't show for our meeting this morning. We haven't talked about Laura's testimony or the defense witnesses or even the summation. All he wanted to know was Ed Haroldson's home number. Which seems to make me excess baggage." Hawthorne swore. "He always *was* an independent bastard. Well, if he wants any more help from me, he's going to have to beg for it."

"You're good at getting people down on their knees, as I remember." Martha's leer tried but failed to be bawdy, which seemed to make her sad.

Hawthorne kissed her cheek. "When this thing's over, remind me to thank you for taking up the slack at the office."

She smiled for a merest moment, then opened the door. "Coming?"

He glanced at his watch. "I'd better stay till Art goes back inside. The Farnsworth woman is prowling around, too. I don't want my cover blown at this late date. Not that it would matter," he concluded bitterly.

Martha started to leave, then stopped. "Speaking of strange women, someone who claims her name is Hygiene has been calling you about twenty times a day."

"Any message?"

"Just that it was personal. Is that really her name?"

He nodded.

Martha tugged at her skirt. "How personal is it, do you suppose?"

His shrug implied fewer stirrings than he felt. "Ex-wife number one."

"Do you find it odd that given the time we've been together, I don't even know the names of the women you've been married to?"

Her expression defied analysis, softened her so extensively that for a moment he wished their time had not passed by.

He looked at his watch again. After extracting a promise that she would come by his house that evening to bring him up to date on the office, Hawthorne shooed her back to work. When he thought everyone had returned to their seats, he eased back into to the courtroom.

Laura Donahue was still on the stand. As the questioning continued, it became clear that instead of acting as her guardian, her attorney had become a thug.

"How would you describe your relationship with your husband at the time of the crash, Mrs. Donahue?" Tollison asked bluntly.

Laura's eyes bulged, the question clearly a surprise. From within the crowd, Hawthorne tensed. Tollison had violated the first principal of direct examination—never ask a question to which you don't know the answer—and worse, had discarded the first suggestion Hawthorne had tendered him—keep the marriage out of the case.

"I . . ."

Laura stammered to silence, desperate for a response that would comply with her oath while avoiding the airing of transgressions she had hoped to conceal. As she swirled in turmoil, Chambers got to his feet, frowned, and opened his mouth to speak. After a moment of silent posturing, he sat back down.

"Please answer the question, Mrs. Donahue," Tollison prompted, suddenly near to hectoring. "What was the state of your marriage at the time of the crash?"

"I . . . Jack and I were having problems," she managed finally.

"Arguments?"

"Silences, usually." She took a breath. "Very long silences."

"How long had these silences been going on?"

Her eyes drifted toward an expanse of ceiling that, though marred by dust and time, must have seemed far more flawless than her life. "For a couple of years."

"Did you consider the problems serious?"

"Very."

"A threat to your marriage?"

"Yes. Possibly."

"Did your husband ever tell you he had fallen out of love with you?"

She looked at Tollison as though it was he rather than Hawthorne who had donned an absurd disguise. "He never put it in those words."

"Did you draw that conclusion nonetheless?"

"Yes. I did. Eventually."

Tollison advanced upon his witness. From where he sat, Hawthorne failed to find a sign in either of them indicative of anything more intimate than dismay.

"What steps, if any, did you take when you concluded your husband didn't love you anymore?"

"I don't know what you mean."

"Let me put it this way." Tollison's voice bore a tactless edge. "Did you have a love affair?"

Her look cried foul, then sought the judge. "Do I have to? . . ."

Frowning at the illicit hint, Judge Powell nodded sympathetically.

Tollison's gaze remained fixed on the woman who had become as much his victim as his witness. "Did you have an affair with another man when you thought your marriage had soured, Mrs. Donahue?"

She closed her eyes and inhaled what seemed to be a poison. "Yes. I did." Seconds later, her eyes flew open and she regarded her inquisitor with an odd conceit. "*Two* of them, in fact."

It was Tollison's turn to be surprised. As emotion warped his adversary's features, Hawley Chambers glanced at his investigator and received a heavy shrug. Hawthorne guessed at least part of the confession was news to everyone in the room.

Tollison struggled with his poise. "Were they brief flings or lengthy relationships?"

Laura Donahue remained defiant. "One of each."

"Did your husband ever learn of either or both of these affairs?"

"One of them. The lengthy one."

Tollison nodded. "How did he react?"

"He was furious. He threatened to beat me up, and he threatened to kill my . . . friend."

"Did he actually try to do either of those things?"

She paused as though she expected him to answer his own question. "No," she murmured finally.

"Exactly when did your husband first confront you with his knowledge of your affair?"

"Early March of last year."

"Shortly before the crash."

"Yes."

Tollison nodded curtly. "Two final points. I show you an item marked Plaintiff's Exhibit Twenty. Can you tell me what it is?"

He handed her the object. Without chancing his gaze, she examined it and nodded. "It's a puzzle. A child's toy, actually. You slide these pieces around inside the square until they make a picture of a cow."

"Since the crash, has your husband ever worked this puzzle?"

She nodded. "It's one of the devices they use to measure the effects of the crash on Jack's . . . on Jack."

"How many times would you say your husband has worked this? Successfully, I mean."

"Twenty. Thirty. Maybe more."

"Thank you. Now, I'd like you to look around and tell me which persons in this room have had occasion to visit your husband since he regained consciousness."

"I don't see what—"

Tollison held up his hand. Laura Donahue did as she was told.

"There's Mr. Chambers, over there. And the assistant beside him—the woman. They came to take Jack's deposition a few weeks ago. And you, of course. And Brenda Farnsworth. She lives in Altoona; she's back there in the corner. The only other one is that man in the front row—he's been spying on us. I pointed him out to Jack one night."

"Your Honor," Hawley Chambers pleaded righteously. "Object to the term *spying*. There's no evidence that anything untoward has occurred with respect to—"

The judge interrupted. "The jury will disregard the charge of espionage. Mr. Tollison?"

"No more questions, Your Honor."

"Cross-examine."

Hawley Chambers slid to his feet, his smile a lascivious implication. "Mrs. Donahue, would you be so kind as to tell us the *names* of the men with whom you had these love affairs you've mentioned? So we can verify your testimony if it becomes necessary?"

Tollison's objection was offhand. "Irrelevant."

"Surely we are allowed to test the credibility of the witness."

"May we approach the bench?" Tollison interjected.

Hawthorne watched as Tollison waylaid Chambers beyond the hearing of the judge. Moments after their whispered colloquy began, Chambers's mouth opened in a vacant exclamation. The judge's eyes narrowed. Unruffled, Tollison whispered a further comment and presented Chambers with a written document. Chambers was as nonplussed as Hawthorne had ever seen him.

After a long moment, Chambers shrugged and turned away. "Withdraw the question, Your Honor," he muttered on the way to his table.

After a second scowl at Tollison, Chambers resumed the fight. "Mrs. Donahue, you've stated that because of your marital problems you engaged in an extramarital affair. Was one of the problems during this period the fact that your husband had *also* engaged in an extramarital affair?"

The crowd rumbled. The effort to match the charge of infidelity with the ghost who haunted the videotape produced collective astonishment.

Chambers's aspect made her speak with insolence. "I believe he had."

Chambers nodded with satisfaction. "Thank you."

The rest of the cross-examination was less sensational—Laura was neither castigated nor praised, her morals neither roasted nor admired. The questioning confirmed that her husband was not in pain, was not depressed or otherwise unhappy, that he was making marked improvement. To Hawthorne, the only unusual aspect was the failure of the witness and her lawyer to acknowledge each other's existence.

When Chambers had finished, Tollison rose. "Two points of rebuttal, Your Honor."

Judge Powell nodded. Tollison regarded his witness.

"Please answer my question carefully, Mrs. Donahue. At any time prior to the crash, did your husband ever *admit* to you that he had engaged in an extramarital affair?"

"I . . . no. Not specifically. But—" She marshalled her credibility. "I was *certain* he'd been unfaithful. A woman *knows* those things. If I hadn't been confident that Jack had strayed, I wouldn't have done what I did."

"You never *saw* your husband with another woman, did you? In a compromising situation, I mean?"

"No."

"And he never told you he had been in such a position?"

"No."

"So your assumption that he *was* seeing other women was just that, wasn't it? An assumption?"

"I suppose you could say that, but . . ."

Tollison nodded joylessly, having sacrificed the woman he loved upon the altar of her honesty, having blackened what they had been to each other without forcing her to tell a single lie.

A moment later, he inflicted a final wound. "I have one more question, Mrs. Donahue. Have you had sexual relations with your husband since he came out of his coma?"

Chambers hurried to object. "Outside the scope of the cross-examination."

"Mr. Chambers went into the relationship, Your Honor."

"I'll allow it."

Tollison turned back to the witness, who appeared to be losing her hold on consciousness. "Have you and your husband had sex since the crash, Mrs. Donahue?"

Resistance beyond her powers, she lowered her head and nodded. "Twice. Dr. Ryan said it might help him recover some sensory . . . his senses. And Jack kept saying he wanted to, so I . . ." She stammered to silence.

"Did your husband proceed to orgasm?"

"Once. The second time."

"Thank you." Tollison turned. "I'm finished, Your Honor."

Overcome with embarrassment, Laura Donahue left the stand only after Judge Powell repeatedly invited her to do so. Stumbling blindly toward the counsel table, as she reached its edge, a strangled cry burst forth and in the next instant she fled the room, gathering her purse to her bosom the way she would a fevered child. When the door closed mercifully behind her, Keith Tollison looked out into the astonished crowd, first at Alec Hawthorne and then at Art Ely. "Plaintiff rests, Your Honor."

As Alec Hawthorne emitted a sound that caused the crowd to silently censure him, Hawley Chambers beamed a smirk born of the realization that his foe had just abandoned the foundation of his case. But Chambers's pleasure was only momentary. As he appreciated the stratagem just employed against him, his cocky grin gave way to the rigor of a grimace.

Hawthorne could only marvel. His pupil had taken a lengthy chance in shunning his expert's projection of lost earnings, leaving pain and suffering the only claim in the case other than punitive damages. But to make the gambit work, he had to play a final trump. Chambers could easily finesse him, but only if he could summon the nerve to rest his case without calling a single witness. Hawthorne smiled. Betting on the predictability of the defense bar and the hidebound conservatism of the insurance companies, Keith Tollison had played his cards the way Alec Hawthorne would have played them had the date been twoscore years before and the court been out in Indian country and the burden been his own.

A s lawsuits often do, SurfAir has condensed to a nugget in the form of a choice that must be made. Because the choice is his and because he has only moments to respond to Tollison's challenge, Hawley Chambers polls his retinue to gauge the direction they wish to take. Tollison is pleased as he looks on. At least he has done this much. At least he has made them sweat.

To delay decision or, better yet, foreclose the need for it, Chambers moves for a directed verdict, the tactic Tollison has feared from the beginning. A solid link is still not made between the defects in the airplane and Jack Donahue's injuries. Tollison does not know whether Dr. Ryan's evidence is enough. All along he has hoped that Hawthorne would somehow rescue him, but the cavalry has not appeared.

Argument takes place in Judge Powell's spartan chambers, beneath a set of woodblock prints that are a primitive backdrop to the sophisticated acrimony. Chambers makes it appear that Tollison has produced no credible evidence at all, that there is nothing for the jury to decide, that the airline is blameless as a matter of law. In response, Tollison argues inferences and deductions suggesting the impossibility that Jack Donahue was injured other than by the grossest neglect, the most extreme misfeasance.

Though Tollison girds himself for failure, the motion is ultimately denied. He would like to take credit for the victory, but the ruling clearly issues because experience has taught Judge Powell to value a jury's acumen above that of the opposing counsel, or even above his own. Twenty minutes after they left it, the men return to a courtroom that has wondered what the hell is going on.

Whispering to his clients, Chambers still can't decide his course. Had it been a criminal case and Chambers the defense counsel, he would certainly have rested, arguing that the state had not obliterated doubt, that its burden had not been met, that further testimony was unnecessary. But it is perilous to waive a defense, even in a criminal trial, and Chambers's dilemma is tougher still, because in civil matters doubt is legitimate; a jury can operate on what amounts to a hunch. The question is whether Tollison has done enough to spark one.

Minutes tick by. Chambers continues a vigorous debate with his assistants and the corporate types. If he is more courageous than Tollison has estimated, the trial will end before Tollison can complete his endgame. It is a pivotal moment. Paradoxically, from within his fatalistic shell, Tollison knows the only serenity he has experienced since he agreed to take the case.

A moment later Chambers makes his move. Beaten by the safe faces that surround him, he will defend his clients the way Tollison has bet he would. In the crowd, a hirsute whistle of relief is audible throughout the room.

The river of self-righteousness flows for three days. Suited, groomed, rehearsed, vice-presidents of Hastings and SurfAir march to the stand and stumble off, victims of their values and the facts and a system of justice that permits the expression of indignation. By the time Tollison has finished with them, they know this is not a case where the blame is circumscribed—no finger points conveniently at pilot or mechanic; if any are guilty, all are. It is a suggestion not many of the vice-presidents can abide, that they have killed a hundred people and maimed a dozen more. But Tollison makes it clear that this is what he believes and what he expects the jury to decide.

The defense is both pat and tedious. Witnesses throw numbers and regulations like rice at a wedding. Though they cast them in impressive jargon, their views are simple, if not simplistic. They have conformed to the custom and practice in the industry so cannot conceivably be at fault. They had no obligation to produce a "crash-proof" plane, a prohibitive task in terms of cost and weight. Accountants to the core, they offer cost-benefit ratios that quantify everything including the value of a life, reduce safety to dollars, cents, and the bottom line. They seem not to notice that their approach is unexceptionable only if their airplanes never crash.

The general is followed by the specific. Speeds and stresses were much higher than Ray Livingood had estimated, far beyond the capacities of the aircraft. In any event, only 70 percent of the seats in the aft cabin came loose, and there is no indication that Jack Donahue's was one of them. The temperatures had been relatively low in the rear of the plane, not hot enough to melt urethane or ignite fabric. Mistite was not workable, the new fabrics and foams were unproven, skin insulations and window improvements did not yield value for the money, evacuation tests done after those Polly Janklow described had been conducted with rigorous realism and proved four exits were adequate in the H-11.

Chambers offers his men as reasonable and prudent, cautious and even Christian in their efforts to safeguard their passengers. Millions of dollars spent on safety, thousands of hours of testing, hundreds of improvements over the years, dozens of instances where the airline and the FAA have anticipated trouble and moved to forestall it. By the time he has finished, it seems impossible that anyone has died or singed a single hair.

At various points Tollison gets angry. "You say it would have cost SurfAir approximately two hundred and seventy-five dollars per seat to have replaced the fabric in the H-11 with more fire-resistant material?"

"Those were the figures I had at the time."

"So on the basis of expense, you decided not to install such fabric?"

"Yes."

"Let's explore that decision a bit. I talked with my travel agent this morning, and she told me that if I wanted to fly to LA and back on your airline, I would have to pay one of *twenty-two* different fares. They ranged from two hundred thirty-eight dollars without restrictions to seventy-four dollars for a child under twelve. Does that sound like the current fare structure to you?"

"Seems okay."

"You're saying that in a rate system as flexible as that, there isn't room to fit the cost of a fire-resistant seat someplace?"

"I'm not a marketing man, but I know the competition over our routes is fierce and—"

"But if you *all* did it—if you and your competitors *all* used fire-resistant fabric—you'd stay in the same competitive position you were in before you added the safer fabric, would you not? You wouldn't be hurt at all."

"I ... I'm not sure."

"And if SurfAir advertised—or even bragged—that your seats were fire resistant and your competitors' weren't, then you might even *improve* your competitive position, isn't that possible?"

"It's hard to imagine that happening, I'm afraid."

"Why?"

"We've found that the end-user of our service doesn't react well to being reminded of the down side to our operations."

"Really? How do they react when they learn what happens to the air inside the cabin when your seats catch fire? Or don't you bother to tell them?"

Then come the engineers, talking of tolerances and specifications, viewing the regulations as sacrosanct as the Constitution. When yet another tries to justify the strength of the seats by deferring to the FAA, Tollison can resist no longer.

"The FAA is God, you seem to be saying. Stick with the feds and you'll be all right. Is that your approach?"

"They *are* in charge of safety, after all."

"The FAA is charged with *promoting* air travel as well as regulating it, right?"

"Yes."

"Those are contradictory missions, are they not?"

"No, I don't think so."

"Money or safety, that's what it often comes down to, doesn't it?"

"No. That's insulting. That's—"

"No more questions."

The doctors—three neurologists and a shrink—are just as predictable. No, Jack Donahue didn't feel pain while he was comatose—that's a contradiction in terms—and he isn't in pain now. The explanation is probably grounded in stimulation of the septum—the so-called pleasure center—resulting from the injury. Yes, with the brain anything is possible, including, in this case, moderate to full recovery, given the range of psychoactive drugs and cellular-implant treatments recently become available. Experiments being done with Parkinson's disease and with rats suffering from a condition similar to Alzheimer's indicate certain brain functions can be regenerated with transplant techniques: cells moved from other organs to the brain, or moved from one place in the brain to another. In such circumstances, the outlook for Mr. Donahue is not all bad. No indeed.

When the last one is on the stand, Tollison stands up. "Have you actually examined Mr. Donahue, Doctor?"

"Yes I have."

"For how long?"

"Approximately thirty minutes."

"When?"

"Approximately a month ago."

"Where?"

"At his home."

"Can you cite to me, Doctor, one case in the literature in which full anterograde memory capacity was regained after an injury to the limbic system such as the one suffered by Mr. Donahue?"

"Uh, no, I can't. However, such injuries are so rare that statistics are of limited utility. I wouldn't be surprised to see such a recovery appear one day soon."

"While you're waiting, Mr. Donahue sits in his room and tries to remember what day it is. And he fails, doesn't he, Doctor? He fails every time."

"The frontiers of medicine expand very rapidly, young man. I'm certain that one day—"

When the final doctor is excused, Chambers looks out into the courtroom. He seems uncertain, even afraid, of the step he is about to take. Finally, he speaks: "The defense calls Brenda Farnsworth."

Her features coiled to strike, her fists clenched at her side, as she marches to the witness stand, Brenda's every aspect is a proclamation that at long last Tollison will get his due. But by the time she takes the oath, the emotion seems halfhearted, as if she realizes that retribution can often be perverse, its results opposite those desired, no matter how fervently.

Chambers takes her through the preliminaries, then asks if she knows the Donahues. "I've known the Donahues for years," she answers, as though describing a lingering disease.

"Are you friends?"

"I wouldn't put it that way."

"Enemies?"

She looks at the jury. "Not yet."

"Did you also know a woman named Carol Farnsworth?"

"Yes."

"Who was Carol Farnsworth?"

"My sister."

"Is your sister alive today?"

"My sister is dead."

"How did she die?"

"She died in the SurfAir crash."

"Did your sister know Jack Donahue, Ms. Farnsworth?"

Brenda's voice seems to contain a boast. "Yes."

"How well?"

"Well."

"*How* well?"

"She was in love with the bastard."

Tollison speaks simultaneously. "Objection, Your Honor. No foundation."

"Sustained. The jury will disregard the statement. Please control yourself, Ms. Farnsworth, or I'll have you removed from my courtroom. The jurors' oath does not require them to endure profanity."

Torn between her war with Tollison and the admonition of the judge, Brenda focuses on the former. The look she gives him encompasses every grudge she has ever held.

Chambers clears his throat. "Do you have reason to believe your sister and Jack Donahue knew each other intimately, Ms. Farnsworth?"

"Yes, I do."

"What reason is that?"

Brenda looks at the jury again, this time eagerly. "From her diaries."

Chambers grabs a sheaf of papers and proffers them. "Are these the portions of your sister's diary to which you refer?"

Brenda shuffles through the pages. "Yes."

"Do you recognize the writing as hers?"

"Yes."

"Move to admit them, Your Honor."

Tollison stands. "These are copies; they are not the best evidence of the diaries themselves."

"I can't *find* the originals," Brenda protests. "My son took them, because he has this thing about my sister. But these are Xerox copies. I made them myself. I—"

Reluctant to have Spitter the engine of her defeat, Tollison elaborates. "Also, Your Honor, the name Donahue never appears in those pages, which would seem to make them irrelevant. They are also hearsay."

"The document states that Carol Farnsworth intends to go to Los Angeles with a man named Jack," Chambers blurts. "What could be *more* relevant?"

Tollison is infuriatingly bland. "Move for a mistrial, Your Honor. Counsel has read from the exhibit before its admission into evidence."

Judge Powell shakes his head impatiently. "The jury will disregard counsel's summary of the purported contents of the diary. No more of that, Mr. Chambers. We are coming to the end of a bumpy road. I want nothing out of either side that would force me to end the journey prematurely."

Taking advantage of Chambers's scolding, Tollison persists. "There is no date, Your Honor. And nothing ties these papers to the plaintiff. If I may voir dire the witness, I believe I can show the document is even less probative than it appears."

Powell nods. "Proceed."

Tollison looks at Brenda until she squirms. "You've known me for a long time, haven't you, Ms. Farnsworth?" he begins quietly.

Her lip curls. "*Too* long," she says, then elaborates. "Forty years, give or take."

"And you've known Jack Donahue, the plaintiff, at least that long as well."

"Yes. Unfortunately."

Tollison hesitates, then turns from Brenda toward the bench. He is as matter-of-fact as if he is ordering his lunch. "Your Honor, may Ms. Farnsworth be instructed to withhold her asides and to answer only the questions that are put to her?"

"You are so instructed, young lady," Judge Powell orders curtly. "I have no appetite for nonsense at this stage of the proceedings."

"Thank you, Your Honor." Tollison turns back to Brenda, who seethes in the heat of her rebuke. "You've also known Mr. Donahue's wife, Laura, since she came to Altoona with her husband almost twenty years ago."

"I've known who she is, if that's what you mean. We're not bosom buddies."

Tollison smiles. "Because we've known each other for so long, and because Altoona is such a small town, I'm in a good position to know whether or not you are answering my questions truthfully, wouldn't you say, Ms. Farnsworth?"

"I don't know what you're talking about. Why *wouldn't* I answer truthfully?"

"We'll get to that in a minute. I just want to be sure you understand that if I detect an untruth, I will call whatever witness and produce whatever evidence that is necessary to show a falsehood has been uttered, including aspects of your life or your sister's life that I might find it necessary to reveal in order to correct a misimpression. Is that clear, Ms. Farnsworth?"

Brenda nods sullenly.

"In other words, we are not playing games."

"I guess not."

Tollison nods briskly. He believes he has dented her armor. "Please answer this question yes or no. Isn't it true that you believe that *each* of us—Jack, Laura, and myself—have done you a disservice? That you feel cheated by each of the people I named? Including me?"

"I . . . no. That is, I—"

"Please answer the question, Ms. Farnsworth. You have a grudge against the Donahues and me for wrongs you believe we have committed against you. Is that not correct?"

She hesitates, then yields. "I suppose it is."

"And you believe the only way open to you to avenge those wrongs is to deny Jack Donahue a recovery in this proceeding. To see to it he gets nothing from this jury."

Brenda shakes her head. "All I want is for them to know the *truth*, so they can—"

"You are inclined to *bend* the truth a little, are you not? To see that we get our due?"

"That's not true. I wouldn't do that."

Tollison allows the jury to see his skepticism. "I'm going to ask you some questions about the so-called diary now. And what I want from you is the truth. Not what you *think* you know, or what you *believe* to be true, or what you *wish* were so. Just the truth. No more, no less. Do you understand?"

His words have cowed her. "Yes."

Tollison's aspect softens. "Jack Donahue has a right to be judged on facts, not fiction. Isn't that right?"

"I suppose."

"Any grudge you have against me, or against his wife, or against him, is not properly a part of this proceeding. Do you agree or not?"

The words are small and timid. "I agree."

Tollison nods and smiles. "Thank you." He waits until she looks at him again, then tries to indicate that the worst is over. "Your sister never mentioned to you that she was having an affair with Jack Donahue, did she?"

The answer is long in coming. When it does, it is after she has considered a lie. "No."

"You didn't find these papers in your sister's effects, did you?"

"No."

"You received them in the mail. From an anonymous source?"

"So what?"

"The pages aren't consecutive, are they?"

Brenda shakes her head.

"You don't know what was on those missing pages, do you?"

"No."

"This is the only portion of the diary you've ever seen?"

"Yes."

"The only proper name on those pages is a man named Jack?"

"Yes."

Tollison regards the jury. "Your sister took trips with men on occasion, didn't she, Ms. Farnsworth?"

The implication rekindles her ire. "What are you trying to say?"

"I'm asking if it was unprecedented for your sister to go away with a man for the weekend."

Her eyes are as bright as patent leather. But after a moment of resistance, she wilts. "She wasn't a nun; she wasn't even married. What's wrong with that?"

"Nothing. One of the men she went away with was a man named Curly Lunceford, was it not?"

"They went to Tahoe a few times, I guess."

"Do you know Curly's real name?"

"Curly. That's all I know."

"His given name is Jacklin, isn't it?"

"I ... so what? She isn't talking about *Curly* in there." She waved the papers at his face. "*You* know Curly; Carol wouldn't put *him* in her diary, for Christ's sake."

Tollison turns to the bench. "I renew my objection, Your Honor. The purported diaries are not relevant, and are clearly hearsay."

"Sustained. The diary is not admitted."

"But—" Hawley Chambers sputters.

"Continue, Mr. Chambers."

Chambers seems about to pursue one of the several lines of inquiry that Tollison's questioning has opened up. But as he is about to stand, he glances at the table where the document Tollison has previously displayed to him still rests. Its potential causes him to remain in his chair. "That's all I have, Your Honor."

Judge Powell shrugs. "Your witness, Mr. Tollison."

Tollison's smile is brief and cheerless. "Thank you, Ms. Farnsworth. I have no more questions."

Brenda Farnsworth twirls toward the judge. "You mean it's *over*? That's all I get to *say*?"

"I'm afraid so."

Public insult has been added to private injury—she is not even wanted here. Her finger is an indictment of her persecutor. "You mean nobody's going to tell these people what he's been *doing* with that bitch? You mean—"

"*Objection*, Your Honor," Tollison roars. "She is about to cause a mistrial."

"*Silence*, young lady," Judge Powell explodes. "Another word, and you will be taken to jail for contempt of this court."

"But I—"

"No! No more!"

The command is violent and compelling, and comes not from the bench but from the rear of the room. Brenda swivels toward the voice, prepared to resist its message, but when she sees who has issued the order, she gasps.

Tollison turns as well. Spitter stands at the back of the courtroom, head shaved, arms crossed, militaristic garb in place. His face is still contorted from his cry; his mother is as pained as if he has shot her.

Brenda tries to speak, but words won't displace her shame. A moment later she retreats from the witness stand and, quickly, from the room. Amid the rumble in the crowd, Hawley Chambers rests his case.

"Rebuttal?" Judge Powell asks.

Tollison nods. "One witness, Your Honor." He turns to speak to the only audience that needs to hear him. "I call John Charles Donahue, the plaintiff in the case."

The door at the rear of the courtroom opens. Spitter disappears. When he returns a moment later, he is pushing a wheelchair. Strapped in it at the waist, the patient—slouched like a drunkard, tilted like a broken puppet—wears an afghan across his lap and a sweatshirt around his chest. Hair sparse, body frail, skin as colorless as soapsuds, he sails down the center aisle on a lake of shock and silence.

At Tollison's instruction, Spitter wheels the chair to a position just below the witness stand, removes the afghan from the wasted legs, and rotates the chair so Jack can face the jury. The clerk stands. With the help of his other, Jack raises his right hand and nods his understanding of the oath. After a further instruction, Spitter retires to the front row of spectators.

"Will you state your name please, sir?" Tollison begins.

"Jaaack ... Don ... a ... hue."

The words are slow but firm, the spaces between them large and full of effort. Given the evidence they have heard, the jury seems amazed that he has managed to do that much.

"What is your address?"

He puffs at air, his lungs reedy and loud. "Oak-view ... Acres. Al ... toooo ... na."

"Are you married, Mr. Donahue?"

"... Yes."

"Is your wife in the courtroom today?"

As though he has lost something precious, he searches for it frantically. "I. Don't. See. Her."

"Do you see anyone else you recognize? Take your time and look around."

So toxic that it itches, Jack's gaze eventually singes every candidate—Chambers, his assistant, Spitter, even the detective.

"No," he says finally. "Except. You. Keith."

By prearrangement, Tollison motions for Spitter to stand. "How about this young man? Do you know him?"

Donahue frowns, for the first time uncertain. He has been asked so much and has failed so often, in some deep uninjured recess he knows questions are frequently a trap. "I. Don't. Think. So. Do. I?" He blinks to clear his vision, as though the problem could be cured by eyeglasses.

Tollison smiles and shakes his head, then gestures toward the jury. "I'd like to show these people how well you're doing, Jack. If you can, I'd like you to raise your left hand and open and close it, like this."

Tollison demonstrates, and Jack does as he is told, slowly and inexorably. After a moment Tollison thanks him and picks up a book from the counsel table. "I want to read you something, and later we'll talk about it. Okay?"

The nod is as slow as time.

Tollison opens the book. " 'The Lord is my shepherd; I shall not want. He maketh me to lie down in green pastures: he leadeth me beside the still waters. He restoreth my soul: he leadeth me in the paths of righteousness for his name's sake. Yea, though I walk through the valley of the shadow of death, I will fear no evil: for thou art with me . . .' "

Smiling giddily, Jack answers without a question. "Biiii . . . ble." In the meantime his left hand, like a distant beacon, has kept opening and closing, beyond the reach of his senses. Tollison walks to his side and squeezes the hand until it stops, then guides it back to his lap.

"That was very good, Jack. In a minute I'm going to ask you about that Bible passage, but first, please tell the jury how you're feeling."

". . . Fine."

"Are you happy?"

He nods.

"Are you happy or do you hurt?"

"Hurt."

"Are you doing good or are you in pain?"

"In pain."

"How do you feel?"

"Fine."

When he is certain the jury has made a match with Dr. Ryan's listing of the frontal lobish symptoms, Tollison reaches for his prop. "I'm going to hand you this little device here and ask if you've seen it before. There. Do you know what that is?"

Jack frowns. "Toy?"

"That's right." Jack's pleasure is extravagant. "Do you know how to work it?"

The pleasure vanishes. "I . . ." He fiddles with the pieces, sliding them to and fro in aimless pokes, then throws the puzzle to the floor.

"That's okay; that one's almost impossible." Tollison picks up the puzzle and takes it away, making sure the jury sees it is the one Laura

Donahue has told them her husband has solved more than twenty times. "Do you know a woman named Carol Farnsworth?"

In the hush of the room, the question reverberates like a curse in a cathedral. Everyone is aghast but Jack. His face is without affect, not possibly disingenuous. "Carol?"

Tollison nods. "When's the last time you saw her?"

He shrugs casually. "Long. Time."

"Where was it, do you know?"

"Al . . . toooo . . . naaa."

Tollison approaches the chair. "Mr. Donahue, did you ever have an extramarital affair with Carol Farnsworth?"

Amid the gasp from the audience, Jack's eyes spring wide and his head shakes violently.

"So your answer is no."

Jack nods repeatedly, his eyes roaming the room to be certain all have understood.

Tollison addresses the judge. "Let the record reflect the witness has affirmed that his answer is no, that he has not had an affair with Ms. Farnsworth." Judge Powell nods, and Tollison turns back to his client. "Thank you, Mr. Donahue. I assume, then, that you love your wife."

"Of. Course. I. Do."

"I don't mean to embarrass you, but I think it would help the jury to know just how your relationship with your wife is going. For example, have you and your wife been able to have sexual relations since the crash?"

Jack's face goes blank. In another moment he begins to cry; he shakes his head as relentlessly as he has opened and closed his hand.

Hot with shame, murmuring a brief apology to anyone who can hear him, Tollison makes himself continue. "Do you know why you've come here this morning, Jack?"

He frowns again, helpless. "I. For. Get."

"Have you ever heard people talk about a plane crash?"

Listless, he shakes his head.

"Has anything happened to you that makes you need medical help?"

He shakes his head again. Suddenly uninterested, Jack seems exhausted—Spitter has executed his assignment.

Tollison continues. "I'm about finished, Jack. I just want to ask you about your wife once more."

His face brightens, the reference obviously a balm.

"Have things always been good between you and Laura?"

His nod is firm and automatic.

"Never had any problems; never accused her of being unfaithful; never threatened to kill her lover?"

His anger is quick. "You. Bad. Keith."

"Yes," Tollison says slowly. "Yes, I am."

It is time to quit, for the sake of everyone, but he has to try for one thing more. "Do you remember the words I read a little while ago?"

The nod is quick but insincere.

"I'm having trouble remembering what it was. Was it this?" He reads the psalm. "Or was it this?—'Fourscore and seven years ago, our forefathers brought forth on this continent a new nation, conceived in liberty and dedicated to the proposition that all men are created equal. . . .' "

Tollison proceeds through the entire address. By the time he approaches the end of Lincoln's eulogy, Jack Donahue is, as Tollison has hoped, asleep. Tollison pretends not to notice, letting the condition persist until all six jurors are aware of it.

As though conscious of the situation for the first time, Tollison puts down his notes and looks to the bench. "In order to speed things up, I'll terminate my questioning at this point, Your Honor, but I'd like a brief recess before the cross-examination to, ah, let Mr. Donahue rest a little longer."

The judge peers across the bench, then excuses the jury. Tollison beckons for Spitter to come forward, suggests that he take Jack to the room across the hall, and asks if he needs help. When Spitter shakes his head, Tollison looks across the courtroom, expecting to see Hawthorne but seeing only Brenda Farnsworth. As Spitter pushes Jack Donahue down the aisle, she falls in behind her son and helps them through the door. When she looks back, her eyes are drained of all but anguish. "I quit," is what he thinks she says.

Stupefied by self-reproach, during the recess Tollison tries to escape his deeds by looking over the checklist in his trial notebook, to make certain he has given the jury everything he has. He is still trying to decipher his notes when he senses Hawley Chambers is sitting beside him.

"Pretty effective. In my younger days I'd have had him hauled to the hospital and tested for sedatives."

Tollison returns to his list.

"Let's talk settlement."

Head still lowered, Tollison enjoys a gust of ecstasy. "How much?"

"Medicals and therapies—any out-of-pocket for Jack—plus half a million mad money."

So he can end it here. They will tell Judge Powell, the jury will be dismissed, and they can all go home. Interest on the money, with luck, could bring fifty thousand a year. Laura could live on that. Laura and Jack both. He would have done his duty.

Tollison shakes his head.

Chambers swears. "How much, then?"

"A million, plus Jack's expenses, plus a quarter-million for my fee."

"It's not worth half that. If you knew your ass from your elbow, you'd realize it."

"Get away from me, Chambers. I've got a summation to prepare."

Chambers stomps off, grumbling. Tollison goes to the conference room to check on Spitter and Jack. Along the way, he sees a stranger beckoning.

"Looks like you're about to wrap it up."

"I didn't even notice you in there."

"I'm getting pretty good at this disguise thing."

Tollison laughs. "Well, have I done all the damage I can do?"

Hawthorne nods. "I tried to get you some help on proximate cause, but the witness died. A stewardess on the flight. Seemed to have come through fine, then zap, a stroke. Dead in a minute."

"Too bad."

"But you did fine without her. Nice job with Donahue, by the way. He your last witness?"

Tollison nods.

"Well, good luck."

Tollison puts out a hand to stop him. "Chambers just offered me five hundred thousand plus the medicals."

"Going to take it?"

He shakes his head.

"Why not?"

"I've come too far to quit, I guess. Think it's a mistake?"

Hawthorne shrugs. "We'll know by tonight." He pats his old friend's arm. "Give 'em hell, champ. See you in the locker room."

Hawthorne disappears down the hall. Tollison rounds up his troops and ushers them back to the courtroom.

The afghan again across his lap, Jack looks happy to be back onstage. The judge invites Chambers to cross-examine. The task is delicate, potentially disastrous, and Chambers knows it.

"How are you feeling, Mr. Donahue?"

"Okaaay."

"Are you worried about anything today?"

Jack shakes his head.

"In any pain at all?"

"... No."

"Good."

Chambers hesitates. Jack is not someone he can bludgeon, but he needs a final thrust that will save his case from this poor creature. "Tell me this, Mr. Donahue. Do you like to fly?"

The question is answered in a hush. "I. Don't. Mind."

"Never had any problems with the airlines?"

He thinks Jack is smiling. "Lost. My. Bags."

"That's all?"

Jack nods a single time.

"Thank you, Mr. Donahue. You've been very helpful. No more questions, Your Honor."

Chambers sits down. Powell looks inquiringly at Tollison. Tollison shakes his head—he couldn't ask a question if his life depended on it. Spitter wheels Jack Donahue from the room.

The judge eyes the jury. "Ladies and gentlemen, the evidence is in. There remains only closing argument and your instructions, then you will retire to reach your verdict. Are you ready to sum up, Mr. Tollison?"

"Yes, Your Honor."

And he does, alone before the jury, stating his case as best he can, giving the speech he gave a dozen times in the wee hours of the night before:

"They could have built a safer plane," he argues after reminding them of what the facts and figures show. "They knew *how* to do it and they knew what would happen if they *didn't* do it, yet they wouldn't spend the money. The FAA didn't *order* them to, so they didn't. As a result, Jack Donahue can't even recognize the man who wants to deprive him of a decent life." He accuses Chambers with a glance.

"Mr. Chambers will argue that his clients did all they were required to do. And he's right, in a sense—we offered no proof that any regulations were violated. But the question is, did SurfAir and Hastings meet their duty to the passengers on flight 617 merely by following the rules?

"In his instructions, Judge Powell will tell you that proof that the regulations were followed *does not automatically mean* that the defendants engaged in reasonable conduct. You can find otherwise. You can decide that following the rules was *not* enough, that the defendants should have done more. If you *don't* do that—if you find that what Hastings and SurfAir did was adequate—there are going to be *more* Jack Donahues in the world, I'm afraid, victims of rules that are decades out of date, victims of airlines that follow them not because they're right but because it is profitable to do so. Put a *stop* to it, ladies and gentlemen. Make them change their ways in the only way that works—make them *pay*, and make it *hurt*."

He pauses for his final burst. "You were told at the beginning of the trial that Hastings earned twenty million dollars in profits last year, and SurfAir earned five. Based on those numbers, my request to you is simple—I submit that two of those millions should be awarded as punitive damages to the plaintiff from Hastings Aircraft Corporation, and half a million should be awarded the plaintiff from SurfAir Coastal Airways. That's a fine of ten percent—ten percent that will be your declaration that passengers in a survivable crash should *survive*. It's as simple as that."

Tollison goes to the blackboard and scrawls some numbers. "If you do find liability—if you find the defendants should have to pay—then you have to award damages. I've told you why I think a portion of those damages should be punitive. Now I'm going to tell you what else I hope you will do.

"First, I hope you will award Mr. Donahue his present and future medical expenses. That's six hundred thousand dollars, according to proof that has not been challenged. That doesn't go to Mr. Donahue, it goes to the hospital and to the doctors, nurses, and therapists who have tried for a year and will be trying for many *more* years to put Jack Donahue back together. I hope you have no problem with that—at the very least, Mr. Donahue should be able to pay his bills.

"I submit that you should also award an amount for pain and suffering. Now, we know Mr. Chambers will argue that Mr. Donahue is in no pain. And maybe that is true. But he *cannot* tell you there has been no suffering. *You* saw the tape—his wife doing everything from moving his toes to evacuating his bowels. Then you saw him. Jack Donahue can't retain a memory for five minutes. He couldn't remember the young man who pushed him into the room, couldn't remember the psalm I read to him, couldn't remember how to do the puzzle. *He can't even remember whether he and his wife had sex.*

"Because of the conduct of the defendants, Jack Donahue lives in a netherworld—a world that makes no sense to him, a world he can't control. You can't give Jack back the powers he had before the crash, but you can give him something. So in addition to punitive damages, I ask you to award Jack Donahue one million dollars to compensate him for his suffering.

"Thank you."

Tollison takes his seat and tries to catch his breath. By the time he is back to normal, Chambers is deep into his argument.

"To award *any* damages in this case would be a travesty. First of all, the only *actual* damages at issue other than the doctor bills are pain and suffering. But Mr. Donahue is *not in pain*. In an important sense, he is not even suffering. He is happy, he is content, he remembers nothing about the crash, and he remembers nothing about his wife's unfaithfulness. His marriage is stronger today than when the plane went down. So where is the damage?

"But even if you do find Mr. Donahue has suffered and feel a small award of that nature is justified, you *must* reject the second element of plaintiff's claim, the punitive damages. The reason is simple—no one did anything *wrong*. To award the sum Mr. Tollison has asked for would be to punish people for doing their jobs the best way they know how. Nothing in this case compels that result. Nothing remotely justifies it.

"Look at the proof. Expensive gadgets, weighty materials, space-age plastics—Mr. Tollison would have every untried, experimental, pie-in-the-sky device anyone ever came up with tossed into an airplane on the vague hope that it would be of help if the plane ever crashed. This isn't the way business is done, or the way it *should* be done. Business can't take those kinds of risks. *Testing* is the answer. The kind of testing done by the FAA and the airframe manufacturers, the kind of slow but certain progress that has marked this industry from its inception.

"The SurfAir crash was a tragedy. But if tragedies aren't fair, at least our system of justice is, because under our system, if there's nothing *wrong* or if it's not your *fault*, then you don't have to pay. The evidence is clear that no one did anything wrong on the night of March twenty-third, and there was nothing wrong with the airplane. On behalf of the wonderful men and women of Hastings and SurfAir, I beg you not to do anything that would make them live the rest of their lives thinking they were responsible for this tragedy.

"I appreciate your kind attention. Mr. Tollison has the last chance to speak with you, according to the rules, but I hope and trust that you will remember what I've said here this afternoon, and will vote to do what fairness and justice demand, which is a verdict for the defense. Thank you."

Chambers sits down, and Tollison stands for the final plea.

"We've been here a long time, so I'll be brief. Mr. Chambers claims his clients didn't do anything, and he's right. They didn't use safe seats or fire-resistant cushions or purchase adequate exits, which means they didn't fly the safest plane available. This isn't pie-in-the-sky stuff— as our evidence clearly showed, this is proven technology, precautions reasonable men and women would take if their interests were as much in safety as in profit. And let's be clear. If you *do* find liability, the witnesses you saw won't have to pay the judgment. No *person* has to pay; only the companies do.

"Mr. Chambers has the gall to suggest Jack Donahue hasn't *suffered* as a result of the crash. If you watched Jack here in court, you know how insulting that argument is, to you and to my client. I could say a thousand things at this point, but I will simply commend to you the words of Shakespeare—'*He jests at scars, that never felt a wound.*'

"I ask that the amount for pain and suffering be one million dollars, and I ask for punitive damages in the amount of two million five hundred thousand, and I ask for the medical expenses. It's a lot, I know. A huge sum, until you look at what's become of Jack Donahue and at the profits made by the companies who flew him to his fate.

"I thank you for your attention during these long and difficult proceedings. I am confident that you will do your duty."

For all but the man they have just been talking about, the tortuous wait begins.

UNITED STATES DISTRICT COURT
NORTHERN DISTRICT OF
CALIFORNIA

John Charles Donahue, Plaintiff,)
              v.   )
SurfAir Coastal Airways Inc.,   )   No. MDL 489
and Hastings Aircraft Corp.,   )
Defendants   )
_____)

FORM OF VERDICT

Ladies and Gentlemen of the Jury:

1. Do you find that defendant SurfAir was negligent in the maintenance or operation of the aircraft on flight 617, or that the aircraft was defective?
   __✓__ Yes _____ No

2. If so, do you find that the negligence or the defect was a proximate cause of the injuries suffered by the plaintiff?
   __✓__ Yes _____ No

3. Do you find that defendant Hastings was negligent in the manufacture or design of the aircraft that crashed on March 23, 1987, or that the aircraft was defective?
   __✓__ Yes _____ No

4. If so, do you find that the negligence or the defect was a proximate cause of the injuries suffered by the plaintiff?
   __✓__ Yes _____ No

   If the answer to questions three or four or both of them is yes, please continue.

   We the jury find plaintiff John Charles Donahue suffered damages in the following amounts:
   Medical expenses _$ 600,000.⁼_
   Pain and suffering _$ 400,000.⁰⁰_

5. Do you find that the conduct of defendant SurfAir was willful, malicious, and in reckless disregard for the rights of the plaintiff?
   __✓__ Yes _____ No

6. Do you find that the conduct of defendant Hastings was willful, malicious, and in reckless disregard of the rights of the plaintiff?
   __✓__ Yes _____ No

IMPACT

If the answer to question five or six or both of them is yes, please proceed.

Punitive damages against SurfAir Coastal Airways $1,000,000.⁰⁰

Punitive damages against Hastings Aircraft Corp. $1,000,000 ⁰⁰

Dated: *April 1, 1988*

Signed: *James L. Ashford*
Foreperson

The jury has been dismissed. Judge Powell has left the bench; the crowd has drifted off to home or tavern. his adversary has extended a grudging hand and threatened to take the battle to a more lofty venue. But within an hour of its advent, the thrill has begun to fade. In the well of the empty courtroom, Keith Tollison ponders the flags of state and nation that flank the bench, symbolic of might and conquest and the attendant pomp that should fit his state but don't. Far less jubilant than melancholy, he tries to think of a place to go where he will be welcome.

Tollison is wondering why neither Martha nor Alec has bothered to share the moment—why, as the foreman rose to read the verdict, he had faced him all alone—when he hears a noise and turns. An attractive young woman strides toward him with a purposeful pace, extending a gilt-edged card, giving him no alternative but to take it.

The engraving is brief and to the point: Victor A. Scallini, Attorney and Counselor-at-Law. "Mr. Scallini has asked me to compliment you on the verdict," she says when he is finished reading.

"Thanks."

"And to ask if you would be willing to come to Los Angeles next Thursday to meet with him."

From where six weeks of strain have put him, Tollison asks, "Why?"

"I believe he wants to offer you a job."

"Why?"

Impatient with the flaw in his reply, she retrieves the card from where he has dropped it. "He believes you could benefit from a future association."

"I don't think I want to work for anyone right now," he manages. "Myself included."

"Mr. Scallini understands that you will want time to unwind. He has asked me to say that he will put you up at the Beverly Hills Hotel and introduce you to some of his friends in the film community if you agree to see him. He is very anxious to discuss the SurfAir case, as well as other matters. He can make you an attractive offer," she concludes, allowing him to believe that she might be part of it. "You'd like it down there," she adds, speaking her own mind for the first time since she entered the room. "I mean, at least the sun shines, you know?"

"I probably would," he agrees.

"So you'll be coming on Thursday?"

He shakes his head. "I don't think so."

"But—"

"I go fishing on Thursdays."

"I see. Well, perhaps when you've rested you will change your mind."

"Perhaps."

She leaves him with a breath of lavender and what he has decided is a far less fragrant opportunity. A moment later Alec Hawthorne—looking like himself—supersedes her.

His approach is oddly courtly. "Mind if I join you?"

"Be my guest."

Hawthorne pulls back Laura Donahue's long-vacant chair and lowers himself into it. "You did what you had to do," he murmurs in the heavy silence.

"It seemed that way at the time."

"Well, I can't say you were wrong—that's a great result, Keith. Fantastic, under the circumstances."

"Thanks."

"This case will have ramifications, you know. Airplanes will get a little safer. Every air traveler in the world owes you a debt."

"More you than me. By a lot."

Hawthorne shrugs. "What did Chambers say?"

"He solemnly swore to appeal, after he cursed my morals and my lineage. He'll never know how right he is," Tollison mutters after a moment.

"You might want to consider a deal—knocking off half a million if Chambers will dismiss the appeal."

"I'll give it some thought."

Hawthorne nods, then seems at a loss for words. "It made me feel young again," he muses finally, "seeing you wing it like that. Reminded me of when the only way I knew how to try a case was to beat up on everyone in sight."

Tollison meets his gaze. "On everyone except the client."

Hawthorne nods.

Tollison suddenly is in need of endorsement. "That's the way it works, right? Sacrifice everything but the client?"

"Sometimes," Hawthorne agrees, but doesn't pursue the ethic to its end. "Why do you suppose Chambers's detective couldn't come up with someone to testify about Donahue's love affairs?"

Tollison shrugs. "People don't like to speak ill of the dead. Maybe in Altoona that includes what's become of Jack."

"What were you going to do if someone popped up and said she'd slept with him a dozen times?"

"I was going to say that a man has a right to know if he's a saint or a sinner, but the crash had taken even that away from him."

"Clever, counselor."

Tollison closes his eyes. "Then why do I feel so shitty?"

Hawthorne chuckles, seems his old suave self for the first time since they had begun to prepare for trial. "Postlitigation depression," he declares. "At this level, the distinction between winning and losing gets a bit opaque."

"I thought that was only true of drunk-driving cases."

"If it's true in life, it's true in court."

"You know what *really* makes me feel lousy?" Tollison says after a minute.

"What?"

"Vic Scallini just offered me a job."

Hawthorne's look is impenetrable for an instant, then he grins. "Try to get your draw in cash."

They sit quietly, amid echoes of the trial. "So how did you keep Chambers from asking Laura who she was sleeping with?" Hawthorne asks finally.

"I told him if he made her answer the question, I was going to have to withdraw from the case. Then I showed him a form for substitution of attorneys that replaced me with Ed Haroldson."

"The phone number."

"Right."

"I'm surprised Ed was willing to take it on. He hates it out here."

Tollison looks at the vacant bench. "I never got through to him. I guess I forgot to mention it to Chambers."

Hawthorne chuckles warmly. Tollison remembers conversations long into the Berkeley nights, when that laugh had been his most reliable relief from the tedium that was law school. "How'd you know, by the way?" he asks.

"About you and Laura? I suspected as much when you brought her to see me. Then your girlfriend pretty much confirmed it."

Tollison is about to inquire about the shape and density of Hawthorne's relationship with Brenda when the door opens at the rear of the room. Martha joins them in six long strides.

When she extends a hand to Tollison, he takes it. Her fingers are straight and smooth, her gesture for the first time giving him the sense that he has just taken a giant step.

"The boys in the office were betting against you," she begins.

"You mean him." Tollison points left.

Martha smiles and nods. "So how are you going to celebrate?"

"I hadn't thought about it."

Her look jostles his mood. "How about a trip to Spokane?"

Too tired to decode, Tollison thinks he has misheard.

"What's in Spokane?" Hawthorne asks.

"A midair." She looks at each of them. "DC-9 and a private plane. Just came over CNN."

Hawthorne nods. "Better get Ray on his way."

"He's in Baja fishing, so I thought I'd go myself. And I thought your friend might enjoy the ride."

They look at him. "Maybe you want to check in with Altoona first," Hawthorne says when Tollison remains silent.

"I know everything I need to know about Altoona." The statement seems to entail an epiphany.

Hawthorne stands and begins to pace, as if Tollison and Martha are jurors about to judge him. "I've been thinking about making some changes in my practice," he says on his second pass. "One of them is the name of the firm."

When Martha doesn't speak, Tollison inquires for her. "Why?"

Hawthorne shrugs. "Because Tollison and Crenshaw has a nice ring to it, I guess."

Tollison frowns. "Who the hell is Crenshaw?"

"Me."

In her normally forbidding countenance, Martha's smile is a votive candle. "And Crenshaw and Tollison rings nicer."

Tollison closes his eyes. "I can't deal with this right now, Alec."

"Why don't you think about it on the way to Spokane," Hawthorne suggests. "We'll talk when we get back."

"What are *you* going to be doing?" Martha asks.

"I've got a date in Maui." Hawthorne gestures toward the rear of the room. Beyond the open door, a stylish woman is standing in the hallway. As they look her way, she waves, then beckons for Hawthorne to join her.

"Who's that?" Martha says.

"My first ex-wife. We're going away for a week. Or a year, depending on how it goes."

Tollison glances at Martha, who might not have heard a word. "Great," he mumbles.

"Think about it," Hawthorne says, and slaps him on the back and leaves the building on the arm of the woman Tollison thinks he has just called Hygiene.

Their eyes nudge above the table. "What the hell," Martha says after a minute. "What have you got to lose?"

He shrugs. "Everything or nothing, I suppose. Maybe by the time we get back I'll have figured out which it is."

She helps him shove his papers into his case. "There's one thing I can't figure," he says, looking at his copy of the videotape that was his best exhibit.

"What's that?"

"How did the guy who pulled him from the plane know Jack Donahue was still alive?"

"The answer to that is walking around disguised as a priest," Martha says on the way to the door. "If he runs true to form, we'll see him in Spokane and you can ask him."

He follows her into the hallway. Long past quitting time, it is as deserted as his wits. For a moment it seems the residue of a disaster he is unaware of, one that will engender more plaintiffs and defendants, judges and juries, lawyers and their clients.

He is about to enter the elevator when he hears the sharp rap of high heels coming down the hall. When Martha sees the source of the interruption, she tells Tollison she'll meet him in the lobby. The elevator doors steam closed, removing her.

"Hi."

"Hi."

"It's finally over," Laura says softly when she has reached his side.

"Yep."

"You won, just like you always do."

"*You* won," he corrects. "By the skin of your teeth."

She twitches to dismiss his amendment, then grasps his arm. "I just wanted to thank you, Keith. I know how hard this was for you."

He tries to smile. "Just so you're not going to forgive me. I wouldn't want you to forgive me, Laura."

She refuses to oblige him. "Are you coming back to Altoona?"

He shakes his head.

She frowns. "Where are you going?"

"Spokane."

"What on earth for?"

"To look at another plane crash."

"With her?" She gestures toward the groaning elevator.

He nods, then leans against the marble wall and slides down its solid coolness till he is sitting on the floor. "I didn't think I'd see you again after what I did," he says as she sits beside him and curls her legs and leans against his arm.

"I was hurt, Keith. I won't pretend I wasn't. I've never been through *anything* like that—you made me feel like some sort of monster. But I understand why you did it—I think I knew even when I ran out of there, but I just couldn't get myself together in front of all those people, knowing what they were thinking about me, so . . ." She shrugs. "Anyway, I just wanted to say there's no hard feelings."

"How's Jack?"

She seems disappointed by the question he has chosen. "He doesn't seem the worse for wear. He's quite perky, actually. Thanks to you, he's got a lot to be perky about."

For an instant he has no idea what she's talking about. "When I saw Spitter wheeling Jack down that aisle," he says finally, impelled to confess at least a portion of his crimes, "I thought, the son of a bitch finally got what he deserves. He really was a jerk, you know."

"I know."

He laughs, beyond gallantry or restraint. "You know what the best part of all this is?"

"What?"

"As close as I can figure from listening to Chambers's experts, there's a chance that sooner or later he's going to be a jerk again."

He expects her to scold him, but she giggles. "I imagine you're right."

"You know what the worst part is?"

"What?"

"I can't wait that long."

She takes his hand and presses it to her breast. "What if I leave him? What if I put his money in the bank and hire some help and let someone else take care of him?"

He leans his head against the wall. "You need to be needed, is what I finally figured out, and when you came to Altoona, I needed you more than anyone in town. But Jack needs you more than I do now. You can't leave him; not completely, not until he's as well as he can get."

"But what about what you said? About waiting the rest of your life for me?"

He finds her eyes. "I loved you even before I realized how virtuous you are, Laura. You may even be a saint. But I can't sit around and watch you do whatever it is saints do, because I'm not virtuous at all."

"Yes you are. You're my champion."

"Champion was a horse." He removes his hand from its warm nest. "I loved you, Laura."

She sighs. "I loved you too."

"But I've given you all I can."

"You're telling me I really have lost my consortium, aren't you?" When he doesn't answer, she begins to cry. "I thought if we won the case everything would be all right."

"It doesn't seem to work that way. At least not for me."

She sniffs and tries to smile. "I remember—even when you win, you lose."

He searches for words that are closer to the truth, at least the truth that is true that instant, but finally gives up. "At least you have three million green things to remember me by."

"Two."

"Three."

"Your fee, remember? Thirty-three percent."

"I already got my fee," he says, and rests his head against the dewy sadness of her cheek.

AFTERWORD

The compromise in California's "tort-reform wars" that was reached at Frank Fat's restaurant in Sacramento on September 10, 1987, proved short-lived: A year later, six additional reform efforts appeared on the California ballot. They ranged from a measure sponsored by legal and consumer groups to roll back insurance rates, to various insurance-industry proposals (backed by a $60 million ad campaign) to establish a "no-fault" tort system in the state and limit attorneys' fee percentages in injury actions to 10 percent of any recovery in excess of $100,000.

On November 8, 1988, California voters defeated all but a Ralph Nader–sponsored proposal that reduced auto-insurance rates in California by 20 percent, and subjected future rate increases to approval by the state insurance commissioner. Several major insurance companies immediately threatened to cease doing business in California and petitioned the California Supreme Court to stay enforcement of the measure pending a ruling on its constitutionality. On May 4, 1989, the court upheld virtually all aspects of the measure, but allowed insurance companies to avoid the mandated rate reductions by showing they would reduce profits below a "fair and reasonable return." The impact of the measure upon consumers remains unclear.

This time, the FAA did not withdraw its proposal to require the installation of fire-blocking materials in aircraft interiors, and the rule went into effect in the summer of 1988. The new materials were quickly credited with saving lives, most prominently in the crash of Delta flight 1141 shortly after takeoff in Dallas on August 31, 1988, in which 13 of the 108 people on board were killed. (All thirteen survived the crash but perished from smoke inhalation. A fourteenth victim died from burns suffered while trying to pull his wife from the wreckage.)

In June 1988, the FAA completed its transition to a new Host computer system at twenty traffic control centers throughout the nation. The system is expected to provide increased speed and reliability, thereby reducing the frequency of near-midair collisions. It is said to operate for twenty thousand hours without an interruption of more than ten seconds.

Frustrated with the lack of progress in other areas of aviation safety, Congress amended the Airport and Airway Improvement Act to require the FAA to increase the number of certified traffic controllers; to develop, certify, and deploy the TCAS II collision avoidance system within four years; to study ways in which aircraft equipment and design could be improved to minimize the danger of fire and explosion; and to consider requiring seats in commercial aircraft to be strengthened to meet the best available testing criteria for crashworthiness. The FAA was directed to submit monthly reports to Congress on the status of those undertakings.

On March 23, 1988, the day the SurfAir trial began, the attorneys general of California, New York, and several other states filed suit against five major liability insurers, alleging they had illegally combined and conspired with Lloyd's of London to artificially induce the so-called liability insurance crisis in order to reduce or eliminate their obligation to insure public agencies and nonprofit organizations. The defendants denied the allegations. The suit is pending.

On October 27, 1988, the Rand Corporation released a study that concluded that relatives of persons killed in air crashes were paid less than half the economic loss they suffered as a result of the loss of their loved ones' future earnings. (If amounts awarded for pain and suffering were deducted from the recovery, survivors received only 31 percent of their economic loss.) The study also found that aviation attorneys typically collected less than one third of the recovery in such cases, substantially less than in tort cases in general.

Trade associations for the airframe manufacturers and the airlines, which had funded a portion of the study, termed it misleading.

AUTHOR'S NOTE

I would like to acknowledge my debt to the following authors for works that have been particularly helpful: Moira Johnston, *The Last Nine Minutes* (New York: William Morrow & Co., 1976); Paul Eddy, Elaine Potter, and Bruce Page, *Destination Disaster* (New York: Quadrangle/The New York Times Book Co., 1976); Jerome Greer Chandler, *Fire & Rain* (Austin: The Texas Monthly Press, 1986); William Norris, *Willful Misconduct* (New York: W. W. Norton & Co., 1984); Carl Solberg, *Conquest of the Skies* (Boston: Little, Brown & Co., 1979); Anthony Sampson, *Empires of the Sky* (New York: Random House, 1984); David Nolan, "Airline Safety: The Shocking Truth," *Discover*, Vol. 7, No. 10, October 1986; Ralph Nader, "The Corporate Drive to Restrict Their Victims' Rights," 22 *Gonzaga Law Review* 15 (1986); Symposium: "Alternative Compensation Schemes & Tort Theory," 73 *California Law Review* 548 (1985); Judith Hooper and Dick Teresi, *The 3-Pound Universe* (New York: Dell Publishing Company, 1986); and Richard M. Restak, M.D., *The Brain* (New York: Bantam Books, 1984). All errors of fact or interpretation, and all adaptations and abbreviations, are entirely my own.

I would also like to acknowledge my use of materials available from the National Head Injury Foundation, and to recognize the members and staff of the Subcommittee on Investigation and Oversight of the House Committee on Public Works and Transportation, Ninety-eighth Congress, whose hearings generated much of the information incorporated in Part Three.

I am also grateful for the contributions of Gerald C. Sterns and Elizabeth Walker Sterns, attorneys-at-law, and for the encouragement of my agent, Esther Newberg, who has been supportive from the beginning. Finally, I wish to thank my editor, Doug Stumpf, whose burden was far greater than it should have been.